Takeoffs
and
LANDINGS

Takeoffs and Landings

LOST IN LONDON, LOST IN PARIS, and LOST IN ROME

CINDY CALLAGHAN

ALADDIN
New York London Toronto Sydney New Delhi

This book is a work of fiction. Any references to historical events, real people, or real places are used fictitiously. Other names, characters, places, and events are products of the author's imagination, and any resemblance to actual events or places or persons, living or dead, is entirely coincidental.

ALADDIN

An imprint of Simon & Schuster Children's Publishing Division

1230 Avenue of the Americas, New York, New York 10020

This Aladdin paperback edition May 2022

Lost in London copyright © 2013 by Cindy Callaghan

Lost in Paris and *Lost in Rome* copyright © 2015 by Cindy Callaghan

Cover illustration copyright © 2022 by Katy Dockrill

All rights reserved, including the right of reproduction in whole or in part in any form.

ALADDIN and related logo are registered trademarks of Simon & Schuster, Inc.

For information about special discounts for bulk purchases, please contact Simon & Schuster Special Sales at 1-866-506-1949 or business@simonandschuster.com.

The Simon & Schuster Speakers Bureau can bring authors to your live event. For more information or to book an event contact the Simon & Schuster Speakers Bureau at 1-866-248-3049 or visit our website at www.simonspeakers.com.

Cover designed by Laura Lyn DiSiena

Interior designed by Hilary Zarycky

The text of this book was set in ITC Berkeley Oldstyle.

Manufactured in the United States of America 0422 OFF

2 4 6 8 10 9 7 5 3 1

Library of Congress Control Number 2022933925

ISBN 9781665907361 (pbk)

ISBN 9781442466548 (*Lost in London* ebook)

ISBN 9781481426022 (*Lost in Paris* ebook)

ISBN 9781481426046 (*Lost in Rome* ebook)

These titles were previously published individually.

CONTENTS

Lost in London

This book, and really everything, is dedicated to Ellie, Evan, and Happy.

Acknowledgments

There are so many very special people I would like to thank:

I am very lucky to be part of two critique groups. Both helped me shape this book. To the WIPs: Gale, Carolee, Josette, Jane, Chris, and Shannon, the last nine years have flown by. You're awesome. To the Northern Delaware Sisters in Crime group: John, KB, Jane, June, Chris, Jacqui, Susan, Kathleen, and Pat, thanks for feedback.

Mom and Dad: Thanks for your continued confidence in me and for your endless support.

To my nieces and nephews: Mikayla, Anna, John, Christopher, Sean, Keelen, Lauren, Nikki, Taylor, Danny, Kelsey, and Shawn. Thanks for all the great material. You're a fun bunch.

To Sue, Mark, and in-laws and out-laws who never fail to ask me, "How's the writing going?" Thank you for your interest and endless ideas.

To my friends, near and far, old and new: You inspire me!

To my agent, Mandy Hubbard: "Thank you" doesn't seem like enough for making my dream career a reality. I appreciate your confidence in me.

To my editor, Alyson Heller, and the whole team at Simon & Schuster: You're a class act! Thanks for everything.

To Kevin: Thank you for supporting my dream career. You're a great partner.

To my readers: None of this works without you. Thank you for reading and for inviting me to your schools, libraries, and book clubs. I love getting your e-mails and letters. I hope you love *Lost in London* as much as *Just Add Magic*.

1

The flyer in my hand said it was a one-week student program in London—as in the most exciting city in Europe. I needed something exciting, anything other than what was called "my life."

Everybody has a "thing." Some people are good at sports, or music, or are popular, or are at the bottom of the social ladder.

Except me. I didn't have a thing. Translation? I was a positively ordinary thirteen-year-old girl who led a boring life. Consider my life's report card:

- I lived in a regular old town without a palm tree, igloo, or palace (Wilmington, Delaware) = blah.
- I didn't do any sports or clubs = yawn.
- I wasn't allowed to wear makeup, ride my bike without a helmet, go to R movies, or attend boy-girl dances = lame.
- I lived next door to my school, where my dad worked = annoying.
- Worst of all, I'd never done anything exciting. When I explained this to my parents, they brought up my trip with the Girl Scouts last year. I didn't think that should count, because it was only two nights and my mom was there. It was totally Dullsville. (I dropped out of Girl Scouts right after.)

This school-sponsored trip was like a miracle opportunity sent directly to me, Jordan Jacoby. *What could be more exciting than London?* (Paris, possibly, but that doesn't matter right now.) I wanted to go to London to become worldly by traveling around that amazing city and soaking in its history and culture.

There was just one problem. Kind of a biggie. My parents.

I studied the London program information on my short walk home from school—across the football field, through a gate, along a short path, and onto the sidewalk that led to my house. My dad was a little ways behind me, walking home too.

Let me give you some advice if your parents ever consider working at your school:

Talk them out of it.

Sabotage the interview.

Recruit someone else for the job.

Do whatever it takes for them to work anywhere other than at your school. Seriously, anywhere. And if they somehow manage to get the job, beg them to change their name and pretend they don't know you.

I love my dad, but walking to and from school with him every day, and seeing him lurk in the hallways, sucked any possible element of fun from my middle-school existence. I couldn't so much as draw on my sneaker with a permanent marker, or talk to a boy, without getting "the look." The you-and-I-both-know-you-shouldn't-be-doing-that look.

Ah, London.

I wanted this trip.

"What are you reading?" Dad walked faster to catch up with me.

"About the school-sponsored trip to London this year. I really, really want to go."

He immediately harrumphed, but I didn't let that stop me. This was going to take persistence. And I could be seriously persistent.

The conversation about the trip went on all afternoon and into dinner. "There has got to be more to the world than Wilmington, Delaware. I've never done anything or gone anywhere."

"Now, that's just not true," Mom said. "You went away overnight to Girl Scout camp. Remember that?"

Oh, yeah. Did I ever.

I tried: "Oh, come on. You never let me do anything fun. And it's only five days."

Then I went to: "We live in an American-centric society. Isn't it important for me to broaden my horizons?" (I'd gotten that from the flyer.)

I added: "I have the assignment all planned out. It's going to be a photo montage of sights with narration. I promise I'll get an A, or maybe an A-minus, on it and I'll weed all summer long to pay you back for the trip."

Finally I went with: "It will be an experience that I will remember for the rest of my life!"

My mom talked about me staying with an old friend of hers who had a stepdaughter about my age. This made me think she was seriously considering it. Then she started talking about the dangers of a foreign city—drugs, kidnapping—and the cost of the trip. It wasn't looking good.

Then—I don't know what happened exactly—but at that moment, on Marsh Road in Wilmington, Delaware, a miracle occurred. They said YES!

I was going to embark on a journey called the De-bored-ification of Jordan Jacoby.

Only, I had no idea how de-bored-ified my life was about to become.

2

A few weeks later I got off my first plane ever. My eyes felt like they'd been dusted with sand. I followed signs toward Customs. There were lots of signs, and my mind wasn't working clearly, so I ended up just following a lady who had been on my flight and hoped that she wasn't connecting to Africa.

After I waited in a line, a customs officer stamped my passport: ENGLAND!

It was official.

I had arrived.

I looked for someone who matched Caroline Littleton's online picture. Instead I found a tall man in a simple black suit holding a sign, JORDAN JACOBY.

"I'm Jordan," I told him.

"Welcome to London. I'm Liam. Shall we get your bags and proceed to the manor house?"

"Sure," I said, half-excited to be taken to the "manor house" by a chauffeur, and half-bummed that Caroline hadn't met me at the airport herself.

"Very well. Off we go." His accent was so sophisticated. I loved it.

I followed him to the luggage claim and then outside, where he opened the back door of a black car with a rounded roof. The first thing I noticed was that the steering wheel was on the wrong side. Well, maybe it wasn't wrong if you lived in London, but it was opposite from the US. I'd never been driven like this, like, *by a driver*. Carpooling didn't even compare.

I wouldn't see the airport again for five days. As far as programs abroad went, this one was short, over spring break. The only requirement was to return with the assignment—a summary of my trip. My grandparents had gotten me a new phone with a really good camera (for pictures and videos) just for the trip. (*Yay for grandparents!*)

13

My parents had agreed that I had to get an A or A-minus on the presentation, and I would spend the summer pulling weeds to pay for the trip. It wasn't the dandelions-in-grass kind of weeding. It was the sweat-and-dirt-and-worms-and-poison-ivy kind. They also gave me some money and an emergency credit card. If I charged anything to the card that wasn't a true emergency, I'd pay it off by spreading fertilizer around our tomatoes. You know what's in fertilizer? It rhymes with "droop."

We drove through London on the wrong side of the road; well, maybe not wrong. I videoed or photographed everything—buildings, street signs, double-decker tour buses, cafés, stores. There was no predicting what I'd need when I edited the montage. And I really wanted it to be good—well, at least A-minus good so that I wouldn't have to do more yard work.

I was going to stay with a friend of my mom's—a sorority sister who she really liked but hadn't seen in years. She was Caroline's stepmom (well, "mum," I suppose). They had discussed the itinerary. It was going to be an amazing week, like palaces-castles-abbeys-gardens-cathedrals amazing. I was going to see and do everything, absolutely everything, and return to Wilmington as a totally different person!

I wondered if Caroline and I would possibly have

time to sleep, because as much as I wanted to see London and begin the process of changing my life from boring to well traveled, I also really needed a power nap. I'd stayed up all night watching movies on the plane.

BTW, there were several movies to choose from, and I picked one that was PG-13.

"First time in England?" Liam asked.

"Yup! I've never been anywhere." This was true if you didn't count Girl Scouts, which I didn't.

"Nowhere, Miss Jordan? Well, you've chosen the best city in the world. I've lived here my entire life." He smiled at me in the rearview mirror, showing a mouthful of crooked teeth. "We should be at the Littletons' house in a few moments."

The city became country. It looked like it'd recently rained. Sections of damp grass glistened in the sun. Liam pulled into a long driveway to a very large Tudor-style house. Ivy clung to its frame; moss padded the roof's tiles. It was fairy-tale perfect, just like I'd hoped it would be.

I didn't have much information about Caroline. My mom had never actually met her. Her Facebook page made her sound so . . . so . . . so worldly. She rode horses, and liked music, shopping, and going out in London with her friends. She was everything I wanted to be. I knew already that we were going to be BFFs, just like our moms.

Liam stopped the car, and I opened the door and got out. The look on his face as he came around the trunk said I should've waited, but I didn't get back in. I was going to walk up to the house, but decided to wait for him to get my bags—well, bag. I only had one suitcase. I flung my backpack over one shoulder and followed Liam to the front door. He opened it and ushered me inside.

I expected Caroline and her parents to be waiting excitedly for me, maybe with balloons, but the house was silent. And beautiful. The walls were trimmed with dark woodwork. Art and mirrors hung on the walls; every surface held a vase of fresh-cut flowers. The room smelled like springtime but a little damp, too, like some of last night's rain had seeped in through the old cracks. This was the closest thing to a palace I'd ever been in. And hopefully in a few short hours I'd be hanging out in London, learning about kings and queens and basically becoming less boring every minute.

Liam led me to a kitchen and waved me to sit at the table. "Energizer?"

I was proud of myself because I knew he meant OJ. The stewardess on the plane had offered it to me. I'd felt dumb when I'd asked her what it was, but now I knew.

"Sure. Thanks. Um, where's Caroline?"

He looked at the clock. "She should be down soon. Mister has already left for work, and Mrs. Littleton—" A Mini Cooper zipped into the driveway. "Oh, there she is."

Through the window I saw a petite woman in yoga clothes run to the front door. "You're here!" she said with the perkiness I'd hoped for. "Let me look atcha." She had an accent like she was from Tennessee or Louisiana that didn't fit with this house or London. "You look just like your mama. Lord, seeing you makes me miss her. How is she?"

"She's fine."

"Well, let's get you some breakfast." She asked Liam, "Where's Caroline?"

"Still in bed, I suspect, madam."

"That child. I told her to go with you to the airport." She smiled at me. "I'm sorry she didn't greet you. She just doesn't understand how much fun y'all are gonna have. I've told her this will be a good experience for her, too, but she's very focused on her friends. I'm sure you understand."

I nodded like I did, but I wasn't so sure. I thought she'd just told me that Caroline wasn't excited that I was here.

"I always wished that I'd had more experiences with

17

different kinds of people when I was thirteen, and I just want that for her."

Liam fixed me a small bowl of berries and added a dollop of white cream, which I assumed was yogurt, but it tasted more like sour cream, so I picked around it to get to the berries. As I started to eat, Liam quietly left the room.

A minute later a girl in pj's with bed head, a sleep mask pushed up to her forehead, and eyes barely open came in and picked up the orange juice that Liam had just poured for me.

I hopped out of my chair, ready to grab her in a totally huge, psyched-to-be-here hug.

She sipped again before opening her eyes and finding me a few inches from her face. "Oh my," she said. Her eyes opened wider. "You must be . . . Jordan?"

"Here I am!" I tossed my arms into the air.

"Yes, you are," she said. And she looked at me from sneakers to ponytail. Her flat expression told me that she wasn't seeing anything she liked, probably because everything was boring. I casually let the smile drain from my face. She sipped the orange juice again.

An awkward silence blew through the kitchen, during which I sat back down and scooped another berry into my mouth. "I'm so excited to be here, like

Christmas-morning-excited. I mean, it's London! A city of castles, real princesses, and knights jousting till death," I said. Then I caught my own zealousness and calmly asked, "What do you want to do today?"

Mrs. Littleton fanned out a handful of brochures that she'd taken out of a drawer. "Here's a load of information about all the places that your mama and I discussed. Y'all can look through to give you ideas of stuff to do. Liam can take you where you want to go, or you can take the train into the city."

"You aren't coming?" I asked. My mom had been pretty clear that Mrs. Littleton would accompany us.

"No," Caroline said. "I explained to her that we can get along quite well on our own. I go all around the city on my own all the time."

Mrs. Littleton said, "Now, not so fast. I want to know where y'all are at." She addressed Caroline, "So call me and text me. It's not like you'll just be going anywhere you want without telling me." Then she faced me again. "You okay with that?"

Caroline was behind her stepmother's back, mocking her by making a mouth with her fingers and thumb. She opened and closed them in a comical way, and I had to chew on my lip to keep from laughing out loud.

I nodded that I was good with that, but I knew my

parents would NOT be . . . if they knew, which they wouldn't, because I wasn't going to tell them.

When Mrs. Littleton turned, Caroline snapped her hand down. "All right," she said. "Then everything is bril." I was pretty sure that was short for "brilliant." I couldn't wait to use that word. Maybe I could mention how bril the energizer was?

"Super," Mrs. Littleton said. "I just know you two are gonna be—what do you kids say? BFFs! That's it. I'm gonna shower. I'll see y'all later. Have fun."

Caroline fixed herself a bowl of berries and swiped the brochures right into the trash. "I'll get dressed. I was thinking we'd go shopping, to Daphne's, of course. I'll be down in a wee bit." She left the kitchen with her berries, but then poked her head back in. "By the way, knights don't actually joust till death anymore, and castles are a bit old and damp." She left.

I didn't think I'd made a very good first impression. And I was really bummed that she wasn't psyched that I was here. I mean, she'd been *asleep*! Maybe she'd get to know me better while we shopped and then she'd like me. I had to work on my coolness factor at the store or mall. And after shopping, we could start on the sights for my montage.

I reached into the trash can for the brochures. Then

Caroline stuck her head in for the second time. I pretended like I wasn't picking in the garbage. "You might want to change and get freshened up before we go," she said. "Liam can show you to your room and give you a call when we're ready to go."

She left me in the kitchen, alone.

3

I managed to find Liam, who showed me to an incredible guest room: all cream-colored with a four-poster bed with a frilly canopy. French doors opened out to a balcony overlooking a field fit for horses trotting in from a fox hunt.

The attached bathroom was marble and silver. I took a quick shower and changed into what I hoped was an appropriate shopping outfit: jeans and turtleneck with a fleece vest.

I looked in the mirror. Hmmmm. Not awful, but not really "London."

Shopping could be exactly what I needed to help me move out of Dullsville, although money could be a problem. I'd budgeted one hundred dollars per day. When I'd transferred the currency, it had felt like I had a lot less money. *Can I afford to shop?*

The way Caroline looked—the way this house looked—money was no object. It was totally crazy to think that I was going to spend a whole week in this mansion!

I looked through my bag and found a scarf that I'd brought in case it got cold. I added it and reassessed. Not much better. Glancing at my reflection in an antique mirror, I decided this was an emergency. A fashion emergency, that is. I twisted around in the mirror, pouting my lips at the girl staring back at me.

Jordan, you desperately need to go shopping.

I brushed my hair and tousled it with my fingers to make it bouncy and full, but it still looked blah. Not "bad" blah, like "ordinary" blah.

I studied my map of London while waiting to be *fetched*. People here totally said "fetched," right? Eventually Liam came to the guest room door. "Miss Jordan? Ready to go shopping?"

I snapped up. "Yup!" I took a second to re-fluff my hair and straighten my fleece vest.

Liam led me to the front door, his shiny shoes tapping on the gleaming hardwood floors. I let out a yawn and tried to shake the fuzz out of my head. I could easily sleep until dinner . . . maybe until dinner tomorrow. And I was hungry, like double-burger-fries-and-a-shake hungry.

Caroline stood by the car talking on her cell phone. She was way more dressed up than me: boots like I'd seen only in a magazine—they went up to her knees—and a skirt that defined the word "mini." I practically drooled over her chunky bracelets. I couldn't see her eyes under bejeweled sunglasses—odd, since it had turned cloudy—but I suspected she wore makeup to match her red lipstick. She looked like she could be fifteen easily. Suddenly even my cute scarf felt worse than drab.

It looked like Caroline would know exactly what I needed to transform. I wondered if I could get that look, if she could teach me to be glamorous.

Caroline clapped her phone shut. "Liam!" she called, and turned to see us. "Oh, there you are." She gave me an extra look over the top of her glasses but didn't comment. "Sam, Gordo, and Ellie are meeting us at Daphne's."

Liam held the car door open, and I got into the back like I'd had a driver all my life. Caroline propped the sunglasses on her head. I was right—eye makeup. "Is Daphne one of your friends?"

"Are you serious? Daphne isn't a *who*. It's a *what*. And it's the most crackin' *what* to shop at in all of London. You wanted to see the sights." She checked her lipstick in a compact mirror. "And, trust me, Daphne's is quite a sight. People from all over Europe, Asia, the Middle East, and even from the other side of the pond come to London to shop at Daphne's. You're going to love it. First stop, lattes. *Oui?*"

"*Oui*," I said, like I had lattes and drizzled French words like "*oui*" into my conversations all the time.

Looking out of the window, feeling a little self-conscious in my basic Old Navy clothes, I felt my mood improve as we drove over the London Bridge . . . THE actual London Bridge. The one the song is about. Then we passed the Marble Arch, and Madame Tussauds—all places I was dying to see. I couldn't wait to visit them all. I snapped picture after picture. It started raining heavily, like nor'easter-heavy raining. I doubted that they called them nor'easters here.

"It's supposed to storm quite hard today," Liam said. "That's why they call it Rainy London."

He pulled over. I looked for a store. "Where is it?" I asked.

Caroline said, "You're next to it."

I squinted. "All I see is this big hotel."

"That's not a hotel. That's eighteen floors of blooming shopping perfection."

"Eighteen? That's a lot of floors," I said, craning my neck to see to the top.

"Yes. And in order to get through all of them, we're going to need some energy in the form of caffeine. So, let the lattes begin!"

"Oui," I experimented. I didn't get a funny look from Caroline, so I think I used it right. *Yay, me!*

I thanked Liam and followed Caroline, like a puppy, through the downpour into the store. I noticed I wasn't the only puppy, but the others were riding into Daphne's inside designer handbags. People toted their pooches along with them. If I were taking notes, I would've definitely written that down.

I hiked my backpack onto my shoulder. I felt a little guilty to be at a big Macy's instead of exploring the sights of London, but there would be plenty of time for that after I shopped. And, really, this little shopping trip was vitally important to the new me.

I glanced at the store directory—a holographic map projected onto a humungous wall. It showed everything that could be found on the eighteen floors, from sun hats to snowshoes, and everything imaginable in between. Every brand I had ever heard of and hundreds—no, thousands—that I hadn't, crowded the directory. The map was in English, French, Spanish, and symbols that I thought might be Arabic. It looked like everything ever made in the world was in this store.

This could be more than a little shopping trip; this might be a complete fashion transformation, even if that meant a summer of shoveling poop.

4

I trailed after Caroline through what seemed like department after department of purses.

"We can come back and you can look for a purse later. You need one." Apparently my L.L.Bean backpack didn't cut it. "But I want to find my mates first. You'll love them. I'm sure Ellie will want to get a mani at the salon here." A mani? I'd never had one.

Salon, hmmm . . . what if I get my hair trimmed? Maybe Caroline could look through those hair books with me and help me pick out a new do?

"Do you know all of them?" I asked. "The floors, I mean?"

"Oh, yes. I've been coming here since I was in my gingham plaid pram."

"What's a *pram*? Like a shirt?"

"Uh, no." I think she rolled her eyes. "It's a buggy, a baby stroller."

She spoke English, but it was like a totally different language. I thought about my baby cousin and decided that the next time I saw her, I was going to use the word "pram."

Caroline walked toward a giant copper cappuccino machine that sat behind a high counter. Three people were waiting for us—a girl and two guys. They offered Caroline hugs, and the girls oohed and aahed about Caroline's sunglasses. Apparently, they were something special.

I waited for her to introduce me. For a second I thought she'd forgotten that I was there, but then she said, "This is Jordan. She's from the States and needed a place to stay, so she's living with us for the week."

Needed a place to stay?

"Actually it's like a study abroad program," I said. "I see the sights with Caroline and her family, and when I get back, I'll do a report about it for school."

"Well, that's exciting," Caroline said like she didn't mean it. "A report for school?"

Did those totally lame words just come out of my mouth? "Actually, I was going to do a photo and video montage of my trip and narrate over it." Her expression said that this didn't impress her either.

A boy dressed just about as well as Caroline (leather ankle boots, blazer over a cashmere turtleneck) said, "At least you'll have something totally brilliant to report— Daphne's. People bite off their arm to come here. You should find plenty to montage—eighteen floors' worth. Can you believe it, eighteen? I know, it's unbelievable, eh?" He stretched out his hand. "I'm Gordo."

"Hi," I said. "I guess you know who I am." I tried to rebound from "school report." "This is bril. I can't wait to shop. Very bril." Okay, maybe one too many "brils," but it was progress.

"Ooh, I love your accent . . . ," Caroline's friend with double-pierced ears and spiky hair said. "It's so . . . different."

"Thanks," I said, unsure if she really meant it as a compliment.

"Where are you from?" she asked.

"Wilmington," I said.

"Is that near Los Angeles?"

30

"Um, yup. It's near LA." Crap, I was reinventing myself as a liar. "Kinda, sorta near it."

"I'm Ellie with an *i-e*," said Spiky Hair. "I'm changing from a *y*. So, it's kind of a big deal."

"Interesting," I said, and I really thought it was. Maybe I'd change the spelling of my name. "How's that working for you?"

"So far it's like a bomb. I feel like a new person already. Which I guess I kind of am. You know, with the *i-e* and everything."

"Yup." I mentally considered this. *Jordan Jacoby . . . Jor? Jor Jack? J Jack? J.J.?* "My friends call me J.J.," I said quietly to test it with Ellie and see if the new name was okay.

"J.J.," Ellie said as if trying it out. "I like it."

Yay! I did too. In fact, it felt like a bomb. Like a whole-big-new-image bomb.

Gordo stopped gushing over Caroline's clothes long enough to order a skinny latte. "Fancy one?"

"Sure. Thanks. I'd fancy one." (I'd just said "fancy.") I'd heard people order coffee drinks whose names went on for half an hour . . . *A double mocha joka jerky over ice with a peppermint twist and a Kansas City pickle on the side.* "Whatever you're having."

"You got it, baby doll," Gordo said as he moved up in line.

31

Baby doll? I was gonna use that one at home too.

Gordo asked, "So, what's your story, J.J.?"

It took me half a second to realize he was talking to me. I was J.J. "Oh, you know, the usual. Regular thirteen-year-old girl." Little did Gordo know that "regular" was an exaggeration.

"What do you like to do?" he asked.

"You know, stuff. Girl stuff."

"Like regular thirteen-year-old girl stuff?"

"Exactly," I said, laughing.

"I see. So, you're not like an undercover secret agent or something? Or a famous movie star pretending to be an ordinary girl to get away from the paparazzi?"

"I'm positive."

Gordo's questions were interrupted when he ordered coffee.

The other guy with them had only looked in the cases of gourmet food. He bought a large bag of jelly beans. "I'm Sam. And for the record, I'm here for the candy, not the shopping." Whether you were in America or England, there was one word to describe Sam, and that word was "cute." He had rock-star blond hair that was longish in the front and buzzed in the back.

"Candy?"

"Okay," Sam said. "You got me." He pushed the longish part of his hair out of his eyes. "I like the pastries, too. I'm in search of a lemon tart from Lively's. It's just over there a bit, around the bend. When it's all clear, I'll get one."

Then he put his index finger and pinkie to his ear and mouth, like a phone. "Ring, bring!" he said. "Hello?" Then he said in a different voice, like it was the person on the other end of the phone talking, "Hi, this is the Truth Society calling. We just heard you tell a lie." And then he said, "Okay, you got me. I'll get at least two lemon tarts." The hand-phone disappeared.

"Um, okay," I said, not sure how to react to this strangeness. "Why do you have to wait for the all clear?"

Ellie picked up her coffee cup and turned around as she slid a bright pink straw through the little hole in the lid. "Because of Sebastian Lively. Lively is with a *y*. He works there for his dad. They own Lively's bakery in town. It's so popular that Daphne's asked them to open a counter here. And he works at it. Anyway, Sebastian is both annoying and evil. He hates us—well, mostly Caroline—because she told everyone he was half-midget and born in a circus."

"I had meant it to be funny," Caroline defended herself. "Turns out he's a half midget with no sense of humor."

Ellie laughed a little too hard. Caroline gave a very subtle head shake that told everyone that the laugh annoyed her. Ellie must've caught on, because she stopped and quickly added, "Sorry."

"Because Sebastian hates Caroline, he automatically hates us, too. So, it's not safe to eat his tarts," Sam said. "Even though Sebastian is a royal jerk—and I do mean *royal*, because he claims that somewhere in his lineage he has royal blood—his family's bakery is still the best."

"The best," Gordo confirmed.

Ellie continued, "Gordo convinced Sam that when Sebastian sees us coming, he spits in the lemon tarts."

"Seriously?" I asked. *Ew.*

"Totally serious." Gordo handed me a big cup that felt light, like it was only half-full. "Sebastian has quite a deviously creative mind."

I sipped the warm coffee drink and refrained from making a yuck-face, because if these cool kids drank lattes, then so could I.

I watched as Gordo used silver tongs to add brown sugar cubes to his drink. When he handed me the tongs, I did the same. The brown sugar dissolved, and I sipped it again. It was better. Good, actually. I liked holding this tall cup with a cardboard protector sleeve on it. The first thing I was going to do when I got home was go to Cup O' Joes and order a latte. My friend Darbie from home would be so impressed.

Caroline and Ellie joined us with their matching icy tan drinks. The straws had red lipstick rings at the top. I wanted to buy a tube of lipstick. I knew the cherry-flavored ChapStick in my backpack didn't make a ring like that.

"Shall we shop?" Caroline asked.

"Yes!" Ellie and Gordo said in unison. Sam ate a jelly bean.

Caroline looked at her watch. "Five and a half hours till closing."

I'd never shopped for five and a half hours! "Power-shopping" had a whole new meaning here.

"Why don't you go on ahead," Sam said. "J.J. looks like she wants a lemon tart."

Gordo narrowed his eyes at Sam. "Be careful." Then he looked at our group, which was about to split up. "Duli for dinner at seven?"

Caroline and Ellie nodded and slurped with their straws.

"Okay," said Ellie. "But for the record I have no respect for a place that ends with an i. It's like they couldn't decide between the i-e or the y. No respect at all."

Gordo whispered to Sam, "Duli is on the fifth floor behind the Persian rugs."

"Thanks. I can read a store map," Sam whispered back.

To me Gordo said, "Don't fill up on lemon tarts. There's lots of fish and chips to ingest. Cheers!"

"Cheers!" I echoed back. Fish and chips didn't sound good to me. I stuck with the usual stuff like burgers (no cheese), spaghetti (no sauce), and pretzels.

When they left, Sam said, "Don't like fish and chips, eh?"

"I love 'em. I can't wait for a dish of fish," I lied again. The un-boring of Jordan Jacoby would now include new foods too!

I followed him across the pretty lacquered floors, and he glanced back at me as we went deeper into the store. "You didn't look like you wanted to shop."

"I didn't?" *Of course I want to shop. How am I going to get a new look without shopping?*

"It's a gift I have. Like a sixth sense. Freaky, eh?" He grinned, and I realized he had dimples, really cute dimples.

"A little, I guess. But maybe it's not working well today, because I kinda would like to shop."

"Huh? Really? Strange. It's never not worked before. You don't look like a shopper."

36

I hope the translation of that didn't mean: "That ugly outfit looks like a hand-me-down."

I smelled it before I could see it: cinnamon and chocolate, cakes and pies baking. The scent entranced me and drew me deeper into the store. But the sight was even better.

It was an absolutely incredible scene, like Willy Wonka incredible. The Hall of Gourmets (kind of like a fancy food court, inside Daphne's) was dedicated solely to sweets. The display went way beyond candy to every type of baked treat you could imagine. A kiosk of bouquets made of cookies stood in the center; another kiosk specialized in cakes stacked five layers high. One cake was a replica of the store, with incredible detail right down to the brick front and windows showcasing dresses, sporting equipment, and toys. One area was floor to ceiling tubes of gummies. A tall ladder on wheels held a man who filled the tubes from the tops. Kids opened the bottom and let the candy pieces fall into their bags.

At the end of the hall I saw letters in glittery lights: Lively's.

It took me a minute to absorb the variety of desserts around me, during which I lost sight of Sam. I turned

37

in every direction but couldn't find him in his red long-sleeved oxford, untucked from his baggy jeans.

Someone tugged on my backpack, and I twisted around, then finally looked down. Sam was crouched down behind a potted plant.

5

"What are you doing?" I whispered to Sam.

"Hiding from Sebastian. He's there, working the counters. The short redheaded kid in the pink apron. If he sees me, I'm a goner."

I couldn't decide if it was better to crouch down or just keep talking, because it probably looked like I was chatting up a giant fern. "Goner? Really?"

"Fine, the Drama Police called, and they said maybe I'm not a goner, but I won't get a tart, which is pretty much the same thing. My blood sugar is low."

"Do you even know what low blood sugar is?" I didn't mention that he'd just pounded a ton of jelly beans.

"No. But mine is probably low, and that can't be a good thing."

Having grandparents who were diabetic, I knew what blood sugar was, but I didn't see the point in explaining it. I looked at Lively's. "So that short guy is Sebastian?"

"Yes. That's the evil bloke."

Sebastian waited on customers, rung them up, and wished them a nice day. "He looks harmless enough."

"Don't be fooled, J.J." Sam said.

I liked the sound of my new name. "I'll get you your tart," I offered. He was right. He was a British drama king hiding behind a potted plant in the Hall of Gourmets.

He said, "I couldn't ask you to do that, but it's a good idea. He won't know you."

I marched toward the line. When Sebastian came to take my order, he was very polite. "Two lemon tarts, please. Actually, make it three." I remembered that Sam wanted two.

He got me the tarts in a totally non-evil way. He used a square of waxy paper to pull them out of the glass case. When he turned to the counter to grab a box, my view was obstructed for a sec. Then he appeared with the box wrapped in red string. I paid for the tarts with some English coins.

Then Sebastian leaned over the counter to hand me my change. He motioned me closer. I leaned in.

"Tell Sam I can see him, eh?" he said, and gave me a totally evil grin.

My eyebrows shot up. I turned toward Sam and realized the potted plant was in front of a big mirror. He wasn't hidden at all.

"Nice try," Sebastian added as I walked away.

I pushed out a smile, my cheeks red from embarrassment. When I got back to Sam, I held up the box. "Success."

He took it.

I added, "Oh, and Sebastian says hi."

"Blast it! He saw me?"

"Afraid so."

He slid his butt onto the ground, blew the long pieces of blond hair out of his face, and rested his head against the pot. He held up the box. "Just take them away so I'm not tempted."

I took the box.

He said, "Do it."

"Do what?"

"Throw it away."

41

"Really?" I scowled. I'm pretty sure I paid at least ten bucks for those things. "That's such a waste."

"Rubbish! That's what this is! We'll come back later when he's gone. But I can't risk it . . . You know, the spit." He kind of gagged like the thought of Sebastian's saliva made him almost puke. I didn't like the idea myself.

I threw away the white box. Total bummer, since I was *starving*. Now I'd have to wait until seven o'clock for fish and chips.

He asked, "Wanna go for a walk or something?"

What I really wanted to do was find Caroline and get started on my new look before we toured the city.

I was going to see and do absolutely everything in a new outfit! I didn't care if I didn't sleep for five days. . . . Oh, the thought of sleep reminded me how tired I was. I really needed to sleep. I also really needed a snack.

"Bring! Bring!" Sam said, interrupting my thoughts. "Anybody home?"

I snapped to attention. "A walk sounds good." My stomach growled. "But I think I'm going to get a cookie."

"You'd better get it from over there. They don't . . . you know." He pretended like he was spitting.

I went to the place with the cookie bouquets and got a big sugar cookie and ate it in three bites.

"Wow," Sam said. He held up his hand with a finger

42

toward his mouth and another toward his ear like a pretend phone. "This is the Hungry Company. Is J.J. there?" He held his hand toward me. "It's for you."

I giggled a little bit. I didn't actually understand the phone thing, but it was funny. I wanted to get to know Sam better. He was goofy, but not in a dorky way. And even a dull American could see he was very good-looking.

"British girls are all itsy-bitsy about their bites of tiny sandwiches. It's so unrealistic. If you're hungry, you're hungry." Then he added, "Let's go. If you've never been here, there's some cool stuff I can show you. Like the Hole."

6

"There's a hole?"

"Well, that's what they call it. It's more like a lift shaft without the lift," he said.

Maybe "pram" wasn't in my pre-trip homework, but I knew that "lift" was an elevator, so that gave me a decent picture.

When we stood at the bottom of the Hole and looked up eighteen floors, I understood what he was trying to explain. It *was* like an elevator shaft, but instead of being surrounded by walls, it was surrounded by escalators that made a square frame. Some department must've been giving away balloons, because a few floated up.

"This is all one store?"

"Yup. One big store that takes up a city block."

Sam hopped on the up escalator.

We rode up one story and stopped on the landing. A glass display case showed what was on that floor. This floor was Toys, so the windows on the landing were decorated with games, puzzles, stuffed animals, remote control planes, and electric cars. Music trickled out from inside the toy department, and a line of kids snaked out the door.

"Every few floors there's something for kids to do while their parents shop. My little sister loves to come with my mom to play dress-up in the Formal Wear Department."

The next floor was Cosmetics and Jewelry, where we could smell the faint scents of various perfumes. The mannequins in the windows were drenched in necklaces and bracelets.

Hmmm . . . maybe my makeover can start on this floor?

Eventually we passed Persian rugs, so I knew that was where we were having dinner. As we walked, I scanned the crowd. People of every color and nationality I could imagine were browsing the store: women

45

with black shrouds over their heads that only allowed a crack for their eyes, men with long black beards and furry sideburns, people with pale white skin to very dark brown skin and black hair.

"What do you think?" Sam asked as we went up another level.

Daphne's wasn't the ginormous London Eye Ferris wheel that overlooked the Thames River (which was one of the things I really wanted to do this week), but I had to admit, it was pretty amazing. "It's definitely bigger than I thought it would be. I don't know of any place quite like it in the US. We have big department stores like Bloomingdale's and Saks Fifth Avenue. It's like this place ate those stores *and* a carnival. Is there anything it doesn't have?"

"A planetarium, a racetrack, and an ice rink. They're working on a cinema and a bowling alley."

I thought he was kidding me, but he didn't laugh. "Seriously," he said. "And a helicopter pad on the roof for people traveling from really far. Later this year they'll let people bungee from off the side of the building."

I narrowed my eyes.

He grinned. "Okay, you got me. I made that one up. Don't call the Exaggeration Patrol. But the others are true, and if I made a suggestion about the bungee, I bet they'd make that happen too."

"Maybe you should."

"Maybe I will," he said, playfully pushing my shoulder.

"We should find Caroline," I suggested.

"Good idea," Sam said. "Let's round up the gang and play a game of Slip Away."

7

"What's Slip Away?" I asked.

"We use the whole store. One group flees and the other searches. Every fifteen minutes the flee-ers text the searchers a clue about where they're hiding."

"It sounds like hide-and-seek."

"Hide-and-seek is for tots. This is way more."

Sam clicked at his phone, which he called a "mobile" (with a long *i*, so it rhymed with "pile"), as we approached the landing of Formal Wear and Kids' Dress-Up Department on the tenth floor.

"They're on their way," he said.

A minute later the golden double doors of an elevator opened. Out walked Caroline, carrying multiple big white shopping bags with the Daphne's logo. Ellie and Gordo came out behind her, each also carrying a bag or two.

Did I miss the shopping?

"Game on?" Gordo asked. His hair had been gelled up like a rock star's, and I think he'd put on eyeliner. They'd gone to the salon! I *had* missed it.

Sam nodded and gave his friend a fist bump.

"Oh, I don't know," said Ellie, examining her cuticles. "I was hoping for a manicure." *Oh, me too!* Maybe I could go home with long elegant nails.

Gordo said, "You can get a mani any day. In fact, I'll come back with you tomorrow if you want."

"Okay, then I'm in," she said.

Caroline sighed. "Fine. But I'll need to find a locker."

Gordo took her bags from her hands. "I'll take care of that for you. There's some by the loo." He disappeared down a hallway with a restroom sign.

"What are the teams?" Ellie asked. "Last time I fleed and this time I want to search. I could be like the captain of the searchers."

"Let's do the coin method," Sam said. "It's the most fair."

Gordo reappeared. "Good plan."

Sam reached into the pocket of his baggy jeans and handed a coin to everyone. "Odd years are searchers. Even years are flee-ers."

I took the coin Sam gave me and looked at the date: 1970. "Even," I said.

"Odd," said Gordo and Ellie. They moved next to each other.

"Even," Sam said.

Caroline didn't say anything but moved to our even team.

"It's three versus two." Sam, Caroline, and I were going to hide.

Gordo said, "You better run. You only have two minutes."

Sam took off.

"I love to search. You guys better watch out," Ellie called after us. "I'm coming after you!"

Caroline tried to keep up with Sam and me, but with her high-heeled boots, running didn't come easily. I almost crashed into a group of women wearing colorful belly dancing pants trimmed with small metal discs that jingled as they moved out of my way.

"Sorry," I said, not losing pace.

We stopped near the tuxedos and huddled. Sam said, "Okay, Caroline go to Toys. J.J., you go to Linens."

Linens? I wasn't going to be able to search for a new look in Linens.

"J.J.?" Caroline asked, forgetting, or not noticing, that I'd changed my name earlier.

"That's what my friends call me." I waited a beat for her approval. I didn't get it. It felt like a sting.

Caroline left without much of a run.

Sam said, "I'm going to Garden." He went to the escalator.

"Wait," I called. "Which way to Linens?"

He pointed to the "lift" and held up six fingers.

"And what do I do when I get there?"

"You text a clue about where you are, like, 'Cover me up, I'm cold.'" And Sam disappeared up the escalators.

"Wait!"

He started walking down the upward-moving stairs. "What?"

"I don't have anyone's cell phone numbers."

He ran down faster and jumped the last few steps to return to the landing. "Gimme your digits. I'll text everyone. Then you'll have 'em all."

I told him my number, and he practically shoved me into the elevator.

Downstairs I found Linens and looked for a place to hide. There were thousands of possibilities. Behind a pile

51

of towels, under a display bed that was wrapped in pretty sheets and comforters, among stacks of blankets . . . But a fake tub caught my eye, mostly because I thought of a great clue: "Rub-a-dub-dub."

I opened my phone and saw a text from Sam. I guess he'd already found a hiding spot, because he'd sent everyone a note that said, "Rhymes with noses." Since he was in Garden, I guessed he was hidden among roses, although it could've been hoses.

I replied to everyone with my awesome clue and pulled back the display shower curtain that partially hid a claw-foot bathtub. When it seemed like no one was looking, I casually pulled the curtain aside and slipped behind it.

The tub was filled with light pink plastic balls that looked like bubbles. I dug a foot in between the balls, and when I touched the bottom of the tub, I put the other foot in too. I carefully sunk into the bubbles until I was completely covered. I only left myself a little crack to watch the back side of the shower curtain so I'd know when someone pushed it aside.

The tub was surprisingly comfortable. Cozy, actually. I wanted to shop rather than play this game, which wasn't as dumb as I thought it would be, but now that I was lying here, it felt good.

I yawned and waited.

8

No one came.

After a long time—I'm not sure how long because I fell asleep—I woke up. I could tell something was different.

Strange.

Dark.

Quiet.

Even a little eerie.

I crept out of my hiding place. The lights in the store were off. There were some dim security lights. I heard a strange slapping sound on the outside wall that was closest to me. It took a minute to get the sleepy fuzz from my eyes and focus on a window. When I did, I saw lots of rain and a flag hanging off the side of the building, flapping viciously in the wind.

What is going on?

I took my phone out of my back pocket and checked it. It was completely blank. *Broken?* I fiddled with the buttons, and the screen lit up. *My butt turned it off!* I dialed the last number that had texted me.

Sam answered, "Where are you?"

"Linens."

"Seriously?"

"Yeah. That's where you told me to go."

Sam said, "Like three hours ago."

Three *hours*? I'd slept in a department store bathtub for three stinkin' hours?

"Where are *you*? Did you get found?" I peeked around a display of purple towels in search of another human. No one was in the dark room. A chill went up the entire back of my boring body, telling me this was anything but dull; it was bad.

"Found? No. J.J., are you off your trolley? The game is over. It's been over. The store lost electricity in this storm. Everyone had to leave. Where have you been?"

What storm? I had a dreadful feeling that I'd just woken up in the middle of a scene from a horror movie, and I was the main character. We had crossed exciting and gone to scary. I wondered if I'd rather be bored. "So no fish and chips?" I asked. I couldn't think of anything else to say, and besides worrying about being slashed by a department store killer, I had food on the brain, in a big way.

"We *had* chips a while ago without you," Sam said. "We thought maybe you found the Dress-Up Department or you got to demo an electric car or something better than dinner." Well, dang. Now I was hungry, scared, sans a new outfit, and *also* bummed I didn't demo an electric car. "We stayed in the store as long as we could looking for you. You didn't answer your phone. What's 'Rub-a-dub-dub'?"

"You know the poem 'Rub-a-dub-dub, three men in a tub'?"

There was an odd pause. "None of us knew what that clue meant."

"What floor are you on?" I asked. "I'll come find you."

"No floor," Sam said. "I'm across the street. The store closed. As in the doors are locked."

My mouth went dry. "What are you saying?"

"I'm trying to say that you're locked in."

If this was a horror movie, really spooky music would've played right at that moment. A lump formed in my throat as I finally grasped the very dire situation.

"I'm all alone."

"Not exactly," Sam said. "There's Ham."

"There's a ham?" A sandwich sounded really good right about now.

"A bloke named Hamlet. He's the night security guard," Sam said.

"I'll find him, and he can let me out."

"No!"

"Why not?"

"DO NOT let Hamlet see you," he said. "He caught Caroline last time we played Slip Away. She got in a heap of trouble. He called her dad, who sent Hamlet a sack of money to let us out of the store's security office. He said he wouldn't do it again; next time he'd ban her from the store."

"Do I really have to stay in here all night?" I asked, panicked.

"That's an option, but we have a plan. We're arranging to rescue you."

"What? How?" Then I heard footsteps coming from Linens. "Someone's coming," I whispered to Sam.

"I know."

"Is it Hamlet? Is he going to take me to security and handcuff me to a chair?"

An arm shoved the shower curtain aside. It was Caroline. She looked royally mad. "There you are."

"Thank God it's you," I said, sitting up. A few plastic bubbles fell out of the tub and rolled across the floor, disappearing underneath a nearby bed.

"You've gotten us into quite a jam."

"I didn't do it on purpose. I fell asleep. You know, jet lag and all."

"What I know is that my friends left the store before it closed, and I stayed in here looking for you, and now we're snookered."

"You got locked in on purpose to look for me?" I guess she had started to like me. She was worried about me.

She continued, "There's no way I could go home to my stepmum without you. If I lost our abroad student, she would make my life miserable. After all, that is her purpose in life."

Or maybe she wasn't concerned about *me* at all.

I followed Caroline to the escalators, which were turned off. We walked down in a crouched position, below the handrail so that we couldn't be seen by anyone (well, Hamlet) who might be on one of the landings.

"Where are you going?" I whispered.

"To the door."

"If the store is closed, don't you think the doors will be locked?"

"Yes, Madam Obvious, I think the doors will be locked." She clucked her tongue like I was a total idiot. She quickly sent a text message. A minute later we were on the ground floor at one of the many sets of big glass doors. We hid behind a tower of boxes wrapped like pretty presents for a party at Buckingham Palace.

Sam appeared on the other side of the glass doors, on the sidewalk in the rain, and started knocking. He looked pretty wet, but it seemed like it had eased up since I'd looked out the window in Linens. When Hamlet didn't come, Sam knocked louder.

I heard a set of feet wearing wet shoes squeak through Purses to the door. Hamlet removed a clunky set of keys from a clip on his belt and turned several locks on the door.

"What is it?" he asked Sam. "Store's closed."

"Thank goodness you're here, sir," Sam said urgently. "I got home from shopping and realized I didn't have my wallet." He made a desperate face. "My mum is gonna kill me. I'm serious. She's loony. If I come home without her credit card, she'll bloody flip." His eyes were surrounded by raindrops that could easily be mistaken for tears.

Hamlet said, "Calm down. She'll understand."

"You don't know her. She's off the north side of the cliffs, if you know what I mean."

Hamlet's eyebrows shot up like he couldn't believe this kid was so afraid of his mother.

"I think I left it at Lively's, which is another problem. If I tell her that, she'll remind me of how fat I am. I'm not supposed to have sweets."

Sam was NOT fat, but the detail added to the picture of his allegedly psycho mother. I had to clap a hand over my mouth to keep myself from giggling.

He continued. "But sometimes I can't help myself. They have the best tarts."

Hamlet patted his chubby stomach. "Don't I know it."

"Can I get it? The wallet, not a tart. I promise, no tarts."

"Sorry, lad. I can't let anyone in after closing. Rules. But wait out here, and I'll take a look at Lively's. If I see it, I'll bring it out, eh?"

Sam shivered more. "Oh, okay, thanks." He gave his teeth a chatter.

Hamlet stood aside. "Come in and stand here and wait. Don't move." He eyed Sam carefully. "I mean it."

Sam stepped inside and stood in front of the unlocked door. As soon as Hamlet was out of sight, we would all dash through the unlocked door.

Hamlet tried to reach around Sam to get to the locks. Sam kept going in the wrong direction and getting in the way. The two of them sidestepped in an awkward dance in which Sam was always in the wrong place.

"Step aside, lad," Hamlet finally said. He released the key ring from his belt, and just as he was about to twist the locks, Ellie came running up to the door.

"Wait," she called, raising her arms like she was protesting.

"We're closed," Hamlet said through the glass door.

"That's my brother." She pointed at Sam. "And . . . and . . . ummm . . . I cannot let you . . . umm . . . You can't kidnap him!" she said, her voice rising about thirteen octaves.

"Kidnap?"

"Yes, that's what I said. Kidnap. Now let him go or I'll call the police right now." She held up her phone.

Ham pushed the door open. "No one's kidnapping anyone."

She made an act of calming herself down. "Oh, okay, then. As long as that's settled." She looked at him and searched for something else to say. "Nice keys. Do you lock all the doors?"

She was being so totally obvious.

"Yeah. That's my job. Now you and your brother, neither of which I am kidnapping, clear off. I'll check for your wallet, but only if you get out right now. Otherwise you'll have to come back tomorrow."

They stepped outside. Ellie casually left her toe in the door, keeping it open just a smidge. Did she really think that was going to work?

Hamlet released the bulky key ring for a third time and reached for the highest lock. He immediately saw the crack in the door. Looking down, he noticed Ellie's foot. "Do you mind?"

She pulled it out. "Not at all," she said.

Hamlet twisted the locks and walked away, turning occasionally to watch them argue on the sidewalk.

Not surprisingly, a few minutes later Hamlet returned empty-handed, and with a slight hint of powdered sugar around his mouth. I turned off the flash and took a picture of the man. I figured that if I was going to photo-document this trip, I might as well start with Hamlet.

Without unlocking the glass doors, he yelled, "No wallet!" He turned away, and his squeaky shoes took him back toward the Hall of Gourmets. My stomach sank.

Sam and Ellie walked away, heads down. Drenched.

Caroline's phone vibrated. She showed me a text from Sam. "Fail. You're stuck."

Caroline didn't send a reply.

"What are we gonna do?" I asked. If my mom found out that I was locked in a department store on my first night in London, she'd make me come home right away. My whole trip would be blown.

She exhaled. "There's only one thing we can do."

"Turn ourselves in to Hamlet?"

"Um, no. Think again."

No escape? No turn-in?

She tapped a few texts. Then she snapped her phone shut and put it in her purse. "Stepmum and Dad think we're sleeping at Ellie's. Ellie, Gordo, and Sam know the cover story and they'll meet us in the morning." Caroline headed for the escalator. "If we're locked in here all night, we're going to SHOP!"

9

Finally! I can get my new look after all!

"What about Hamlet?" I asked to the back of her head.

"There are eighteen floors. We'll just have to stay a few behind him as he does his rounds."

"What about the security cameras?" I pointed to one mounted on a wall in a corner.

"J.J., this may be the luckiest day ever, because those cameras are not on. There is usually a little green blinking light. Perhaps when the electricity is out, the cameras go out too."

"I guess that is lucky," I said, staring at the camera. She was right; nothing was blinking.

We walked up the escalator and stopped when we heard Hamlet humming "A Spoonful of Sugar" from *Mary Poppins*.

Caroline said, "We canNOT get caught. That would ruin my life. Got it?"

Caroline and I stayed a floor behind Hamlet, so we would know where he was. While he did his security thing on the floor above us, we stopped at Cosmetics and Jewelry.

Just enough light from the moon and a few emergency bulbs allowed us to see. We wandered over to one of the counters, and Caroline found a white smock and a palette of colors. "Might as well give you a makeover."

Maybe Caroline's sixth sense was better than Sam's, because it was like she was reading my mind. Or maybe I really looked like I needed a makeover, which sort of hurt my feelings, even if it was the same thing I'd been thinking all along.

"You could use a bit more color around your eyes," she said, and proceeded to brush powders onto my eyelids. Her art project continued with liner, mascara, fat brushes of bronzer and blush, and finally lipstick.

Before I looked in the mirror, I told myself this was

the first glimpse of the new me. I could wash it off if I hated it. I just really wanted to love it. She spun the stool around. "Voilà," she said.

I opened my eyes. "Wow!"

"I know, eh? There was, like, this totally cute person just waiting to come out."

Well, she didn't say that right, but maybe a compliment was hidden in there. The colors she'd chosen were natural. They brightened everything—my eyes, my skin. It looked really good.

"Wait till we get to the salon and I can do something with your hair."

That definitely didn't sound nice. I'd always liked my hair, but now I thought it could use a refresh to go with this face.

We spritzed the perfume testers as we walked by. We got back on the frozen escalators and walked up until we heard Hamlet humming on the floor above Shoes.

Caroline was drawn to the Shoe Department like a cat to a bowl of warm milk—which reminded me of how hungry I was.

She tried on several shoes that were on display, then approached a door behind the cash register.

With a display boot in her hand, she said, "The stuff in the back is always the be-all. Come on."

I wasn't sure about "be-all," but I think she meant that the shoes in the back were really good.

She turned the doorknob, and we went in. She did something on her phone, and it let out a strong glow. "Flashlight app," she explained. The light revealed towers and towers of shoe boxes. She grinned. "Hello there, my darlings. I'm here, and I'm going to try you all on. All you size thirty-sevens, that is."

Thirty-sevens? Clearly they had different sizing in England than we did.

She showed me how to find the style number on the display shoe and then on the box. The boxes were well organized, so finding what we were looking for was easy.

Moments later I was strolling around in brown flats.

Caroline looked at the shoes I'd chosen. "I'll pick some for you. Do you usually wear jeans like that?"

"Sometimes I wear leggings."

"Of course," she said, like leggings were not the be-all.

I found a mirror and studied my made-up face while I waited. Maybe I'd buy some makeup.

Caroline returned with three boxes. "Try these."

I opened one, then the others. "These are all heels. I wear jeans."

"Who says you can't wear heels with jeans? It's not like they're stilettos."

I hesitated, but I tried on the peepy-toed shoes. (I think that's what they're called.) I walked a bit. They weren't bad. In fact, they were easier to walk in than I thought they'd be. My legs felt longer. I looked in the mirror. Heels looked good with jeans. Who knew?

I guess Caroline did, since I actually liked all three pairs that she had picked out for me.

Caroline tried on really outrageous boots, like with glitter. Somehow they worked for her. After trying a few more on, she came back into the room with a big paper shopping bag. "They look really good. You should take those."

"What? Steal them? No. No way."

"No. Not steal. There's no need to nick. We have an account here. We can just set everything aside and ring it all up in the morning when the store opens."

"Seriously?"

"Quite." We continued to try on shoes—lots of them. I even snapped some pictures so that I'd remember the ones I liked but had left behind. I also shot a short video of our feet in different shoes walking up and down the aisle between the towers of shoes.

We continued to stay far enough from Hamlet as he went about his rounds. We made another stop in Teen Fashions.

Caroline picked out all kinds of clothes for me. I stayed in the dressing room, and she threw stuff over the top.

I paraded around like a runway model, feeling transformed. One shirt didn't have straps (none!), another had swinging fringes, some pants were tight to the ankles, others swayed while I walked. I felt glamorous. Pretty. Totally un-boring.

After an hour of mixing and matching, I decided to wear a new pair of skinny jeans, a long tank top, and a wide belt that rested just below my waist. I added a pair of boots I'd just gotten. They were high—like horseback riding boots. I loved this outfit too much to take it off. Caroline managed to snip the tags and gathered them in a small bag, so that we could pay for it all later and get the security tags removed.

After a little while I'd filled two more shopping bags and taken another video of myself by holding my camera out and trying to capture the outfit.

Finally we were at the salon. Caroline added the flashlight app to my phone, so we had two. I sat in a beautician's chair and spun around in it. She held up a device that looked like a small sandwich maker. "This is a flat iron. It should be your best friend."

She took a section of my hair and put it between two pieces of flat metal, then clamped them shut, sandwiching my hair in between. Then she pulled gently and the iron slid from the crown of my head to the tips of the hair.

"If you do that at home, it will come out pencil straight. Of course, it's not hot now because we don't have electricity." I thought my hair was straight already. She brushed it out and sprayed it with some stuff that made it look supershiny.

Then Caroline took a small piece of my hair and rubbed a stinky-smelling cream on it.

I stiffened. "What is that? Chemicals?" I'd never had any chemicals in my hair. What if she didn't know what she was doing?

"Relax. I've watched my stylist do this a hundred times." She held up a jar of hair lotion that clearly said "blond" on it. "If you don't like it, you can always put the color back in."

"What? You're taking color *out*?" Maybe I wasn't meant to handle un-boring. My heart pounded.

"It's all the rage. Trust me on this. I know what I'm talking about."

A minute later she washed the small section of my hair in the sink and combed it out. I had a streak of blond hair. I couldn't stop staring at it, because I didn't believe it. . . . It looked fantastic, red-carpet fantastic. I *never* felt this glam. And I liked the way it felt. She put in a couple of bobby pins, and the hairstyle looked even better.

On our way out Caroline took a flat iron and added it to my bag. That's when we heard something.

Someone was humming "New York, New York."

We froze.

10

With no time to hide, we clicked off the flashlight apps and stood perfectly still. *Perfectly.*

Hamlet was an older man. He shuffled along without stopping at the salon, steadily proceeding to the next escalator, which he was forced to walk up, since it wasn't moving. Once he was past us, Caroline said, "Do you know what that means?"

"What?"

"He has already checked all the floors above us. We can go all around now and not worry about getting caught."

"Don't you think he'll come back?"

"Why would he? He's done his thing. It's not like people are just going to materialize and gallivant around dressing up and making over."

"It isn't?"

She laughed. "No. Now, let's go to the Dress-Up Department and gallivant."

"Like in dresses?" I asked.

"Not in any ordinary dresses. Wait until you see this."

I followed her up another floor, to Formal Wear. The landing area was set up like a prom with a disco ball, and mannequins in tuxedos and glittery gowns. We ran past the racks of dresses until we got to a back corner that was a medieval castle. It wasn't decorated to look like a palace; it actually *was* a palace built *inside* the store. Mannequins of knights stood guard.

Caroline walked over a bridge and into the palace. It was packed with trunks of crowns, necklaces, scarves, and scepters. Shelves of Styrofoam heads wore wigs: straight red hair, blond braids, jet-black pixie cut.

Along the walls were hanging displays of every kind of gown you could imagine. Some were bustled and bunched up at the back, while others had long trains draped behind them. There were also costumes for boys and men: a British policeman uniform; a yeoman uniform, which was a one-piece black kilt with red trim and an embroidered red crown on the chest; and a royal guard with a red jacket, black pants, and a hat that looked like a giant black Q-tip.

This palace was like the biggest box of dress-up clothes imaginable.

I chose a wig that was a half mile high in tight brown curls, and a velvet gown suitable for a coronation, then disappeared behind a pretty white screen with little pink flowers painted all over it.

Caroline grabbed a tight, red satin dress with spaghetti straps and a hot pink wig. She played music on her mobile and we changed, and then we danced around in our fancy outfits.

I put my phone on a ledge and set it to video-record us dancing around. But the ledge was low, so I probably cut our heads off. I didn't care. It wasn't like this would go into the montage. I was having the best time of my life and I wanted it photo-documented. "I love this place," I said.

"If you think this rocks, I can show you something even more fab."

"No way. Better than this?"

"Follow me." She went toward the Hole and paused. "Shh."

I stood silently.

She listened. "No humming. No squeaky shoes. The coast is clear. Let's move on." She ran up the escalator.

I tugged up my dress and followed her toward the Children's Department. I couldn't imagine what we were going to do there until I saw it: a trampoline the size of my backyard. It was surrounded by an enchanted garden.

Caroline kicked off her shoes, climbed on, and started bouncing. I joined her, jumping higher and higher. Finally I held my breath and gathered the layers of my gown in one hand and flipped backward, landing triumphantly on my feet.

"Wow! How did you learn to do that?" she asked.

"Gym class, I guess." I plopped on my butt and popped up. "Try that."

She did, and she giggled the whole time.

I tried to get some real action videos with my phone, but with all the bouncing and wig hair, I'm not sure what I got.

I bounced myself sweaty and eventually flopped onto the springy floor, flat on my back as I tried to catch my breath.

"Something wrong?" Caroline asked.

"I'm pooped."

"I'm a bit zonked myself," she said. "I know where we can crash for the night . . . like real princesses."

"Really?"

"The Furniture Department is just one floor up."

"And they have beds?"

"Big, beautiful beds."

"I'm there," I said.

A few minutes later we were back in our regular clothes and tucked into side-by-side king beds. We chose two that couldn't be seen with a quick glance from the hallway. And for a little extra insurance, we took a wooden screen like would be used to separate a room into two parts and relocated it to shield the beds.

I sank my head onto a feather pillow and almost fell asleep instantly, thinking about my first day in London. I had set out for an experience to change my life, but got so much more. I was changing my life *and* my image. This trip *had* become an adventure. It had been a wonderful day, trapped-in-a-mega-department-store-slash-carnival wonderful.

Caroline had started out not liking me, but now I thought she was my friend. "I had a great time today," I said. "Thanks."

She said nothing.

I turned to look at her. Her eyes were closed and she was breathing deeply.

I started falling into a dream about *The Wizard of Oz*, when I realized I wasn't dreaming. Someone was humming "Over the Rainbow."

11

I peeked under the oriental screen and saw Hamlet's wet shoes making their way over to us. Apparently he didn't go to sleep. He *did* go through his rounds a second time.

I grabbed a few big pillows and covered Caroline with them as my heart climbed into my throat. I did a good job, because I couldn't even tell she was in the bed.

His steps got closer, and my panic rose higher in my stomach. I pulled the comforter back up so my bed would look made, and then I got down on my belly and crawled under it.

Hamlet came right up to the screen and switched songs to "Tomorrow" from *Annie*. I held my breath and prayed Caroline wouldn't move or snore. I could see the thick soles of his squeaky orthopedic shoes come behind the wooden screen. A few more steps, and I could reach out and touch his toes.

Then he turned and left.

By the time he was at "I just stick out my chin and grin and say . . . ," it sounded like he was back at the Hole.

I got back into bed and fell asleep.

Quickly.

Deeply.

It seemed like I was only out for a few seconds when Caroline woke me, but according to my watch it was eight a.m. "You sleep like the dead. I thought I'd never be able to knock you awake," she said. "Let's get out of here."

I put my shoes on, made the bed, and got my backpack. We walked down the frozen escalator all the way to the Purse Department. "You going to pick one out?" Caroline asked.

I thought my pack worked just fine for me. "Sure. I mean, you're sure we're going to pay for it?"

"I promise we'll pay for it. I don't know if I can say the same for breakfast, though."

"What breakfast?"

"The one we're going to take from Lively's. And, J.J., I do mean 'take,' like steal. Sebastian can't spit on it if he's not there, and technically you paid for tarts yesterday that were rubbish; so he owes you."

When she put it that way, I didn't feel bad about taking tarts from Sebastian. However, even though Caroline and I had an awesome night, I believed she'd probably been very mean to Sebastian and deserved to be cut off from his tarts.

I picked out a purse using a very scientific method I like to call eenie-meenie-miney-mo. Caroline nodded her approval, so I guess I'd eenie-meenie-ed a good brand and style.

From behind the counter at Lively's, we slid the pastry case open. Caroline took a scone and bit into it with an "Mmmm."

I took one too. I had to agree. It was like dessert-for-breakfast good. Caroline threw a big white box at me. "Fill that."

"Really?"

"For as long as he's been withholding these awesome treats from us, yes. Fill it."

I took my backpack off so that I could reach inside the case. I chose a mix of different pastries so that it wouldn't be obvious that we'd ransacked the shelves.

Caroline took out my phone and made a video of me half inside the case. She narrated a pretend documentary, "Desperate for carbs after a long night of mischief while locked inside Daphne's, the creature snatches countless pastries—"

An overhead light came on and surprised her.

"Ohmigod the power's back on. Get your bum out of there," she whispered. "We gotta hide from the security cameras."

I removed myself from the case and followed Caroline to a hiding place that was *not* in front of a mirror but behind a stone statue of a naked man with leaves covering the . . . essentials.

It was a half hour until opening, and the store workers filed in to prepare the Hall of Gourmets for the day.

I thought for sure a worker would spot us and know we'd been there all night, but nobody came to our little corner behind the naked statue. We hung out for another twenty or thirty minutes after the store finally opened and customers entered. Then, very calmly, as if we'd just done some early-morning shopping, Caroline casually

walked to a register and paid for the items we'd accumu-
lated throughout the night.

Sam, Ellie, and Gordo were waiting for us on the
sidewalk.

"You survived?" Ellie asked. "How was it? What did
you do? Ohmigosh. I have majorly good news—I found
my turtle earring that I thought I'd lost." She pointed to
her ear. "I was getting out of the shower and—POW!—I
saw it on the floor in the corner. I mean, what are the
odds of that? And—"

Caroline cut her off. "It was a nightmare being locked
in the nirvana of shopping all night, but we survived."

Gordo said, "Now, *that's* good news."

Ellie said, "J.J., I love your hair like that."

My cheeks warmed. "Thanks," I said, shrugging like
it was no big deal. At least it was dry now. And I could
try out that flat iron when we got back to Caroline's
house. In fact, I was psyched to try it. "We had a ton of
time to kill."

I caught Sam staring at me. Self-consciously my
hands went to my newly-dyed hair. "Something wrong?"

"No," he said. "Um, how did you make out? You . . .
look . . . look different."

"*Good* different?"

"Um, there was nothing wrong before, but yeah,

81

good." This time he turned his head, allowing longish hairs to cover his face.

My insides jumped up and yelled, *Yay!* I had no idea what it would feel like to get a compliment like that from a boy. A cute British boy. And it felt—well, it "took the biscuit." They say that, right?

I said to Sam, "You look good too." He did in an untucked, crisply ironed oxford.

I held up the Lively's box. "I got something for you. No spit."

"Aces!" He took the box and popped a lemon square into his mouth.

I asked him, "What is that sound? Is that the Hungry Club calling?"

Sam laughed at my impersonation of him.

Ellie and Caroline slowly inched themselves away from us and talked in whispers. I was a little bummed that I wasn't included in their secret chat.

I figured since I had just had an incredible night with Caroline, we were friends, right? And rather than standing with the boys, I could move over to the girls' area and see what was going on, right?

I could be like: "Hey, guys, latte?"

Or maybe: "What's up, girlfriends?"

Perhaps: "That was so awesome, eh?"

I decided I'd go with: "It's gonna be hard to find something to top that today, huh?"

I took a step closer to the whispers and was ready to give my line, when I heard Caroline saying, "It was soooo boring . . ." Quickly I turned before they could tell that I'd heard.

She didn't have a fun time last night? There's no way she was that good an actress. She must have been talking about something else. I pretended to look through my Daphne's bag and listened hard to see if I could get anything else.

Ellie said, "She's from a small town in America. Things are different there."

"Yeah. Lame," Caroline said. "It was like she'd never been in a store before."

"But isn't that exciting for *you*? You can, like, teach her. You know, like in that vampire movie. When Priscilla, the two-hundred-year-old vampiress, had to show the new vamp how to hunt."

"Oh, I love that picture," Caroline said. "But she's not a newborn vampire."

Sam called over to me, interrupting me from eavesdropping on the rest of the conversation. "Hey!" He was holding up his cell phone. "It says it's you calling." I wasn't making a call. "Are you dialing me with your bum?" he joked.

Instantly my hands went to the back pocket of my new skinny jeans. No phone.

He picked it up and listened. His expression changed from amused to annoyed. "Hello, Sebastian."

Sebastian? From my phone? Where is my phone?

I looked around.

My backpack—it wasn't here.

I had left it in the store.

At Lively's.

My stomach plunged to my knees. I'd left my backpack at the scene of the crime!

Sam's expression flattened. "He's sending us a list." Touching the screen of his mobile, he saw it and read it out loud for us. "It says: salon, trampoline, unmade beds, costumes, shoe department, and stolen electronics . . ." Sam looked at me and Caroline. "What's he talking about?"

Gordo asked, "What the heck did you guys do? And why did you steal stuff?"

Caroline assured him, "We didn't steal anything."

Sam added, "And there were items taken from the bakery."

"Except a few items from the bakery," Caroline said. Gordo gave her a questioning look. "Seriously."

Gordo said, "He must think it was you guys."

Ellie added, "Tell the midget to prove it!"

"How does he have your phone?" Caroline asked me with an angry tone.

"I must've left my backpack behind his counter."

"That's just bril, J.J.," Caroline snapped, and it hurt. All the wonderfulness of the most exciting night I ever had in my life melted into a bazillion pieces like it never happened.

Ellie said, "That doesn't prove anything. You could've left your backpack there yesterday. Someone saw it lying around and tossed it behind Lively's counter like it was a sack of tomatoes." She said it like *to-mah-toes*. "And no one saw it until the morning."

Gordo corrected her, "Potatoes." *Po-tah-toes*.

"Exactly," Ellie agreed.

"Simply genius," Caroline said to me, not listening to the possible *po-tah-to* explanation, which I thought was good.

Well, she may be mad at me, but this definitely isn't boring.

Ellie looked at Sam's phone some more. "I'm loving that wig."

12

"Wig?" Caroline barked. She snatched the cell phone out of Sam's hands. "Oh, how great is this? He has the photos and videos. He can prove we were in the store last night."

Sam spoke to Sebastian on the cell phone, not his finger-phone. "I'll come in now and get the backpack and the mobile. And I'll pay you for the sweets. You should take it as a compliment; we love them."

Under her breath Caroline said, "It's *you* we hate."

Sam seemed to be listening to Sebastian. "Hang on. Calm down. I'm gonna put you on the speaker so everyone can hear your ranting." He pushed the button and held the cell phone out for us to hear.

Sebastian was already talking. "—don't bother coming in to pick it up, because I'm not giving it back."

Gordo said, "Don't get your knickers in a twist, Sebastian boy. We can work something out."

"Yes, we can, Gordo. I already have."

"What do you mean?" Sam asked.

"Here's the deal," Sebastian said. "I have a paper due in four days. It's about the demotion of our poor planet Pluto. You guys are going to write it for me. I will get two hundred and fifty words of this paper e-mailed to me at eight o'clock every night for three nights. Then, on Friday morning I'll e-mail it to my teacher. If I don't get them—"

"If you don't get them, then what?" Gordo tested him.

"I'll tell you!" Sebastian snapped. He paused, drawing out the suspense. "I'll tell everyone that you guys committed the crime in the store last night! And then, oh my, I wonder what they'll do? Maybe arrest you? Maybe ban you from the store?"

Caroline looked shocked, even horrified by these threats. Her eyes narrowed and her mouth crinkled with anger.

Ellie smacked her hand over her mouth to cover her own shock. Then she shot out questions: "Really? Would they seriously do that? What exactly would that mean? Like banned from the store *forever*?"

Gordo took Ellie's hands in his and lifted them up to her mouth. Quietly he said, "Shh. Please?" That seemed to work well, because she pressed her lips tightly together and nodded.

"Okay. Fine," Sam said. "Continue with your threat, which doesn't really make any sense, because nothing was stolen except a few tarts, which I offered to pay for."

Sebastian continued, "From the photographic proof in my hand, it looks like two of your merry band were in this store after closing, making a terrible mess, and I can only conclude that if they were here when the electronics were stolen, then they were involved. I'm quite sure the police will see it that way."

"But we didn't steal anything," Caroline chimed in.

"So, it's purely coincidental that you were in the store on the same night there was a major theft. Maybe you believe that, but I'm not so sure that the authorities would understand. I find it hard to believe myself," he said. "Look, as long as I get my two hundred and fifty words each night, you have nothing to worry about. And they'd better be good. No plagiarism."

Ellie yelled to the phone, "You're a cheater!" Gordo touched a finger to her lip, and that reminded her she was supposed to be quiet.

Caroline asked, "So all we have to do is write your blooming paper and we can forget about all of this?"

"Well, there's one more teeny tiny little detail."

Sam growled, "What?"

"I need at least a B-plus, and no one—I repeat, NO ONE—can know that I didn't write it. This paper is vitally important to my future. Do you *capisce* what I'm saying to you? Very important."

We grumbled our understanding into the phone. "Yeah, yeah, we *capisce*," Ellie said.

"I've copied the videos and photos onto a flash drive. By the way, how stupid can you be to create evidence like this?" he asked, not waiting for an answer. "The paper is due via e-mail at ten Friday morning. And because it is critical, the teacher is going to be checking references and grading pretty quickly."

"Why is she grading it so fast?" Sam asked.

"Did you miss the part when I said 'vitally import-ant'?" Sebastian barked. "Once I get my grade, we'll meet and I'll give you the flash drive. For now Ellie can come in and get this phone. No one else. I can't stand to see your ugly gobs." He continued, "If you are even one millisecond later than eight o'clock each night, I'll make you an instant Internet video sensation." He laughed evilly.

He had us. He totally had us in a you-are-my-puppet sort of way. We had to do this for him or we'd possibly get arrested.

This was definitely not boring, but ending up in a British prison was not the kind of life-changing experience I was looking for on this trip. I could look forward to being locked in my room, with the exception of school or weeding, for the rest of my life. Suddenly I was keenly interested in Pluto.

"Why can't you do the paper yourself?" Sam asked.

"That's none of your beeswax either. Just do it. Fast."

"He's bluffing," Gordo said to Sam, loud enough for Sebastian to hear.

The phone made a jerking sound on the other end. Sebastian said, "Oh my goodness gracious, what just happened? What did I do? Did I just accidentally upload one of those incriminating videos? I think I did." He ended the call.

Caroline hissed, "He didn't."

Sam showed us his screen. It was a video of me and Caroline—well, our feet—trying on shoes. Lots of shoes. The clip didn't show our faces.

"Un-bloody-believable," Caroline said. "Let's do this ridiculous Pluto paper for that pastry midget. We can work at my house."

Things were getting more un-boring by the minute. Maybe a little too de-bored-ified.

"First I'm getting that phone," Sam said. He stormed into Daphne's and came back a few seconds later with a flush to his cheeks and no phone in his hands.

Gordo patted Ellie's back. "Can you handle it?"

Ellie made a muscle with her arms. "See these guns?" She walked into the store. A minute later she returned with a mini multicolored layered cake.

"What is that?" I asked.

"A petit four. Isn't it cute? It's like a little rainbow baby sandwich made of cake. Wanna bite?"

"No, thanks," I said, but I was still hungry. I had heard about this thing called a full English breakfast. Supposedly everyone ate it. Where was it now? None of my new friends knew how popular it was, obviously.

"No luck with the phone?" Gordo asked.

"Oh, that." She popped the remaining little morsel of petit four into her mouth and reached into her back pocket. "Here you go."

"How'd you do that?" Gordo asked.

"I have my ways," Ellie said. "But don't get too excited.

He showed me the flash drive, a little plastic worm. It's very adorable, actually. And fitting, because he's like a worm." She handed me my new phone with the hi-res camera, and I thought that maybe the decision to do a photo montage of my trip wasn't such a good idea after all.

13

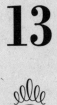

Sam asked, "Don't you think he's made other copies of the videos and photos?"

"We'll have to worry about copies later," Gordo said. "But I think we shouldn't trust anything Sebastian says."

We crammed into a taxi, which made me feel like I was a gum ball inside a machine. It took us to the Metro station. "It's a fifteen-minute train ride to Brentwood," Sam explained.

We sat on the train, and I couldn't help thinking for a second about the Hogwarts Express. Of course, this was nothing like Harry Potter's train. It was shiny and modern, with half of the seats facing one way and the other half facing the other way.

"Shh," Sam said. "Look at the telly." He indicated a flat screen in the front of the train car. Two news reporters stood in front of Daphne's.

The female reporter said, *"Shortly after opening this morning, Daphne's employees discovered that several thousand pounds' worth of electronic equipment was missing. The investigation is just beginning and we'll certainly report details on this case as they unfold."* The name "Skye Summers" was written on the screen under her face.

The male reporter, Cole Miles, said, *"Indeed, Skye, what does surveillance footage from the Daphne's security system show?"*

"It seems that with the big power outage last night, the whole system was down. Authorities are presently looking for the night watchman for answers," Skye said.

Cole said, *"More on the Daphne's theft later. But now to sports. Let's talk about football."* The screen switched to a scene of what I would call a soccer game.

"There really was a theft last night," Caroline said. "What are the chances of that?"

"You tell us," Ellie said.

"What do you mean?" Caroline asked.

"I mean, why would you take that stuff? It's not like you need it."

Caroline snapped at her, "We didn't steal anything. Do you see any stolen electronics?"

"No," Ellie said sheepishly.

"Exactly." Then under her breath I think she said, "Idiot." *What kind of person calls her friend an idiot?*

Gordo said, "The police will figure this all out. Don't worry your pretty little fashionable heads about it."

I forced a smile. I hoped Gordo was right, because the videos and photos that Sebastian had would surely put Caroline and me at the scene of the crime *during the crime.*

From the train station we walked a few blocks to meet Liam, who was supposedly picking us up after we'd all met for breakfast following the sleepover at Ellie's. On the ride I clicked an e-mail to my mom and dad. My mom had probably scrubbed every surface of the house worrying about me.

Approaching the manor house, I was again reminded of how big and fabulous it was. Ivy and moss crept everywhere.

We planted ourselves in her kitchen while Caroline got her iPad. "I cannot believe Sebastian has the nerve to blackmail me. He is more of a weasel than I thought. Just thinking about him makes me feel all icky." She rubbed her arms.

Liam brought us an assortment of juices and baby-size muffins. *Yay, Liam!* I was starving, so I popped one into my mouth whole. I saw Sam look at me, and I thought he was going to call the Hungry Police, but he didn't. The next muffin I took, I broke and ate in smaller pieces.

Mrs. Littleton stepped into the kitchen. "Oh, hi there, gang. Jordan, I got an early text from your mama. She was a wee bit angry when she got your message that said all y'all have done is shop and have a pillow party."

"Pillow party?" Caroline asked, confused.

"You call it a sleepover, but we used to call that a pillow party in my sorority days," Mrs. Littleton said.

I thought for sure that Ellie was going to blow our cover story. She fiddled with the lace table runner. "The pillow party was very . . . pillowy. We had a pillow fight and a pillow pile and um . . . ah . . . uh . . . We made a fortress out of blankets and pillows."

I was officially impressed. I doubted that Ellie with a *y* would have thought so fast on her feet. The fortress was an especially good detail.

"Really? A fort?" Mrs. Littleton asked.

"Yup," Ellie said. "That was J.J.'s idea. Apparently

Americans like to build stuff with blankets and pillows."

"J.J.'s?" Mrs. Littleton looked at me to make sure I was J.J. I nodded. "Cute," she said.

Caroline said, "This was after we spent a positively perfect day at Daphne's."

Mrs. Littleton said, "Did you hear the news that there was a break-in last night? The telly said there had been some mischief and a theft—jewelry, I think."

"Electronics," Ellie corrected her.

Caroline said, "J.J. got some nice additions to her wardrobe. I mean, look at her. Better, eh?"

"I did think there was something different about ya. I thought it was just the blond streak in your hair. Do you think your mama is going to be okay with that?"

"Oh, yes," I lied. "She is totally into exploring new fashion." I really hated lying. "I don't know when you saw her last, but she has become quite a collector of shoes, like Jimmy Choos. Ha! That rhymes." (Last night I'd learned that Jimmy Choos were a really hot brand.)

"A bore," Ellie said.

"What?" I asked. "What did you say?"

"We call someone who collects lots of shoes a *shoe bore*."

"Okay. Right. Well, that's what she is," I lied again. "A bore from a shoe store. Ha!" I did it again.

Mrs. Littleton said, "Well, it sounds like y'all have had great fun. But your mama was peeved that you were shopping instead of working on your school assignment."

Caroline mumbled something like, "Heaven forbid we take a break from studies over school vacation."

"She was?" I asked.

"I haven't heard her so mad since we got splashed with a hose at the homecoming football game. Ohhh, we had been having such a good time until that happened."

"My mom had fun?"

"Oh, all the time! She loved it!"

I was sure she had my mom confused with someone else from college.

Mrs. Littleton said, "But don't worry. I took care of everything. I promised her that you would spend the rest of the week hitting all the places on your list. To calm her down I told her y'all would text pics to her from each sight."

"You can't be serious?" Caroline asked, as though the idea of checking if she was lying was completely absurd, even though she had *just* told a whole story about a sleepover party that never happened. "She wants to spy on us? Why doesn't she just send a babysitter to trail around after us?"

I was totally embarrassed. Even though I was on the other side of the world, my parents were still looking over my shoulder.

"If that's an invitation," Mrs. Littleton said, "I'd love to go with y'all."

"Yay!" Ellie said. "You'll be like one of the gang, except older and more . . . more older than we are."

Caroline pursed her lips in anger, but spoke in a careful and controlled voice, "Um, I think NOT."

Mrs. Littleton said, "Caroline darlin', I gotcha a little something. Come on into your daddy's office so I can give it to you."

"What is it?" Caroline asked.

"Ooh, it's a surprise."

Caroline followed her stepmother out of the room.

"What do you think it is?" Ellie asked.

Gordo shrugged. "Could be anything. Remember the time she got a Vespa scooter? Her mum didn't even know she was too young to drive it."

They returned very quickly. Caroline was smiling.

"What was it?" Sam asked.

"What?" she asked.

"The surprise."

"Oh, it was kinda like a secret surprise. No biggie, really," Caroline said.

"No biggie," Mrs. Littleton confirmed. "So, lemme just get my coat and I'll come along with y'all today."

Caroline said, "As much fun as that would be, I think it's a richer adventure for J.J. to experience London with us, just us, friends her own age." She put her arm over my shoulder and said to me, "You are going to have an awesome time."

"Well, I want J.J. to have the fullest experience possible," Mrs. Littleton said, like it was a big sacrifice for her not to hang out with us.

"That's what we all want," Caroline said. "We'll certainly text you pictures from each sight we visit. Oh, and those pics will be perfect to use for your photo montage assignment." I thought Caroline had quickly changed her mind about sightseeing.

"It'll be heaps of fun, I'm sure," Mrs. Littleton said, and exited the kitchen.

There was a moment of silence. "I think that went well," Ellie said. "She bought the whole fortress thing."

Caroline announced, "I'm going to take a shower. Can you start on planet Pluto? We have to do a super-good job on it so that those videos stay under wraps. If we get discovered, it would be very bad for me."

Gordo said, "Daphne's couldn't ban you for long. You're their best customer."

"Well, I don't want to risk it. Besides, I have more to lose than shopping."

"Like what?" I asked.

"A lot," she said, offering a nonanswer.

As if commanded by the queen bee, Gordo took the seat at the iPad and began telling us what he was writing: "I am Sebastian Lively, and I am a jerk. I am not the one writing this paper because I'm a cheater . . ."

"Stop that," Caroline said. "Don't joke around."

"You're smart," Ellie said to Gordo. "Can't you just whip it out or something?"

"Of course he can," Sam said.

"Bril," Caroline said, and left for her shower.

"Sure," Gordo joked. "I'll write a research paper in the next few minutes while you pals just hang out."

"That works for me," Ellie said. She didn't get that Gordo had been kidding. At least, I'm pretty sure he was.

Gordo googled some sites and sent pages to the printer at the other side of the kitchen. Sam read them over and tossed out random Pluto facts that made me think maybe this could be a good paper.

When Caroline returned to the kitchen, she was surrounded by shower scents. Her wet hair was combed out and hung lower than it had last night. She wore new clothes: a flowy peasant blouse, black jeans, and ankle

101

boots with a heel. I noticed that she had also put on a new palette of makeup. "J.J., Liam left you fresh towels."

As much as I was enjoying working on the paper with Sam and Gordo (Ellie really wasn't into it), I left. I was excited to use my new hair straightener, and makeup, and to wear another new outfit. As I walked down the hall to the bathroom, I heard Sam and Gordo talking about the solar system, and the printer hummed.

I also heard Caroline say to Ellie, "Look, we need to make sure J.J. has a good time, and we have to keep the Bakery Bozo off our backs."

Ellie said, "Where I am, fun follows, and the boys have Pluto under control. No worries, Carrie."

"Don't call me Carrie," Caroline said.

"Gotcha," Ellie said.

I was so happy to hear that Caroline wanted me to have a memorable visit to London. She was sincere, wasn't she?

14

I felt like a celebrity in my new duds, makeup, and straightened hair. I found Ellie thumbing through a fashion magazine while Sam and Gordo huddled over the iPad. When she saw me, Caroline checked me out from hair to shoes. A quick jump of her eyebrows told me she was pleasantly surprised with my look. She dropped her feet from the kitchen table to the floor and said, "She's back. The American of the week." To her friends she said, "We're off to see the sights of London!" Her words sounded excited, but something about her tone said otherwise, I think.

"Oh, yeah," Ellie said. She put on a crocheted wool cap. It was so cute. I never thought of wearing a cap like that. It covered her spiky hair but let her double earrings show. I wanted double earrings and a cap. Maybe I could get those today.

Sam finally stopped reading and caught a glimpse of me. He didn't look long, but brushed some longish hairs in front of his face and packed the iPad in a pack with one strap that he hung diagonally across his chest.

Thankfully, I had my new purse, or I might have been jealous of that pack. I really preferred having free arms, but I liked having a stylish purse too. I flipped my fab hair over the strap. It felt good.

Gordo said "Ooh lala" about my appearance. "Sit tight. I need a minute to freshen up if I'm gonna hang with this one." And then he locked himself in the powder room.

When he returned, his collar was snapped up and I smelled a hint of cologne. We were ready for Liam to take us to the train station.

"Where are we going first?" Gordo asked, looking at his reflection in the steel refrigerator and moving a hair to where he wanted it to be.

"I suppose we should ask J.J.," Caroline said. "This week is all about her."

Normally that would've made me do a *Yay, me!* But something in her voice sounded just a little sarcastic. No one else seemed to notice, so maybe I was being overly sensitive. So: *Yay, me!*

"I'd like to go to the Tower of London," I said, with very little confidence that was the right answer. "I've been dying to go there." Then I laughed because I said "dying." "Get it? Because King Henry killed so many of his wives there?"

Gordo and Sam cracked a bit of a smile at my joke. I didn't think Ellie got it, but she laughed anyway, probably to be polite.

"Then off we go to the Tower," Caroline said. "If we make it quick, we'll have time to see the new zombie picture."

"Oh, right!" Ellie said. "I absolutely cannot wait to see that picture. I hear it's scary and gory. 'The bloodier the better,' that's what I always say." She got her face very close to mine, looked me in the eye, and said, "OOOOH! I am so excited. After the picture maybe we can get manis. I really need one. Look." She held out her hand with chipped black polish.

"Ditto," Gordo said. He held out his hand too, but he didn't have chipped polish. "My cuticles are so bad."

"TD," Ellie said about his nails. No one knew what

105

she meant. "Total Disaster," she explained to our questioning faces. "Duh."

"Not me," Sam said. His nails were bitten as low as they could go.

"That's fine," Caroline said. "You can work on the Pluto project while we're mani-ing. We've totally got to stay on top of that. I swear if I get in trouble because of that rat, I can't be responsible for what I'll do to him."

Sam didn't seem bothered by being told he'd be working on a research paper. He said, "This assignment isn't hard. I don't know why he can't do it."

"Fab," Caroline said. "Then everything is peachy. We'll jet through the Tower, catch the zombie picture, and get manis."

"Sure," I said, but honestly, I didn't like the idea of rushing through the Tower of London to see a movie I could see at home, or rent on DVD. But getting my nails done sounded like a treat.

As we walked to the car, Caroline added, "I would love to think of a way to get even with the Swine of Sweets for making us do his work for him."

No one commented that Caroline had said "us" even though she wasn't doing anything for the Pluto project. I wondered about a way we could get our videos back and also make sure Sebastian got caught for cheating.

Caroline would probably be psyched if I came up with a plan.

Liam dropped us at the train station, and I followed the gang to the right platform.

Suddenly Gordo stopped and pointed to a screen overhead. "Look at the telly," he said.

The reporter named Skye said, *"As we reported earlier today, there was a break-in at Daphne's, during which some sophisticated electronic equipment was stolen. After a thorough inventory, it was determined that the loss was greater than originally suspected. A selection of power tools was also taken. The combination of items leads authorities to believe the robbers may have been collecting tools necessary for other crimes."*

"What exactly are the items that were stolen?" Cole asked.

"That information hasn't been released, Cole. But an interesting video has been attracting a lot of attention on the Internet. Let's go to the clip."

They ran the video that Sebastian had uploaded of Caroline and me trying on shoes.

"You can see by the date and time stamp that this video was taken at Daphne's. No faces are visible in this clip, but the audio suggests it's a local and an American girl."

Cole asked, *"Are you saying these are the robbers?"*

"Authorities haven't said that, but these girls were in the store after closing on the same night," Skye said. "I know I'd like to be loose in Daphne's after closing, Cole. Can you imagine?"

"No I can't, but I'd love it too. For now, let's take a look at the weather."

"That blasted Sebastian!" Caroline said. "Look what he's done. He's tied us to this robbery."

"Was it heavy?" Ellie asked Caroline.

"What?"

"All that stuff?" Ellie asked. "Where did you put it?"

"For the love of the queen! We. Didn't. Steal. Anything!" Caroline barked.

Ellie cowered a bit from the volume, then softly asked, "Are you sure?" Then, after seeing Caroline begin to boil red, loudly she said, "Never mind! I didn't just say that. I swear, I didn't. I heard it, so someone said something, but it wasn't me. Maybe it was a ghost."

"Maybe we should go to the police," I suggested, trying to take the heat off Ellie.

"And tell them what, exactly? That we stayed in the store after closing and ran amok in every department all night long on the same night there was a major theft, but we had nothing to do with it? That sounds like it will work," Caroline said. "Truly bril idea, J.J."

108

"Maybe we should tell your father," Gordo said. "He's involved with Her Majesty's government, isn't he?"

Caroline looked at Gordo like he was stupid, a total moron.

"You know what?" Gordo asked. "Bad idea. Forget I mentioned it," Gordo said.

"Gladly," she said. "Look, no one can think we did this." She asked Sam, "Can we get this Pluto project done early? And get the flash drive back? I don't like the idea of the Dork of Danishes having photographic proof we were in Daphne's that night."

"Early?" Sam asked. "Sebastian was quite specific about the schedule." (He said "schedule" like "sheh-dyul.") "If we stick to his deadlines, we should be fine." He said to Caroline, "You just can't do anything for three days to make him mad."

15

We stood in front of the Tower of London, which was much more than a single tower. There were multiple Gothic castlelike buildings in the complex.

"Let's get a photo," Caroline said. "J.J., you stand right in front here."

Gordo already had his arm around me with a toothy grin exposed. I hadn't noticed before, but braces must not be popular here, because they needed my orthodontist's digits. Except Caroline, of course, who seemed effortlessly perfect.

Ellie crouched down in front of me and stretched her arms wide as if to say, *Ta-da!*

Gordo reached out to a man walking by and said, "Excuse me, mate. Would you mind snapping our photo?"

The man agreed. Gordo had an arm over Caroline's shoulder and the other over mine.

A second later we had a great shot. It was totally going into my photo montage.

"Let me text this to the stepmummy and Mrs. J.J., and we can move on." Caroline fiddled with the phone. "Maybe this is what it's like for a prisoner to have a tracking anklet that follows their every move."

Was she really comparing texting sightseeing pics to our moms to being a prisoner?

Gordo must've been thinking the same thing, because he asked, "A little dramatic, eh?"

Maybe Caroline liked dramatic. I could do that. "I know, right? It's like going around with a big green ogre on your back."

Ellie jumped in at the mention of an ogre. "Maybe one that just ate a village of trolls. I think I saw a picture like that once. He popped the little trolls into his mouth like they were chips."

Sam studied the castles. "I'm psyched," he said. "For

the sightseeing, not the troll eating. And that's saying something, because I like eating."

"I think we know that," I said. "I guess we need to get tickets to go in."

Caroline sighed. "We don't have to go in, do we? We can just hang out here and mock all the tourists walking by. I mean, unless you want to." She said it like it was a ridiculously lame idea.

What can I say? I mean, of course I want to go in. I'm in London to see the sights, DUH!

I needed to make this more interesting than an average field trip.

I got an idea.

"Mocking the tourists sounds superfun," I said to Caroline. "But I thought maybe you'd want to see the Crown Jewels. And, Ellie, I thought you might want to see the ghosts that haunt this place. Sam, the brochure I read said they have an assortment of royal chocolates in the gift shop."

"I'd forgotten that the Crown Jewels were here," Caroline said, reconsidering. "We didn't see them on our school trip."

Ellie said, "We didn't see any ghosts then either. They probably don't take schoolkids to the truly ghostly parts of the Tower, eh?"

112

"What are we waiting for?" Sam asked.

Yay, me! I had gotten them a little interested.

We passed through the stone archway, on top of which was an iron gate that would be dropped to protect the royal court from threats.

Inside the Tower walls my eyes feasted on the old stone buildings. I imagined ladies in layered lacy dresses, maybe a poor fellow locked in a stockade, and a stray dog scampering for a scrap of bread.

We took a long bridge that passed over a grassy path. I overheard a tour guide, who was dressed in a yeoman's tunic, saying that the plush greenway was once a moat. I took lots of pictures.

"The deep water was like a security system," Sam added. "It was probably filled with man-eating fish."

"Now, *that's* cool," Ellie said. "Too bad they filled it in."

Caroline's mobile rang. She answered it and spoke for just a second in hushed tones that I couldn't decipher. "It was Stepmummy. She got the picture, and noticed J.J. wasn't all smiles. I assured her you were having a grand old time." Then she asked, "So, where are the jewels?"

I looked at the map. "For the Jewel House we need to go this way."

"Then let's head over there." Caroline hooked her

arm into mine and walked with me like we were Dorothy and the lion parading down the yellow brick road. (I would be the lion in that scene.) I was continuing to follow the directions, when I saw something that I thought Ellie would be interested in. It had that horror-movie feel to it. "See this tower?" I asked her. "They call it the Bloody Tower."

"Awesome," Ellie said. "Let's go in."

"Oh, yes! Let's," Caroline said excitedly, too excitedly? Or was she actually getting into this?

We walked inside the Bloody Tower. A cool feeling of death and despair was everywhere as I followed the signs and led the group up a narrow spiral staircase surrounded by stone walls. Velvet ropes blocked us from a small room that held only a few pieces of furniture: an ornate wooden chair, a writing desk, a small wooden bed against the wall. There was light from just one square window.

"I don't see any ghosts," Ellie said. "What a rip-off."

We followed the gloomy corridors, whose silence felt very haunted. The corridors were narrow and bendy. Occasionally there was a mirror in the corner, angled so that you could see if someone was coming from the other direction. I didn't like the eerie feeling in this place. I walked fast until I made it outside to the warm sun.

I continued walking in the direction of the jewels,

but then I saw the Tower Green. I stopped and stared at the square patch of grass. It was smaller than I'd imagined, considering what went on there.

"What is it?" Sam asked me. "What's wrong?"

"This is the Tower Green. It's where they held public executions," I said.

Caroline said, "That's what the medieval times were all about. Maybe it's novel to you because Columbus hadn't even discovered America yet. But we know all about it."

I didn't know what to say; this *was* new to me. Maybe they'd seen it all before, but I hadn't.

Caroline looked like maybe she realized her comment was insensitive, and tried to gloss it over. "But that's why you're here, isn't it?" She smiled. "To see our wonderful history."

I stared at the Green. "I especially like Anne Boleyn's story. It's so romantic and tragic," I said.

"I love romance," Gordo said.

"I love tragic," Ellie said.

"Go on," Caroline. "Tell us what you know about her."

I was a little apprehensive because I couldn't tell if she really wanted to hear the story. "Well, King Henry was married to Catherine when he fell madly in love with Anne, one of her lady's maids. Henry and Anne married, and their love was true and deep. They had a daughter who later became queen. But after they had been married for several years, King Henry began courting Lady Jane Seymour and he wanted to marry her. So that the new marriage could be legal, he told everyone that Anne had bewitched him to make him fall in love with her. Anne was locked away in the Tower and eventually executed—in this exact spot right here." A chill went through my entire body, and for a moment no one spoke.

"Positively gruesome," Ellie finally said with a sparkle in her eye.

I took a picture of the grassy area. "Here, let me get a picture of you on the Green," Caroline said, and took my phone. "Now smile really big." She clicked the picture, handed the phone back to me, and said, "Send that to the mums too."

I did.

"Now, how about the jewels?" Caroline asked again.

We entered the narrow stone corridor of the Jewel House. It was dark and damp. Security cameras along the halls reminded me that modern surveillance was in use, not that we were planning to do any dress-up or trampolining.

The main room that housed the jewels was also

guarded by security men, the no-nonsense-no-tunic kind.

Caroline got dangerously close to one of the glass cases that shielded from potential theft crowns and scepters adorned with enormous gems. A guard cleared his throat, and Caroline stepped back.

I went to click a picture, and the guard told me I couldn't in this room.

I said, "I would love a time machine so that I could go back and see these actually being worn at a big celebration with dancing and live music and court jesters." As soon as I said it, I wished I hadn't. Caroline didn't think about things like time machines.

Apparently Gordo did. "And knights with swords and shields."

Caroline said, "But I'm not interested in living without air-conditioning or cell phones or Jacuzzi tubs or TV. No thanks. I'll pass."

"I don't need a time machine," Ellie said. "The MoviePlex takes me to all sorts of places in time. That's the same MoviePlex that's showing *Bloodsucking Zombies* at four o'clock, which we can make if we leave *right now*." She sang "right now."

"Yes!" Caroline said. "I mean, as long as J.J. is okay with that. I think you're going to absolutely LOVE this picture. It's all the rage."

"Okay," I agreed, and I liked that Caroline had checked with me. She had been totally nice and attentive to me today, and initially she hadn't even wanted to come.

"Right after we check out the gift shop," Ellie said. "I never leave anywhere without a souvenir."

"Fine," Caroline agreed. "We'll all get souvenirs."

Gordo bought a little knight figurine, Sam grabbed some chocolate, and even Caroline got a few postcards. I chose a London bus key chain to put in my new purse.

Ellie got a three-foot-tall pencil with a big crown eraser, and a tiara that she wore out of the store.

Outside the Tower walls, we were back in modern London; I followed the gang underground via stairs in the sidewalk. In medieval times this might have led to a dungeon, but today I suspected it went to something like a subway. Not like I had ever actually been on a subway, but I'd seen them on TV and in movies.

"This is the Tube," Sam said.

The Tube? How British. I imagined myself in a New York subway one day and saying to the person I was with, *It's nice, but it's not like the Tube in London. Have you ever been on the Tube? Well, I have, and I can tell you all about it, if you'd like.* Or maybe I'd be back at school and someone from our lame school paper would interview me about this trip and I could say something like, *Well, we took the Tube from sight to sight. Don't you know what that is? Well, let me explain . . .*

The walls were white, with different-colored stripes indicating the routes. Sam seemed to know which underground train to get on. I sat on a hard plastic seat. Ellie was in front of me, holding on to a metal pole. The train took off through the tunnel, which was kinda like an underground tube. I guessed that was where it got its name. The train moved so fast that Ellie kept bumping into me.

"Sorry," she said. She took her phone and clicked four or five pictures of everyone acting silly. Then she held it out and took one of herself in her tiara, which she hadn't taken off. "I'll text these to you so you'll have them." She frowned. "Drat! No signal down here."

We emerged from underground, and I felt my phone vibrating in my new purse. I looked at it. I figured it was the pictures Ellie had just sent, but it wasn't. "Oh no," I said. "It's Sebastian. He wants his pages at five o'clock instead of eight."

"Can he do that?" Ellie asked. "Just change the time?"

"No," Sam said. "He can't. Tell him he's a twit and we'll get him the pages as agreed."

I texted Sebastian back, leaving out the part about

the twit and writing much more politely than any of them would have.

He immediately replied.

"What did he say?" Gordo asked.

"It's just a link." I clicked it, and it went to an online video. I held it out for the others to see. They had to crowd around me. Sam's cheek practically touched mine, and I felt the wisps of the longish part of his hair on my face.

The video began to play. The background was Daphne's. The video was familiar. You could clearly see two people in costumes, jumping on a trampoline. There were no faces, but I could hear my own voice and Caroline's.

"That looks like fun," Ellie said. "Can we do that?"

"Blast it!" Caroline groaned.

16

We sat on the curb outside the MoviePlex. Sam tapped out words that Gordo dictated based on the printouts he had. Gordo also told him where to add a citation.

Ellie fidgeted and kept looking at her watch. "It's almost four o'clock. I'm going to miss the previews. I hate missing the previews. Can't you go any faster?"

Sam picked up his hand-phone and looked at Ellie. "It's the Shut Your Piehole Factory; they want to talk to you," he said.

She closed her mouth and huffed over to Caroline

and started imitating Sam on his finger-phone. Caroline sent Ellie to buy tickets. I really hoped this movie would involve popcorn. I wouldn't mind a hot dog, but that might be too much to hope for.

Finally Sam said, "Okay, it's sent to the pastry jerk. We overachieved, my friend. Two hundred and fifty-six words." He gave Gordo a high five.

Ellie rushed us through the theater. I passed a poster for *Bloodsucking Zombies*. It was a gruesome image of a walking-dead person with blood dripping from his mouth. I noticed it was rated "15." A quick glance of the other movies and ratings told me that meant it was for kids fifteen and older. A little beat of excitement pulsed through my veins. Ellie handed me a ticket. I guess she'd passed for fifteen, which wasn't really surprising. "My treat," she said.

I thanked her.

I sat between Ellie and Sam. After only a second, Sam got up and left. "BRB," he whispered.

Ellie said, "You know I started 'BRB'?"

"Yeah?" I asked.

She nodded. I think she believed that she had started the abbreviation, but I didn't think so.

The theater darkened, and a few previews later, blood started splattering everywhere.

Ellie was entranced. Something on the ground

caught my eye. Her feet were glowing. She saw that I was staring. "Glow-in-the-dark socks," she said. "Very popular."

"Really?" I had never heard of them. I glanced down the row. Gordo's feet were kicked up onto the chair in front of him, and a smile covered his face. I think Caroline was checking her watch. It was like she always wanted to be somewhere else, but her friends were all here. It didn't make sense to me. In some ways I wanted to be like her—she was so pretty and had cool clothes and everyone wanted to be around her. But I didn't think she was that nice to her friends. She'd been really nice to me all day, but it felt different than it had at Daphne's. It was like she was . . . *acting*.

Sam came back with a bucket of popcorn and a mega-huge soda.

"Help yourself," he whispered into my ear.

"Did you hear my stomach growling?" I whispered back.

"No, but I can only imagine after hanging out with those guys all day."

"Why don't they eat?" I asked.

He said, "Too busy, I think."

Ellie shh-ed us. Sam and I stared at the screen with our hands occasionally meeting in the bucket. I had to think about something other than the blood and guts on the screen for a second:

- I was in London, staying in a mansion.
- I'd just come from seeing the Crown Jewels.
- I now sat at a movie, sharing popcorn with a totally cute British boy.
- Oh, and I had on hot new clothes and makeup, and had a great new hairdo.

This had been a pretty successful trip so far, except for being blackmailed by some guy to do his homework. And that there were videos of me (faceless, thankfully) online in connection with a robbery.

Yup. I'd say smashingly successful so far.

The movie was terrible, but the popcorn was good. I learned a new English word that I thought maybe I would try to use while I was here.

They sat through all the credits. When the house-lights came on, they still didn't get up.

"That was so good," Ellie said. "I totally cannot wait to see it again. Did you see that bloke's fingers go into the blender? He didn't even feel it. I think I want to be a zombie when I die."

"Too true," Gordo said. "But with better hair."

Caroline said, "That picture had better win some major awards. I love Riley Goodwin; he is so cute."

Sam asked, "Which one was he?"

"Are you kidding?" Ellie asked. "You're just having a laugh, Sam, right? Everyone knows who Riley Goodwin is. The hot zombie. The one who never wore a shirt."

"How can a zombie be hot?" Sam asked. "I mean, they're dead. They must smell terrible, and random body parts just fall off and tumble to the ground."

Gordo said, "Just 'cause they're dead doesn't mean they should completely neglect their hygiene, does it? Half of them had bugs crawling out of their ears or nose or eyes. That's not hot. But even I have to admit that Riley Goodwin is a good-looking guy."

Then Sam held his thumb and pinky to his ear and mouth like he was making a phone call. "Hi," he said. "I am looking for the Hot Zombie Club. Can you help me? Oh, you can't because zombies aren't hot? Okay, thanks. That's what I thought too."

Ellie shooed Sam and continued talking to Caroline. "Do you think he owns a shirt that isn't ripped to shreds?"

"I hope not," Caroline said. She looked at her watch. "Latte?"

Gordo said, "The sooner the better."

Caroline asked me, "You think your mom will be okay with us stopping for a warm beverage, or will you miss too much sightseeing?" She sounded like it was a totally normal question, but it was mean, right?

"I think she'll be okay with that."

We walked to a small coffee shop next door. Gordo, Ellie, and Caroline all shared a sandwich. Sam and I each got our own scone and passed on the latte.

"I suppose we'll head to the train, and we can do yet another fabulously touristy thing tomorrow," Caroline said. I wasn't sure she really meant that touristy things were fabulous. "That new reality show about the cooking club is on tonight, right? I cannot wait to see it. They're going to have a live online chat during the show."

Sam said, "It's only seven o'clock. And it's not raining. It's a good night to go to the Eye. Is that on your list, J.J.?"

"Oh, yeah," I said. "I really want to ride that big Ferris wheel."

Caroline exhaled like this was terribly inconvenient for her reality TV schedule. She pushed out a smile. "Maybe we should save it for tomorrow?"

"Why don't you stay here," Gordo said. "Look, they have a telly." He indicated an ancient TV in the corner near the cappuccino machine. "We'll come back and get you when we're done. Your stepmummy didn't say you had to be in every picture. We'll take J.J. and we'll text the photo."

Hmmm, I thought. *It might even be more fun without her.*

"Fine," she said. "Ellie and I will hang here while you ride that wheel."

Ellie pouted. "I sorta want to go."

"That's just fab," Caroline said. "Then we'll all go, won't we?"

17

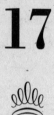

London was lit up under the night sky like a perfect postcard. I was looking up and wondering which light was Pluto, when I saw the London Eye in the distance.

A regular Ferris wheel from a Wilmington carnival was like a dwarf planet compared to this gigantic wheel.

Once we were right under it, Ellie looked up. "It looks even more massive up close, doesn't it?"

"I suppose we should get a photo for the mums," Caroline said. She tapped a passerby to take it. "Smile big, J.J.," she said as we posed.

I looked at the photo on the screen, and it showed the five of us but didn't capture the wheel or the River Thames behind us. "You can't tell where we are," I said.

"We can get a better shot from up top," Sam said.

We moved up in line, which Gordo called the queue. Caroline said, "Let me guess. You read all about the London Eye before you came."

"Yes," I said, embarrassed.

"Please enlighten us," she said.

This felt like a pop quiz for which I didn't know the answers. I looked down at the brochure as if I needed it to give me the information, which I didn't. "It was built to be the biggest Ferris wheel in the world, and it was until two bigger ones were built, one in China and one in Singapore."

Caroline looked up. "Bigger than this?"

It seemed that I knew something that Caroline hadn't learned on a field trip.

Our turn came up faster than I expected, even though the Eye turned very slowly. The Eye didn't even stop to let us on. We walked onto the clear plastic capsule that was like a big bubble with a long bench down the middle.

"How long does this take?" Ellie asked.

"A half hour for a rotation," I said.

We were off the ground and above the river. The panoramic view of the city was beautiful and amazing, and I sent my mom and dad a mental thank-you for letting me go on this trip. "Oh my gosh," I said. "Look at the lights of Big Ben and the Palace of Westminster. I want to go there so badly."

My four new friends soaked in the view. "It really is spectacular," Gordo said. Ellie took my phone and asked another capsule passenger to take our picture. The person didn't speak English but understood what she was asking.

Under her breath Caroline said, "You'd think the least these people could do is unbutton the top of their oxford shirts. Maybe the top button is in style in their country, but not here."

The tourists showed no sign of hearing or understanding her, thankfully. That would've been so embarrassing.

We stood with our backs to the capsule's glass wall so that Big Ben was in the picture. It came out great. I texted the proof of our stop at the London Eye to our moms.

"I wonder why they call it Big Ben," Ellie said.

How can she not know this? "The biggest chiming bell of the clock tower is called Ben and gives the tower its nickname."

"Why 'Ben,' and not 'Bob' or 'Burt'?" Caroline asked.

"There is the name of a politician named Benjamin Somebody inscribed on the bell," I said.

"You seem to know a lot about this stuff," Caroline said. "What else do you know about the clock?"

I thought she was joking, maybe setting me up to be mocked, but her face showed no indication that she was anything but serious. "Well, it's the only tower with four faces of a clock. And it's known for its accuracy. It's been lit and has kept good time for a hundred and fifty years. During the First and Second World Wars the lights were turned off to protect it from attacks. Also, only UK residents can go in."

"Bummer, eh?" Caroline asked. "We'll just have to focus all our fun time elsewhere. I'm sure you have other places we can visit on that list of yours."

"I'd love to get a picture in front of it," I said, even though I knew it would be an unpopular idea.

"Sure thing," Sam said on behalf of his friends.

Caroline's glare said that he did not have the authority to make a commitment like that on her behalf. "Maybe we can fit it in one day," she said coldly.

Needless to say, we didn't get that picture.

18

The next day at breakfast Mrs. Littleton asked us, "Where are y'all going today?" She looked like she had already been to yoga.

I said, "I was thinking Madame Tussauds."

I caught Caroline puff out an annoyed exhale. "Bril," she said with a smile that I didn't believe.

"Maybe I'll come along," Mrs. Littleton said. "Just let me get a quick shower."

"Oh," Caroline said, looking at her watch. "I wish we

could wait, but we were supposed to pick up the others about five minutes ago."

"Oh, drat! Well, have fun," Mrs. Littleton said. "Before ya go, I just wanna talk to Caroline for one smidgen of a second."

Caroline followed Mrs. Littleton to the hallway. I could hear a hushed conversation. As promised, they returned to the kitchen in a smidgen of a second. "Will we see you for dinner?" Mrs. Littleton asked.

"Unlikely," Caroline said. "We'll probably go to some London icon; you know, to make sure J.J. has a superepic time here in London."

It was amazing how her mom kept trusting us. I never had this much freedom at home.

Liam was waiting to drive us to the train station. I was already hungry because the berries and tea from breakfast hadn't been enough to fill me. I couldn't wait to see Sam, both because I was starting to really like hanging out with him—okay, so maybe I was starting to like him—and because he'd be into getting a snack with me.

From two blocks away I could see the huge green dome. I knew from my pre-travel research it was Madame Tussauds, the famous wax museum. It's the home of tons of wax figures of famous people, like Tom Cruise,

Angelina Jolie, politicians, athletes, and any other star you could imagine. It's been visited by famous people and tourists for almost two hundred years.

"Oh, blast," Caroline said. "Look at this queue." We were in a long line of people waiting to get in. She looked at her phone. "There's no new videos uploaded, so those pages must've met the pastry pest's standards."

"Did you say 'pastry'?" Sam asked. "Because I think there's a shop right around the corner. It's not as good as Lively's, but it's all right."

"Sounds like something we should check out," I said.

Ellie said, "We'll get in the queue while you get something to eat."

Sam and I crossed the street, which is harder than you'd think when people are driving on the wrong side of the road.

Sam asked for two scones. I ate it as slowly as I could, which was kinda fast. It really hit the spot.

We rejoined the gang, who had inched up in line a bit.

Gordo said, "Let's work on the next set of pages now. We can't do anything else while we're standing here."

Ellie said, "Give me the Pad-i, and I'll type today."

"Pad-i?" I asked.

"Yeah. Like 'Pad Thai,'" she said.

I asked, "What's wrong with 'iPad'?"

"I thought it might be fun to change it. You know, see if it catches on," she said. "Who knows, maybe I'll start a whole new trend. You know I was the first to use 'BTW'?"

"I didn't know that," I said. Ellie nodded, confirming that it was her. I wondered if Ellie could single-handedly rename the Apple suite of products. I doubted it, but I admired her for trying.

"You go for it," Gordo encouraged Ellie.

Caroline examined her nails.

Ellie fished the tiara from the Tower of London out of her purse and set it on her spiky head. She checked her reflection in the museum's tinted windows.

Caroline looked at her. "Seriously?"

"What?" Ellie asked. "Don't you like it? I wonder why women stopped wearing them."

"Because they look dumb," Caroline said.

Ellie didn't take it off. I thought maybe she was trying to start another trend. I loved that Ellie wore it even though Caroline had just said it was dumb.

The line inched forward.

"Are you a good typer?" I asked Ellie while she touched the iPad screen, which Gordo held for her.

"Not really, but I like to do it. I'm not a good tap

dancer either, but I like to do that, too." She clomped her feet around and smiled.

Caroline's foot was tapping, but it was much less enthusiastic than Ellie's. "Let's get a photo now," Caroline said, "so we can take off quickly when we're done." I wondered why she was in such a big hurry.

Sam asked the lady in front of us to take our picture. Caroline once again reminded me to smile big. I looked at the picture on the small LCD screen before sending it to the mums.

Caroline said, "We've got the shot. Do you wanna skip this and just go see the zombie picture again? This place gives me the creeps."

"But a zombie movie doesn't?" asked Sam.

"That's different," Caroline said. "That's Hollywood. This place is, like, actual spookiness right here in front of us."

"Too true," Ellie added. "That's what I like about it. Can you imagine if you'd been locked in *here* overnight instead of Daphne's?"

"Shhh!" Everyone shushed her.

"Sorry. But *that* would've been a bomb."

Gordo said, "I haven't been here since I was a kid. I liked it then, and I wanna see it again."

"Same," Ellie said.

"Do they have food?" Sam asked.

"Yes!" we all assured him.

"Speaking of food," I said, "if you ever want a lemon tart again, we should work on those pages."

It seemed like everyone had ignored Caroline's suggestion to go to the movie. Her toe tapping and watch-looking indicated that she didn't like that, but for some reason she didn't make a big deal about it.

Sam read a few lines from a printout he still had in his pocket, and Ellie used the touch screen to type. Every few words she said "Oops" or "Wait a sec."

And then, just to tease her, Sam would talk really fast. "Slow down, Sam," Ellie told him, but he sped up again, even faster. Sam dictated, "Pluto was a planet until recently, when astronomers decided it was too small and stripped it of that title."

"That's good," Ellie said. "I am totally writing that— stripped it—it's very dramatic and really makes you feel bad for the sad little dwarf planet. Kinda like Sebastian is a dwarf person."

I admired that even though they were waiting in line for some touristy thing, writing a school paper for someone else—an annoying bully who spit in their tarts— they were still having fun. I really liked these guys. I looked at Caroline fiddling with her phone, and I didn't understand why they'd want to be friends with *her*. But I did understand why she would want to be friends with *them*.

Once again Ellie was nagging Sam to slow down, when I heard something familiar. With a start, I realized it was my own voice coming from the phone of the girl behind us in line.

Motioning for everyone in our group to be quiet, I tilted my head toward the girl.

We heard Caroline's voice too—and lots of laughing.

It was the trampoline video clip that Sebastian had uploaded.

19

The girl behind us in line, the one chomping on her chewing gum, held her phone out enough for us to listen and watch. It was the news reporters again:

The anchor named Skye said, *"The recent theft at Daphne's remains unsolved, but it's believed that these two people are responsible."*

They flashed a still photo of our feet midjump.

"As you can see, there are no images of the suspects' faces. But from the voices, it's assumed to be two girls—an American and a Brit. Police have reviewed the surveillance

cameras from the night in question, but since the storm knocked out the electricity, there is no recording."

The reporter named Cole asked, "Skye, what about a backup generator? Surely a store as high-tech as Daphne's has a backup system?"

"Indeed. They do have a generator, which was disconnected. The Daphne's security team said the heist was well thought-out, because these girls chose a night when a storm killed the electricity, and they also knew how to disconnect a generator."

"They sound like smart and experienced thieves," Cole said. "What happens next?"

"The authorities will comb the videos before power was lost to see if they find a pair of girls matching these feet," Skye said, and the screen filled with the shot of our feet again.

"Can you believe it?" Bubble Gum said. "They recorded themselves and then put it on the Internet. It's like they *want* to get caught."

Then her friend with a pierced nose said, "Why would they want that? They'll probably go up the river if they get caught."

"I can't imagine it will take that long to identify them," Bubble Gum said.

"Then what?" Pierced Nose asked.

"Bring them in for questioning, I guess," Bubble Gum

said. "I'll make you a bet that they have the American-British robber pair in custody before morning."

Pierced Nose said, "No way. The police aren't that good. I'll take that wager."

"What shall we bet?" Bubble Gum asked. "Tickets to the Riley Goodwin picture?"

"YES!" Pierced Nose agreed. They shook on it.

I whispered, "What are we going to do?"

Gordo said, "All right. Starting now you're not American, J.J."

Ellie asked, "How about Chinese? Can you do a Chinese accent?"

"That's a good idea," I said. "But even if I could, I don't think I can *look* Chinese."

"You haven't tried."

Sam said, "Why don't you just be English? From Manchester."

"I guess I could try that," I said.

"In the meantime it wouldn't hurt for you to lie low," Sam said.

Caroline said, "We're standing in the queue at a museum. It doesn't get much lower than this."

"I know!" Ellie raised her hand like an eight-year-old in school. She waited for Caroline's acknowledgment to allow her to talk. "One word. 'Disguises.' I am the best

141

at disguises. We had a costume party at my school, and I won the prize for the best costume. I went as a royal guard with a homemade hat. I made the hat with pillow stuffing and painted it black. It was, like, four feet tall. Tell her how awesome it was, Sam."

"It was actually quite good," Sam agreed.

Ellie said, "I thought everyone was going to make their own and wear them to school the next day, but it didn't catch on that way. That's the thing with starting new fads, sometimes they catch on and sometimes they don't—"

"Anyway," Caroline interrupted. "Back in the real world I suppose a little camouflage wouldn't be a totally awful idea."

"True," Gordo agreed.

Ellie said, "I don't want to totally freak you out, but look." She pointed to two policemen coming down the street. "Duck!"

Caroline bent down as if she was tying her shoe, which was silly because she was wearing boots with zippers. "Stop pointing!"

I stuck my head into my purse like I was looking for something very important that was way down at the bottom in the corner. I continued to hunt until Ellie said, "They're gone. You can climb out of your designer bag now. I've never actually seen someone try to fit inside a handbag. You gave it a good go. Let me try."

She took my purse and bent her head down into it but didn't get very far. "You're better at it. One time I tried to see if my foot would fit into an orange juice container. My foot was smaller back then, of course. I got my foot in but couldn't get it out, and since I couldn't walk with it on my foot, I had to hop around until my dad could saw it off—the plastic orange container, that is, not my foot, obviously, because I still have it. See."

She held up her leg and showed us her foot, like it would be news to us that her foot was still there. Caroline's eyes said she was irritated by Ellie's moronic behavior, but I got a laugh out of it—something I definitely needed at the moment.

"We know all about the ol' foot-in-the-orange-juice-container story," Caroline said. "But right now we have something to take care of. Can you boys stay in line and save our places?"

Gordo studied how far we had left to go before we got into the wax museum. "You'd better be quick."

As we girls set out to buy disguises, I overheard Bubble Gum say, "I wish that was me. How awesome would it be to stay in Daphne's overnight? Those two chicks are my heroes."

She was talking about me! Boring old me was her hero!

Then Pierced Nose said, "You aren't kidding. I'd love to have an exciting night like that, except I wouldn't steal anything."

"Come on," Ellie said, and she ushered us away.

"How are we gonna get out of this?" I asked. "My parents are going to be superangry if they find out the police are looking for me."

"We need two things," Caroline said. "Disguises, and to get those videos from the Tart Fart so that he can't upload anything else to the Internet, or turn anything over to the police."

Ellie was laughing so hard that she had to hold herself up against the brick wall of the building we were going to walk into. "Tart Fart! That's a good one, Car. I LOVE it."

"Caroline," she corrected Ellie.

"Ahhh." She exhaled and caught her breath back. "Right. Sorry about that." She was slightly more serious as she held the door to the Shamrock Boutique open for us. "Maybe if you apologize for breaking in and stealing the electronics—"

"We didn't break in!" Caroline said loud enough to draw attention from the four customers and store lady.

"And." She lowered her voice but said very firmly, "We. Didn't. Steal. Anything."

"Jeez," Ellie whispered. "You don't need to yell about it. Okay, you have five minutes for the ultimate disguises. I'll be over here by the earrings for free consultations."

"Why are you whispering?" I asked.

"Because I don't want her to yell at me again."

I went right for a soft pink wool cap with a really big flower pin affixed to it.

"Yes, that is perfect for you," Ellie whispered very loudly across the store. I looked at a rack of sunglasses, touched a few, and chose a pair. "Yes," she hissed again. She could whisper pretty loudly. "Those shades would be perfect for you."

"You can stop whispering," I said across the small boutique.

"Oh, good. I didn't like it."

The sunglasses were like two postage-stamp-size lenses held together by a thin metal frame.

"Really? You like these?" I put them on.

"Totally bohemian," she said. She added a feathery scarf and wrapped it around my neck several times.

Caroline had tucked her hair under a red French beret, put on a well-worn denim jacket, lifted the collar up to cover the bottom of her face, and added her big white sunglasses with the rhinestones that she already had in her purse.

Ellie slid a credit card across the counter; it amazed me the way these girls could charge stuff. Before we left the boutique, something caught my eye. A woman working there was piercing a little girl's ears. The little girl was squeezing her eyes shut and hugging a stuffed bear into her belly, when there was a *POP!* The store lady shot an earring into her ear with a handheld gun gadget.

"Are you done?" the little girl asked.

"All done. That didn't hurt, did it?"

"No, uh-uh."

If she could do it, so could I. I'd never be able to get the second hole at home.

"Wait!" I called to Ellie and Caroline. Then I asked the store lady, "How fast can you give me second holes?"

The store lady popped her gun. "Less than a second per ear."

I sat and pointed to a pair of earrings. The little girl handed me her bear. The store lady loaded the gun, and *POP!* She reloaded, and *POP!* And I was done.

On the sidewalk Ellie touched my back and my sides, and patted my purse. "What are you doing?" I asked as she did the same thing to Caroline.

146

"Just making sure you didn't steal anything from that nice little store," she teased.

"Oh MIIIIIGod! Do you listen?" Caroline asked.

A few minutes later, after Gordo oohed and aahed over my earrings and our disguises, we entered Madame Tussauds on the lush carpet and followed the path to the first display—a random selection of US presidents.

Ellie stared. "Blimey! They look so real. I want to kiss one of them."

"NO KISSING!" a voice behind us bellowed.

A figure stood perfectly still in the corner. Ellie walked toward her. "She looks like an actual person." Ellie moved her face very close to the guard's to examine her.

"I AM a real person," the guard said, shocking Ellie so much that she fell to the ground.

She stood up and rubbed her butt. "That hurt," she said.

After I took a picture of the guard, we moved to the next display. It was the cast of *Bloodsucking Zombies*, dressed up like they were at an awards show.

Ellie said, "I just love them. I wish they were here right now, because I want to meet them."

"Me too," Caroline said. She continued to lead the

way past countless wax celebrities. She stopped at a display of people I didn't recognize. It was a group of ladies from Victorian times standing in front of Madame Tussauds in the evening. The wax lampposts looked like they were lit with oil, and the sidewalk appeared to be cobblestone.

Caroline's mouth hung open. "Their dresses are incredible."

Gordo read a plaque that was just inside a velvet rope keeping us back far enough so our breath wouldn't touch the figures. "Says here that these gowns are all handmade. Guess who made them?"

"Who?" Sam asked, chewing a soft pretzel that had materialized in his hand.

"Daphne," Caroline guessed.

"Yup," Sam said. "It says that she started her fashion empire by first hand-sewing party dresses that she sold at the front of Madame Tussauds. Then she was hired as the official seamstress of the museum. Her dresses became so popular that she expanded her business and it continued to grow. Her wax likeness is in the next hall."

"Let's see it," Ellie said.

"Can we get a photo first?" I asked.

Sam nudged me. "Manchester."

"I dare say," I said. "Might we snap a photo in front of these dear mannequins?"

Sam wiped the longish hairs out of his face. "Um, we'll work on that."

We passed several displays until we got to one of a young Daphne, who was plainly dressed, no makeup. She held a little girl's party dress in each hand—one red, one blue. They were elaborately decorated with every embellishment imaginable—beads, sequins, and lace. The plaque said, MS. DAPHNE WHITWORTH, FUTURE PRESIDENT AND CEO OF DAPHNE'S.

"She looks so ordinary. I expected someone far more chic," Caroline said. "You know, my dad knew her before she died. Her daughter is in charge of the store now. My stepmum claims to be her yoga friend, but I don't believe her."

Gordo said, "It's possible. My mum knows her. Her name is Sophie."

"Here's a picture of her." Sam held out his phone.

We all looked over his shoulder. "I think I'm in love," Gordo said.

"Me too," I almost said. She was dressed casually, in jeans and cute sneakers. She was a natural beauty. Of all the fashion looks I'd seen so far in London, this was my favorite. It was like she wasn't even trying to be beautiful. She just was. That was exactly the style of pretty I wanted to be.

Gordo stared at the phone's screen. "Sophie Whitworth. I'd love to meet her!"

"So would I," Caroline said. "My dad, as you know, has connections, and he hasn't ever been able to get us a meeting. She leads a very private life."

"If your faces get identified from the surveillance cameras, you might be meeting her," Sam said.

"Where are we going now?" Ellie asked. "All I want to do is soak my tired tootsies in a hot tub and get my toes done."

"Sounds good," Gordo said.

"*Oui,*" Caroline said. "Let's do that."

I had never actually had my toes done. If this was a week of adventure, maybe I should be open to exploring the concept of pretty toes to match my new look.

"What about Pluto?" Ellie asked.

"We can work on it there while our toes are drying," Gordo said.

"I know the perfect place," Caroline said. "No one will recognize us. J.J., you are going to LOVE this."

Something strange, and wonderful, had happened

over the last two days. Was Caroline finally starting to care about making sure I had a good time? I didn't know what that stuff was that she'd said to Ellie, but thanks to our adventure in Daphne's, maybe she was finally starting to like me.

20

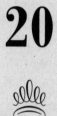

We arrived at Salon London. It was a simple shop with three mani stations and three pedi chairs. The windows were covered with heavy, dusty drapes. Incense sticks burned on the floor next to a little Buddha statue. We were the only customers in the place.

Sam said, "I think I'm gonna go find a sandwich."

"What?" Gordo asked. "You're not going to get your feet soaked?"

"I'll pass," he said. "J.J., do you want to go look for a sandwich with me?"

"Actually," I said, "I'd like to check this out."

"Fine, I'll get you some chips. These girls will go all day without eating. And I'm including Gordo in that statement."

"I heard that!" Gordo said with a smile.

A man came out and gestured to the chairs. Before long, Caroline and I were soaking our feet. Ellie and Gordo were nearby with their fingers dangling in bowls of soapy water. I didn't realize how tired my feet were until a small woman wearing long false eyelashes started rubbing them. It felt heavenly. Now I knew why Ellie wanted to do this.

Another woman walked around carrying a selection of nail polish colors. I chose a light pink. Caroline casually shook her head. I chose again—red—and showed it to her for her approval. She shook her head again. This went on until I held up a dark blue.

She chose gold, and Ellie black. Gordo was going with clear.

After an amazing foot massage with scented lotion, I sat with my feet under a fan. Caroline switched places with Gordo. I opted to skip the manicure because I was starting to worry about money, and I didn't think I could sell this to my mom and dad as an emergency. I flipped through a magazine until Sam returned. He held a grease-stained paper bag.

"Chips," he said.

I opened the bag. It was filled with french fries. "What's on them?"

"Salt and vinegar."

It didn't sound good, but I was hungry and I had mentally declared that I was going to give everything a try. . . . Well, not anything raw or gross.

Hesitantly I tried one.

"Quite good, eh?" Sam asked.

"It is. Thanks."

He sat next to me and looked at my toes. "Blue?"

"Caroline picked it out. Do you like it?"

He shrugged in a way that said *I don't really care but I want to be polite, so*: "Sure."

"How are we on today's word count for Sebastian's paper?"

"Still about eighty short."

"We can do that in no time," I said.

He reached into his back pocket for a rolled-up bunch of paper. "Be my guest. You just tell me what to type."

I scanned the pages for another tidbit or two about Pluto's composition. That was all we really needed for eighty words. "How about the idea that Pluto is one of thousands of objects that make up a ring far, far away from the sun. Pluto is the largest of these objects that form a belt in the universe."

He typed. "Okay, that's good." He tapped more words than I had said, obviously trying to stretch it out to eighty words. "Almost there," he said.

"Okay, use this. 'It is similar in composition to the other objects in the belt.' And 'made mostly of ice.' You have to footnote that section with this reference." I pointed to the website name on the paper.

"Read it to me," he said.

I gave him the website information that was in the top margin of the paper.

"Perfect. Done." He sent the pages. "The little poop gets it early today."

The footnote gave me an idea. "Are you making a bibliography?"

"Yes. Of course. Don't you use bibliographies in America?"

"Duh. Yes. But that just gave me an idea of how we might be able to rat out Sebastian." I explained my idea to Sam.

"I like it," he said.

"Do you think we can do it?"

"Maybe," he said. He reached into my chip bag and

put a handful into his mouth at once. I took some too but only ate one at a time.

"How many places are left on your list?" Gordo asked me.

"I want to see the Royal Mews, Westminster Abbey, Buckingham Palace, the London Dungeon, the Changing of the Guard, and Saint Paul's Cathedral."

Caroline called over from the pedicure chair, "Isn't that a little ambitious for three days?"

"We have nights, too," Sam said.

I excused myself to use the ladies' room. I left the bathroom door open a crack while I washed and dried my hands. I could see Caroline and Ellie in a serious conversation. Caroline's back was to me, but I could see her using her arms to talk.

I heard her saying, ". . . so we're spending our entire week standing in queues. Could it get any more boring? I swear that if Stepmum hadn't promised me a trip to Jamaica as long as J.J. had a great time, I'd bag this whole thing. You know the Mash-Up concert is tonight? And we're not going to it. I mean, really? I am bored out of my blooming mind!"

Caroline had just confirmed all of my greatest fears. I suddenly felt like an imposition and a bother. Worst of all, my de-bored-ification plan clearly wasn't working.

21

Ellie looked over Caroline's shoulder and noticed me.

"Is that true?" I asked angrily. I held back the tears that were coming. I did NOT want her to see me cry. I couldn't believe that I'd thought she'd actually been having fun. I'd totally fallen for her act. She didn't want to be doing any of this, and she didn't like me. She was pretending in exchange for a trip to Jamaica.

Caroline turned around.

I said, "I mean, is it true for all of you?" Ellie was staring at the floor, Gordo dried his nails, and Sam ate a black and white cookie that he'd gotten from somewhere. I didn't know where, but I wished I had one.

"Have you all been promised something in exchange for hanging out with me? Would you all rather be doing something else?"

"Of course not. I'm having a crackin' time," Gordo said. Then he looked at Caroline. "Although, I don't much care for standing in queues."

Sam licked a finger and tossed me a bag. "I think you know how I feel about shopping and salons. I actually quite prefer the sights." He looked at Caroline. "The queues don't bother me."

Ellie studied her feet.

"Ellie?" I asked.

"I like the sights, and I also like getting my nails done. I liked the zombie picture, and I also liked hearing about Anne Boleyn. Can I just say that I like it all?"

Her indifference clearly annoyed Caroline, who huffed. She sucked in a breath like she was about to explain herself, but I didn't want to hear it.

I stormed out of the salon. When my feet hit the cold sidewalk, I realized that I was barefoot. And I didn't know where to go. My mind raced through the last few days: the whispers when she talked to Stepmummy, making sure I smiled big, agreeing to do stuff that I knew she didn't want to.

I contemplated jumping on a red hop-on, hop-off bus destined for somewhere—anywhere—but I realized I didn't have my new fancy purse either. I wasn't going anywhere except back into that salon.

Maybe the old Jordan would run away, but J.J. wasn't going to, although I really wanted to. I was going to find a way to make this week memorable for Caroline, whether she liked it or not. If being blackmailed by Sebastian and potentially chased by the police wasn't enough, I really didn't know how to take things up a notch on the exciting scale.

"J.J.!" someone yelled. It took me a minute to realize he was talking to me. I turned to see Sam jogging down the street after me. "Hey!" he said. "I think you forgot something. You can't go far without these." He held up my shoes and purse.

I slipped my shoes onto my feet and instantly felt the polish smear. *So much for having pretty toes.*

"Thanks," I said.

"No biggie. But I have something else that might help."

I opened the bag and found a black and white cookie. "Oh, this is so great. Thanks." I wiped a tear out of the corner of my eye. "She's a terrible person, right?"

"If I thought that, I wouldn't hang out with her. I think she's trapped inside the body of someone who started acting like a terrible person a long time ago, and now she can't get away from it. If you notice sometimes, she forgets to put on the act and she's totally normal."

"I thought she liked me when we were at Daphne's. I mean, we had an awesome night."

"Maybe we all pretend to be someone we're not sometimes," he said. "You think Gordo likes going out to watch football and eat wings with me? No, he'd rather be at a museum or reading or something, but he acts like a sports fan when we do that."

I thought about how I was pretending to be someone that I wasn't. "I guess I get that."

"And even though she told Ellie that she was tired of standing in queues, I don't believe it. You can't tell me that she didn't like seeing the Crown Jewels, or the Daphne dresses at Madame Tussauds. She's not that good an actress. That was real." He was still holding my purse. He swung it over his shoulder and pushed out his hip. "How about we skip the rest of the salon activities and make a run to Buck-P."

"Buck-P?"

"Yes, the palace. As in Buckingham," Sam said. "Or we could go to the London Dungeon, but that's really more fun after dark."

The mention of the London Dungeon gave me an

idea, an exciting, fun, and totally un-boring idea that would get even with Caroline for making me feel like a joke. I would play a good one on her. As we walked to the bus stop, I explained it to Sam.

"You're so creative. First you have an idea to nail Sebastian and now a plan to prove to Caroline just how much fun an American exchange student can be?" He picked up his finger-phone. "Can I talk to the man with the plan? Sorry, I meant *woman* with the plan. Oh, never mind. She's right here." He actually said "Click" as he hung up his fingers. "It takes the biscuit."

I was pretty sure that was a biscuit I wanted to take.

Sam knew exactly which bus to get on and led me up the staircase inside. The second floor of the bus was open like a convertible, no roof. Sam chose a seat near the front, and I sat next to him. He handed me a little plastic bag of earphones. "Might as well have some fun on the way," he explained.

Sam opened his bag and plugged the earphones into a hole in the seat in front of us. I did the same and suddenly heard a British voice telling me about the streets we were driving through.

We went through an intersection that the voice said was called Piccadilly Circus, which wasn't a circus at all. It was just an intersection where a bunch of streets came together. *How can they do that? Call it a circus when it isn't?*

Whoever named it had done a really bad job.

We passed the Marble Arch, which is a white marble monument on a large traffic island. A long time ago it stood in front of Buckingham Palace. Historically, only members of the royal family were allowed to pass through the arch in ceremonial processions. But now it's out for everyone. At least that's what the voice in my ears said.

Right before we hopped off the bus at "Buck-P," I noticed an Internet café. I made a mental note about the location because we needed to go there to plant the seeds needed to nail Sebastian. But there was one biggie of a problem with that plan. I needed someone who could build a website.

I crossed the street with a crowd of tourists, and I stood in awe as I stared at the palace. As the queen's official London residence, it was heavily guarded, and was so large that it frightened me. We passed through the golden gates and got closer. It was even bigger up close. I took several pictures, including a handful of the royal guards.

Sam went on a search for food while I thought about my plan for Caroline. It would take place tomorrow night at the London Dungeon.

Tomorrow was going to be a very big day.

22

Sam and I walked into a lobby that looked like it could've been in a grand hotel in Washington DC. The floors were white marble with speckles of gray. The wallpaper was textured velvet. I wanted to touch it, but I figured that was a big no-no.

We followed the tour guide up a set of stairs on one side of the lobby; a matching set of stairs climbed up the other side. They wrapped around toward the center and formed a balcony on the second floor to what the tour guide called a state room.

I stopped to look at a gigantic painting of a ship and the ocean. I wondered if it was one of the ships the explorers had taken as they'd set out in search of the New World. It was really bizarre to think there was a time when people didn't know America existed.

"J.J.?" Sam asked.

"What?"

"The group is leaving us. Come on."

I didn't realize that I'd stopped walking. I glanced behind me for one more glimpse of the painting before catching up with the group. The tour guide described the value of the queen's collection of gowns, many of which had been sewn by Daphne. "Today Daphne's daughter, Sophie, makes clothes for the royal family sometimes, and Daphne's granddaughter, Rose, is learning the family trade. Both Sophie and Rose frequently visit the palace to have tea with the queen, and to fit her gowns."

We stopped at a state room, which looked like a ballroom—a very grand ballroom. It was fit for a queen to entertain guests and host ceremonies. The floor was adorned with an oriental rug; the ceiling was high and carved in elaborate designs. In the front of the room there were three steps leading up to a platform on which two thrones sat—actual real thrones. Behind them was a long heavy red curtain. My parents would love this, so I sent them a picture. Of course, there were tons of security people and one of them was in the picture too. I figured it would help them think I was safe.

At the end of the tour I checked my cell phone messages and found one from Liam. He said he would pick me up whenever I was ready to leave. He said I shouldn't rush. I guess Caroline had told him to fetch me. I needed a chauffeur in Wilmington, Delaware; I really did.

Liam gave the horn a light tap when he saw us among the crowds of tourists lingering in front of the palace. It was a long ride out of the city. We dropped Sam off, and I went back to the manor house. Liam said, "Miss Caroline is home, lying down. She said she left sight-seeing early due to a terrible headache." He didn't sound like he believed it. "She explained that Sam was accompanying you. Mr. Gordo and Ellie went home. Mr. and Mrs. Littleton are at a government function tonight, and I made you a shepherd's pie for dinner."

"Thank you, Liam. I'm hungry and tired."

The evening was quiet. Caroline was in her room

and I didn't see her. I was alone for the first time in a few days, and I actually enjoyed the quiet.

Before I went to sleep, I double-checked my plan to pull an awesome and memorable prank on Caroline. It certainly wouldn't be a quiet day tomorrow.

23

The next morning I slept until nine o'clock. I felt well rested for the first time since my arrival in London. It was my second-to-last day in England.

On my way down a massive hallway, I passed Mr. Littleton's home office. It sounded like he was in there. I wanted to introduce myself, but I didn't want to interrupt.

As I debated whether or not to go in, I overheard him talking on the phone. "Daphne's, Incorporated, released its quarterly earnings today. Profits were down for the eighth straight time. Tell the police commissioner that . . ."

The rest was muffled like he was moving around while he talked on the phone.

Interesting. While Daphne's dresses were remarkable, the store was having money problems. I also wondered what Mr. Littleton's job was that he was talking about Daphne's profits and a police commissioner.

Caroline and Mrs. Littleton were in the kitchen sipping tea and flipping through magazines. They sat as far apart at the table as they could possibly be. "Well, good morning, sleepyhead," Mrs. Littleton said. "All the fun catches up with ya, doesn't it?"

"Yes, it did."

I looked at Caroline, who was staring out the window. I could feel the tension between us like I could feel the grumbling in my belly.

"Caroline's headache is all gone, so y'all can have a day filled with sightseeing. Where do you still need to go?"

"I was thinking we would go to the Royal Mews, and tonight I made reservations at the London Dungeon." I swear I saw Caroline's eyes roll back in her head. "I have a feeling it's going to be a very memorable night."

I had an extra bowl of cereal they called muesli. "Are you ready to go to the Mews?"

Caroline said, "It'll probably take a while for the

168

others to get ready, a few hours at least. Maybe we can go later."

I ignored her and fixed my lipstick. Liam pulled up in the driveway and parked near the front door. He walked around the black car and opened the door for Gordo, Sam, and Ellie.

"What were you saying?" I finally asked Caroline, putting my lipstick back into my purse. She just gave me a dirty look and went off to grab her bag.

Mrs. Littleton said, "Well, I think it's great for you to get an early start on the day." She walked over to her bag, which looked fancy. She took out several bills and handed them to me. "Today is my treat. Y'all go to the Mews, have lunch, and do the Dungeon thingy. This should cover it."

I tried to protest, but she said, "Nonsense. You're our guest, and I haven't treated you to a thing yet. Have fun!" She put her purse away and headed toward the hall. "Just remember to text the pictures." She winked at me.

"No problem," I said, and thanked her. I looked at the bills in my hand. What a normal person would've seen as a few hundred pounds, I saw as my ticket out of spreading poopy fertilizer.

24

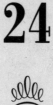

We took the train into the city. Sam asked me, "Did you tell them your idea to nab Sebastian?"

"What idea?" Caroline asked.

I explained it. "You think it'll work?" I asked.

"Unlikely," Caroline said.

"We need to create a website," Sam said. "Can you do that?" he asked Gordo.

"I guess. People do it all the time," Gordo said. "A few hours at an Internet café, and I could probably figure it out. It can't be rocket science."

"Couple of hours?" Ellie guffawed. "Seriously?"

"I think," Gordo defended himself. "I've never done it before."

"Well," Ellie said, "I have. I could do it in twenty minutes. Piece of cake."

"Did you say *cake*?" Sam asked. "Great. Now I'm hungry."

I asked Ellie, "You know how to create a website?"

"Sure. I have one."

"You have a website?" Caroline asked. "How come you never told us?"

"I didn't think you'd be interested."

"What kind of site?" I asked.

Ellie took the iPad from Sam and touched the screen. "Elly's Inventions and TC Ideas and Stuff."

"What's 'TC'?" I asked.

"'Totally cool,'" she said. "I need to update the name." She tap-tap-tapped, and presto! It read: "Ellie's Inventions and TC Ideas and Stuff."

"I give trendy ideas to people all over the world," Ellie continued. "Where do you think the idea for glow-in-the-dark socks came from? Dyeing white cats purple? All my ideas that are now being done everywhere. A website is powerful."

Sam added, "You are full of surprises."

"I'm officially impressed," Gordo said, and he bowed down to her. As he stood himself back up, he saw the screen in the front of the train. "Check out the telly," Gordo said.

"Top news story today. An attempt has been made on the Crown Jewels," Cole the reporter said.

Skye said, *"Cole, this is major. And I understand there is some connection to the Daphne's heist, is that right?"*

"There is," he said. *"Investigators believe the equipment stolen from Daphne's was used in the attempt. In addition the security cameras at the Tower of London were temporarily redirected so they couldn't capture the robbers' image. However, they missed something."* The telly showed a blurry image.

"Is that one of the ghosts that supposedly live in the Tower? Cole, are you telling us that the spirits tried to steal the Crown Jewels?"

"Although that would be an interesting story, that's not what I'm saying. This is a reflection from one of the mirrors that tell you if someone is approaching from around a corner in the narrow corridors. Seems one of the thieves was unknowingly captured in the mirror's image," Cole said.

Skye asked, *"Do the police think the 'Daphne's Duo,' as the pair of girls in the Internet video are now referred to, are responsible?"*

172

"*The girls are among the suspects in this failed attempt,*" Cole said.

"*So what's next?*" Skye asked.

"*Video analysts will cross-check visitors from Daphne's with the Tower of London and see who visited both sights over the last few days. We can expect this to be a very long list of suspects, Skye.*"

"*Long indeed. Thanks, Cole.*"

"That's incredible," Gordo said.

I added, "And we were just there."

25

The Royal Mews were the queen's riding stables and were part of Buck-P. I'm actually not crazy about horses. They scare me a little. I only picked this place because I'd seen the Internet café yesterday.

We walked through the tour of the Mews, which showed us both old and new motor cars and horse-drawn carriages. The horses were often out in the country training and resting, but today they were here in London, so that was kind of a big deal to the people who fancied horses.

As we were leaving, a straight-faced royal guard approached us. "Pardon me."

Regardless of the beret and postage-stamp glasses, I thought for sure we'd been identified from the Internet videos. From the expressions on everyone else's faces, they thought so too.

"Are you Caroline Littleton and company?"

"Nope," Caroline said, looking at her feet.

The guard didn't believe her. "Miss Littleton, your father has arranged a VIP tour for you and your friends."

"VIP?" Ellie asked. "Ha-ha-ha! I said 'pee'!"

"We just finished our tour," Caroline said.

"A trail ride is a unique experience reserved for only very special guests."

"Wait a minute," Gordon said. "Your dad can pull strings with the queen but can't get you a meeting with Daphne's daughter?"

I was still stuck on this VIP thing. "Like, a ride on one of the queen's horses?" I asked. "Shut up!"

The guard looked confused. "That won't be necessary. You can talk whilst you ride. Please follow me."

"Is he serious?" I asked.

"Quite," Caroline said. "You know how to ride, right?"

"Ride a horse? Of course." I let out a little awkward

laugh. "That rhymes." Hopefully I covered up my nervousness.

"Good. Then you won't embarrass me," Caroline said. I figured there was a high possibility that I would embarrass her.

We followed the guard, who delivered us to a stable helper. Gordo walked next to me. "You've never ridden, have you?"

"Shh," I said. "How'd you know?"

"I think you rhyme when you lie."

"I do?"

"Don't worry. I won't tell anyone," he said, and pretended like he was locking his lips.

"What am I gonna do?"

"You don't have many options. I say, 'fess up or fake it'?"

"I think 'fake it,'" I said.

"Me too," Gordo said.

"Stay between me and Sammy. These horses are really well trained. They should just stay in line."

"And if they don't?"

"How far could they go? This place is all fenced in and protected by the royal guard."

I said, "That doesn't make me feel better."

"Just keep your eyes on me. I'll help you."

"Okay."

Sam came over. "Is this totally boss, or what?"

"Saddle or paddle, that's what I always say," I said.

Sam looked from me to Gordo. "Oh, bloody mess. She doesn't know how to ride, does she?"

Sam saw right through me. "I am going to fake it," I said. "Gordo said it will be fine."

"All-righty. Good luck with that," Sam said. "Make sure you tighten your helmet."

We walked to the stables, which were clean, like just-mopped-and-dusted clean. The groom, which is what they called the stable helper, got us on the horses. I was behind Gordo and in front of Sam. I handed the groom my phone and asked her to take a few pictures of us.

After I sent those photos to Mrs. Littleton, we waited to be led to the trail. My horse dug his big nose into anything he saw, while everyone else's stood in line. "Pull up," the groom said, but I didn't know what to pull— my legs, the saddle, the horse's mane. "Pull up," she said again when the horse stuck his snout into a bucket of brushes, knocking it over.

I looked at Gordo, who demonstrated what it looked like to pull up on the straps that held a very uncomfortable-looking gadget on the horse's face.

Gordo mouthed the word "harder" to me, and I pulled up as hard as I could. This beast was strong, but the tug made him lift his head and stay in line.

The groom and her horse slowly walked out of the stable. The five of us followed. I swayed from side to side on the strong black horse. The ground looked far away, farther than I thought it would when I'd been standing on the ground. I was a little scared, but it wasn't too bad—I could do this, I could totally ride a horse. How hard could this be?

Then the groom kicked her heels into the sides of her horse. It began to trot. Caroline's and Ellie's followed. Gordo kicked his heels, and his horse took off. And mine started to go faster without me even kicking.

Someone yelled, "Ahh!"

When I realized it was me, I tried to stop, but my body jerked with each trot, and with each jerk I couldn't help letting out a grunt. I held the saddle and reins for dear life.

My helmet bopped around on my head until it covered my eyes.

My horse ran faster and my body sagged off the saddle.

My left foot came out of its stirrup as I fell to the right.

178

I pictured myself falling off and getting trampled to death. Caroline would be beyond embarrassed, but I wouldn't care because I'd be dead, and Ellie would have her fill of blood and guts until the sequel to *Bloodsucking Zombies* was released.

"Gordo!" I called. "Help!" Then, as if the horse could hear me, his stride began to break. The reins felt slightly looser in my hands.

"You're okay," Sam said. He and his horse were very close to me, trotting right by my side.

I moved my helmet out of my eyes.

"That was so freakin' scary," I said, out of breath and almost crying. "You're like a cowboy. How did you know how to do that?"

"I've been around horses since I was little, so it wasn't a big deal. I was watching you closely because I didn't think faking it was gonna work."

"Well, it's a big deal to me. I thought for sure that my insides were going to be stomped out. At least that would take the news coverage away from the videos for a while," I said. "I don't know what I was thinking to believe that I could just hop on and ride a horse. It was a bad idea."

"I'm not going to disagree with you. I should've stopped you."

"Thanks." We approached the stable while the other kids were going down a path. "Did Caroline see?"

Sam and his horse casually led me back to the stables. "Not a thing," he said. "I'm sure."

26

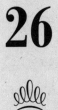

We had to pull Ellie away from the horses. She kept kissing them and thanking them.

"It's their job," Caroline said. "You don't have to thank them."

Gordo said, "Besides, these aren't the talking kind of horses. So they don't understand you anyway." He was teasing her, but I didn't think she knew that.

"Let's go across the street to the Internet café now," I said. That was really where I'd wanted to go all along.

"Yes!" Sam said. "I'm getting a sandwich. Tuna. Possibly with bacon. Maybe soup, too."

Gordo said, "You're going to be a human trash compactor before long."

"That day is not today, Gordo. You want soup too? And maybe we can share a little cheese plate, eh? You wanna?" Sam asked. I think he knew Gordo wouldn't eat soup and a cheese plate.

"Maybe a cup of soup," Gordo said. "*If* it has noodles."

On our way Ellie asked me, "Where do you think they keep the talking horses?"

I said, "I don't think Gordo was serious."

"Why?" Ellie asked. "They probably have to keep them away from the crowds."

And this is the girl who was going to build the website?

At the café we all got soup and sat at a big booth in the corner. Ellie stared at the café-supplied computer. "Now, what exactly do you want me to do?"

I explained my idea. "Create a website that will be a reference in the bibliography. When the teacher checks the site, she'll find our message explaining what Sebastian has done. We'll ask her to *temporarily* give him a B-plus until he returns what he has of ours. She'll e-mail us that she's gotten our message, and we'll reply when it's all clear to give him an F for cheating."

"Why don't we just e-mail the teacher now?" Caroline asked. "In fact, why didn't we do that three days ago and skip writing the paper?"

I said, "Because he would've posted our videos all over the place."

"Right," Ellie said. "I can do this superfast. But how will the teacher know to go to this site?"

I explained, "She'll check the references."

"You think she'll check every single one?" Gordo asked.

"The URL name is going to be important. It will have a subtle clue that the teacher will notice but Sebastian won't. The clue will make her think, 'I better check this one out.'"

"Like what?" Ellie asked.

"Maybe 'www.dwarfplanetpluto.com, "The depressing truth about Pluto," by I. M. Acheater.' Get it?" I added. "Like 'I AM A CHEATER.' The teacher probably knows the Pluto websites that students use for this project, but when she doesn't recognize this one, she'll look it up."

"And when she does," Sam finished, "she'll find our message."

"What if Sebastian decides to check it out too?"

Caroline asked. "He's a twerp, not an idiot."

"Too true," Ellie said. "It could totally backfire on us, in which case your late-night videos will be Internet sensations and you'll be in the tank for grand theft."

Caroline yelled, "We didn't steal anything!"

Ellie added, "It's your word against theirs."

"WHO!" Caroline yelled. "Who is 'they'?" She seemed frustrated with Ellie.

Ellie said, "You know, the popo, the police!"

Sam asked Caroline, "Are the police going to believe you? I mean, you *were* in the store the night the stuff was stolen."

Gordo pushed his unfinished soup cup aside and nibbled his baguette. "I don't think this is gonna work."

Sam took the soup cup and drained it into his mouth. "Bummer." He wiped the corner of his mouth on a cloth napkin. "It sounded like a good idea."

"It can still work," Ellie said.

We listened to her idea. There was a 50 percent chance it would involve talking horses and a 50 percent chance it would be brilliant. "We'll hold the bibliography until right before the paper is due and make him meet with us in order to get it. We can meet him at Lively's tomorrow morning and exchange the bib for the flash drive with the videos.

That way he won't have time to check the references."

Caroline asked, "And what if he doesn't like this idea and he blasts more evidence of us at Daphne's? The next batch might include our faces."

"If he did that, he wouldn't get his bibliography, and without that he won't get a B-plus," Ellie said.

We all looked at her.

"Why are you all staring at me?" she asked. "I think it'll work."

"It will," I said. "You're a tiara-wearing-glow-in-the-dark-sock-and-zombie-loving genius."

"Thanks. Give me a half hour. It will be a bomb-diggity," Ellie said with a proud smile.

We watched every tap she made on the computer. She stopped and peered up at us. "I can't work under this pressure. Why don't you go shopping or something?"

Caroline said, "You don't have to ask me twice." She tossed her purse over her shoulder, flipped on her white rhinestone sunglasses, and tucked her hair back into the red beret.

"Ditto," Gordo said. The two of them left, arms hooked together.

Sam and I moved to a different table. "Wanna share a piece of pie?" I asked.

He said, "I don't know. Let me think. Do I want pie? Am I even hungry? Oh, this is a hard decision. Maybe I should call the DUH, YES, I LOVE PIE ASSOCIATION."

"Funny," I said. "I'll get it." I returned with one plate and two forks.

"Think it'll work?" I asked.

"I think it just might," he said.

"Done," Ellie announced. "Easy peasy." She left the booth where she'd been working and came to sit with us, picking up a fork from another table on her way. She took a wee teeny bite of pie. "Oh. That is so good, I could have another bite." She took another teensy-weensy bite, and said, "Yup. Still good."

"Since that's done, I can tell you my secret plans for tonight," I told Ellie. "I'm going to need your help to make this a night Caroline will never forget."

She dropped the fork and slapped her hands over her ears. "La-la-la. If it's a secret, don't tell me. I'm terrible at keeping secrets. I don't mean to be; I just can't remember what's secret and what's not. So, don't tell me. I trust you guys. Let's just assume I love the idea and it will be a great night."

"Okay. I won't tell you."

Ellie dropped her hands and continued to take itsy-bitsy bites of the pie, until it was gone.

Sam didn't stop her but watched with surprise.

Then Ellie rummaged through her purse for a lip gloss and applied. When she was done, she looked at the plate. "Oh my, Sam, it's all gone." I don't think she realized she'd eaten the whole thing.

"It's all right," Sam said. "I wasn't hungry anyway."

27

On our way to the train, we passed a store where Caroline "had to" stop. She and Ellie went in while Sam and Gordo searched for a loo.

"I'll wait here," I said. "And look in the windows."

I strolled about half a block, to where I stumbled on Lively's main location. Immediately I knew I wanted to get Sam a lemon tart since Ellie had eaten all the pie.

Sebastian was behind the bakery counter taking muffins out of a pan. "Oh, look what the wind blew in," he said to himself but loud enough for me to hear. "Where is the rest of your mob?"

"Shopping."

"How come you're not with them?"

"I wanted a snack."

He placed the pan down and picked up another. "Oh, bloody blast it!" He dropped the pan. It made a loud *klunk-klank* on the ground. He held out his hand. "Wonkers! That was hot."

I marched right behind the counter to see the burn. "Come to the sink." I turned the knob of a big stainless steel sink and guided his burned hand under the faucet.

"Ah, that feels good," he said.

"Do you have ice?"

"In that chest." His eyes directed me to a giant freezer that opened like an army trunk. I broke off a chunk of ice. "Grab some butter, too, will you?"

"Ice. I read that ice is better for a burn than butter." I wrapped the ice in a paper towel, guided his hand out of the water, and set the towel on the red spot. "How does that feel?"

"Not bad. Not good, either, but not bad." He looked at me. "Thanks. My mum has ointment in the back. I'll put that on and bandage it." Sebastian went into the back of the store, and I lost sight of him.

"Hello?" a voice called to me from the customer side of the counter. I looked at a woman in a purple pantsuit and facial wrinkles down to her elbows. She said, "I'll have a prune Danish and tea."

"I . . . ummm, errr . . ."

"Two lumps of sugar in the tea, dear."

"Two?" I put what I was pretty sure was a prune Danish on a plate, and tipped some hot tea into a dainty cup. I looked around for sugar, found a canister, and plopped in two lumps. I put the plate and cup on the counter, but the lady was gone. She had sat herself down and was tucking her legs under a table.

I brought the items to her.

"Oh, thank you. You are so sweet."

Sebastian still hadn't returned. I went back to the scene of the burn, scooped the broken bits of blueberry muffins off the floor, and put them into the trash. I found a broom and was sweeping when Sebastian appeared with a bandage on his hand. His eyes widened when he looked at me cleaning.

"You're cleaning up my mess?"

"I was just helping." I thought maybe he was mad. "And that lady. She wanted a Danish—"

"You served Mrs. Sawyer?"

"I guess so."

"Why are you trying to be so nice to me? Do you want something? Did Caroline send you here?"

"I'm not *trying* to be nice. I *am* nice."

Sebastian seemed to accept this explanation as he sent me on my way with two free tarts.

But was I nice? I'd just made sure he'd get an F.

28

The London Dungeon lived up to its name. The outside was lit with medieval torches. The building was windowless and gray. Standing outside the bleak and dreary attraction, Ellie said, "Thank you! Thank you, J.J., for bringing us here. This is like a real live horror movie that we are going to go in. I swear life can't get better than this."

The London Dungeon was a cross between a haunted house, an amusement park ride, and a history lesson. It was like walking, or riding, through London's haunted history, which was presented with elaborate scenes and live actors that tried to scare you.

I looked at Caroline, who let out a yawn, which she covered with her fist. *You better get your yawns in now,* I thought. *Someone might get a little extra scared tonight.*

Sam looked at his phone. "Okay. I just sent Sebastian the last pages except for the bibliography. I told him we'll meet him tomorrow morning at Daphne's at nine o'clock and trade it for the flash drive."

Everything for Sebastian was ready. And we were on the cusp of entering what could've been hell.

A bald man dressed in a black gown like an executioner directed us to enter the damp dungeon.

Ellie said, "The best night EVER!" And she jumped around.

Inside was like a dark, scary cave. We walked a narrow path and looked at the horrible scenes in each crevice. They were disgusting displays with actors in very realistic costumes being executed, tortured, and locked in stockades and cages. It was truly horrific. Sometimes someone would jump out at us and try to catch us to bring us into their deadly world.

The medieval times were gruesome and barbaric. I'd been in London for four days, and I'd been so busy transforming myself, taking pictures and videos, writing a paper about Pluto, hiding from the police, shopping, setting a trap for Sebastian, *and* planning this charade for Caroline that I hadn't noticed the obvious—this place was superold, older than anything in the US. They had way more history all around them than we could ever have. That was the history I'd come here to see.

I could hear the sound of water as we progressed through the cavernous halls.

A woman dressed in rags screamed in my face, "Get in the boat! Hurry!" Fake blood dripped down her face and stuck in her matted hair. I stepped into the boat. The flat-bottom was filled with about an inch of water that soaked right through my sneakers. The boat wobbled from side to side, and I thought for a second I might go overboard. We all made it onto the craft and sat real close together on two rows of bench seats that didn't feel strong or sturdy under my butt.

Ellie was giddy with excitement. She still didn't know the plan, so I whispered into her double-pierced ear, "Whatever happens, just go with it. It's all part of the secret plan that I didn't tell you."

"Got it."

The boat floated down the indoor river toward fog and screams. It got darker, and Ellie said, "I think I just tinkled."

Gordo, who was sitting next to her, said, "No, baby doll. I think that was me."

The boat disappeared into the tunnel. The actors around us screamed in pain. One guy with a huge zipper scar on his face tried to climb into the boat with us, but Sam pushed him away. I heard Gordo let out a blood-curdling howl, then shout, "Get off me! Get away! Ahhh!"

"What's the matter?" Caroline asked.

It was all part of the plan.

Sam yelled like someone had cut off his arms or taken away his last cupcake. "No! No! Oh my God!"

I joined in with my own shouts of terror.

Caroline frantically asked questions, "What's the matter? What's going on? Ellie, where are you?"

No one answered, because we all snuck out of the boat and left Caroline all alone.

"Gordo? J.J.?" She was crying now. "What's happening?"

From our hiding place I saw the boat float past a scene of King Henry's daughter, who was known as Bloody Mary.

The boat came out of the tunnel to where candles hung on the walls. I saw Caroline looking around her and realizing that she was alone. All alone in the horrible cavern. She called to the ghoulish actors, "Help me! My friends are gone! They've been taken." But they ignored her and continued on with their show.

I laughed so hard that I thought that I might tinkle. We walked along a narrow and ghoul-less path to get to the end of the ride before Caroline, and we hid in the darkness.

At last the boat bumped the edge of a dock. Caroline jumped out. She looked at the empty boat and screamed to everyone, "Call the police. Oh my God! Oh my God, they're all gone."

We let her go a minute longer before coming out from the shadows. We all burst out in laughter. It was we-totally-got-you-with-this-joke laughter.

There was no way she could EVER forget this night.

29

Caroline didn't think the joke was as funny as the rest of us did. Even the actors and people who worked at the London Dungeon thought it was hysterical.

"Why would you do this?" she asked Sam and Gordo.

"J.J. set it up," Gordo said.

Sam said, "It was priceless." He held his hand up for a high five. "Up top." I smacked it.

"You?" she asked me, moving very close to my face. "Why?"

"You said this was a boring week," I said. "The only reason you were nice to me was so that you could go on a vacation. Now the joke's on you."

She pursed her lips and held in whatever it was she wanted to say as we made our way to the train.

As with every other train ride, the telly was on in the front of the car. Once again the news involved us.

"*It's unbelievable, Skye. Another robbery. This one was quite successful. Two famous Daphne dresses were stolen last night from Madame Tussauds.*"

"*Last night, Cole?*" Skye asked. "*Why are we just hearing about this now?*"

"*The blue and red dresses were replaced with imitations. The swap wasn't discovered until midday. Oh, and guess where the fake dresses came from?*"

"*I'm gonna say the Dress-Up Department of Daphne's. Looks like it was the Daphne's Duo again.*"

"*Actually,*" Cole said, "*authorities think the real mastermind might have uploaded videos of the duo just to throw investigators off his or her scent.*"

"*It did, indeed,*" Skye said.

"*Now the police are looking for the source of the uploaded videos with hopes that it will lead to the true mastermind behind this recent string of robberies.*"

"Do you know what that means?" Gordo asked.

"They think Sebastian is the real mastermind," we all said, and had a gut-busting laugh.

"Do you think the police will actually look for him?" I asked.

"Who cares?" Caroline asked. "Let the little poop get in trouble. Uploading those videos without our permission is probably illegal somewhere."

"If it's not, it should be," Gordo agreed. Then he asked, "Do you think it's strange that we've been to all three of the places where there have been crimes?"

"They're three of the most popular tourist attractions in England," Sam said.

"Well, I think that is smashing news," Ellie said.

Sam asked, "That they think it's Sebastian?"

"That they think it's anyone other than the Daphne's Duo here." Ellie indicated Caroline and me. "I gotta be honest, I thought it was you guys all along."

30

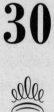

We huddled under umbrellas outside Daphne's at 8:55 the next morning. It wasn't raining hard but spitting enough to return the curl to my flat-ironed hair, which I'd pulled back into a braid. I'd ditched the crocheted cap, and Caroline had lost her beret.

At precisely nine the doors opened and we raced to Lively's. Sebastian wasn't there. The lady behind the counter introduced herself as his mom. I was dying to tell her what Sebastian had been up to. Sam, on the other hand, took advantage of the situation and ordered lemon tarts without spit. Mrs. Lively was so nice, she didn't even charge him.

"How did Sebastian get to be such a creep?" I asked Sam. "His mom seems very kind."

"Dunno."

Mrs. Lively said, "I called Sebastian to tell him that his friends were here looking for him. He said he was on his way."

"Pardon me, Mrs. Lively," Ellie said. "I see you have a computer there." She indicated behind the counter. "I'm looking for a grade from my teacher. Would you mind if I checked my school account really quick? I'm so nervous about this grade."

"Well, I suppose that would be okay. I understand how important your grades are," she said. "You know, Sebastian is handing in a critical paper today. His scholarship depends on it. You help yourself." She placed a glass of juice on the counter for each of us. We hadn't even asked for them.

Ellie walked behind the counter.

"What do you mean about his scholarship?" Sam asked Mrs. Lively.

"Sebastian has to keep a B-plus average or he'll lose the scholarship he needs to attend your school."

"Oh." Sam tugged me, Gordo, and Caroline away

from Mrs. Lively. "If Sebastian gets caught cheating, or gets an F, he'll lose his scholarship."

"He's a cheater," Caroline said. "He deserves to fail and to lose his scholarship."

"If everyone got what they deserved, you'd be locked up somewhere for spending the night at Daphne's," Sam said.

"You know that was way different. I'm not a jerk and a blackmailer," she said.

Gordo said, "Sebastian and I used to be science lab partners. He was fine until you started talking rubbish about him."

"Are you joshing me? He's evil," she said. "You're just gonna have to trust me on that."

No one said anything. It seemed like Caroline's friends weren't willing to "just trust" her the way they used to or the way she wanted.

Ellie came out from behind the counter.

"What was that about?" I asked her.

"I asked myself, if I was Sebastian, would I just hand over all my videos to you guys?"

Gordo asked, "And what did you answer yourself?"

"No. I would make a copy."

Sam said, "Which you just found."

"I did. And I replaced it with this." She pointed to

her phone's screen. There was a video of Ellie. Her hands were in front of her mouth and she pretended she was playing a clarinet. "Hmm doot doot doo."

"What's this?" Sam asked her.

"It's that new Mash-Up song played on an invisible clarinet. Can't you tell?"

Gordo said, "That doesn't sound like Mash-Up at all."

Sam ignored the insignificant debate. "What did you do?"

"I replaced the video of Caroline and J.J. with their bums in the pastry case with this," she said. "I left the old file name so he'll think he still has it, but he has Invisible Clarinet instead." Then she added, "BTW, in the cloud he has another folder called 'Caroline Heart.'"

"Ooh, someone has a crush," Gordo said.

"Heart?" Caroline asked. "I think I just barfed in my mouth."

Gordo started a slow, steady clap. We all joined in. She smiled a huge yes-I-know-I-am-awesome smile.

"He can't get us now. We're free," Caroline said.

Sebastian came into the Hall of Gourmets, nearly a half hour late.

"You're late," Caroline said. "I guess you're not too worried about having that paper in by ten o'clock."

"Patience, Cruella," he said. "It's actually not due until eleven. I just wanted you to wait for me."

"You're a real creep," Caroline said.

"And you're a snob," Sebastian said back.

"Oh, blast!" I yelled, using my new British expression. I'd spilled my juice down the front of my shirt. Everyone looked at me. "Sebastian, can you show me the sink, please?"

He huffed like it was terribly inconvenient, then led me to their kitchen and to the sink. I turned on the water, and he was about to walk away. "Wait," I said. "Remember when I said I was nice?"

He nodded.

"Well, I did something not very nice." He listened. "You're gonna get an F as soon as you hand over the flash drive. And then you'll lose your scholarship."

"No I won't. I have insurance."

"Not anymore." His forehead creased in the center. "Turns out Ellie is a computer wiz. Your insurance is gone." His face turned a dark shade of red.

He smashed his fist into his hand. "I'll still get them." His evil mind looked like it was racing for a new plan.

"How about you don't?"

"What do you mean?" he asked.

"Take the B-plus. Keep your scholarship."

"You said you made it so I would get an F."

"I can undo that." I hoped I could. "And when I do, let's just drop this, okay?"

He thought and picked at the bandage on his burn. "What's in it for me?"

"Seriously? You get to stay in school, keep your scholarship, and get a B-plus on a paper that you didn't even write."

He picked some more.

Sam handed Sebastian a small red flash drive. "Now hand over the flash drive."

Sebastian took it out of his pocket. "Here you go. One worm chock-full of incriminating videos and pictures. It's all yours."

Caroline took the worm and squeezed it in her fist.

Sebastian disappeared behind the pastry counter, but not before glancing at me.

"We should check it," Sam said. "Make sure it's the right worm." He put it into the iPad and started watching the video of us dancing around in costumes. "You two had quite a busy night."

"Then our mission is complete," Caroline said. "By this time tomorrow he'll be tossed from school."

I felt sick to my stomach. I knew he cheated, but jeez, this was extreme. "Wait," I said. "We can't let him get kicked out of school."

Caroline said, "Yes we can. We have the flash drive. Let's just go."

I pushed some more. "This isn't worth him losing his scholarship over."

"You don't know him like we do. He's wicked. Now let's get out of here and do something fun. J.J., apparently you're the Queen of Fun. What do you have up your sleeve today?" She didn't sound like she really thought I was the queen of anything.

I asked Ellie, "Is there anything you can do?"

Caroline said, "I said we're leaving it."

"No," I stated firmly. "We're not going to make him lose his scholarship."

She narrowed her eyes into little slits. "What did you say?"

I wanted someone else to say something, but no one did. My heart was racing. I felt sweat in my palms and armpits as Caroline continued to drill me with her nasty stare. "Ellie, what can you do?" I asked.

"Jeez, I perform a few computer miracles, and now you guys think I'm some kind of fairy godmum. Oh, let me wave my wand and—Poof!—it's all good now."

"What about changing his grade in the school computer?" I asked.

"I have ethical standards, and that crosses the line."

"You can do that?" Sam asked.

"Maybe I can, but I don't. If I did, I would've changed your science midterm. You mixed up meiosis and mitosis. I mean, come on, Sam, use your head!"

"What? How did you know I missed those questions?" Sam asked.

"I might snoop from time to time. But that's not important. What we're talking about is where I draw the line. No grade changing."

Sam shook the confusion out of his head. "You are one weird chick."

"Gimme the iPad," I said, and I handed it to Ellie. "Can you make our URL actually go to the real article, so it's all fine?"

Ellie thought for a second, tapped the screen a few times, and said "Uh-huh." Then she handed the tablet back to me. "There you go. Just like you wanted. Fixed," Ellie said. "Now, does anyone want me to change a pumpkin into a carriage?"

"So it's all good, then," I said. I looked at Caroline, who I knew disapproved of everything I had done. I tried to lighten the mood. "I mean, besides the grossness of Sebastian's crush, of course. That's not good."

There was an awkward pause of quietness.

"Well," Caroline finally said. I was sure her next words would be harsh and hurtful. I squared my shoulders and prepared for the blow. "It's done, then." She un-narrowed her eyes. "I didn't think you had it in you, J.J."

I waited. The lashing was coming; I just knew it. I saw Ellie cringe as she waited for it too. "I expected you to be more of a slug. But you've proven me wrong."

Wait, what just happened?

Gordo studied Caroline with great suspicion in his face. "Who are you, and what have you done with Caroline?"

"Oh, shove off," she said.

He raised his eyebrows. "It's Caroline."

"This is one of those unusual times when things didn't pan out like I'd planned. I didn't mean for you to overhear me at the nail salon, but it was the truth." She continued. "My stepmum bribed me to hang out with you because I didn't want to. I don't really like hanging out with new people. I like my life exactly the way it is. I wasn't interested in prancing around London from sight to sight entertaining a stranger during my week off from school."

Well, at least she was honest. I hadn't really considered that my arrival might have botched up her week.

"Your mom called, and my stepmum said yes, and the rest was on me. No one even asked me if I wanted to be your hostess and tour guide."

I hadn't even thought that she wouldn't be psyched about our week. "So you were promised a trip to Jamaica in exchange for schlepping me around?"

She nodded. "Not a bad deal, eh?"

"I guess."

"What I didn't say at the salon, and maybe I should've, is that I've kinda liked it. I mean, I've lived in this city all my life and I never knew there was a wax figure of my favorite person at Madame Tussauds," she said.

"And the truth is that the whole London Dungeon thing was . . ."

It was coming now. I was going to get a full verbal assault.

"It was freakin' amazing! I mean, I *totally* believed that you had been slashed. I'll be talking about that forever. And the night at Daphne's was pretty awesome." She tossed her beautiful blond hair over her shoulder and put on her big white sunglasses. "I suppose I should thank you."

"You want to thank *me*?"

"Yes. I just did," she said, and rummaged through her purse for her mobile, probably to see who had texted in the last hour. "Should we get going to the abbey, then?"

"Bril," I agreed. Things with Caroline felt good, and I was glad Sebastian would keep his scholarship.

31

The day was dreary and rainy. Everyone was fine with heading home early. Even me. I had to admit that I was exhausted. And maybe I was a little depressed that this would be my last night in Caroline's house, which was like a palace to me.

"It feels good to have all of the Sebastian stuff over with," Ellie said.

Caroline said, "And since the police think our video was just a diversion from the real thief, I feel like I can watch the telly without cringing."

"But the real thief is still out there," Sam said.

"Speaking of the telly, look," Sam said. "It's Skye and Cole with the news."

"*This just in. A priceless painting was stolen from Buckingham Palace,*" said Skye. She showed a shot of the painting. It was the one of the boat.

"*Let me guess,*" Cole said. "*The tools used for this heist were the ones stolen from Daphne's.*"

"*You got it.*"

"*Do the police have any leads on the robber or robbers?*"

"*As you know, they have been cross-checking the surveillance footage from all the sights: Daphne's, the Tower of London, Madame Tussauds, and now Buckingham Palace, and they've narrowed down the potential suspects,*" Skye said.

"*That is wonderful news. What about the mirror image from the Tower of London?*" Cole asked.

"*As soon as it's released, you'll see it here,*" replied Skye.

"I kinda hoped they'd figure out who it was before I went home," I said. "But I'm just glad they don't really think it was the Daphne's Duo."

"You're going home with a cool story to tell," Gordo

said. "Being suspected of trying to steal the Crown Jewels? It doesn't get any more exciting than that."

"Too true," I agreed.

It was dark when Liam woke me. "Miss J.J., it's time to get ready to go to the airport."

I packed my things and was filled with a satisfaction that I had done what I came for, plus so much more. I'd had a major adventure that I'd never forget, I felt totally un-boring, and most importantly, I'd made four new friends.

I figured I could google the UK news from home to see updates on the crime spree that had plagued London since my arrival.

I brought my things to the living room, where Mrs. Littleton was in front of a seventy-two-inch TV screen, twisting her body in a yoga pose.

"Liam is gonna take you to Heathrow. Gimme a hug now."

I did, and I thanked her for everything.

In the grand marble foyer of the mansion, Caroline waited with a suitcase of her own. "Are you coming with me to Delaware?"

She rolled her eyes. "No. It's a gift." She pushed a case

with a pretty floral pattern on it and the word LONDON written across the top.

"Oh, thank you," I said. I pulled it by its handle. "Why is it so heavy?"

"I might've filled it with the stuff you wanted but didn't buy from Daphne's."

"Are you serious? That's amazing. I love, love, love it." I smiled. "Thank you so much."

I walked out the front door of the fantastic manor house and turned to take another look at it. I wanted to remember all the details. I hoped that someday I would visit this house again.

Liam held the car door open for me. I would have to get used to not having a driver back home.

Ellie, Sam, and Gordo were in the car. "Hi, guys! You all came to say good-bye?"

"Of course," they said in unison.

And off we went to the airport.

At the terminal we said good-bye. "I'll text you," I said to Caroline.

"Of course you will," she said, like I would be so fortunate to text Caroline Littleton, but I knew what she really meant was "I can't wait."

"All right, baby doll. You stay cool," Gordo said.

"I will."

"Seriously, it's been a totally epic week," he said. "You are one of the most interesting and fun people I've ever met."

Ellie was tearing up.

"Ellie," I said. "It'll be okay."

"I'm just going to miss you so much."

"We'll be friends on Facebook so we can always see what the other is doing," I said.

I knew Ellie and I were going to be friends forever.

Sam took my hand. "I wish it had been longer than a week," he said.

"Me too."

A boarding call for my flight bellowed overhead.

"You have to go," he said. He picked up his finger-phone and mouthed the words, "Call me."

"I will." With a wave I headed home with my over-priced purse, a bag full of new clothes, and a new attitude.

32

I spread out in my seat, which I found out Mr. Littleton had upgraded to first class for me as a special treat. Have you ever sat in first class? It's *very* nice, like reclining-seat-my-own-TV-phone-WiFi-slippers nice.

I clicked picture after picture of my trip and arranged them in the order I wanted. I typed captions under each, describing Anne Boleyn and showing the yeomen who guard the tower in their uniforms.

As I was going through, I noticed something strange about one yeoman in the photo. I paused for a second,

216

then moved on to the Crown Jewels. Then I explained a bit about Madame Tussauds' history and showed pictures of some current celebrities whose likenesses were frozen in wax, adding more captions along the way. I also added the pictures of the cast of *Bloodsucking Zombies*.

Right before I moved off to the next photo, my eye caught the face of a man in the background. To anyone else he would just look like another tourist, but I recognized this man. It was the same man who had been in the yeoman's uniform, or maybe it wasn't a uniform at all; it was a COSTUME.

I combed through the rest of my photos, carefully looking for the man in the other pictures. And finally, near the end of the album, I found him—a.k.a. Hamlet, the night security guard at Daphne's—at Buckingham Palace dressed as a royal guard, another costume from Daphne's Dress-Up Department.

I pulled out the air phone from the seat in front of me, and I took out my credit card. This *was* an emergency. I dialed a number I'd had in my wallet in case I ever needed it while I was in London. I needed to call Mr. Littleton now.

"It's Jordan Jacoby," I said. "I know who the thief is, and I have proof, photographic proof. I'm sending it to you right now." I paused. "Did you get it? Do you see what I'm talking about? That's the night security guard from Daphne's. His name is Hamlet."

I landed in Philadelphia. After navigating Customs like the experienced international flyer that I was, I was met by a man in a black pin-striped suit and a red tie.

"Excuse me," he said with a British accent that I didn't expect in Philadelphia. "I'm Mark Salyers, the British ambassador. Mr. Littleton sent me. He's very appreciative of your help. Can we talk for a minute?"

"Um, okay," I said.

"Follow me."

I spent the next hour with Ambassador Salyers.

By the time I got home, it was already on the news. Hamlet was in custody. My allegations were confirmed with his image clearly reflected in the mirror at the Tower of London. And the local reporter said that I, J.J. Jordan Jacoby, was offered the gratitude of Her Majesty.

The ambassador had been very kind to me. He said I was welcome in England anytime, and he personally arranged for me to have VIP access to any of the city's sights and palaces. This meant that I didn't need to buy tickets or wait in the queue.

• • •

On Monday at school I gave my presentation in a new outfit from Caroline. I'd put the presentation in a really neat web-based program that Ellie had taught me to use.

I started, "While the Royal Mews are the official stables for the queen . . ." I was in the middle of a pretty good presentation when my mobile . . . err . . . cell phone rang. Whoops.

"I am so sorry. This phone is still new. I thought I'd turned it off," I said to my teacher, embarrassed.

When I glanced down at the phone, I almost hit the floor.

The caller ID said SOPHIA WHITWORTH.

SIX MONTHS LATER

"*Top story today is about everyone's favorite store, Daphne's,*" Skye said.

"*Indeed it is, Skye,*" Cole said. "*To increase its business the store has decided to stay open all night long for what it's calling Pillow Parties.*"

"*That's brilliant, Cole. I know I want to go. Do you know who the mastermind was behind this idea?*"

"*Tell me, Skye,*" Cole said.

"*An American girl named J.J. This is the same girl responsible for identifying the perpetrator behind a rash of thefts that plagued some of our most beloved landmarks just a few short months ago. She is truly an amazing young woman,*" Skye said.

"*Let's show a clip of J.J. and her friends with Sophia and Rose Whitworth at a ribbon-cutting ceremony for the new Slumber Party Department.*"

Lost in Paris

Pour ma mère et mon père. Merci pour tout. Je vous aime.

Acknowledgments

Ooh la la, so many fab people to thank:

A writer girl can't do much without *formidable* critique partners and writing pals: Gale, Carolee, Josette, Jane, Chris, and Shannon, and the Northern Delaware Sisters in Crime group: John, KB, Jane, June, Chris, Janis, Susan, and Kathleen.

Special thanks to Chris Lally, the mastermind of plot, who always meets me when I'm in a panic. Many of the ideas incorporated herein came from her beautiful head.

Thanks to my friends, who are super supportive of this life and listen to me talk about fictitious people, places, and situations.

A thousand *merci*s to my literary dream team, who just "get" me: Mandy Hubbard, literary agent, and Alyson Heller, editor. Without them, none of this works.

As always, to my family: Ellie, Evan, Happy, Kevin, my parents, nieces and nephews, sister, sisters-in-law, brothers-in-law, and mother-in-law, thank you for your continued encouragement! Extra-special thanks to my daughter and Parisian travel-mate, Ellie, for sharing the City of Light with me. "We'll always have Paris."

To teachers, librarians, and most of all, my readers: I love getting your e-mails, letters, pictures, selfies, posts, and tweets. . . . Keep 'em coming! I hope you love *Lost in Paris* as much as *Lucky Me*, *Lost in London*, and *Just Add Magic*.

To all of you above, and those I've somehow forgotten (*pardon!*): *Je vous souhaite santé et bonheur!*

1

I traced my finger over the gold emblem of my new pass-port. It was blank, but it would have its first stamp very soon. A stamp that said FRANCE!

My brothers were playing in a lacrosse tournament overseas, which meant that I got to go to . . . *wait for it* . . . Paris!

While the boys were off playing lacrosse, Mom and I planned to tour the entire city—the City of Light. That was what they called Paris. What I wanted to do most of all was to take a boat ride down the Seine—that was the river that flowed through the center of the city. My dad had to stay behind for work, so he would miss all the fun. *Quel dommage!* That was "bummer" in French, I thought, or maybe it was "it's too bad," or "scrambled eggs."

Giddy with excitement, I placed the passport back onto the middle of the kitchen table, so everyone could see it. It had my name, Gwen Russell; my picture; and my birth date, indicating that I was thirteen. "It's beautiful, isn't it?" I asked Mom for the umpteenth time.

"Yes, it is. It'll look even better with a stamp in it." She looked at her cell phone. "The boys just texted. They'll be home soon with pizza."

By "boys" she meant my three older brothers. There were four kids in our family. I was the youngest and the only girl, the only one who stepped on the mat when she got out of the shower, the only one who took her shoes off at the door, and the only one who'd never traveled overseas. But not for long.

I pulled up the latest Shock Value video on my tablet and turned the sound waaaay up. I grabbed a broom, played air guitar, and sang along. I didn't sing when the boys were around because they told me I was terrible, but when they weren't around, I belted it out. I knew every word to this song.

Shock Value was only THE most amazing band. I

dreamed that one day I'd get tickets to one of their concerts. I wanted to see Winston up close. He was my total fave band member. Maybe because he was the youngest, but also because he was the cutest with a capital *C*. But I doubted I would ever get to see them in person, since tickets to their shows were like a bagillion dollars. A girl could still dream, and I did. I wasn't the only one nuts about Shock Value. My brothers and parents loved them too.

When the video was over, I played it again with the volume lower and jumped over the couch with a notebook in which I wrote song lyrics. I called it my Lyrics Notebook. Creative, huh? I jotted:

I'm going to Paris.
Café au lait.
I can't wait for France.
To stroll along the boulevards.

I admired my work. Okay, so maybe these weren't the best lyrics, but I was getting better. Maybe one day I'd write a song for Shock Value.

As I studied my notebook, the door to the garage slammed open, and Josh (seventeen), Topher (sixteen), and Charlie (fifteen) walked in, each carrying a pizza box. The kitchen instantly filled with the smell of boy sweat and garlic. They stacked their slices three high, grabbed extra-large Gatorades, and headed toward the stairs, where I knew they were about to play hallway lacrosse in between showers and burping.

"Come on, Gwen," Topher said on his way up. "We need a goalie."

The goalie was the one who kept the ball from rolling down the stairs.

"I'll be there in a little bit." I pointed to my mom. "Girl talk, you know."

"No. I don't know." He flew up the stairs two at a time.

I sighed.

I said to Mom, "Tell me again about the flight."

CRASH! It sounded like the ball had knocked something over.

"We're leaving tomorrow evening, and we'll fly all night on the red-eye," Mom said.

"AWW!" cried Josh. I was pretty sure he'd caught an elbow to the gut.

I ran up to see the boy drama. No one was dead.

I hung out, and as the hallway lacrosse game whirled around me, I put my earbuds in, played a Shock Value song, and imagined myself in front of each fab sight in Paris. Mom and I really needed some quality girl time. ASAP!

2

I'd never been on a plane ride that long before. It felt like I had just slept in a shoe box, but one glimpse of Paris and I didn't care.

As our taxi zoomed, with a capital Z, through the streets, the highway and buildings near the airport gave way to the Paris I had always imagined. The city was already alive with people in the middle of their morning routines. I could see the beautiful cobblestone streets lined with beautiful buildings that just screamed Paris—and definitely didn't look like Pennsylvania! All the storefronts had chic-looking everything: window displays, awnings, and shoppers—many with their dogs in tow.

Finally, we arrived at our hotel. The Hôtel de Paris lobby was small, cozy, and warm—maybe too warm—like, stuffy, and I wanted to open a window. In a modern city of glitz and fashion, the Hôtel de Paris felt like a time capsule from another century. The lights of the antique chandelier were dim, and a candle on the check-in desk reminded me of wildflowers. The drapes were heavy and dark, the furnishings were something out of a museum.

After a long late-afternoon nap (in four-poster beds) to recover from staying up all night watching airplane movies, we walked the boys to the hotel restaurant for dinner with their team, while we joined some fellow tourists gathered in the lobby. Mom and I were taking a special evening tour.

Mom skimmed over our itinerary. "We're in group C," she said, pointing to a sign.

It was a diverse bunch of about a dozen people—old, young, men, women, all different nationalities, shapes, and sizes. They flipped through brochures and unfolded maps.

A guy who looked a little older than me, wearing a shirt with the hotel's logo, came over. He was cute in a soccer player–like way: a few inches taller than me, with sun-bleached hair pulled away from his face and tied into a ponytail. "*Êtes-vous Américaine?* Are you American?" His accent was adorable and totally added to his cute factor.

"Yes. I'm Gwen Russell."

"Ah, someone was looking for you." He scanned the people in the hotel lobby and pointed to the familiar face of Brigitte Guyot. I'd met Brigitte in Pennsylvania when she and her family were living in the US for work that her dad was doing with my dad. We all hung out and became friends. She was like the big sister I never had, kind of a lot older—nine years. But then her dad's job moved them back to Paris.

He added, "You are going on the night tour to *la côte d'Albâtre*. It is . . . er . . . egg salad."

"Egg salad?"

"Um . . . how do you say? . . . *Formidable*?"

"Excellent?"

"*Oui.* Excellent! We say *excellent* too." He pointed to his name tag. "My name is Henri."

"You work here?"

"*Un peu* . . . er . . . a little, when I am not in school."

He turned me in the direction of a podium where a woman stood. "Listen carefully. She does not like it when people do not listen," he said. "I see you *plus tard* . . . er . . . later?"

"Yes," I said. I knew a little more than basic French, because I'd studied it in school and listened to some CDs, but mostly I'd learned it from Brigitte and her parents when they were in the US.

Brigitte was exactly like I remembered, except maybe a little older. Here's the deal: Brigitte was very nice but a little *unusual*.

Her brown hair was longer now, past her shoulders, and she was still very thin. She was tall—very tall, in fact. It seemed like her legs were longer than the rest of her body. Her glasses were square and thick. Her pants were pulled up too high, and she'd buttoned her shirt all the way up to her neck. Her unusual style actually made me smile, because the thing was, it suited her. She was kind of a quirky girl.

I hoped my outfit described me in a way that said, *Bonjour, Paris! Gwen Russell is in the house!* With three brothers, I was no expert in fashion, but I'd gotten sandals, hair clips, and lip gloss for this trip. Those were big advancements to my wardrobe.

Before I could talk to Brigitte, a small woman wearing a crisply starched uniform and a name tag identifying her as Madame LeBoeuf stood behind the tour guide podium. She glanced at the clipboard in her hand.

"Welcome to the Hôtel de Paris," she said with no

234

French accent at all. If anything, from her drawl, I'd have guessed she was from Alabama or Louisiana. "Tonight we will travel by bus to"—she paused at the French location—"*Atretat*, which is on the *coat de Albetross*." Man, she'd butchered *Étretat* on *la côte d'Albâtre*. She continued, "Where they launch the lanterns." She clapped twice to get the attention of a couple who was talking. She pointed to her ears and mouthed, *Listen up.* Henri wasn't kidding. She was serious about paying attention. "I will be joined tonight by my assistant." She waved to Henri, who was lifting a tapestry suitcase onto a cart.

Henri waved back, but his mouth gaped open for a second like this was a surprise to him. He forced a smile.

I was psyched to hear this because I wanted to talk more to Henri. He was cute, French, and seemed about my age. Plus, if he was as *sportif* as he looked, we had something in common.

I was good at most sports. Kind of by accident, really. You see, I'd been recruited for every backyard game my brothers played. Whoever was "stuck" with me on their team pressured me to be tougher, faster, and stronger. This meant that I made every team I tried out for. Now I was a three-sport girl: soccer, basketball, and lacrosse. It also meant that I often had black eyes, fat lips, and bruised legs. I'd had more broken fingers than anyone—

boy or girl—in my school. I had a few girlfriends, but mostly I hung out with the boys.

Recently, I'd been trying to be more girly. My hair finally reached my shoulders, and my mom had bought me some trendy new clothes, which I'd brought with me.

Madame LeBoeuf continued, "You must stay with the group at all times. Raise your hands to ask questions. Speak slowly and clearly so that everyone can hear. Capeesh?" she snapped. Then she said, "If you require the facilities, now would be the time. We're leaving in five. That's *minutes*, people!" Her yelling definitely had a southern twang, proving there was nothing French at all about Madame LeBoeuf except her name. I used the translation app on my phone. *Le boeuf* was "beef." Kind of a perfect description of her too.

Everyone in group C scampered to the bathroom. But not me. This woman wouldn't scare me into going when I didn't have to. Instead I went to see Brigitte.

She hugged me, instantly transferring hair or fur or something strange and fuzzy from her shirt onto my new V-neck tee, which I'd tucked into capris.

"Gwen! The little sister I never had." I figured Brigitte was probably twenty-two years old now. "I am so glad you are both here," she said to Mom and me. "You are going to have a wonderful trip!"

236

"Are you coming on the night tour?" Mom asked her.

"Yes! I wouldn't miss it. I've lived here all my life and I've never been to *la côte d'Albâtre*," she said. "Besides, I want to hear all about every little thing going on in Pennsylvania."

Brigitte led us outside to the tour bus. I didn't get on the bus right away because I heard a familiar sound and started to wander toward it. A guitar.

There was a guy with a full beard, knit cap, wild hair, and sunglasses (at night), strumming and singing. The words were in English, something about running away. He stopped singing after lyrics about leaving worries behind. Brigitte nudged me to get on the bus. I did, but I wanted to come back later and hear more. In my town, no one hung out on the street and jammed like that.

Many seats were already taken, so all three of us couldn't sit together. Henri called me over to sit next to him. Yay! Brigitte sat with Mom, and the two of them began to chatter.

I looked at the guitar guy through the window. "Is he there a lot?" I asked Henri.

"Every day. I see him at other places too. Do you like music?"

"I love it. My fave band is Shock Value. Do you know them?"

"Everyone knows Shock Value. They are very famous in France. One of the guys is French."

Together we said, "Winston!" He was the only French member of the band.

We shared a laugh. "They're big in America, too."

Henri asked, "You hear of the legs?"

"The legs?" I asked. Then I pointed to my legs. "Legs?"

"*Non. Non.* Not legs. It is like a story that I tell you and then you will tell another person . . . how you say? . . . Leg—"

"Legend?"

"*Oui!* Legend. You hear of the legend of the lanterns?"

I loved a good legend almost as much as I loved Shock Value. "Tell me."

"Parisians, they fly lanterns to the night sky at Étretat to welcome *l'été* . . . er . . . summer," Henri explained. "If you make a wish as you let your lantern"—he raised his hands over his head and then made a pushing motion— "out of your hands, it will come true."

And at those words, I knew exactly what my wish would be—an awesome week in Paris.

3

As the bus lurched down the streets of Paris, Henri asked me questions about my home and my school. I told him about my best friends, Lily McAllister and Addison Harper. And I asked him questions about France and his job. I thought it was pretty cool that he had a job at age fourteen. It was because friends of his parents owned the hotel.

"I play football," he said. "You call it soccer."

"I know it!" I said. "Me too!" I didn't add that I could play *football* football, too, and I knew how to box, wrestle, and lift kinda heavy weights. He didn't need to know that.

"I scored a winning goal today," he added.

"That's great! Congratulations."

"My friends were on the other team, and they are"—he made a growling face—"about me."

"They're mad?"

"*Oui.*"

"We call that sore losers," I said.

He nodded at the new term, but I didn't think it actually made sense to him.

Our chat was cut short because Beef, who was driving, called Henri in her loud, husky voice.

He hesitated to respond, like maybe she would forget.

She bellowed, "Henri!" again.

"Are you afraid of her?" I asked him.

We studied her. She had pulled a paper clip off a stack of stuff set on the armrest. She unfolded it and used an end to pick at her teeth.

"A little," he said as he reluctantly made his way up the aisle to the driver, where he listened to her.

While he was away, I took my notebook out of my drawstring backpack and crafted a few lyrics:

> *I met a boy in France.*
> *He told me about a legend.*

I planned to make a wish.
And let it sail away on a lantern.

In Étretat, we parked at a dirt field leading to the top of a rocky cliff.

Beef handed everyone in group C a paper lantern, and Henri followed her with candles and a lighter. There were a lot of other people launching lanterns off the edge of the cliff, and many other tour buses parked on the dirt.

I took a candle from Henri and stuck it on a poky thumbtack thingy inside the paper lantern. He lit it with his long lighter, careful not to burn the paper. I walked to the rope line that held people back from the edge of the cliff, and just like Henri had pantomimed, I pushed my lantern out toward the stars, letting it catch in the breeze. I watched it glide into the sky, which was blacker, with brighter stars, than in Pennsylvania. And I made a wish.

All the tourists in group C and hundreds of others threw their lanterns into the sky too. It was cool how the wind got under the lantern's paper edges and lifted it, as if the flame was hanging by a parachute. It looked like a swarm of slow-moving fireflies gliding in the blackness until the twinkle of the lanterns blended into the sparkle of the stars.

241

Henri stood next to me. "Did you wish?"

"Yup. And I'm very good at keeping secrets," I said.

"I will tell you mine. I cannot hold a secret."

I said, "No. Don't. Then it won't come true."

"It still might," Henri said. "No one knows."

"I'm still not telling you mine."

"D'accord," he said. "My wish was—"

I put my hand over his mouth. I don't think I'd ever actually touched a boy's lips, besides JTC's (that's my abbreviation for Josh, Topher, and Charlie). And when I covered their mouths with my hand, they would lick it. So gross. I moved my hand away before Henri could consider doing the same. "Don't tell me," I said.

He slouched like he'd given up.

I didn't know how long wishes usually took to come true, but these lantern ones seemed to take effect fast, because I was already having an awesome time in France with Henri.

Just then he blurted out, "I wish Les Bleus win the World Cup!" And he ran away.

Leave it to a boy to waste a wish on soccer!

I chased him and caught him easily.

"Mon Dieu, you are very fast for a girl."

I smacked him in the arm. He rubbed it. Maybe I'd run a little too fast and smacked him a little too hard. I

242

could hit JTC as hard as I wanted, but I had to be more careful with other boys. "Now they're going to lose and it's going to be all your fault."

"They cannot lose." He rubbed his arm. "They are *formidable!*"

My phone vibrated in my pocket. This only happened when I got an important update in my Twister social media account. I looked at the notice flashing on my screen. It was from Shock Value. It said, *Concert: Shock Value has added one additional spot to their tour. PARIS. One night only.*

"Shock Value is coming to Paris!" I practically yelled in Henri's face.

My phone vibrated again. Another Twist from Shock Value. It said, *Paris concert SOLD OUT.*

"Holy cow! It's already sold out," I said.

"A cow?" Henri asked.

"Sorry. It's just an expression in English. Kinda like 'oh my gosh!'"

The phone vibrated for a third time. *What now?* It said, *Shock Value ticket contest! Follow the hunt around Paris and win tickets to the special one-night engagement in Paris.*

"Check this out." I showed Henri.

"Cow!" he yelled.

I looked at my watch. We'd only been here for fifteen

minutes, but we had to get on this contest, like, double pronto.

"We've got to get Beef to get this train moving."

"Train?"

"Bus. Small van, actually," I clarified. "We've gotta start looking for those tickets!"

Henri waved me ahead. "Ladies first."

Yeah, my wish had already started.

Beef leaned against the van, going with the paper clip again. "Hi there," I said. *"Bonjour,"* I added. "I kinda have to get back to the hotel, like now."

"What's the rush?"

"You see, there's this band; I really like them. They're called Shock Value."

"Who doesn't love Shock Value?" she asked. "I love that one they call Clay. Too bad he quit. Anyway, they're still great." She looked at her watch. "But we're on a schedule, and this bus don't move until it's time."

"Right. I totes agree with you on Clay, and schedules. I love to be on schedule," I said. "But the band, Shock Value, they're having this contest for tickets to a one-night concert they just added right here in Paris. And—"

Beef dropped her paper clip, jumped into the bus, and started honking the horn. She took her phone out and brushed her finger across the screen, scanning

244

pages. She honked again and again. Then she stood on the ground next to the hotel bus with a megaphone. "Let's go, people! We're cutting this excursion short because musical history is being made. Shock Value has just announced a new concert and I wanna get tickets. Let's go."

Everyone hustled to the bus as directed. I grabbed Henri's shirt and tugged him to run faster.

We sat near Mom and Brigitte and waited for the last few people to get on the bus. "Let's go, Wheels," Beef called to a man in a wheelchair, who was taking longer than everyone else. He was hardly secured when she threw the bus into drive and skidded through the gravel parking area.

Now she wore a headset thing that dangled a microphone in front of her mouth. "For those of you less adept at social media than *moi*, I'll fill you in on the four-one-one Twisted from Twister.com." She aggressively navigated around other cars pulling out of the lot. I had to hold tight to the seat in front of me so that I didn't fly into the aisle. "Shock Value has announced a one-night concert in Paris and a contest for tickets."

"They haven't been quite the same since Clay Bright left," Brigitte said.

"Who's that?" Mom asked.

Brigitte explained, "Clay was their guitarist and he wrote their music. One day he quit—"

I interrupted. "He didn't just quit. He disappeared. Like, totally off the grid. Even his bandmates, who were also his best friends, claim they've never heard from him."

Brigitte nodded and continued, "The band didn't replace him. They're still the most awesome band around. It's impossible to get tickets."

"Who's talking?" Beef barked. "Listen up, people, or you'll miss the critical deets. The show sold out in four minutes, a new record. But front-row tickets and backstage passes are being given away to three lucky people who follow a trail of clues that the band has left around Paris. If you haven't noticed, I know pretty much everything about Paris, so those babies are as good as mine."

"Mom, we absolutely have *got* to get tickets," I said. "I'm in Paris; they're in Paris. It's like it was meant to be." I didn't wait for a response.

"Where's the first clue?" I called to Beef.

"Seems like *someone* wasn't paying attention to the instructions before we left the hotel," she snapped. "The world would be total chaos if people just called out anytime they wanted."

I raised my hand, but she didn't call on me.

"The first clue will be released at nine tomorrow

morning. For those of us participating in this treasure hunt, we have to prepare before getting a solid eight hours of shut-eye," Beef said. "I know you all want to be on my team. But, there are only three tickets, and since we don't have time for a formal application process, I'll pick."

Beef was scary and mean and picked her teeth with a paper clip, but she was a tour guide. Who would know more about Paris? *Please pick me!*

She looked at the man in the wheelchair. "Wheels, there's something I like about you. You're with me, but we're gonna have to add a little horsepower to your motor. I know a guy."

The man in the wheelchair didn't seem to understand any of this. Henri leaned over and whispered in his ear. Wheels clapped when Henri finished; apparently he was a fan. But, really, *I* was their biggest fan, so I should totally get those tickets.

The man in the wheelchair pointed to a young lady with a stethoscope dangling around her neck. "Fine," Beef said. "She can come too."

Looked like Gwen Russell wouldn't be hunting on Team Beef.

My mom whispered very softly, "I don't want to get in trouble for talking, but do you think we should try to get tickets?"

"Really? Are you serious?" Shock Value—Alec, Winston, and Glen—occupied every inch of every wall in my bedroom. I knew every word to every song. "YES! I think we should try to get the tickets!"

"Let's do it!" she said. "The boys are leaving at nine o'clock tomorrow morning for lacrosse, so we're free."

I couldn't believe it. Less than a day in Paris, and I was in the running for tickets for Shock Value—AND I was going to see the city in the coolest way possible!

And Mom was actually on board with this plan! I didn't know who had swapped my mom for this totally cool lady, but I was pretty sure it had something to do with a lantern and a certain wish.

4

The lacrosse bus was parked in front of the hotel ahead of schedule. The driver put up his hand and stopped JTC from getting on the bus. He came over to talk to my mom. *"Bonjour, madame. Je crois qu'il y a un problème."*

Mom didn't speak French, but she understood "problem."

"Les garçons—et un parent," the bus driver said, trying to explain.

Mom held up her palm. She walked away and came back with Brigitte, who'd been waiting in the lobby when we got off the elevator. Brigitte began speaking to the driver in French. Then she said to Mom, "The boys, they need a parent."

"Oh. Oh my."

Brigitte explained this to the bus driver, who replied something in very fast French.

Brigitte said, "Yes, they can go with the team, but they must have a parent with them."

Mom looked at me. "I guess you'll have to come too. I'm so sorry we can't do the treasure hunt. Maybe we can still buy regular tickets."

"It's sold out, remember?" I said. "I'm not going to another one of their tournaments. I could do that in Pennsylvania. We're in Paris!"

I thought of a few lines of lyrics:

> *Wishing on paper lanterns does NOT work.*
> *Don't let the French tell you it's true.*
> *Because it's not.*
> *It's not.*

Topher called out the bus window, "Yo, Mrs. Russell, you're holding up the team!"

She motioned that she needed one minute. As I like to say, her *one minute* finger.

250

While she thought, Charlie yelled out, "Paris is sweet, huh, Gwenny?"

Right now I hated JTC. They always ruined everything.

"Well, you can't just hang out alone at a hotel in a foreign country," Mom said.

"I won't be alone. I'll be with Brigitte." I grabbed Brigitte's hand. She looked at me in surprise.

Mom studied the two of us.

"It is a good idea," Brigitte said. "I will take care of her like she was my very own sister. You go to the game. It is fine."

"Are you sure?" Mom asked her. "Don't you have to work?"

"No problem." She smiled. "She can go with me to care for the pets."

"What pets?" Mom asked.

"My job—a business, actually. I care for people's pets while they are out of town. It is called 'Boutique Brigitte—Pour les Petits Animaux.'"

"You do? I love pets," I said.

"*Oui.* I have a minivan and everything!" Brigitte explained. "And we can look for the clues. But work comes first." She shooed Mom away. "Go. *Allez!*" Brigitte had just climbed, like, four notches on the cool scale.

"Okay," Mom said. "But, Gwen, seriously, Brigitte's job is her priority."

"I get it," I said. "We can do both." Brigitte had lived in Paris her whole life, except for the two years in Pennsylvania, and she had a minivan. I still had a shot at those tickets.

Mom took out her wallet and gave me money.

Josh called out, "What's that for? I want money!"

Charlie added, "What's she doing that she needs cash?"

I said, "I'm getting front-row seats to Shock Value."

"Yeah, right," Topher said. "That'll happen right after Charlie can make a shot from outside the box."

Charlie punched Topher, and a wrestling match ensued.

"I have to go," Mom said. "Behave. Brigitte has a job to do, and *that* comes before the Shock Value tickets, understand? Please try to be low maintenance."

"I can totally do low maintenance," I said.

Mom got on the bus.

Charlie called out the window to Brigitte, "It's okay if you lose her."

I stuck out my tongue.

The bus pulled away, and Brigitte said to me, "I won't lose you. Just stay close. Be like my . . . how do you say? . . . shadow."

"Got it."

Henri pushed an empty luggage cart to the curb. "Is everything *bien*?"

I thought about telling him that the whole wishing-on-a-lantern thing was a charade, but when he flashed me this super-cute smile, I forgot what I was going to say. "What are you up to?" I asked.

"Up?" He looked at the sky.

"I meant, what are you doing?"

"I have to shave the courtyard."

"What?"

"You know"—he made a scissoring motion with his fingers—"give the plants a haircut."

"Oh. Trim the hedges."

"Right." He smiled. "Are you looking for the tickets?"

"Yeah. With Brigitte," I said. "Will I see you tonight?"

"If I am still shaving . . . er . . . trimming, maybe we can get *le gâteau*."

I knew *le gâteau* was cake. "Deal!"

Cake with a cute French soccer player? Potential front-row tickets to Shock Value? Maybe those French legends really were true.

5

At exactly nine a.m. the lacrosse bus full of boys and parents pulled out. Brigitte and I leaned over my smartphone and looked at the Shock Value site on Twister.com, and . . . *wait for it* . . . there it was:

> *You cannot make me laugh nor cry. If you touch me, you will find that I'm cold. I cannot embrace anyone to get warm. People travel far and wide to see me, and despite my flaws, they're awed by my beauty.*

"What do you think it is?" I asked Brigitte.

"I do not know," she said.

"You're from Paris. How can you not know?"

"I do not do the tourist things. I run a pet-sitting business." She glanced at her watch. "In fact, we need to get to little Fifi before she leaves a little pee-pee on her apartment floor."

"Now?"

"Yes. I have a schedule," she said. "I will go to get the petmobile. That lacrosse bus took my usual spot. The petmobile gets priority parking at most hotels and apartments," Brigitte said. "You stay right here and try to figure out that clue!"

"Okay." *Petmobile?* I went back inside to a rack of booklets and brochures and grabbed everything I could. Maybe there was something in here that would help. A white paper was taped to Beef's podium; it said, *All tours will be led by Étienne.* Seemed she was serious about this contest.

Then I typed a search into my phone using the words of the clue. I tried different combinations, but just got junk.

Beef whizzed out of the hotel, standing on the back of the wheelchair like she was on a carnival ride. She zipped along the sidewalk to the Hôtel de Paris bus, whose ramp was already lowered. The wheelchair flew into the bus like a race car. Apparently, her guy had come through with the horsepower. A third person, the young woman who still had a stethoscope, followed them, much more slowly since she was weighed down with a gigantic hiking backpack. There were three sleeping bags affixed above and below the main pack. Pots and pans hung on the bottom and jingled as she waddled toward the bus. She also had a big duffel bag in each hand.

Wow, Beef was prepared with a capital *P*. How were we going to compete with her? She was focused only on the hunt, while we had to run a pet business at the same time.

"Wait, Professor Camponi," the woman called. "It's time for your medicine."

"Get in!" Beef called to her, already pulling away. The woman had to jog and jump into the moving bus.

Through the windows I saw the woman hand Professor Camponi—which was a much better name than Wheels—a bottle of water and a pill. Then the bus peeled out with a screech and she fell into a seat.

Where was Brigitte? If we hurried, we might be able to follow them. I looked down the boulevard to the right and left, but didn't see Brigitte, and now I'd also lost sight of Beef. Following was no longer a possibility.

I mumbled the words of the clue. Then from behind me I heard someone singing the same lines, as though they were lyrics. I recognized the voice. It was the guitar player with the beard, knit cap, and sunglasses.

He stopped singing. "Good stuff," he said.

"How do you know those words?"

"I have Twister.com too." He patted the front pocket of his worn jeans, indicating that even a sidewalk guitarist had a smartphone.

"Do you know what it means?"

"Of course," he said. "It's one of my favorite things to see in Paris. I may be American, but I've been all around this city. I'll help you out."

6

I waited for Brigitte on the sidewalk. Suddenly I heard a really loud rumble. The contraption that drove up the boulevard to pick me up was an unbelievable sight. I blinked, but it was still there.

It was a white minivan covered with black paw prints, like a gang of cats and dogs had stepped in black paint and run all over it. Stuck to the front was a basketball, colored to look like a pink cat nose with wire whiskers sticking out the sides, and on the roof were two pointy ears. The van stopped in front of the hotel and it actually barked! Yes, barked.

I had a whole new appreciation for my mom's old minivan.

I hustled into the passenger seat and buried my head in my hands. "To the Louvre," I said.

"You figured it out?" Brigitte asked. She checked her seat belt and adjusted her rearview mirror, then her side mirror.

"Yes. Come on. We've gotta go. Beef left in a hurry."

"Beef?" Brigitte asked.

"Sorry. I meant Madame LeBoeuf."

"Ha! *Non*, I like Beef better," Brigitte said. "Okay. Here we go." She adjusted the side mirror again, put on her directional blinker, and rolled down her window to point to the road she was easing out onto.

I looked at the cars around us. "You look all clear," I said as a hint to speed up.

"To the Louvre," she said, but she didn't drive any faster.

Did she not realize what was at stake?

She continued at the pace of a turtle with three broken legs all the way to a parking spot near the Louvre. We dashed out. Brigitte managed to run faster than she drove. Through three giant arches I caught my first glimpse of the great glass pyramid of . . . *wait for it* . . . the Louvre! Even though I was in a hurry, I had to stop for

259

just a second in the huge courtyard to marvel at where I was standing. The pyramid was framed on three sides by a breathtaking building.

"It's like a palace," I said to Brigitte.

"It actually *was* a palace for hundreds of years until Louis the Fourteenth moved the king's home to Versailles. Then it became the place to keep the royal art collections. As kings grew the art collection, the building's size grew too," Brigitte said.

I looked at her with surprise at this little history lesson, because she'd seemed to know nothing when she'd looked at the first clue. "What?" she said. "I am French. Of course I know about the Louvre."

"Well, it is amazing."

"Masterpiece," she said. "It is large and most magnificent."

"It is." I wanted to stay longer—I could've spent the entire week in this one spot—but the hunt . . . the hunt. We had to move quickly. We made our way to the ticketing lines and were immediately sucked into crowds of tourists and what looked like other Shock Value hunters.

"Mon Dieu!" Brigitte said. "This line will take all day."

"Isn't there a shortcut?"

"It looks like Beef has already found one." She craned her neck to indicate Beef riding on the back of the wheelchair to the spot where people needing extra assistance didn't have to wait in line. The nurse lady, whose backpack had been replaced with Beef's fanny pack, held a clipboard and ran to keep up with the speeding chair. Beef seemed to have thought this all out.

"What are we gonna do?" I asked.

"I have an idea of my own."

Brigitte struck me as a person who followed the rules exactly, so I was skeptical. "You do?"

She reached into her back pocket and pulled out a little black book that said ADRESSES on it.

"What's that?" I asked.

"It's the list of clients for Boutique Brigitte—Pour les Petits Animaux."

"How is that going to help?"

"People love their pets. . . ."

"Sure."

"They love people who take good care of their pets. . . ."

"Okay."

"And they are willing to help them. . . ."

"All right."

"One of them works here," Brigitte said.

Now I caught on. That little black book was like a list of secret helpers. I didn't know how many clients Brigitte had, but I hoped she had one who could help us with every clue. *That* was something Beef didn't have.

Brigitte dialed her phone. *"Bonjour*, Monsieur Willmott, *c'est Brigitte,"* she said. Then she explained that we were on the hunt for Shock Value tickets and needed to beat the crowd to the clue—Monsieur Willmott must have interrupted her, because she suddenly stopped talking and listened. Her expression was serious like it wasn't good news, but then she grinned.

"Merci! Merci beaucoup!" She hung up. "We're in!"

"We are? How?"

"Follow me. We need to make a little . . . how do you say? . . . delivery."

"Delivery?" I followed Brigitte back to the petmobile. "We don't have time to make a delivery."

She threw open the back door and tossed an empty brown cardboard box out. She scribbled over the label that said SHAMPOOING POUR CHIEN and wrote the address for the Louvre. And added *Attention: M. Willmott.* Then she climbed in the back of the van and took out two black lab coats. They were covered with pet fur.

"This is the closest thing we have to a delivery uniform." Then she put a baseball hat on each of our heads.

There was no way this was gonna pass as a delivery company uniform. She said, "Make a business face, like this." She pushed her smile down, squinted her eyes a bit, and forced wrinkles onto her forehead. Then, in a lower voice, she said, "Delivery for"—she glanced at the box—"Monsieur Willmott." When she was done with the little charade, she laughed with a snort.

She was actually a pretty good actress, but I didn't believe the act would work, especially if she let a snort slip out.

She closed up the petmobile and ran ahead with the empty box. "What will you say to Shock Value when you meet them?"

I hadn't had time to think about it. What would I say? Before I could answer, we were at a door that said LIVRAISONS. I knew that meant "deliveries." Brigitte pushed a button. A security guard answered the door.

She wasn't gonna fool this guy.

He looked at the box, glanced up at a security camera that probably made sure no one other than real delivery people came through the door, and asked, "*Livraison?*"

Brigitte nodded.

He winked, moved aside, and let us pass.

We were in!

The security man took the box and directed us down a corridor with another wink. Maybe he could tell I was American, because he directed us in English, "Go that way and turn right."

Brigitte gave him a tiny hug and said, "*Merci*, Monsieur Willmott."

We raced down a small hall and turned right as he'd said. When we emerged into the museum, we were among a smaller crowd heading up the stairs to admire the famous statue of Venus de Milo:

> *You cannot make me laugh nor cry. If you*
> *touch me, you will find that I'm cold. I*
> *cannot embrace anyone to get warm. People*
> *travel far and wide to see me, and despite*
> *my flaws, they're awed by my beauty.*

Venus de Milo couldn't embrace anyone, because she didn't have arms. They'd been broken off and lost somewhere in time. Clearly, the guitarist in the knit cap wasn't the only one who knew this answer, because a bunch of what had to be other fans crowded around a girl wearing a royal blue Shock Value shirt, but I just stared at the statue. She was so pretty, chiseled perfectly from marble, yet she looked like she'd be soft if I touched her. She had been sculpted in the likeness of Aphrodite, the Greek goddess of love and beauty. And she really was beautiful.

I snapped back to the contest and realized that the girl in the Shock Value shirt was explaining the next part. "The first ten teams get the next clue. Go stand on a number." On the floor sat round rubber pads, each with a number—one through ten. The spaces numbered one through four were occupied. I jumped for number five only to be beaten by a girl who had pierced everything on her face. I didn't want to mess with her. As I stepped on number six, the tip of my new sneaker squished as it was run over by a speeding wheelchair.

"Ow!" I yelped.

"Too slow," said Beef.

"I was here first," I said.

Beef, Professor Camponi, and the nurse lady squarely occupied space number six. I suppressed the urge to clobber them like I would if Charlie blocked the last piece of pizza from me, but Brigitte calmly pulled my furry lab coat to space number seven.

"All ten people get a clue," she said. "Space number seven is okay."

"It was the principle," I said. "She is pushy and bossy and I don't like her."

Once all ten spaces were filled, the Shock Value representative handed each team a small royal blue gift bag. "Welcome to the contest," she said. "You are the ten teams competing for the three front-row seats and passes to Shock Value's special one-night engagement in

Paris this Friday. You'll get to see all the backstage action during the concert and maybe catch a glimpse of Winston, Glen, and Alec themselves."

Glimpse?

I wanted more than a glimpse. I wanted to meet the band.

"A Shock Value rep will meet you at each clue's location to give you the next bag. The first team to successfully follow all the clues and make it to the end of the trail will get the epic treasure!"

Everyone on the ten teams clapped.

She continued, "So, good luck. The next clue is in that bag. Make sure you give me your names and cell phone numbers; then you can take the bag and go!"

Everyone opened their bags except Beef, who tossed a business card to the Shock Value rep, fired up the chair, hopped on the back, and whizzed away from the beautiful Venus de Milo.

7

Brigitte bent to tie her shoe. "What is it?" she asked me without looking at the clue.

I held it up. "It's like a little model of a building." I looked at it. "Not a building, really, because there aren't windows . . . it's like a monument, maybe. We have one in Washington DC called the Washington Monument. There are words on the side." I turned it. "'It's time to fly' is etched along the side." I put the little building in my pocket.

Brigitte stood back up. "It's time to fly," she repeated, and thought.

"Does that mean anything to you?"

"Nope. Nothing." She looked at her watch. "We'll think about it on the way."

"Where?"

"Fifi. Pee-pee. Remember?"

I didn't like the idea of disrupting our search now, but since we didn't know where to go next, "To Fifi," I agreed.

On the short drive over, we brainstormed different ideas. "It's time to fly." I put it in Google, but didn't get anything useful. "These are harder than I thought," I complained.

"Which one is your favorite?" Brigitte asked me.

"Which what?"

"Band member. Alec, Winston, or Glen?" she asked.

"I can only pick one?"

"Only one."

"Winston," I said. "How about you?"

"Alec."

"Why Alec?"

"He is British! I love the Brits!" she said. "Why Winston?"

"He's the cutest. And the youngest," I said. "And I love his French accent."

The Shock Value members were a mix of ages. From youngest to oldest there was Winston (16), Alec (20), and Glen (26). Clay was thirty when he disappeared. The two oldest, Glen and Clay, were also the two Americans of the band.

Shock Value won a big TV talent contest three years ago and came out with an awesome (with a capital *A*) song. When Clay disappeared a year ago, they stopped recording and touring. Everyone was surprised they didn't replace him. Then a few months ago they released a new album without Clay. The music sounded a little different, but it was still fab.

Brigitte drove past a huge church. I could see the giant spires and what looked like little monsters etched into the sides. Based on pictures, I could tell it was Notre Dame Cathedral.

"Look at those scary statues," I said.

"We call them *gargouilles*," Brigitte said.

"Sounds exactly like what we call them, gargoyles," I said. "Isn't it convenient when French and English words are the same, or almost the same?"

"*Oui.*" Brigitte giggled, and we made a list of words that were the same in both languages: *ski, bizarre, important, zoo, menu, garage*. And, most important to me, *boutique*!

"We're here." Brigitte pulled up in front of a four-story apartment building with beautiful iron balconies that looked *très chic*. A doorman came to the petmobile and opened my door for me. *"Bonjour,"* he said in a husky voice, *"Brigitte pour les petits animaux.* Fifi is waiting for you."

"Merci, Philippe," Brigitte said. "We won't be long. We're on the hunt for those Shock Value tickets. Did you hear about the contest?"

"Of course!" Philippe said. "If I had more time, I would try it myself."

"Ask him if he knows what the clue means," I whispered to her.

"Ah, Philippe, do you know what 'It's time to fly' means? It's our clue."

He rubbed his chin. "Time to fly . . . time to fly . . . *l'aéroport*? The time of a flight?"

Hmmm. That sounded possible.

"Maybe," she said. *"Merci."* I followed her to the elevator, which was like none I'd ever seen. We stood on a platform, and Brigitte pulled a caged wall down in front of us. The elevator rattled as it brought us to the fourth floor. I held on to the waist-high railing for support. "Orly is one of our airports," Brigitte said. "Very big."

"It may not be a big airport."

"True." She lifted the cage and walked to the first door in the hallway. She pulled a gigantic key ring out of her lab coat pocket. The rounded end of each key had a rubber cap. And each cap had a name written in slim black letters. She found Fifi's key.

A white, puffy, fluffy, yappy pup ran to the door. When it tried to stop, it slid across the hardwood floor until it hit the wall with a little thud. Fifi didn't seem to mind. She redirected toward us and yapped more.

"*Bonjour*, Fifi!" Brigitte talked in a baby voice. She pulled a leash out of another lab coat pocket and put it on the pooch. "*Comment vas-tu? Est-ce que tu étais une bonne chienne? Allons-y,*" she said to Fifi.

We went back down in the elevator and walked down the boulevard, which was lined with many more buildings like Fifi's. We turned a corner at La Boulangerie Moderne, a French bakery whose outside walls were painted brick red and trimmed in gold paint. The red-and-gold awning was decorated with the name and phone number in beautiful cursive.

With the smell of croissants in our wake I saw a brilliant building that made me think I was suddenly in Italy, not France. "Wow! What's that?"

"The Panthéon."

"What is it?"

"It is one of my favorite places in Paris. Actually, it wouldn't be fair to all of my other favorite places if they

271

heard me say that. But I like it a lot." She lowered her voice. "It holds the remains of important people. You know what I mean by *remains*?"

"Like, the bodies?" I asked.

"Corpses," she added to make the idea of it more gruesome.

"Maybe we won't go in there," I said.

She perked back up. "Besides the remains, it is a very beautiful mausoleum. And I love the story of why it was built."

"I like a good story," I said. "Tell me."

"King Louis the Fifteenth was very sick. He made a vow to God himself. He said that if he recovered, he would replace the ruined church that used to be here with a magnificent building. Then, he did recover! And built this. It looks over all of Paris." As quickly as she'd given me the brief history lesson, she refocused on Fifi, baby-talking more in French. She was more interested in the dog than in the incredible historic building in front of us. Maybe she was used to walking around seeing ancient stuff and buildings like this, but I wasn't.

While I thought the Panthéon was beautiful and I wanted to learn about it, it didn't have anything to do with "it's time to fly."

"Wait," I said. "Gargoyles fly, don't they? Maybe 'a

time to fly' is sending us to a gargoyle in Paris." I googled "gargoyles in Paris." Hmm. "There are hundreds across the city. Way too many to check out."

"Maybe it's about telling time. Like a watch," she said.

"Of course!" I yelled. "That's brilliant. Is there a famous clock tower?"

"There is! Gare de Lyon, but maybe that is too . . . like, too easy . . ."

"Obvious?" I asked.

"Right. Obvious," she said. "I was thinking that Paris is home to the most famous watches."

"Is there a factory?"

"No, a store," she said. "Cartier!"

8

"What about Fifi?" Brigitte asked.

"This is a race, Brigitte! Bring her. Hurry!"

We ran to the petmobile. For having such little legs, Fifi could run fast.

Brigitte retrieved a gadget from the back of the van and strapped it into the backseat. She set Fifi into the thing, which was very like an infant car seat, secured a harness over Fifi's fluffy paws, and clicked the seat belt. Fifi could only be more protected if we wrapped her in bubble wrap, but I didn't mention that because it wouldn't have surprised me if Brigitte had bubble wrap in one of her pockets. Brigitte got in the front and ever so cautiously pulled out into traffic, checking her mirrors over and over, rolling the window down, and pointing to the spot she was moving to.

I thought about explaining the part about the race again.

She drove with both hands firmly clenched around the steering wheel, and she leaned in close to the windshield. I didn't want to break her concentration and I didn't want to make her angry. After all, the only reason I was able to participate at all was because she'd agreed to be my "babysitter." And it was pretty awesome that she had a car and was interested in this hunt too. If she quit on me, I'd be in a major jam.

Even at our snail's pace it didn't take long to arrive at the Cartier store in la place Vendôme. Brigitte parallel parked right in front of the Cartier store. When she backed up the petmobile, it made a *Beep! Beep! Beep!* that attracted even more attention than the average minivan dressed like a cat-dog.

There was no sign of the Hôtel de Paris bus. Either Beef had already been here or, hopefully, we'd beat her. I had a good feeling about this place. Beef had probably gone straight to the obvious clock tower.

I glanced around for some sign of a Shock Value rep; I didn't see one. Maybe she wouldn't be dressed in a blue shirt at each location. Maybe she'd even be hidden or undercover, like as a store employee.

Each of the windows was decorated with white lights and displays of watches on black velvet wrists. A half-moon awning covered every window, with the word *Cartier* written across it in posh script.

In a word, this place looked *fancy*.

Brigitte examined me, and then herself. "Wait. We can't go in like this." She opened the back of the petmobile. She scavenged around and found a purple sequined beret, which she put on my head, slightly off to the side. If you looked at it closely, you could tell that it had two ear holes. Then she took three leashes, braided them together, and wrapped them around my neck like some *nouveau* fashion statement. She took her lab coat and tied it over her shoulders like a cape of sorts, unbuckled Fifi, and tucked her under her arm like an accessory. If you didn't look *too* closely, we could possibly pass for two chic gals shopping for an upscale watch. For a last touch I grabbed a pair of postage stamp–shaped sunglasses with wire frames from the bottom of a box of junk. I wiped off the smudges that were probably from the last dog who'd worn them, and set them on the end of my nose.

We marched into the exquisite watch store like we totally belonged. I walked to the counter, glancing down at the bejeweled watches.

"Can I help you?" a man in a pin-striped suit asked. He eyed me with a mix of curiosity and disgust.

I peered right over the top of the sunglasses looking for the girl from Shock Value. She was nowhere. Maybe this guy worked for the band. I whispered, "It's time to fly," like it was a secret password, and slid the glasses back over my eyes to conceal my true identity.

He paused, maybe considering if I was worthy of it. Then he asked, *"Pardon?"*

I repeated, in case he was just checking to see if he heard it right, "It's time to fly."

He exhaled as though I'd annoyed him. "Can I help you or not, *mademoiselle*?"

I guess not.

I whispered to Brigitte, "I don't think this is the place."

She nodded, and like a customer who couldn't find anything suitable, she stuck her nose into the air, tightened her grip on her white fluffy dog, and marched out.

If Brigitte didn't succeed as Paris's premier pet sitter, she might seriously have a future in acting. As Brigitte buckled Fifi up, I said, "That was embarrassing."

"Nah. We'll never see them again. Besides, I always

figure they have seen some person more odd than me," she said. She put the van in drive and focused on the road. "Where are we going?"

"I can't help but think that I've seen that monument in one of my tour books. Let's go back to the hotel and I'll look it up."

"*Bien.* That is not far."

Again, Brigitte drove like a snail on a leisurely ride. I was glad she was a safe driver, but it bugged me that she didn't realize that we were in a hurry! It seemed like every car was flying by us. Some honked. Brigitte just waved at them and smiled.

I ran into the Hôtel de Paris and lingered for just one extra second in the lobby to see if Henri was working, but I didn't see him. I was about to race up the center staircase when I heard, "*Salut!*" I turned to see Henri standing in the fireplace, covered with soot. "How are you?" he asked.

"Great! What are you up to?"

He looked up for only a second, then remembered that I didn't mean "up." "I am dusting the fire chimney." He looked at my hand. "What is that?"

"It's a clue for the Shock Value treasure hunt. It's some monument with a message: 'It's time to fly.' We're trying to figure out what it means. I'm going up to get a book to see what it is."

"It is not a monument."

"It's not?" I asked.

"*Non*. It is an *obélisque*."

"What's that?"

"It's tall and stone. When the sun shines, it makes a dark mark on the ground."

"Like a shadow?"

"Right. That is it! A shadow to tell the time. Like before clocks."

"Like a sundial?" I asked. "Or an obelisk?"

"*Oui*, but a very big one," he said. "It is in la place de la Concorde."

"Do you know how to get there?" I asked.

"*Bien sûr*." Of course.

9

I dragged Henri to the petmobile, careful not to pull too hard or run too fast. Brigitte was letting Fifi pee-pee.

"It's time to fly," I said to Brigitte. "Henri knows what this is and where to go." I opened the back door for Henri, picked up Fifi, and put her on his lap.

"You are all dirty," Brigitte said to Henri. Was she worried he might soil white fluffy Fifi? "Buckle Fifi up, please," she asked him.

He messed around with the seat belt and the dog harness, and the whole time Fifi licked him on the face.

He didn't appear to enjoy the bath, but it washed off some of the ash.

Henri directed Brigitte to la place de la Concorde.

"I know where it is. I just can't believe I didn't recognize it. I guess because it was so small," Brigitte said.

"You drive very slow," Henri said to her.

"I am careful and safe."

"It feels very slow," he said again.

"Safe," she corrected.

I think he might have said "slow" again under his breath.

"*Là-bas!*" Henri shouted. Fifi barked.

There it was. A tall obelisk surrounded by an oval boulevard. Two magnificent fountains occupied where the twelve o'clock and six o'clock spaces would be if this whole oval were, in fact, a huge sundial. I saw a royal blue shirt in the distance. "Pull over. I'll run and get the next clue."

Brigitte honked the barking horn to get people to move out of the way. Henri and I jumped out before the petmobile came to a complete stop and ran across the cobblestone street that became a sidewalk.

The Shock Value rep stood at the base of the obelisk. "Hi there," she said. "Good to see you." She handed us a royal blue bag. "Good luck."

A woman holding a microphone, followed by a

cameraman, walked over to me. *"Bonjour,"* she said. "I'm Murielle duPluie, covering music news. Can we ask you a few questions?"

Did they want to interview us because we were in first place? We must be pretty far in the lead for this to be news. OMG, I was going to make the French news! *How cool is that?* "Okay," I said.

"What is your name and where are you from?"

"I'm Gwen Russell, from the US—U-S-A!—and I'm Shock Value's number one fan."

"Can you tell me, Gwen Russell from the USA, how does it feel to be in last place?"

Last place? "Well, I wasn't . . . I didn't . . . ," I sputtered. I was going to be a laughingstock on the French news. I was representing my country, not unlike an Olympic athlete, and I was letting all Americans down.

Murielle duPluie asked, "What is your strategy to get back in the game?"

"Umm . . . we need to find the clues faster, I think."

"And how do you plan to do that?"

"We, umm . . . we . . ."

Henri came into the frame of the camera and said, "She has me on her team. I am Henri and I am *formidable* at puzzles and soccer. I am the team's . . . how would you say? . . . A missile that no one knows about."

"A secret weapon?" Murielle duPluie asked.

"*Exactement!* We will see you, Madame duPluie, at the next clue, and we will not be last," Henri said.

He'd saved it. Maybe I wouldn't be a total embarrassment to my country. But now the pressure was really on. We'd made a public declaration not to be last. All eyes were on us.

Henri and I were walking toward the petmobile with our royal blue bag when two people blocked our way.

"Ha! ha! *Bonjour*, Henri," said a guy wearing a Paris Football Club shirt. "Your car barks."

"It is a petmobile," Henri clarified defensively. "*Bonjour*, Sabine," he said to the girl with him. It was the girl with the piercings who had occupied space number five at Venus de Milo.

She asked me, "Is Henri on your pet team?"

"I am helping them," Henri answered for me.

Soccer Guy said to me, "You don't have a chance." He laughed. To Henri he said, "You got lucky at the game, but it won't happen again. Not at soccer and not at this contest." Then he made a mean bark.

A car screeched to a halt. Sabine and the guy laughed and barked as they got into it.

Another boy in a soccer shirt was driving. He yelled out the window, "*Salut*, Henri! How does it feel to be in last place?"

They drove away with squealing tires.

"Who are they?" I asked.

"They are the . . . what did you call them? . . . sore losers," he explained. "Sabine and I, we sort of . . . how do you say? . . . go together?"

"Date?"

"Dated. But now she dates Jean-Luc. The other guy, the driver, is Robert."

"And you don't like them?" I asked.

"No. They are very mad that my soccer team is good."

"They sound like jerks," I said. "We have a saying in the US when we compete with people like them. Game on!"

"I like that." He repeated, "Game on!"

10

We got in the petmobile and Fifi instantly licked Henri's face like he'd been gone forever and she'd missed him terribly. He didn't smile as he tried to wipe his face.

"What was that all about?" Brigitte asked.

"We're in last place," I said. "That was a reporter who wanted an interview."

"Did you mention Boutique Brigitte? It would be good for business for that to be on the news," she said.

"Um, it didn't come up," I said.

"What is in the bag?" Brigitte asked.

Henri asked, "If the game is on, am I in the game? Like, on the team?"

"I don't think my mom would mind. Besides, how can she actually be on the team when she isn't here to help?" I asked.

"I am here to help," Henri confirmed.

"What about your job?" I asked him.

"It is like bending rubber."

"What?"

"My boss, he is friends with my parents and he bends for me."

"You mean it's flexible."

"*Oui*. And bendable."

"Then it's official. We three will be a team," I said.

Henri gave me a high five. "*Formidable!* Now, what is in *le sac*?"

I opened the bag and took out a key hanging by a royal blue ribbon.

"*Une clé,*" Henri said.

"I wonder what it goes to," I said. "A door somewhere? A secret room? And inside we'll find the next clue."

"Not a hotel," Henri said. "They use cards."

"True," I said. "Do you think this is the last clue and Shock Value will actually be there? Like, we'll open the door and they'll *pop out*?"

286

"Or, maybe the key is to a box or a locker," Brigitte said.

"The band cannot fit in a box or locker," Henri said.

"Where would we find lockers?" I asked. "Train stations?"

"*Oui*, and bus stations and airports. But the lockers at bus stations and *metro* stations are like . . ." He pantomimed twisting right and left with his fingers. "And numbers."

"A combination?"

"*Oui*. Combination," Henri confirmed.

"Or you put in money and then take an orange key out of the locker. The key has a number, which matches the locker," Brigitte said. "Does the key have a number?"

"No," I said. I rubbed my fingers on the rough edges of the key.

"Well, while you're figuring it out, we need to feed . . . feed . . ." Brigitte looked at her clipboard for her next client. "Sylvie."

I guessed Sylvie was another dog. Brigitte put the petmobile in drive and crawled into traffic, her nose inches from the windshield. She drove so slowly that I realized that earlier she *had* been hurrying.

"And maybe *un petit morceau de gâteau*?" Henri asked.

What was it with boys and food? My brothers couldn't

go fifteen minutes without eating, and Henri had been hanging with us for an entire hour. He must've been starving. I had to admit, a little cake even sounded good to me right now.

"There is a shop in Sylvie's building," Brigitte said. "We feed her first."

She parked in front of another apartment building. This one was newer and more modern than the other building. It was very clean and stark white, from the first to the eighth floor, and lacked the decor, details, and golden embellishments of Fifi's building and la place Vendôme, which both seemed hundreds of years older.

I put the ribbon and key around my neck and continued thinking about what the key could open. Brigitte put Fifi in a little pink purse and handed it to Henri. "You can carry Fifi," she said. The doorman at this building also nodded like Brigitte was an important guest and we were too because we were with her. He held the door open for us.

When we got to the apartment, Brigitte said, "Wait here. The owners don't like it when people walk around here." She took a pair of plastic booties that looked like shower caps out of a lab coat pocket and slid one onto each shoe. With her big key chain she unlocked the door to a foyer that could've popped out of a magazine. Everything was white—walls, tile, furniture—and it smelled like Mom's Pine-Sol cleaner. She walked down the hall and into a room, where she spoke in French. "*Bonjour*, Sylvie. You are so pretty. Are you hungry? Here you go." She waited. "Do you think that's yummy? Yes, you do." She came out of the room with a giant snake wrapped around her shoulders like a pashmina.

I shrieked and jumped back.

"Whoa!" Henri yelled. "That is a snake!"

My eyes bulged. "Do you know it's around your neck? Could it strangle you?"

"Do not be silly. Sylvie is very gentle. And isn't she pretty? She likes it when you tell her she's pretty."

"Pretty snake," I said to Sylvie. *Please don't kill Brigitte, or me, or Henri,* I thought. Sylvie's neck stretched around something round, like an egg or tennis ball.

"What's that?" I asked. "A tumor?"

"This? No. Not a tumor. She just had lunch. A rat."

I held back the urge to gag. I hoped she hadn't taken that out of her pocket too. Were there more rats in the petmobile?

"Let's get her out for a while. I think she's lonely," Brigitte said. "She likes to be around people. We will take her with us for cake." She looked at the snake. "Do you like the sound of that? *Le gâteau?*" She lifted Sylvie's head for us to see. "She is smiling. She likes cake."

We were really going for cake with . . . *wait for it* . . . a six-foot snake.

"Fab," I said. "It'll wash down that mouse."

"Rat," Brigitte corrected me.

Brigitte slid the booties back off her feet and into her pocket, took an empty canvas bag from a hook, and locked the door, and the four of us went to the lobby, where there was a small *boulangerie*.

I anticipated a negative reaction to Sylvie followed by terrible embarrassment, so I was super glad when Brigitte curled her up and put her into the canvas bag and zipped it almost all the way shut. Through the opening she said to Sylvie, "You are very pretty."

11

All the desserts looked so good. I ordered a cream puff with chocolate sauce. Brigitte got a baguette, and Henri salivated over a slice of strawberry savarin. We sat, and Brigitte dropped pieces of bread into the canvas bag sitting in the chair next to her. "It's not as good as the rat, eh?" she asked through the hole in the bag.

I examined my phone. "Let's see where the other teams are." I opened Twister.com. "I don't know why I didn't think of this sooner," I said as the site opened. I scanned it. "Looks like no one has made it to the third clue yet. That's good. This is our chance to get in the lead." I took the key off my neck. "We've just gotta get there first, and I want another chance with Murielle duPluie. If we come in first, she'll have a good story about a team going from tenth to first place. Wouldn't that be great?" I finally took a bite of my puff. Henri's plate was empty.

I peeked into the canvas bag to see that the first several inches of Sylvie's body were in the shape of a baguette.

"May I see *la clé*?" Henri asked.

I took the key off my neck and gave it to him.

He studied it while I ate, not like my brothers, but as fast as I could in a ladylike way, because I didn't want my puff to end up in Henri's stomach or Sylvie's neck.

Brigitte took a place mat and turned it over. She pulled a pencil out of another lab coat pocket. That coat was amazing. It was like a Mary Poppins coat. "Let's play a game." She made blank dashes and a hangman symbol. "Pick a letter."

"Game? We don't have time. We need to concentrate on that key," I said.

"A quick game exercises the brain," Brigitte said. "It will think better when you are done."

"I love games," Henri said. "I pick *A*."

She wrote in *A*s where they belonged.

How could they be playing a game at a time like this?

It didn't last long. Henri guessed it was "Sylvie is a pretty snake."

He looked at the key again. "There are a lot of books at the hotel. Let's go there and look for ideas."

Since we didn't have any other leads, we decided to go back to the hotel.

"We will return Sylvie to her home first?" Henri asked Brigitte.

Brigitte asked Sylvie, who was still in the bag, "Do you want to go home, my sweetie?" She glanced at the snake's face. "No, she does not want to go home yet."

Fifi licked Henri again. "How about Fifi?" he asked.

"She is having so much fun. She will love the old hotel," Brigitte said as we got back into the petmobile and secured Fifi into her car seat.

Henri huffed like he wasn't happy to be driving around with a pooch and a snake. Maybe I could change the subject. "I love the old hotel too."

"It was a mansion for guests who could not fit in the king's castle at the holidays," Henri said. "When the city grew up, the hotel, it stay the same as before."

"I like that it feels old. Do you like working—oh no." I cut myself off when I saw who was waiting at the front of the hotel.

"*Mon Dieu,*" Henri said at the sight of Jean-Luc, Sabine, and Robert.

"Oh, look," Brigitte said. "There are your friends." She honked the barking horn and waved to them like they were well acquainted. "*Bonjour!*" she called out the window.

Henri sank into the seat, but there really was no way to hide in the petmobile. "What are they doing here?"

I said, "Maybe they feel bad about what happened at la place de la Concorde and they want to apologize."

"*Pfft,*" Henri said. I think the English translation of that would've been "no freakin' way."

We pulled into one of the hotel's four parking spots.

"Can you get Fifi?" Brigitte asked Henri. "Put her in her pink *sac*. She likes riding around in that." Her cell phone rang. "I will come in *un moment.*" She answered it, "*Boutique Brigitte—Pour les Petits Animaux.*"

Henri walked toward his three former friends with a white puffy pup in a pink bag over his shoulder. He stood up straight. "*Comment?*"—What?—he asked them, as tough as possible.

"*Beau sac,*" Jean-Luc said.

"Pink is your color," Robert added.

"Stop it," Sabine said to them. "Pink is the new black." Then to Henri she said, "We came to see how you were doing with the key." Now she was trying to be nice? Something fishy was going on here. Fish? Would that be Brigitte's next pet?

"Really?" Henri asked.

"You know, six minds are better than three," she said.

"Like a partnership?" I asked.

"*Pfft*," Henri said.

"Yeah, *pfft*," I added. "We're way close to solving this clue. We're not gonna help you."

Brigitte, who finished with her call, joined us with Sylvie's bag, the snake's head now poking out through the hole for air.

Jean-Luc's, Sabine's, and Robert's eyes popped out at the sight.

"Afraid of a pretty little snake?" I asked them. "There's no way you'll be able to go to where this clue leads if you're afraid of stuff."

"*Comment?*" Henri asked me.

"Oh, don't worry," I said to him. "I won't give it away. Even if I did, they would be too afraid to follow through."

Just then the lacrosse bus pulled up. Perfect timing. We all stood and watched the muddy, tired American lacrosse team get off.

I could see Mom sitting in the last row of the bus. I took out my phone and sent her a quick text that, if things went the way I hoped, would help with this little thing I was doing to Henri's so-called friends.

JTC each offered me a high five on their way by.

"Victory," Josh said.

"Another win," Topher said.

"We advance to the next round," Charlie said.

They followed their team into the hotel.

Mom came up to us and glanced at her phone like I thought she would when she heard my message arrive. She said to me, "An abandoned metro station? I don't think so, Gwen," she said.

"Shh—Mom," I said, and bent my neck toward our three competitors, like she'd spilled some majorly secret and important beans in front of the opposing team.

"What? It's too dangerous. And sorry, but I'm too exhausted to go with you. We can talk about it tomorrow." Then she looked at Brigitte. "Pretty snake." She petted Fifi and departed.

Sabine, Jean-Luc, and Robert whispered to each other.

Jean-Luc said, "Since your mommy won't let you go to the old *metro* station at night, we will go on ahead and just beat you to another clue. Then we will tell the other teams where to go, and you will be last again."

They walked off, laughing. Robert barked.

"I do not know what . . . what was that?" Henri asked.

"I knew that was exactly what my mom would say, so I made up something to text her. And, presto, those three morons are off on a wild goose chase," I said.

"They are chasing a goose? Is that like a duck?" Henri asked.

"No. Sorry. It's just an expression. It means that they are off in the wrong direction, wasting their time."

"I am glad they are chasing ducks," Henri said. "You are . . ." He pointed to his head.

"Thanks," I said. "I have three older brothers who've taught me pretty much every trick in the book."

"What book?" Henri asked.

"Never mind. Sorry, there isn't a book."

"Yes, there is," Henri said. "Inside. Let's look for the key in the hotel books."

"Okay," I said.

"Do you want to go in the hotel?" Brigitte asked Sylvie, who was still nestled in the bag. "She does."

12

Brigitte and Henri went into the lobby, but I walked to the corner where Knit Cap was. He was singing, "It's time . . . my time . . . my time to fly . . ."

The words were familiar, but the tune wasn't.

Coincidence?

"Did you write those lyrics?" I asked.

"Yup. Ages ago. But I couldn't finish it. I'm good at the music, but not the lyrics."

"That's funny. I'm just the opposite. I write lots of lyrics, but not music," I said. "But those words you were

298

just singing. Do you know they were part of the Shock Value contest?"

"Yeah. It's all over Twister.".

That made sense.

Then he asked me, "If you write lyrics, then you must sing?"

"Um. No. Not so much," I said. "My brothers say that I sound like a dying hyena when I sing."

"You know," he said, "sometimes brothers say things that aren't true just to be mean." He strummed. "Give it a try: 'It's time to fly.'"

My brothers did a lot to be mean; that was true. I glanced around, and no one I knew was in earshot.

He coaxed me again. "It's time to fly," he sang.

I inhaled deeply and softly sang, "It's time—"

"Louder."

I inhaled again. "It's time to FLLLLYYYYYY!"

Knit Cap took his sunglasses off and looked at me with widened eyes. "O-M-G."

"That bad?" I asked. "I told you. Hyena."

"No. Your brothers stink. You're really good. Try again." He played the lead again and I sang.

People walking by threw money in the open guitar case. "If you hang with me, I'll be rich," he said.

"Unlikely," I said.

He craned his neck toward my royal blue bag. "The key?"

"Yeah. Any ideas what it might open?" I asked. "I want to get there first so that Murielle duPluie can do a story about us in first place!"

"I have a few ideas," he said. "It's a game, so there might not be an actual lock."

"Duh." Of course. "Lock is too obvious," I said. "But what else could a key lead to?"

"That, my new singing friend, is the question. You need to think deep. You're like a poet if you write lyrics. Musicians and poets think really deep. That's why you know what I'm saying." He strummed a chord. "Good luck."

"Thanks," I said, and walked toward the hotel door, even though I wasn't entirely convinced that he knew what he was talking about.

13

The old hotel lobby was cozy and dimly lit, but bustling with chaos tonight—infested with a sweaty lacrosse team and their parents. In a particularly dark corner Beef, Professor Camponi, and his nurse huddled around the key like it was a crystal ball and they were waiting for it to reveal its secrets.

Professor Camponi scratched his chin and looked off in the distance, thinking deeply.

Henri watched them too. "Do you think we can check the book of tricks and send them to get the ducks?"

I grinned.

"I think we can come up with something," I said. My mind searched through all kinds of tricks my brothers had played on me. Like the time JTC sent me an invitation to MaryEllen Marini's costume party, which might have been okay if I was actually invited to her party and it had been a costume party.

"You work here," I said, still thinking through the details. "That'll be a big help with this."

"Is that what the trick book says?" he asked.

At some point I'd have to tell him again there wasn't an actual book of tricks. But now that I thought about it, maybe there should be. "Do you have any royal blue paper?"

"I think I can find some," he said.

I waited for him as he fetched the paper.

Brigitte looked at her watch. "I need to bring Fifi and Sylvie home. I will leave you two in charge of the ducks, okay?"

We agreed.

Brigitte said, "I will pick you up in the morning after I go to the Cliquots. I have an important pet delivery to make for them."

"That sounds good. My mom won't let me out anymore tonight anyway," I said. "Brigitte, thanks for taking me on this hunt. I know you have your job to do, but I wouldn't be able to do it without you."

"That is what big sisters are for," she said. Then to Sylvie and Fifi she said in French, "Come on, precious babies, I'll put you to bed." She called as she left, *"Bonne soirée!"* A few seconds later I heard the bark of a horn as she drove away.

"I have it," Henri said about the paper.

"Is there a place where we can work?" I asked.

"I know a place. It is perfect." Henri walked into a corner of the lobby and slipped behind a tree in a flower-pot. The wall was lined with dark woodwork and busy with elaborate oil paintings of royalty. He pushed in a piece of wood molding. That triggered a slim section of the wall to shift aside, providing a narrow entrance. Henri squeezed through it. After a quick glance behind me, when I saw the lacrosse team and parents all chatting and distracted, I did the same. It was totally Scooby Doo.

The wooden door slid closed after me, and we were in pitch black. "I can't see."

"Un moment." Henri turned on a flashlight app on his phone and led the way through a narrow passageway.

"What is this?"

"Halls behind the walls. They lead to . . . you know . . . tubes under Paris."

"Tunnels?"

"*Oui*. Tunnels."

"What for?"

"During wars, people needed to hide and move around in secret," he said. "But today it is just halls." He stopped at a section where we could hear people talking on the other side.

"Listen," I said. It was Beef.

Henri moved a playing card–size piece of wood affixed to the inside of the wall. It revealed several holes, each a bit bigger than a pin. He turned off his flashlight and squinted to look through a hole, and I did the same. We spied into the lobby.

Beef spoke to Professor Camponi. "I've got to get those backstage tickets. Don't you understand?"

The nurse answered, "You must really love Shock Value."

"Who doesn't love Shock Value? But, it's more than that. So, so much more," she said, without offering the deets. "I just need the good professor here to solve the clues to make sure I win. Capeesh?" Professor Camponi nodded. "Good. Because if you don't, it's bye-bye to the free tours, and you won't be able to give your grand-daughter the tickets she's wanted since the last concert."

"When was that?" the nurse asked.

"The one our friend Clay Bright didn't make it to," Beef said. "Camponi's only granddaughter was going to that concert, which was obviously canceled when Clay decided to go all Houdini and disappear. She never got to see her favorite band. Now Grandpa has a chance to be her hero. I'll get a backstage pass and he can get the tickets," Beef said. She turned to look at Professor Camponi directly. "You got that, Camponi?"

Professor Camponi nodded and gave a thumbs-up.

14

Henri slid the wooden card back in front of the holes and turned the flashlight on again. I was about to talk about what Beef had said when Henri put his hand over my mouth and whispered, "Shh." He walked further down the secret corridor and into a small, dark room. With matches from his back pocket he lit candle sconces hanging on the wall. It was an old office with worn and cracked leather chairs. Dust and cobwebs covered every surface.

Who would need an office hidden behind the hotel walls?

Henri took his sleeve, pulled it down over his hand, and used it to wipe off a large section of the desk, where he set the royal blue paper and black pen.

"This is a great hidden room," I said.

"I love that it is like . . ." He made an "oooooo" sound, like a ghost.

"You mean scary."

"Yeah. You think?"

"With three older brothers I've been scared by the best of them. It takes a lot to freak me out."

He nodded, but I didn't know if he understood "freak out." "What are you going to write?" he asked.

"I'm gonna write a letter to myself." I wrote, *To Gwen Russell.* "It will be from a Shock Value representative. It'll have information about the key. When Beef sees a royal blue message for me, and she hasn't gotten one, she won't be able to resist reading it."

"And she will go look for the duck that you write about in the note?"

"Exactly."

"I am glad you have older brothers," he said.

I wrote the rest of the note in my most grown-up handwriting. It said:

307

Most people from Paris know there is a basement in Orly airport with lockers where employees store their belongings. Since you are American, we thought it was fair for us to tell you because you would have no way of knowing this.

Good luck.

From,

The Shock Value Team

Henri asked, "She will go to Orly looking for a basement that is not there?"

"Right. Plus, she'll think that they're somehow giving me extra help because I'm American, and that will make her mad. If she's mad, maybe she'll make a mistake."

I folded the note and gave it to Henri. "Can you put this out on the front desk tomorrow morning? Place it where you're sure she'll see it."

"*Oui.*"

Henri blew out the two candles and led me through the secret corridors back into the lobby, which was now empty. My phone vibrated. I looked at the text. It was from Josh. He said Mom was looking for me. I said, "I have to go."

"*Bonne soirée*, Gwen," Henri said.

"*Bonne soirée*, Henri," I said. "Thanks for your help."

"You can wait and thank me when we are in the front row!"

I ran up the center staircase, taking the steps two at a time. I slowed and turned my head to look back, and at the exact moment, Henri turned his head and our eyes met.

15

When I came down in the morning, my mom and JTC were ready to leave for the next round of lacrosse games.

"Behave for Brigitte," she said to me, and she gave me money for lunch. "And wish your brothers luck."

"Bonne chance," I called to JTC. They shoved several mini breakfast tarts into their mouths, stuffing their cheeks like chipmunks, and gave me the peace sign.

One quick look at the front desk and I immediately saw the royal blue paper. I made myself a plate of grapes and tarts, pretending I had no idea it was there.

Beef entered the hotel through its huge wooden door, which was complete with tarnished golden handle and hinges.

I concentrated on my grapes and looked out the window for the arrival of the petmobile. I wondered if Fifi and Sylvie would be with us today. As embarrassing as that van was to drive around in, I'd grown strangely attached to it and its passengers. After a while you got used to its unique appearance and odor.

Beef was instantly attracted to the blue paper. Without hesitation she walked toward it and spoke to the concierge. "Hiya, Étienne, how're you doing this fine morning?"

I backed up behind the tree in the flowerpot.

"*Bonjour*, Madame LeBoeuf. It is a beautiful day."

"I see you have this note for one of the members of my next tour. I'd be happy to deliver it for you."

"I thought your tours were canceled today, Madame."

"You are on the ball, Étienne. They were. But I will see this girl this morning. And I'd be happy to deliver this for you."

"*Oui, merci*, Madame LeBoeuf. That would be kind of you."

"Don't mention it. Unless I ever need a favor, in which case I'll mention it. Ha-ha!" She took the note with a big smile. "I'm just joshing you, Étienne."

"Oh. Ha-ha. Joshing. I understand." He smiled broadly.

I saw her slide the royal blue note into her pocket, scan the lobby, and leave.

From my view through the tree leaves, I saw Knit Cap sitting cross-legged in an armchair, studying the people and activity while sipping coffee that was for hotel guests. It seemed like he made himself right at home in the lobby, which was strange because he wasn't a guest. He'd watched what Beef had just done. Then he found me between the greens and raised his cup in a gesture that suggested he knew the trick I'd just played. Of course he didn't have his sunglasses on inside, and without them there was something familiar about his face.

I came out of my hiding place.

"That had something to do with the key?" he asked.

"Yeah," I said.

"Good for you," he said. "Now you're playing the game. And remember that games and puzzles are more challenging if they provide misdirection." He stood and swung his guitar over his shoulder and went on his way.

Then I saw the petmobile drive up the boulevard.

Did I say I was becoming attached to the petmobile? The basketball nose was now a beak, and large foam feathers had been stuck to the sides. The horn announced Brigitte's arrival with a *Squaaawk!*

I ran out front to see what this transformation of the petmobile meant. Tourists photographed the wheeled bird, but the locals didn't seem to notice or care.

Brigitte took a while to find the perfect parking spot, just like she seemed to do everywhere in Paris. *"Bonjour!"* she called to me. She had on a green lab coat today, which was equally as dirty as yesterday's black one. This one was speckled with white and black droplets that I suspected were bird poop. On her head she wore a hat with a long beak.

"Good morning," I said. "How about we talk in the van?" I thought that would get us away from the onlookers—including Knit Cap, now strumming—who had gathered.

"I would love some tea," Brigitte said, and walked toward the lobby.

She said hello to Étienne and briefly discussed the bashful personality of his pet turtle. Then he made her a cup of tea and placed a scone from the complimentary breakfast bar on a china plate. She and I sat on a sofa in the lobby. It seemed that everywhere we went, Brigitte was treated like royalty. It's true: people like people who care for their pets.

Henri joined us with a plate stacked a foot high with scones, muffins, and mini bagels. He was such a boy!

"The book of tricks worked," he said.

"What book of tricks?" Brigitte asked.

We filled her in on what we'd done while trying to spy on Beef, who sat in a leather armchair with her feet propped on an ottoman, toggling between her watch and her smartphone.

"I bet she's looking up stuff about the airport," I said.

"No, thank you. I do not like bets," Henri said. "Usually someone loses." I really needed to watch my expressions around him.

Beef put her phone down and whipped a pocket-knife out of her fanny pack. She twisted a toothpick out of it and went at her teeth—poking and picking.

I touched the key around my neck and felt each groove and bend. When my fingers felt a small nub at the end, through which the ribbon was looped, I took it off. I rubbed the nub and, squeezing a little, turned it. It twisted like a cap on a tube of toothpaste.

It opened.

"Look," I quietly said to Brigitte and Henri, but they were already watching. I turned the key upside down, and a tiny piece of rolled paper slid out. I screwed the top back on and unrolled the paper.

"It says: '*I leap off* is written here.'"

I looked at Henri and Brigitte for a reaction but got

314

none. Brigitte shook her head like *I don't know,* and Henri shrugged his shoulders.

Henri said, *"La bibliothèque?"* The library? "Everything is written there."

"I guess it could be. Or a plaque somewhere?" I suggested.

Neither of them had any idea. I keyed the phrase into the search engine on my phone. Nothing.

"I guess we should go to the library," I said.

"That is good," Brigitte said. "I can drop the Cliquots' pets off at the groomer on the way."

"I thought you were a groomer too." We headed out to a beautifully sunny Paris day.

Henri lagged behind.

"Not for this kind of pet," Brigitte said. Based on the feathers and beak I had a feeling I was going to find some kind of bird in the mobile.

I got into the front seat and turned to look behind me, and I did in fact find a bird. Correction: birds. Blue and orange parrots. Three cages full.

Brigitte hopped into the front seat, buckled up, and checked the rearview, each side mirror, and the rearview again. When Henri came to the mobile, his pockets were stuffed with something. I knew what it was because I had brothers. Food.

He climbed into the backseat and Brigitte asked, "Ready to go?"

Then every bird, all twelve of them, repeated, "Ready to go?" "Ready?" "Go?" "Ready to go?" They weren't in unison.

Henri jumped back in shock. "They *talk*?"

"The best kind of feathered friend," Brigitte said.

"Fantastique," Henri muttered, but I sensed he meant *un-fantastique*.

When Brigitte backed out of the parking spot, the petmobile made a *Beep! Beep! Beep!*

A dozen parrots mimicked, "Beep! Beep! Beep!"

Henri, who was closer to the flock, covered his ears. On his hands' way to his ears, he popped a mini muffin into his mouth.

"Here we go," Brigitte said.

"Here we go!" "Here we go!" "Here!" "Go!"

16

Brigitte pulled into a lovely cobblestone alley with creeping ivy and flowers. She honked the *Squaaawk!* horn to scoot a few stray cats out of her way. She opened the mobile's back door and carried one cage of four birds through a small door next to a faded sign covered almost entirely by vines. The sign said BAIN D'OISEAU.

"Bird bath," Henri translated for me.

"Bath?" "BATH?" "Baaaath?" "BAAAATTH?"

The remaining parrots did not like the idea. Brigitte

came back, and when she heard them yelling, she asked, "You told them?"

"Not exactly. They kind of overheard us talking. You might want to explain to them that eavesdropping is rude," I said as she carried in the second cage, which contained four nervous birds yelling about a bath.

"They are freaking out," Henri said, using one of my expressions.

I agreed, "Yes, they are."

"They're freaking out!" "Freaking!" "OUT!" they said. One shouted, "Baath?" and the remaining three started flipping out about the bath all over again.

Once Brigitte brought the last cage inside, the pet-mobile was filled with beautiful quiet, and I was able to think about "I leap off." But the quiet didn't help. I still had no ideas where that might be written.

Brigitte drove to the library via a road that ran parallel to the Seine, the main river flowing through the center of Paris. I watched a tour boat glide down the water.

"I really want to take one of those river tours," I said.

"Want me to stop at the ticket station?" Brigitte asked.

"No thanks. Winning this contest is more important."

We arrived at the library. "Wait," I said when I saw Jean-Luc, Sabine, and Robert parking.

"Do you think they found 'I leap off'?" Brigitte asked.

318

"Let's watch them for a second," I said. "Stay still and they won't even know we're here."

"I'll just back into this spot behind the bushes," Brigitte said. She put the petmobile in reverse and *Beep! Beep! Beep!*

Jean-Luc, Robert, and Sabine looked over and had a good hearty laugh at the van's new ensemble. They cupped their hands by their noses like beaks and hooted.

"Owls hoot," Brigitte explained to us. "Not parrots. They are so stupid."

"Let's just get in there and find the book where 'I leap off' is written before they do," I said.

On my way out, my foot stepped on a paper on the petmobile floor. It was the place mat that Brigitte and Henri had played hangman on.

It's a game.

Puzzle.

Misdirection.

"Hang on," I said. "I don't think 'I leap off' is written in a book. Well, maybe it is, but that's not the clue."

Brigitte said, "But it says—"

"We've been thinking about this wrong. Each clue needs to be solved, like a puzzle." I wrote, *I leap off is written here* on a blank section of the place mat. "Do you know what anagrams are?"

"Letters that are like . . ." Henri pantomimed stirring something in a bowl.

"Mixed up," I said. "Letters have to be rearranged. Maybe if we rearrange these, they will reveal the real clue."

I played with the letters:

At top.

Irish.

Brigitte added:

Pet Fifi.

White leaf.

"That's the idea," I said. "We just have to make them into a location."

"I can," Henri said as though it took no effort at all.

"You can. *What?*"

"You cannot see it?" he asked.

I looked at the letters. "No! What is it?"

"I will give you hints and you figure it out," he said.

Jean-Luc, Sabine, and Robert ran out of the library and to their car.

"No!" I yelled, louder than I meant. "Maybe they've figured it out. We are in a huge hurry! Just tell us what it is."

He looked disappointed with my anger.

"I'm sorry," I said. "I just really want these tickets."

"D'accord," he said. "It's the Eiffel Tower. You have a few letters left over, but it's pretty close."

"Very close. Too close to be wrong. Let's go!"

Brigitte skipped the triple mirror check and recheck and pulled out with a lot more power this time. The power of a sloth!

"First place, here we come!" I called.

17

Brigitte passed one side of the Eiffel Tower. We couldn't park on that street, so she made several turns until we came up on the other side. Under one of the iron lattice archways a girl in a royal blue shirt—different from the last one—was waiting, stretching her gum out of her mouth with one hand and scrolling on her phone with the other.

Brigitte couldn't park here either, so Henri and I jumped out and sprinted toward the girl.

When Blue Shirt looked up from her phone, we were in her face.

"Whoa," she said, startled. "Where did you come from?"

"We ran," I gasped.

She reached into a box and took out a royal blue gift bag. I peeked into the box. There were nine others.

We were first!

"Where is Murielle duPluie?" This was my chance to redeem myself to the world. After all, I was representing the USA! "Does she want to interview us?"

"Nope. She's chasing another story today."

"Maybe we could give you a statement or something to send to the TV news," I suggested. I really wanted public attention for this achievement.

"Nah. That's okay." She went back to her phone. "Good luck," she added without looking up.

"What is the clue?" Henri asked, but I was still thinking about my missed moment in the spotlight. If Murielle duPluie wasn't going to report on us, then I had to take matters into my own hands. *Isn't that what social media is for?*

I logged onto Twister.com and typed in a post: *Hello! Can't tell you where we are or where we're headed, but this team is . . . wait for it . . . in first place!*

That was a good start, but I still wanted the shout-out on TV!

"Come here. Hold up the bag—we're gonna do a sel-fie." I snapped a pic of me, Henri, and the bag without getting the Eiffel Tower in the background. The longer we could maintain a lead, the better.

Back in the petmobile we opened the bag.

> *I keep the torch lit for all to see,*
> *The apple of their eye,*
> *Tall and strong for liberty,*
> *I watch the birds and planes fly by.*
> *48-51-0/2-16-47*

A surge of excitement flowed through my veins. "OMG! I know this! I know the answer to this clue!"

"So fast?" Henri asked.

"Yes. It's the Statue of Liberty! She has a torch and she's the symbol of liberty. And the part about the apple—that's what we call New York City, the Big Apple, and that's where she is. She stands on an island where she can watch birds and planes fly by."

"That sounds like the right answer, but we cannot go to New York for the next clue," Brigitte said.

"True," I agreed. "Do you have something like a Statue of Liberty here?"

Henri laughed. "Actually, we have three."

18

"There are *three* Statues of Liberty in Paris?" I asked. Wow, the one in New York Harbor had suddenly become less special. "At least we're in the lead, so we'll have time to go to all of them."

"We don't have to," Brigitte said.

"We do!" I agreed. "We have to be first. We're gonna beat Beef."

"I mean we only have to go to one of the statues," Brigitte said. "The correct one."

"How will I know which one is correct?" I asked.

Brigitte pointed to the numbers. "I use these kinds of numbers all the time to find my customers' homes."

"Like a cell phone number?" I asked.

"No. They are coordinates for a GPS," she said. "They are the exact location of the next clue."

"Well, what are we waiting for? *Allons-y!*" I said. "Let's go!"

Brigitte took a gadget out of the glove box and punched in the numbers from the clue. Instantly, a voice told us in French to turn right. Brigitte, hands clenched on the ten o'clock and two o'clock positions on the wheel, did as the voice said.

We were only a few blocks away from our destination when an alarm sounded from Brigitte's watch. She pushed a little button to make it stop. She swung the petmobile into a U-turn.

"What are you doing?" I asked.

"It is time to pick up the birds from their baths."

"But the statue?" I whined.

"Work first," she sang as if I would totally understand.

Fine, I understood, but there was a lot at stake here besides a few wet birds.

She maneuvered through the steep winding streets of Montmartre, past street-side painters and people sitting outdoors sipping cappuccino.

Each of the three of us grabbed a birdcage from the *bain d'oiseau* and put the flock in the back of the minivan. The birds smelled good, like soap and flowers. "Here we go, guys," Brigitte called back to them. "To the Île aux Cygnes to get the next clue."

"Clue!" *"Cygnes."* "Guys." "Go!" The gang sounded less energetic than they had on the way to their bath this morning.

"Usually they nap after their—" She whispered "bath" very softly, so they wouldn't hear the word. "If you're quiet, they'll probably fall asleep."

We were ready to go, but Henri was nowhere to be found. I looked around the busy street until I saw the back of his head. He was at a small table-like wagon on the side of the road, paying a man. I joined him to see the table layered with rows of croissants. Henri held a bag open for me. "Croissant?"

While I was a stranger to the croissant, I had never met a pastry that I didn't like. So I took one and bit into it, and was pleasantly surprised by a warm, sweet glob of chocolate hiding inside the flaky, buttery roll.

"It is good, *non*?" Henri asked.

"*Non.* I mean, *oui.* It's very good."

Back in the petmobile the three of us rode in croissant-induced silence. Other cars whizzed around us. We passed the Eiffel Tower and drove onto a bridge that crossed the Seine. Brigitte pointed off the side of the bridge to a small protrusion of land, but I was already looking at it. It was an exact replica of our Statue of Liberty. I couldn't believe my eyes. It was like her twin, her smaller twin.

"Pull over," I said. "I think we're first!"

"First!" "First!" "First!"

"Shhh," Brigitte said. "You woke them up. They get cranky if they don't get a nap. And you would not like them when they are grouchy."

"Sorry. But this is a race! Can you just pull over and let me out?"

"I cannot stop here," Brigitte said. "I will park ahead. We will have to walk." She eased into a parking space, painfully slowly.

"Or run," Henri said. "Race you!" He took off toward the statue.

I chased him. This time I ran as fast as I could, but I couldn't catch up. I wasn't trying to be girly; I seriously couldn't keep up. Was I getting slower? It was one thing to pretend to be slow; it was another to actually become slow.

Henri stopped at the Shock Value rep. It was the same girl from the Louvre.

"*Bonjour,*" Henri said.

"Hi," I gasped. "Are we first?"

"Yes, you are. You really are a comeback story," she said.

"Where is Murielle duPluie?"

"On another story," she said. "Here is the last clue. Don't get too comfy with first place; this one is really hard."

"Jeez, can't Murielle duPluie send someone else?" I groaned. "This is major music news."

Brigitte caught up with us. Totally out of breath, she asked, "What does the clue say?"

I read:

> "XX marks the spot. Number eighty-three is
> the place. In the Garden of Names."

I looked at them. "Do you guys have any ideas?"

They both shook their heads.

I looked off in the distance. I could see the Eiffel Tower, and dark clouds starting to roll in. They looked nasty.

Brigitte saw them too. "Let's get the birds home," she said.

We hustled to the petmobile, where our feathered friends were still snoozing. We closed the doors as quietly as we could.

I read the clue out loud again. "'XX marks the spot.

Number eighty-three is the place. In the Garden of Names.'" Still no one had any ideas.

One of the birds said, "Eighty-three! In the garden!" in its sleep.

Another answered, "Okay, Sammy," in its sleep. "Deliver the flowers."

"They talk in their sleep?"

"Yeah. They say some funny things sometimes. Stuff they've overheard. Their owner is a florist. So they say stuff they hear from the store or the cart."

"What cart?"

"The owner has a flower cart. The birds who are well behaved get to hang out on it on nice days. They love it," she said.

The rest of the afternoon we spent my lunch money on crepes smothered in Nutella and took the birds around the city. As the afternoon turned into evening, we planned to take the tired flock home.

Brigitte drove at her usual glacial speed that I was starting to get used to when rain started hitting the windshield hard.

"Oh no," said Brigitte.

"What is the matter?" Henri asked.

"I do not like driving in the rain." Brigitte's hands trembled on the wheel.

Henri said, "It is okay. Take your time. We can stop at the hotel if you turn up there."

Just then a car flew past us and splashed water onto the windshield. Little tears formed in the corners of Brigitte's eyes.

"Almost there," I said to reassure her. I could see the hotel up ahead.

She coasted into her preferred parking space and turned off the ignition. "I cannot drive anymore in this weather. I will have to call the Cliquots to come and pick up the birds and they will probably fire me."

"You can bring the birds inside and wait for the rain to let up," I said.

"I do not think birds are allowed in the hotel," Henri said.

"What if no one knows they are there?" I asked.

"I have heard them. They are very . . ." Henri made a beak with his hand and mimicked the birds. "Go! Guys! Clue!" Just as he started yelling "Baaa—" I put my hand over his beak.

"But there is a room where they can stay," I suggested. "A very quiet room where no guests will see them. Can't we go there?"

"We will have to"—he tucked his head into his neck and made a swaying motion from side to side, then hid his face behind his hands—"around so that no one will see the birds in the lobby."

"Like, sneak?" I asked.

He nodded.

"Piece of cake," I said.

"*Le gâteau?* Where? Where is the cake?"

"I meant it will be easy to sneak them in."

"Really?" Brigitte asked. "There are twelve of them."

"But there are thirty lacrosse players coming in soon. They are waaay louder than some birds. Trust me," I said. "Call the Cliquots and tell them you don't want to drive the birds in the rain and you will keep them for the night and bring them home safe and sound in the morning. They won't fire you. They'll probably be glad that you are so safety conscious."

"Okay," she agreed.

I looked at my watch. We had about a half hour until the boys would be back. "Henri, I think the lobby could use some vacuuming. Let's go do that."

"Vacuuming?"

I made a motion like I was vacuuming, but maybe it looked more like I was mowing the lawn, because he didn't understand. I said, "Vrooooom," as though I was sucking up dirt. He looked like he still didn't understand. "You know when the floor is dirty and you use a machine to suck up the dust?"

"What does the machine sound like?" he asked.

I said, "Vroooooomm." And I made a face like sucking up dirt.

He smiled. "Vroom. I like that. I never saw someone act like a vacuum before."

"You know the word 'vacuum'? Why didn't you say so?"

"Because it was more fun to watch you vrooom." He mimicked my face.

I punched him.

Darn.

Too hard again.

I really had to work on that.

"Sorry," I said when he rubbed his arm.

"Pas de problème," he said. No problem.

19

Henri put on his hotel shirt and name tag. I wore a lab coat. If anyone asked, we would say that I worked for a cleaning company. Who knew that a few lab coats would come in so handy? I also donned some rubber gloves that Brigitte had in the back of the van.

"What are we going to do?" he asked.

"Move these chairs and plants to make a barrier that will be difficult for people to see behind. It will look like we are moving all of these things to vacuum behind and under them. Then we'll bring the birds in the front door, behind our barrier, and through the secret door," I said. "But in case someone happens to see through our barrier, it would be good to cover their cages." I looked up at the heavy drapes. "Do you think we can get one of these down for a little while?"

"Yes. I take them down to clean them. I can do it."

"Great," I said. "Once we move this stuff, we just need to wait for the team to arrive. When they come into the lobby, everything will be chaotic and loud. That's the perfect time to move the birds in."

He took down one of the drapes, which wasn't nearly as heavy as it had looked hanging up. I delivered it to the petmobile while he started sliding the chairs and potted plants. The rain was still coming down hard, so I ran. I jumped into the van and brought Brigitte up to speed.

"I spoke to the Cliquots," she said. "They were glad that I wasn't driving in the rain with their babies. They also said to make sure they get a good night's sleep."

"We can do that," I said.

"After we get them settled, they will look for dinner. I have food."

"When we move them in, can you cover them with this?" I handed her the fabric and she agreed.

On my sprint back to the hotel, I saw Knit Cap playing his guitar under an awning. I stopped to listen. He was singing a song about running away again—seemed like his theme—but then he paused at the same point that he did the other day. "Why do you stop when you get to that part?"

"I don't know how the rest goes," he said. "I don't have any more words."

"Words are my specialty," I said. "How about:

> *"I could go to Japan,*
> *I could go to the sky,*
> *If only I could fly."*

"Wow. You're really good at this stuff." He strummed and added my words into his tune and then repeated "If only I could fly" several times as the refrain. It totally worked.

"That's good," I said.

"Good? It's better than good," he said. "Will you sing it with me?"

"Really?" I asked. I totally wanted to sing with him.

"Sure. A continuation of what we started yesterday." He played a chord and another and started it for me: "I could go to—"

I picked up: "Japan. I could go to the sky . . ."

He harmonized with me. We sounded great together. Really great!

When we finished the few lines, he said, "You have an amazing voice."

"Thanks." I think I blushed. Then I offered, "You can have those lyrics if you want."

"Thanks. That's a nice offer, but I want to write my own material," he said. "But tell me, how did you come up with that?"

"I like to start with a rhyme. This time with 'fly' and 'sky.' I make those two sentences and then fill in the others," I said. "But I keep a notebook and jot things down when they come to me. That would probably help you a lot."

I reached into my pocket where I'd stashed the few extra pieces of royal blue paper in case I needed them today. "This will help you start," I said. "It's easier to write lyrics than to try to just think them up."

"Wow. I'm gonna do that," he said. "Cool beans." He strummed and sang, "Cooool beansss."

"How long have you been playing?"

"All my life," he said.

"You're so good. Why do you play out here on the street when you could be at a club or something?"

"Been there, done that. As soon as I started playing for money, it wasn't about the music anymore; it was about the show and the publicity. I just love the music," he said.

"Me too," I agreed.

Then he said, "By the way, great job with the diversionary tactic you played on the Beefy lady. Too sly."

"Funny. I call her Beef too," I said. "I would've loved to have seen her face when she realized there were no basement lockers at the airport."

"I saw her mug when she got back here this morning," he said. "Wow, she was fuming. I think maybe she's onto you."

"She is?" Oh no, I never thought of what would happen if she figured out it was me. Beef didn't seem like a good person to have on your bad side. "I think I'll avoid her until this contest is over."

"And maybe even after that, like, forever," he suggested. "She is still furious about that TV reality show, and that was years ago."

"What happened?"

"She was a contestant on a super-popular talent discovery show. She lost, obviously, and never got over it."

"Is she a good singer?"

"Really good, actually. Country music," he said. "She still hopes to make it big, and I hope she does. Everyone deserves their big break."

Henri came outside and called to me, "I need help, Gwen."

"I have to go," I said to Knit Cap. "We're kind of doing something in there."

"Have fun, Gwen," he said. "I hope you win."

Henri had the lobby arranged perfectly. He asked, "Were you talking to the guitar player?"

"Yeah. His music is good," I said. "And he's nice."

"He is there all the time. I do not understand why someone who plays so well just stands on the street," Henri said.

"Because he loves the music. When he played for money, he said, it wasn't about the music anymore." Henri started pushing a vacuum along the edge of the newly exposed wall. "What are you doing?"

"Cleaning," he said with a grumpy tone. "Étienne asked me what I was doing. I told him. He got me the vacuum machine. So now I vacuum."

I smiled. The floor was kind of dirty behind all of this stuff.

Suddenly headlights flashed in the hotel window where the drapery was missing. "I think the team is back," I said.

The boys unloaded the bus from the front and back at the same time, shouting, "Vic-to-ry! Vic-to-ry!"

I signaled Brigitte and she took the first cage out of

the van, covered it with the fabric, and brought it to the door. As the boys entered the hotel, she handed the cage to me and I dashed along the pathway with it. No one even noticed me. I could hear the birds under the drape saying, "Vic-to-ry!"

I set the birds down in the secret hall and went back with the drape.

Brigitte brought in the next cage and we did the same thing.

When she came to the door with the third cage, the boys had a whole lacrosse game going on in the middle of the lobby. Étienne was telling them they couldn't play inside. They argued that it was raining outside and champions had to play.

We scooted the third cage in without issue.

Once the birds were all secured behind the wall, the three of us moved the furniture and plants back to their original places, which were now clean. I helped Henri rehang the drape and watched Knit Cap through the window as he jammed and jotted notes. He was way too good to be playing on the street.

JTC paused in their indoor game long enough to ask, "What are you doing, Gwen?"

"Oh, hey. Just helping straighten things up down

here. Like a little volunteering. No biggie. Congratulations on your win. That's exciting!"

"It's more than exciting!" Josh and Topher ran toward each other and crashed into a chest bump. "*It rocks!*" They high-fived after the body check.

Charlie asked, "How's the hunt for the tickets going?"

"It's going pretty well—"

Topher said, "Only you would waste your time in Paris playing some contest that you're never gonna win when you could be sightseeing."

Josh added, "Most girls would kill to shop in Paris."

"She's not a regular girl," Topher said. "She doesn't like shopping." The two of them moved away with their lacrosse sticks and tossed a ball back and forth. Étienne tried to get the ball, and they had a laugh playing monkey in the middle with him until the coach took the ball and all the sticks and made the team sit "like gentlemen" for dinner.

Before Charlie joined them, he said, "I think you're a regular girl. A guy would look funny in those capris and sandals." That was the closest thing to a compliment I could ever expect from JT or C.

Before he disappeared into the dining room, Josh called to me, "Hey, tell Shock Value I said hi. Especially Winston."

"I like Alec," Topher added.

"Dream big," Charlie said.

I sighed. "Sorry you had to see that," I said to Henri. "They can be such jerks sometimes, maybe most of the time, but sometimes they're nice. I just can't always tell which way it's gonna go. Usually when they're together like this with friends, it goes jerky."

"I understand," he said. "I have Jean-Luc, Robert, and Sabine. When they are together, they are . . . how you say? . . . jerky." I smiled. It was nice to have someone who kind of understood. I guess it didn't matter whether it was Paris or Pennsylvania—there were some things, like "jerky" groups, that were universal.

20

We uncovered the birdcages, fed the birds, and let them check out their temporary bedroom.

Henri lit the sconce candles before going on a search for pillows and blankets.

I texted Mom that Brigitte got a room in the hotel because of the bad weather and I was staying with her.

I heard Henri's voice in the lobby on the other side of the wall, so I slid the playing card–size wood chip aside and peeked in.

"Where have you been?" Étienne asked in French.

"I am doing the treasure hunt for the Shock Value tickets," Henri said in French, but I understood. I hadn't realized how much better my French had gotten in just a few days.

"Why are you doing that? You are probably the only person I know who doesn't like Shock Value," Étienne asked, again in French.

Henri shrugged.

Étienne said, "It is the girl, isn't it? The American. You like her?"

"We are having fun playing the game. She is not like other French girls I know. She likes sports."

"And you think she is pretty?"

"Oui. Elle est jolie." Henri smiled.

I knew *jolie* meant "pretty." Henri thought I was pretty? And he was playing this whole game, missing work, and running all over Paris in a petmobile with a fluffy dog in a pink bag over his shoulder looking for tickets to see a band that he didn't even like? For me?

The birds were awake now, but calm and full-bellied.

"They talk less when they are calm," Brigitte said. "This is a good room for them, because there isn't a lot for them to see or hear."

I stopped listening through the wall when Henri came in with sleeping stuff. It seemed like the birds were still listening, but they weren't talking. I figured as long as no one mentioned that they were taking a bath, they would be quiet.

Henri returned stocked with everything we needed to camp out in the old office, including a board game and a white box wrapped in a pink satin ribbon. "Here." He handed it to me.

A gift?

I pulled the silk ribbon, easily untying it. Lifting the lid, I discovered rows of delicate little cookie-like sandwiches. Each one had three layers—the outer two pieces were the same color, and the middle layer was different.

"What are these?" I asked.

"Have you never seen a *macaron*?"

"Yeah. I've seen them made with a lot of coconut and dipped in chocolate."

"Ah, that is not a French *macaron*." He pointed to one that had two dark brown layers sandwiching a whitish one. "That is espresso and cream." He pointed to another, which had a dark brown layer between two red pieces. "That's chocolate and raspberry." And he went on to name each *macaron* in the box, lying next to one another, creating a rainbow of colors: peanut butter and marshmallow, white chocolate and peppermint, pistachio and almond, etc. . . .

I took the cherry and vanilla one—it was about the

size of an Oreo—and bit it. It was crunchy and airy at the same time. "Mmmm. It's good. I want to try them all."

"Of course," Henri said. "They're little." He took the other half of the one I'd just bitten. I bit into another, and again he took the other half, until I'd eaten half of a dozen flavors!

"It's official. I like French *macarons*," I announced.

Henri smiled. "Me too."

Then we spread the blankets and put the pillows in a circle with enough room for a board game. Henri tossed me the dice to go first.

I heard voices in the lobby, but since they weren't bothering the birds, I ignored them and rolled. Double sixes! I was off to a good start.

Brigitte took her turn; then it was Henri's.

"Wait," I said. "Listen."

"It's just guests," Henri said.

"Not just any guests. I know that voice," I said. "That's Beef." I got up from my pile of blankets and walked over to the wood that blocked the pinholes. I slid it aside to see Beef talking to Professor Camponi.

It was the middle of the conversation. "You really let me down today. We're not gonna get those tickets." I wasn't positive, but I thought Beef might've wiped a tear. "I can't believe I let that girl outsmart me."

21

The next morning, the birds were fluttering around in their cages.

"They're hungry," Brigitte said through a yawn. "I'll feed them and get them back home on my route today. I also need to pick up today's client."

I didn't want to know what she would come back with. Kangaroo? Hippo?

She put food in their cages.

"We need to finish this hunt in first place. Then Murielle duPluie will report on us and I won't be an embarrassment to my country," I said. "This clue could be our big break."

"Big break!" "Win contest!" "Meet Shock Value!" "Get my big break!" "Sing for them!"

"What did they say?" Henri said.

"Something about singing for Shock Value and getting their big break," I said.

"I've never heard them say any of this," Brigitte said.

I peeked through one of the pinholes. Beef and Professor Camponi were in the lobby, talking. "They must have just overheard it. That's why Beef wants to win so badly, so that she can sing for them. I guess she thinks they'll love her and she'll make it big."

"That is not going to happen now," Brigitte said. "She is so far in last place, she won't catch up."

"Because of the book of tricks," Henri added.

"Because of me," I said. I hadn't played fair, and I'd ruined this woman's dream. Sure, I wanted to win, but I felt terrible about my little maneuver.

22

We waited until the lacrosse team once again passed through the lobby, creating total chaos. Étienne might have seen me scoot out with the last cage, but by then we were in the clear.

Henri and I waited outside the hotel for the pet-mobile, which Brigitte had parked around the corner. Her preferred parking didn't last overnight.

People pointed down the boulevard, so I figured it was approaching. I saw the snout first.

Did she really have a pig in that minivan?

A voice behind me asked, "Pig day?"

"Looks that way," I said to Knit Cap, who'd walked up next to me.

"Should I ask about the birds?" He nodded toward the cages on the sidewalk next to us.

"I wouldn't."

"Fair enough." He strummed and sang, "Fair is fair. Hair is hair. And I'd know you anywhere."

"Hey! Look at you go. Good job with the rhymes."

"You were right. It's a good way to start." He whipped the blue pages out of his back pocket. "Filled all these pages with rhyming lyrics."

"Then you're ready for lesson two."

"Lay it on me," he said.

"Here it is: Not everything has to rhyme."

"Hmmm, really? So, I could do something like ... ." He played a few chords.

> *"Run away,*
> *Be free,*
> *Be yourself,*
> *And leave your worries behind."*

In a way it didn't matter what he sang, because his voice was so hypnotic. But the chords were soothing and the lyrics flowed with them perfectly. "That's exactly what I meant," I said. "You could write all along, couldn't you?"

"I used to. I surely used to, but I've had a block that I couldn't get past for a long time. Your idea of rhymes and a scratch pad were just enough to unplug the logjam in my brain," he said. "Thanks a lot."

"You are very welcome. Maybe someday you'll write a song about me?"

"Maybe I will." He strummed a few notes.

I smiled because I liked them. They were fun and upbeat and kind of caught the essence of me.

Brigitte honked the petmobile horn at me. And, yup, it oinked!

"That's my cue," I said. "I gotta fly."

"To the last clue?"

"How do you know it's the last one?" I asked.

"Oh, I don't. It was just intuition." He picked at the strings and strolled down the street, singing about a girl. It sounded like the girl could be me.

Henri had loaded the birds in with . . . wait for it . . . a pig. The van was stuffed.

"Where to?" Brigitte asked.

I still felt bad about Beef, but we couldn't both win. It was going to be hard enough for just me to win. "To the next clue," I said. "I'll read it again. '*XX* marks the spot. Number eighty-three is the place. In the Garden of Names.'"

"Let me see *le papier*, please," Henri said. He looked at the paper. "This is not *XX*. It is how we number the *arrondissements* around Paris—they are like sections, or neighborhoods. It is Roman numbers. We need to go to the twentieth *arrondissement*."

"Awesome. Could eighty-three be a street? Like Eighty-Third Street?" I asked.

"Our streets are not numbered," Brigitte said. She cracked her window.

"*Mon Dieu*. What is the smell?" Henri asked. He rolled his window too. And then I did the same.

"*Excuse-toi*, Norman," Brigitte said to the pig. "Sorry, that happens after breakfast sometimes."

"Where is he going?" I asked.

"What do you mean?"

"I mean, where are you dropping him? Does he have a tap lesson or snorting practice or something?" I asked.

"No. He likes to ride around with me. It is his big day out. One day a week is Norman's Day of Fun," Brigitte said.

The birds said, "Day of fun!" "Day of fun!"

Great, I get to spend the whole day with Norman the

farting pig. Poor Henri was in the backseat, closer to him. Right now he hung his face out the window and made no indication he was coming back in anytime soon.

"If eighty-three isn't a street, what could it be?" I wondered aloud.

"Section eighty-three!" "Flowers to section eighty-three!" "Carnations!" "Section twenty-four!" "Section nineteen!" "Flowers!"

"What are they talking about?" I asked Brigitte.

"I do not know. Something from the flower cart, I think," Brigitte said.

"They seem to know section eighty-three."

"Section eighty-three!" "Section thirty-four!" "Tombstone!"

"Flowers on a tombstone?" I asked them.

"Carnations!" "Roses!" "Pansies!" "Tombstone!"

"Of course," Brigitte said. "The flower cart goes to Père-Lachaise, the biggest and oldest cemetery in Paris. The graveyard and gardens are divided into sections that are numbered."

"The Garden of Names," Henri said, "is like a garden of names on the tombstones."

"Makes sense to me," I said. "Let's go."

"Let's go!" "Let's go!" "Let's go!"

23

Brigitte extended a ramp from under the van for Norman to walk down.

"What are you doing?" I asked.

"It's Norman's Day of Fun. He won't have much fun locked in a petmobile all day, will he?"

Norman waddled down the ramp, and Brigitte strapped on a leash.

"The birds?" Henri asked.

"Bring one cage. They can sit on the flower cart, if it is here."

Henri said to the birds, "Who wants to come?"

"Come!" "Who!" "Who wants!"

He scrunched his mouth from one side to the other, clearly having trouble deciding which birds should come along. He pointed to them. "Eeny, meen—"

I grabbed the cage closest to the door and ran on ahead.

We found Monsieur Cliquot at the entrance to Père-Lachaise Cemetery. He kissed Brigitte on each cheek and took the cage from me. "*Bonjour*, Marlène. *Bonjour*, Jacqueline. *Bonjour*, Gary . . ." He greeted each of the birds by name as he let them out of their cage and perched them on top of the cart while they stretched their multicolored wings.

"*Bonjour*, Norman." He gave Norman the tops of some red carnations to eat.

"Will they let him inside?" Brigitte asked Monsieur Cliquot.

He gave her a small bouquet of yellow roses. "Get your ticket from the first teller. That is Monique. Give her these and she'll let him in."

"Thank you," Brigitte said. "I'll bring the other birds home later."

"*D'accord.*" He wished us luck with the rest of the hunt.

Brigitte gave Monique the flowers as Monsieur Cliquot

had advised, and voilà, pigs were welcome to roam the Père-Lachaise grounds.

With map in hand, we set out for section eighty-three, with Norman leading the way. Someone needed to explain in pig language that we were racing against the clock here. Norman checked out every smell the way you'd expect a dog to, and he nibbled flowers off the grave sites, generating dirty looks. At this rate it was going to take us forever to find section eighty-three. We had major ground to cover!

This cemetery was bigger, and more beautiful, than any I'd ever seen. I estimated that the walk to section fifty-two was probably a mile. Norman slowed down, and I expected that soon he'd need to rest. I plucked a few dead flowers from a grave and used them to lure Norman along. "Come on, boy. Good pig," I said, while I was thinking, *Just hurry up, you stupid pig!*

"Many famous people are buried here," said Henri.

"Like who?"

"Chopin and Molière," Henri said.

"I know Chopin was a great musician, but I don't know Molière," I said.

"That is because you are not French," Brigitte said. "Molière was a very famous playwright and actor. You probably know Jim Morrison."

"I've heard of him," I said.

"He was an American musician. Very popular," Brigitte explained. "Ah, section eighty-three," she announced.

It was not hard to find the grave we were meant to find because it was surrounded by royal blue shirts. Camera flashes snapped in our faces as we approached.

We were first! Even with the pig slowing us down, we'd won!

But then I saw Jean-Luc, Sabine, and Robert talking to Murielle duPluie. They smiled broadly when they saw us.

Seriously? My heart dropped.

Now we wouldn't get the tickets or backstage passes, and I wouldn't be featured on the French news.

A girl in blue said, "You are the first team to arrive with a pig."

"But the second team to arrive," I pointed out glumly.

"Yes, second. Second is good. Only the first and second get a chance at the box," she said.

Wait, what? "The box?" I asked.

"Yes. The game isn't over for you," she said. "There is one more challenge, and only the first two teams get to try it."

"Are you kidding?" Robert asked. "We were here first!"

"So you get to try with the box too." She smiled like this was exciting news, but Jean-Luc, Sabine, and Robert glared at her. Clearly, they hadn't seen this twist coming.

Murielle duPluie looked into the camera, shining her white teeth, and said, "It seems this contest is not over, Paris."

A microphone appeared in my face. "Hi there," she said to me. "Murielle duPluie with *Music News*. What are your names?"

I stared into the camera. "We are Gwen—from the US—and Henri and Brigitte—"

Brigitte interrupted me. "From Boutique Brigitte—Pour les Petits Animaux."

Murielle ignored her and asked me, "How does it feel?"

"It's amazing, like, with a capital *A*," I said. "I am so happy to be representing my country at this event. I mean, we're talking front row, and backstage passes!"

"Are you aware that Shock Value has sweetened the deal?"

"Sweetened?" Was that even possible?

She reached down and held up two identical boxes. Each had four drawers. The outside of each drawer had a different type of lock. "The first team to unlock all four of these gets an additional bonus ticket and invitations to a VIP reception with the band after the concert, in their greenroom. That's a total of five tickets!"

"With the band?" I repeated.

"Yes! Like a private party!" Murielle confirmed. Then she added, "Of course, I'll be there too." She pointed to the boxes. "You'll see that each of these drawers is locked. You need to use all the clues you've gathered so far to open them."

She gave one box to Robert, Jean-Luc, and Sabine, and the other to us. "The clock is going to start." The Shock Value rep gave Murielle duPluie a nod. "Now!"

I took our box and set it on the tombstone. "Okay." I pointed to a lock on one of the drawers. "This one looks like a regular keyhole," I said. I took the ribbon from my neck. "Easy, as long as this key works." I slid it in the hole and turned.

Click.

The door slid open, and inside was one Shock Value ticket.

"One down," I said.

Henri looked down.

"It's an expression," I said. "It means we're done with one."

Brigitte studied the other three. "What do you think about those?"

One of them was a hole about the size of a dime. Another was a number pad, one through ten. The last was a twisting combination lock.

I glanced a few feet away at Sabine, Jean-Luc, and Robert, who were also huddled around their own set of locks, whispering. "Where are the other clues?" I asked Brigitte.

Brigitte took them out of her pocket. "We have la place de la Concorde, the Statue of Liberty, and then the one that led us here."

"The Statue of Liberty and cemetery both have numbers, but not la place de la Concorde," I said. "Do you have the obelisk?"

She reached into her lab coat pocket, where, of course, she had the obelisk, and probably a shower cap, crowbar, and bottle of maple syrup.

"Do you want to do it?" I asked her, and pointed to the dime-size hole.

Brigitte slid the model monument into the dime-size hole and turned it.

Click.

"Two down," Henri said.

"Now the numbers. The twisting combination of my gym locker is three numbers."

"Then let's use the clue for the cemetery. It is the twentieth *arrondissement* and section eighty-three. We need a third number," Brigitte said.

"Is there a grave number?" All three of us looked

around. There wasn't. "Row?" Nothing. "How about year? When did he die?" I indicated the grave we were standing at.

Brigitte looked. "Last year."

I tried that combination of numbers, but it didn't work. I looked over to see how Robert, Jean-Luc, and Sabine were doing. They were already on the last drawer—the number pad. We were so close.

Think, Gwen, think.

"How about his age?"

"Whose?" Brigitte asked.

"The dead guy."

It took her a few seconds to calculate. "Twenty."

"Oh, that's so young. Poor guy." I tried twenty, eighty-three, twenty.

Click.

It opened.

The third ticket was in the drawer.

"Let's try the GPS coordinates on the number pad," Brigitte said.

"Yeah. Yeah." I waved my hand in front of the number pad. "Hurry!"

Jean-Luc, Robert, and Sabine were arguing. It looked like they had the Statue of Liberty clue, but maybe it was ripped up, or someone had thought it was trash.

Whatever had happened to it, now there was a section of paper missing, so they didn't have all the coordinates. The boys were yelling at her in fast French. She worked her phone. Probably to find the GPS numbers.

Brigitte referred to the paper and pushed in the keys. It opened easily. We had the fourth ticket!

"You did it!" the Shock Value rep said, and gave us the fifth and final ticket.

All three of us shot our hands in the air. "Done!" I yelled. And I launched into a hip-rotating happy dance complete with hands swinging over my head. Brigitte and Henri copied me, although we probably could have benefited from a little practice. We all high-fived.

"Belly bump?" Henri asked Brigitte.

She took a step back and walked into him for a chest bump, but once she hit Henri, she fell flat on her back.

Henri and I reached down and helped her up. She brushed dirt off her butt.

"We won!" I yelled to both of them again, because it was worth saying again and again. "We WON!"

"Bravo!" Murielle duPluie cried, and dragged her cameraman over to us. "Are we ready to roll?" she asked him.

"Ready. And . . . action."

24

"This is Murielle duPluie reporting live from Père-Lachaise Cemetery, where the American underdog Gwen Russell and her friends have just won the contest for tickets to Shock Value's special one-night engagement."

She put the mic into my face again. "How does it feel?" she asked—her signature question.

"Fantastique!" Brigitte said.

"Formidable!" Henri said.

"Oink," Norman snorted.

"Incredible!" I yelled. "I cannot wait to meet Winston, Alec, and Glen." Then I added, "U-S-A!"

"I'll be reporting all the backstage action from the VIP reception at the concert tomorrow." She paused and flashed her perfect smile.

The cameraman said, "Cut! That's great!"

"*What?*" Jean-Luc yelled at Murielle duPluie. He looked at the Shock Value lady and again asked, "*What?* Are you *kidding* me?"

"I can translate," I said. "I mean, if you wanted me to."

Jean-Luc got just an inch from my face. "No," he said. "I do not need a translation." Then Jean-Luc took a step backward, landing his foot right into a pig present that Norman had so perfectly placed at his feet.

Good pig!

"Aw! Gross!"

Robert said, "You are not getting into my car with those shoes."

"So disgusting!" Sabine said.

Jean-Luc said, "Get that stupid pig out of here."

"Or *you* could just leave," Brigitte suggested. "We still have to talk to the Shock Value people about winner business."

Jean-Luc harrumphed and walked away, sliding his feet on the grass.

364

Brigitte, Henri, and I enjoyed a high five, and we all petted Norman. After a short meeting with the Shock Value people to sort out all the deets for the next day, we began walking back to the petmobile.

"OMG!" I said. "This is just perfect. I made the news, I won the contest, and now I get to attend a VIP reception with the band."

If it was so perfect, why did I feel bad? One word: Beef.

"The only thing that could be better is if Clay Bright was there," Brigitte said.

"Too true," I said.

Henri said, "I wonder why he vanished and ran away."

"Maybe it was all too much, the pressure," I said. "And he just wanted to leave . . . to leave and . . ."

"What?" Henri asked. "Leave what?"

"His worries behind," I said. "And fly away." I get quiet, allowing my thoughts to race around the inside of my head.

Henri and Brigitte didn't notice my silence and kept talking. Brigitte said, "I guess we'll never know what happened to him."

I didn't respond right away. "We could ask him," I said.

"Ask who what?" Brigitte asked.

"We could ask Clay Bright why he disappeared," I said. "I know where to find him."

25

We went back to the Hôtel de Paris and walked up the boulevard to my friendly neighborhood guitarist.

"You're him," I said to Knit Cap.

"Who?"

"You're him!" I said again.

"Who?"

"Clay Bright," I said.

Henri studied him closely. "And you are not missing."

"It took you long enough to figure it out," he said. "I thought you were, like, a huge Shock Value fan."

366

"I am! But look at you. You're hanging out on the street. AND I thought you were missing!" I said. "What are you doing here?"

"This is my life now. It's all about music. That's what I was born to do."

"Being in the world's most popular band wasn't doing that for you?" I asked.

"It wasn't about the music anymore. It was photo shoots and perfume and T-shirts. Heck, I started buying music instead of writing my own. That was the last straw for me."

"So you just hang out here every day?"

"Yup. You know, I've been playing here for a year and Beef never recognized me."

"The costume is *très bien*," Henri said.

"Thank you. My mom made me the cap. You know, no one actually told me I was good or had real talent before you came along. It was always 'how many arenas can you sell out' or 'make sure you don't cut your hair before our next photo shoot.' It was never about the actual music. And you helped me get past my writing block." He strummed a few chords and began singing the most beautiful lyrics about making friends with strangers and being found.

"That's amazing," I said. "You're better than ever!"

"I don't know how I can thank you."

"I do," I said.

"Just ask," Clay said. "What can I do?"

"Get me another ticket to tonight's concert."

"Another?"

"Oh, yeah, we kinda won the contest!" I said.

"That's great! That's exactly what you wanted."

"It totally is."

"You are going to have an awesome night." He paused and crinkled his brow like he was thinking deeply. "Man, I miss those guys."

"You might have the chance to see them sooner than you think."

"Why?"

"I'd like you to help me get Beef in front of Shock Value," I said. "To give her the opportunity for a break."

"How will I do that?"

"By asking Alec, Winston, and Glen," I said.

"You mean, you want me to come out of hiding?" Clay asked.

"You're ready," I said. "Don't you think?"

Before he could answer, Brigitte asked, "Can you do a commercial for Boutique Brigitte—Pour les Petits Animaux? I mean, after you come out of hiding, of course."

"Sure," he told Brigitte. "But can it wait until next week?"

"That would be okay," she said.

"So, you'll do it?" I asked.

"It's time for me to fly back," he said. "Home to my boys. Let's go tell them."

"Tell the boys? As in Alec, Winston, and Glen?" I asked. I couldn't believe I was going to get to meet them, like, today.

Clay nodded. "We'll have to swing by my house first so I can change my clothes."

"Then *allons-y* to your house," Brigitte said. "I'll drive."

"Seriously?" Clay asked. "In the pet van?"

He was going to need a limo or something. He was Clay Bright. He was used to traveling in style.

"I've always wanted to ride in that thing," he said. "Is the snake in it?"

"No. But we can get her," Brigitte said. "She is such a pretty snake."

"Too true," Clay added. He secured his guitar in the case and clicked it shut.

On the way to the van Henri asked him, "Your mom has seen you since you have disappeared?"

"It would be pretty weird if she made me a sandwich every day but couldn't see me."

"Who else knows?"

"Just my mom. And, now, you guys."

He helped Brigitte with Norman's ramp, then got in.

"After my house, we'll go find the boys," Clay said. "They're the ones who can get you the ticket you need."

"You know where they are?" I asked. "You haven't talked to them in a year."

"I know all of their habits."

"So where are they?"

"Uncle Alphonse's garage. He lives in Essonne."

"You know who is on the way to Essonne?" Brigitte asked.

Clay nodded, then asked, "Is Fifi here?"

"No, but we can get her too. And we'll have to bring the birds!"

"Oh, yes. Please," Clay said. "Let's get them all."

Seconds later, Sylvie was in the van, hanging around Norman's neck like a scarf. Before I knew it, Fifi was sitting in Henri's lap, licking his face. She wasn't snug in her car seat because Clay Bright was in that space.

We left the animals in the car and went into a brick row home, where we found Clay's mother in the living room, sitting at a drum set. "Hi, honey," she said.

He gave her a kiss. "Hi, Ma. This is Henri, Gwen, and Brigitte. They just won the Shock Value contest. They need an extra ticket for some lady named Beef so she can play for the boys and maybe get her big break into musical stardom."

"Sounds good, honey." She pulled headphones over her ears. "I made tuna sandwiches." She jammed on the drums. Terribly and loudly.

Clay said, "Just give me a sec." He really was only gone for a sec, and when he returned, the only thing he'd changed was his cap. He took sandwiches out of the refrigerator and put them into a brown paper bag.

Clay lifted one of her earphones. "Wanna come?" he asked his mom.

"You're going to see the boys?"

He nodded.

"And not hide anymore?"

He nodded again.

"Sounds like a hoot." She put her drumsticks down and unplugged the earphones without taking them off. On the way out the front door she grabbed a white button-up sweater that looked like a librarian's. It didn't go with her cheetah-print leggings and spiky heels.

"Nice ride," she said when she saw the petmobile. She stuck her hand out, waiting for someone to put something in it. When no one did, she looked at us. "Keys?"

"It is my pet van," Brigitte said.

"Cool. I like it. But I'll drive. I always drive," she said.

Clay confirmed, "She always drives."

Brigitte took out the keys, but before she could give them to Mrs. Bright, the woman snatched them and got in the van. As we were still piling in, she peeled out. I fell into the seat with Henri, and Norman squealed.

Mrs. Bright yelled back, "Buckle up, amigos!" And floored it.

Finally, someone who could drive!

Mrs. Bright whizzed around corners, changed lanes, and honked the oinker generously. She appeared to know exactly where she was going. We left the city of Paris for the first time and traveled along the hilly French countryside. The grass was dark green, and slender fir trees lined both sides of the narrow road for miles. We all managed to crack our windows to let fresh air in and stale pig smell out. The animals were quiet and sniffed at the new scents in the air; even Sylvie gently swayed her head from side to side over Norman's shoulder. The pet van followed a sign with an arrow pointing toward Essonne.

Essonne was a picturesque village with many gardens, small rivers, and bridges. There were more bicycles than cars on the gravel streets, but that didn't slow down Mrs. Bright, who took tight turns and kicked dirt out from under the van's tires.

Brigitte held on to a hanging hook near the car window with one hand and braced herself on the dashboard with the other for the entire ride. I was sure she wanted to say something, but except for a few whimpers, nothing left her mouth.

Mrs. Bright skidded into the unpaved driveway of a small stone cottage with white shutters and beautiful window boxes filled with colorful wildflowers. There was a trellis adorned with grapevines, underneath which sat a wrought-iron table and chairs. Sitting in the chairs were Winston, Glen, and Alec!

They saw Mrs. Bright and hopped up to greet her. Then they saw three strangers get out of a van, and last, they saw Clay. Their eyes widened in shock.

"No way!" Alec yelled, and ran into Clay's arms.

"*Incroyable!*" Winston ran his hands through his hair over and over.

"I should kick your butt right here, right now, man," Glen said. "But I'm just so glad to see you, I'll do it later."

"It's a date," Clay said, and he hugged his friend. "Look, guys, I know you probably have a lot of questions, and I'll tell you everything, but I need a favor."

"Now?" Alec asked.

"I guess it doesn't have to be *right* now, but since I'm here . . ."

"It's just that Murielle duPluie is on her way here to

do an interview. You know, a sit-down thing before the concert," Glen said. I loved that Glen talked like a New Yorker. If I wasn't at a beautiful cottage in a village outside of Paris with the most popular band in the world, I might have been a little homesick.

"An interview?" Clay asked. "That sounds perfect."

"For what?"

"A public reappearance?"

26

The petmobile was hidden.

Norman roamed and nibbled the grass with Sylvie on his neck. The two had become fast friends.

Winston's uncle Alphonse spoke to the birds who were still in the van in French and let them sit on top of the trellis to enjoy the sun.

Fifi had little interest in the country, and stayed glued to Henri's lap in the cottage kitchen, where we drank cappuccino. Uncle Alphonse didn't talk much, but rather busied himself around the kitchen, wiping, straightening, and refilling our cups. He pulled up a paint-chipped stool and motioned for Clay to sit on it. Then he took a razor from a drawer, wiped it on his pants, and went to work on Clay's beard.

When we heard Murielle duPluie's news van on the gravel, we spied out the window: She shook hands with the three current members of Shock Value and explained, "This is going to be live."

"That's right, man. Just like a good concert," Glen said.

Murielle duPluie looked at the cameraman. "Are we ready, Kevin?"

"Ready. And . . . action!"

"This is Murielle duPluie, and I'm coming to you live from Shock Value's secret practice location." She sat between the three handsome musicians under the trellis. "Are you guys excited about tomorrow's big show?" She put the mic in front of Glen, who seemed like the leader.

Glen said, "That's an understatement. This is going to be truly epic."

DuPluie asked, "More than usual? How come?"

Alec moved the mic in front of his own mouth. "I guess the best thing we could do is show you," he said. "You're gonna love this."

"Yes. We'll show you." Winston stood. "Come out, *mon ami*," he called to Clay.

Clay Bright walked out of Uncle Alphonse's cottage. His hair had been cut and his beard shaved, he wore a clean shirt tucked in, and a guitar hung on his back. He looked like a totally different person. The Clay Bright everyone knew and loved.

Murielle duPluie stared at Clay. Her lips didn't move. Shock? Amazement? Awe? It was anybody's guess, but the famous Murielle duPluie froze once she saw Clay Bright.

"He's returning for the concert," Glen said, helping her out.

Alec asked, "You're back, buddy. So great to see you. Where the heck have you been?"

"Sorry, but I needed to run away for a while, to find the music again. It's hard to explain, but I'd lost it," he said. "But I'm back now, and I missed you guys. And I missed the fans."

"So did you find it? Have you been writing?" Glen asked.

"I did," Clay said. "And yes, I have been writing quite a lot. Want to hear something new?"

"Would we?" Glen looked at Murielle duPluie. "What do you think? Would your viewers like to hear a new Shock Value song from Clay Bright, who has just returned to his band?"

"Uh-huh," she said, still in her frozen smile.

377

"Great!" Clay played a short section of the song about running away. "I'll be playing that one tonight," he said to Glen.

Murielle duPluie finally cleared her throat and looked into the camera. "There you have it. Musical history. Clay Bright is back and will rejoin Shock Value tonight," she said. "Follow me, Murielle duPluie, on *Music News* live throughout the evening. Remember, you heard it here first." She didn't move her stare from Clay.

Kevin, her cameraman, said, "And . . . cut."

27

The petmobile was loaded with me, Brigitte, Henri, and Natalie—Professor Camponi's granddaughter. We gave her one of the extra front-row tickets that we'd gotten for opening all the boxes. We gave Beef the fifth and final VIP ticket. For this event Brigitte had agreed, reluctantly, to leave any nonhuman friends behind. "Fifi will be so sad to miss it," Brigitte had said.

"We'll tell her all about it," I'd said. She didn't feel good about it until Henri suggested that we record parts of the concert and play it back for Fifi later.

I recognized the arena, the Palais Omnisports de Paris-Bercy (the locals called it POPB), from my tour books. It had a unique pyramidal shape and really cool walls that were actually covered with sloping lawns.

Brigitte navigated the van into the crowded parking lot and rolled down the window to pay the attendant for parking.

"*Bonjour*, Brigitte," said the parking attendant.

"*Bonjour*, Monsieur d'Argent. How is the little angel?"

"Ah, *très bien*. He is getting big." He handed her a bright red VIP parking sticker. "Put this on your window and you can park anywhere."

"*Merci*, but you see, I have two more buses behind me. One is from the Hôtel de Paris, and the other one carries a very noisy lacrosse team."

He stretched his neck around the petmobile and looked at the two buses behind us. "Ah! I see. Shock Value told me about them. They will have to sit with the maintenance crew in the mezzanine section. The view is obstructed, but it's the best we could do with the whole place sold out. We forgot that they would need to park." He scratched his bald head. "But for Brigitte, it is no problem." He took out two more red stickers. "I will give them these." He winked at her.

"*Merci*, Monsieur d'Argent. Thank you so much."

"For the girl who cleans Antonio's teeth, anything."

We drove on.

"Antonio?" I asked.

"Baby alligator," she said. "So cute and cuddly."

"Right," I agreed, "a cuddly alligator."

We flashed our backstage passes to every agent. Each one seemed like they were expecting us and the huge crowd of people who trailed along behind us. Of course, they couldn't all sit in the front row or go backstage. So Étienne and the apartment doormen who had driven in the hotel van were led to the balcony, while the lacrosse team and their families were directed to a long empty row up high in the nosebleed seats.

As we parted ways, I heard one of the lacrosse players say to Josh, "Your sister rocks."

Another player said, "She's cute, too."

Topher said, "Dude, gross."

I guess my new outfit, which Étienne had helped me select from the hotel store, looked good. It was a denim miniskirt and scoop-neck Shock Value T-shirt. A few days without contact sports and my legs were practically bruise-free. I'd taken some extra time to blow-dry my hair. It had never looked so good. It was amazing what some spray and a few rhinestone clips could do.

The last of our crowd of guests to walk away were Jean-Luc, Sabine, and Robert. That's right: I asked Shock Value for tickets for them, too. And they gave them to me because they were so appreciative that I'd convinced Clay to come back.

Sabine said, "I like your hair jewelry."

"Thank you," I said. "Enjoy the show."

Jean-Luc said, "You are okay, Henri, to get us these tickets."

"It does not mean that I will not beat you in the next game," he said.

"No, you won't," Jean-Luc said. "That will never happen again."

"Maybe we should bet—" Henri said.

I interrupted, "No. Let's not. Someone usually loses when you bet." I tugged Henri toward the front row. "Are you glad now that you invited them?"

"Maybe," he said. "They are going to get mad again when I score the next goal."

"Probably," I said, "Let's go."

Mr. Camponi's granddaughter, Natalie; Beef; Henri; Brigitte; and I were given the full backstage tour before being escorted to our seats—all of us except Beef, who was asked to stay behind with the band.

Natalie oohed and aahed at everything. From the

front row I saw Murielle duPluie in the wings, where she was reporting live.

Alec, Winston, and Glen took the stage. The audience cheered, "CLAY! CLAY!" After making us wait just long enough, Clay came onto the stage, and the four original members of the band, with Beef on the tambourine, launched into their most beloved song. The audience, including me, Henri, Brigitte, and Natalie, went nuts.

The set continued through Shock Value's classic songs. They danced, and the audience sang along. Everything about the concert was perfect.

Then Clay stood at the mic and said, "It's good to be back with my three bandmates and all of you here in Paris!"

The crowd screamed.

He continued, "Finding the courage to come back wasn't easy. I had a little help, actually. You see, I met a stranger who inspired me." The audience listened in silence. "This new friend also helped me find my way back to my love of writing music, and I think maybe I helped her discover something she didn't know about herself." Was he talking about me? "She had no idea that her voice rocked, because her older brothers . . ." He shaded his eyes from the spotlights and looked up into the mezzanine section. "They're up there somewhere.

Anyway, they told her she couldn't sing." He picked a guitar string. "Gwen, I want you to come up here and sing the song you wrote."

No! Freakin'! Way!

Was he seriously doing this?

"If it wasn't for you, I wouldn't be here right now." He started playing the familiar chords. "Let's rock."

Glen tapped the security guards in front of the stage. "Her," he told them, and pointed to me.

Two muscular security men lifted me onto the stage.

I tugged my skirt down and brushed a lock of hair over my ear.

The crowd cheered for me. For *me*! I thought I could hear JTC, but I couldn't see anyone because the lights totally blinded me.

Clay continued plucking at the sequence of chords. I swung my hips to the familiar and catchy tune.

Glen came over and hung a mic on a wire over my ear. He looked me in the eye and said, "Deep breath."

I took one.

Then he said, "You got this," and he strummed his guitar. Alec boomed on the drums, and Winston pounded on the keyboard.

I was so into the beat that when Clay started the first words, I joined right in. He lowered his voice and let me take over the song. "I could go to Japan!" I sang the whole verse; then Clay joined in to harmonize the second time through. The rest of the band hummed in the background. Beef clanked the tambourine.

I danced and walked across the stage, finally belting out, "If only I could fly!" Both of my hands were in the air.

Clay yelled, "Yeah!" and gave me a big hug. He whispered, "Thank you," in my ear. Then he announced, "Good night, Paris!"

The lights went out and I was escorted backstage. Natalie, Henri, and Brigitte were already in the greenroom. The band was right behind me.

Alec signed an autograph for Sylvie and one for Fifi, and Winston posed for countless pictures with Natalie. Even Beef was there. I listened to her live interview with Murielle duPluie.

Murielle duPluie asked, "So, how was it?"

"Well, you know, Murray—"

"Murielle," Murielle duPluie corrected her.

"It's like a nickname that I made for you," Beef explained.

"I don't like it, but how was it?"

"It was like I always imagined it would be. I can't thank Shock Value enough for giving me my big break. Now I have a question for you, Murray. Where do you get your hair done? Because it is fab and I was thinking of getting a little trim." She fluffed her very short waves.

Murielle duPluie's mic-less hand went to her hair. "Why, thank you. I can give you some names."

"Well, that would be appreciated," Beef said. She was definitely a smooth talker. "And how about that little lady?" She indicated me with her thumb. "My new friend. Wasn't she amazing?"

Murielle duPluie focused the mic on me, and Beef moved straight to a plate of shrimp cocktail.

"Hello, Gwen," she said. "I'm live with *Music News*. Can I ask you a few questions?"

"I'd like that," I said.

"I think the world is wondering, 'Who is Gwen Russell and what's her story?'"

"It's a super-simple story, really," I told Murielle duPluie. "I came to Paris and I made a wish on a lantern that I tossed off the cliff at la côte d'Albâtre."

"What was your wish?"

Henri interrupted, "Do not tell her. It will not come true."

"It's okay," I told Henri.

"Well?" Murielle duPluie asked.

"I wished for the best week ever in Paris."

"And did you have it?" she asked me.

"I got to spend time with my old friend and surrogate sister, Brigitte, and her gang of pets. I won the Shock Value scavenger hunt. I not only met the band, but I returned their friend and bandmate to them—not many people can say they've done something like that. He convinced me to start singing, and it turns out I'm pretty good. And"—I took Henri's hand—"I made a great new friend."

"So your wish came true?"

"You bet it did," I said. "Wait. Actually, don't bet. Someone usually loses."

The cameraman pushed in closer to Murielle duPluie. She stared straight into the camera, at her viewers, and said, "There you have it, music fans. A wish on a lantern ends in musical history. I'd say that's a successful trip to Paris."

28

The next day was my last in Paris. I couldn't believe it.

I entered the cozy lobby and watched tour group D gather by the podium to be briefed by Beef. The tour group was considerably larger than mine had been. It seemed that Beef's recent musical success attracted tourists. I noticed that in addition to her fanny pack and clipboard, she now also had her tambourine hanging from her belt.

Henri was leaning against a wall near the grand front door of the Hôtel de Paris. His hair was combed back and tied into a ponytail; his striped oxford was pressed and untucked. He had one hand shoved deep into a front pocket, and the other waved to me.

"Hi," I said. "You aren't working today?"

"No. Not today. Étienne gave me the day with no work."

"Off."

"Off what?"

"Off work. That's what we call a day with no work, a day off."

"Then off," he said. *"Allons-y."* Let's go.

"Where?"

"You aren't done with your great week in Paris."

"I'm not?"

"No. There's something you need to see." He took my hand. "Come on."

I went with him outside to the front of the hotel. I looked for Clay Bright, but he wasn't there. Then I looked around for the petmobile, but I didn't see it barking, squawking, or oinking nearby.

"Where is Brigitte?"

"She was picking up new rats for Sylvie."

"Yuck," I said.

"Yeah. Yuck."

Henri stopped walking at a yellow Vespa scooter and handed me a helmet from the back.

I said, "I don't think my mom—"

He put it on my head. "I already talked to her and JTC. The boys convinced her that you can go with me for an hour."

"Really?"

He buckled the strap and tapped the top of the helmet. "Really." He kicked a leg over the scooter and fastened his own helmet. "Get on."

I straddled the seat and wrapped my hands around Henri's waist. He flicked a switch and something with his foot, and we cruised down the boulevard. We stopped near the edge of the Seine—right near the fleet of tour boats I had seen when I had first arrived.

"A river cruise?" I asked.

"*Oui,*" Henri said. He slid a plastic card out of his pocket. "A gift," he said. "From Professor Camponi. For taking Natalie to the concert." He waved me ahead of him onto the boat.

I stepped on and climbed up to the top deck, Henri following close behind.

The boat sailed down the river that flowed through the center of Paris. We went under what seemed like a million bridges. It was so cool to see the city we had been running around from the water—the Louvre, Notre Dame, and a bunch of other sights we hadn't gotten to see. Henri pointed to buildings and told me what he could about each.

"Guess what?" he asked me.

"What?"

"Les Bleus won the World Cup."

"So I guess that proves it," I said. "Lantern wishes come true whether you tell them or not."

He squeezed my hand and held it for the rest of the ride while we slowly sailed down the Seine.

Lost in Rome

This is a book about sisters, so this is for Sue as well as all my other special gal pals whom I consider sisters.
In the pizza of life, sisters are the pepperoni.

Acknowledgments

Writers often ask me for advice, and I always tell them to find trusted partners. I'm lucky to have this in Gale, Carolee, Josette, Jane, Chris, and Shannon, and the Northern Delaware Sisters in Crime group: John, KB, Jane, June, Chris, Janis, Susan, and Kathleen.

Thanks to my friends, who understand that I talk to imaginary people and are fine with it.

Mille grazie to my literary agent, Mandy Hubbard, and editor, Alyson Heller. Sometimes we're so like-minded that it gets scary.

As always, to my family: Ellie, Evan, Happy, Kevin, my parents, nieces and nephews, sister, sisters-in-law, brothers-in-law, and mother-in-law, thank you for your continued encouragement! Special thanks to my niece Taylor and daughter, Happy, who for the low, low price of a diner breakfast helped me plot out a Summer Rome-ance with Extra Cheese.

Also a *grazie* goes out to my helpful translators: Shari, Eddi, and Vic.

To teachers, librarians, and, most of all, my readers: I love getting your e-mails, letters, pictures, selfies, posts, and tweets. . . . Keep 'em coming!

1

❧

I'd been planning to be a counselor-in-training at Camp Hiawatha, but there was an issue with fleas, mice, lice, and snakes and the camp closing, leaving my summer *wide open*.

The only question was, what would I do with all my free time? Thankfully, my parents were able to make alternate plans.

"It's all set," my mom said.

"For real?" I asked.

"Totally for real," Dad confirmed. "Your great-aunt Maria can't wait to have you."

My great-aunt Maria was my dad's aunt, and she was more than *great*, she was my favorite relative in the adult category. She was sweet, nice, an amazing Italian cook, and she owned this insanely cute pizzeria. Plus, I always felt like she and I had some kind of special connection—like a bond or something. I can't explain it exactly.

Oh, and that pizzeria she owned? It just happened to be in Rome. Rome, Italy!

Basically, Aunt Maria is all that and a plate of rigatoni, if you know what I mean.

"When do we leave?" I asked.

"Tomorrow morning," Mom said. "But this isn't going to be two weeks of sightseeing and touristy stuff. I told her you wanted to work."

"At the pizzeria?"

"Yeah," Dad said. "She's planning to teach you how to make her signature sauce."

"The secret sauce?" I asked in awe.

"That's the one," he added. "*I* don't even know how to make it."

"That's a major deal," Mom said.

Just then a girl who looked a lot like me—long dark curly hair, light skin, brown eyes, except she was taller, prettier, older, and more stylish—walked into our parents' room, where we were talking. A cell phone was glued to her ear.

"It's on!" I said.

"For real?" she asked.

"For real!"

She pumped her fist in the air. "I'll call you later. I'm going to Rome! *Ciao!*" She hung up the phone, looked at herself in the full-length mirror, fluffed her brown curly locks, and practiced, "*Buongiorno!*"

Maybe I should tell you who "she" is: my older sister, Gianna. She's like my best friend. There's no one I'd rather be with for two weeks in Rome. Next year she'll be a junior in high school, where she is most often seen with a glitter pen and scrapbooking scissors.

Me . . . not so much. I'm more of a big-idea gal. Then she builds or glues or sews or staples my ideas into reality.

This fall she'll start looking at colleges. She's excited about it, but the idea of her leaving home makes my stomach feel like a lump of overcooked capellini. Maybe some sisters fight, but Gi and I are tight. (Okay, *sometimes* we fight like sisters.)

Mom said to Gianna, "I told Lucy that you girls are going to work at the pizzeria."

"I love that place," Gianna said. "I hope it's exactly the same as I remember it."

"Do you think she still has Meataball?" I asked. I had visited Aunt Maria and her pizzeria years ago, and I vaguely remembered her cat.

"The cat?" Dad asked. "He has to be dead by now, honey. But maybe she has another cat."

"Gi, she's gonna teach me how to make her sauce."

"Just you?"

I shrugged. "Maybe she loves me more."

Mom said, "No. She loves you both exactly the same."

"Maybe," I started, "she wants me to take over the pizzeria when she retires, and I'll be the Sauce Master, the only one in the entire Rossi lineage who knows the ancient family signature sauce. Then, when I'm old, I'll choose one of my great-nieces to carry on the family tradition. And—"

Mom interrupted. "Lucy?"

"What?"

"This isn't one of your stories. Let's bring it back to reality."

"Right," I said. "Reality." But sometimes reality was so boring. Fiction—*my* fiction—was way better. I'm pretty sure I'm the best writer in my school, where I'm a soon-to-be eighth grader.

Gianna asked, "You're totally gonna teach it to me, right?"

"It depends on if I have to take some kind of oath that could only be broken in the event of a zombie apocalypse," I said.

Dad suggested, "And let's try to cool it with apocalypse-related exaggerations, huh? Aunt Maria probably doesn't 'get' zombies and their ilk."

"Roger that, Dad," I said.

"I'm going to pack," Gianna said. "I can bring a glue gun, right? That's okay on the plane, isn't it?"

"I'm pretty sure they have glue guns in Italy. Or maybe you could refrain from hot-gluing things for two weeks," Mom suggested.

"Ha! You're funny, Mom," Gianna said. "Don't lose that sense of humor while the two of us are spending fourteen days in Italy!"

Gi and I looked at each other. "ITALY!" we both yelled at the same time.

We would've screamed way louder if we'd had any idea how much this trip would change the future—mine, Gianna's, Aunt Maria's, Amore Pizzeria's, and Rome's.

2

STAMP!

The customs officer, who sat in a glass-enclosed booth, pounded his stamp onto Gianna's passport.

I slid mine through a little hole in the glass, and he did the same.

New stamps in our passports!

"Yay!" Me and Gi high-fived.

A few moments later my eyes caught a paper sign that said LUCIA AND GIANNA ROSSI.

The lady holding it wasn't Aunt Maria. She was as

different as possible from our older Italian aunt. She was young, maybe twenty-three, and was all bright colors and peculiarities. Her head was wrapped in a dark purple scarf that hung like a long tail down her back. Her sunglasses were splotched with mismatched paint, and her pants were unlike any that I'd ever seen: one leg was striped and short and snug (maybe spandex), while the other leg was flowery, long, and flowing (possibly silk).

We made our way over to her and her sign.

"Are you Lucia and Gianna?" she asked without a trace of an Italian accent. She was as American as me.

We nodded.

"Buongiorno!" She hugged us just like Aunt Maria would have: tight, and extra long. "I'm Jane Attilio, and I've come to take you to Amore Pizzeria. *Andiamo!*"

Gi and I looked at each other, unfamiliar with the word. Maybe she didn't know that we didn't speak Italian.

"Let's go!" Jane added with a big smile. With one hand she dragged my wheely suitcase. With the other she took Gianna's hand and led us out of the airport. "We're going to have an incredibly awesome two weeks."

Jane Attilio effortlessly crammed our bags into her small European automobile (a Fiat) and whizzed us— and I do mean "whizzed"!—through the streets of Rome.

While Jane's driving was fast, it was no crazier than everyone else's. I would've buckled up twice, if that was possible.

We passed ancient and crumbling buildings and statues, monuments and ruins. When traffic stopped, we were next to a big stone wall, where a very long line of people stood.

"What are they doing?" I asked.

"Behind that wall is Vatican City. Those people are in the queue to go in." Jane pointed to a half-moon of gigantic stone columns. "That plaza is Saint Peter's Square. See that big dome behind it? That's the Basilica. People travel very far to get in there."

"So cool," I said, and snapped a picture with my cell phone.

Jane navigated the roads onto a white marble bridge called the Ponte Principe Amedeo Savoia Aosta, which took us over the Tiber—a river that ran right through the middle of the city.

Finally Jane's little car halted at the end of a cobblestone alley. "Amore Pizzeria is down there," she said.

Gianna started getting her bags out of the car and setting them down on the street.

Jane said, "That's okay. Leave your bags. I'll drop them off at Aunt Maria's apartment. It's not far." She hugged us both again, real hard. "She is so excited to see you girls. You're all she's talked about since she found out you were coming." Jane got back into the car and yelled, "I hope you'll be able to cheer her up."

Why does she need cheering up?

3

~~~~

Ahhh! I recognized the smells of roasting garlic and simmering tomatoes from my great-aunt Maria's signature secret sauce. I hadn't smelled it in years.

"Lucia! Gianna!" Aunt Maria called from the kitchen through a big rectangular opening in the wall. The hole was for passing hot food from the kitchen to the dining room. It had a ledge where the cook could set plates while they waited to be picked up. "The girls are here!" She shuffled out.

Aunt Maria looked older than I remembered; her

hair, which used to be black, was now peppered with gray. She grabbed hold of me—thankfully, her snug embrace hadn't changed. She switched to hug Gianna and then back to me again. Either she'd shrunk or I'd grown—probably both—but now I was taller than her.

I said, "It's good to see you, too." After three rounds of embraces, Gianna and I were both dusted with flour from her hands and apron.

She stepped back and studied us from head to toe. "Look at you." She grew teary. "You are so *bellissima*, beautiful." She lifted the tomato-sauce-speckled apron and wiped her eyes. "I am so happy you girls are here. You are like a breath of the fresh air." She took us each by the hand and led us to a table. "Look at how skinny you are. I am getting you the pizza." She frowned at our figures, then hustled behind the counter. "Sit. Sit. It will take me one minute."

I hadn't been to Amore since first grade. Even though I didn't remember the visit well, I knew the familiar scent of spices seeping out of the walls like ghosts of old friends.

Now the pizzeria looked worn, like Aunt Maria had tried to redecorate at some point but hadn't finished. Paint covered the exposed brick wall. The chairs and tables needed attention—they were chipped, stained, and a little wobbly.

A picture of my great-uncle Ferdinando hung in the center of a wall covered with framed photos that looked like they hadn't been dusted in months, maybe years. There was a ledge holding trinkets that seemed to be layered with a thin coating of Parmesan cheese.

Aunt Maria returned with two plates and three bottles of Aranciata (an Italian orange soda that I love!). Not sure why she had brought the extra bottle. "*Mangia, mangia,*" she said. "Eat, girls."

Crispy crust.

Aunt Maria's signature sauce.

Steamy, melty mozzarella cheese.

Ooey, gooey, cheesy, and crispy.

It was, like, delicious with an ice-cold glass of *mmmmm*.

We had totally hit the jackpot with these temporary summer jobs.

Let me tell you about Amore's pizza, because it's different from American pizza: First, they're round, not triangle, slices. It's like everyone gets their own small individual pie made specifically for them. And the toppings are different. The ones she brought out were smothered with roasted garlic.

"It's quiet in here," Gianna commented.

"*Sì*. There are not so much customers." Aunt Maria sighed sadly. Maybe this was why she needed cheering up. "You like the pizza?"

"It's as good as I remembered," I said through a mouthful of cheese.

Aunt Maria nestled herself into a chair across from us and exhaled as she took her weight off her feet. "I have something to tell you." She looked us both in the eye. "You cannot work here."

Splat! Those words landed like a meatball plopped onto a plate of spaghetti.

"What?" Gianna and I asked together.

"Well, one of you can," she clarified. "But not both."

One of us has to go home? But we just got here!

"How come?" Gianna asked. "What's wrong? We promise we'll work hard."

"It is not that. It is the Pizzeria de Roma." Aunt Maria spat the name. "It's an old pizzeria in the piazza by the Fontana del Cuore." That's the Fountain of the Heart. "Now it has a big new flashy sign and shiny new forks," she said. "Everybody go there. They see it right there in the piazza!"

"How's their pizza?" I asked.

"You think I know?" She pinched her fingers together and flipped her wrist back and forth as she spoke. "I never go."

"Then how do you know that they have shiny forks?" I asked.

"Signorina Jane Attilio. She live upstairs." Aunt Maria pointed up. "She see them when she walk past."

Gianna and I looked at each other. "Are you going to send one of us home?" I asked.

"No. No. No. You stay. Signorina Attilio, she says one of you can help her. She is very busy."

"Oh great," I said. "Let me guess. She works at a funeral home, or a toothpick factory, or vacuuming dirt out of USB ports?"

(I didn't think there was really any such thing as a toothpick factory.)

"What is this 'ports'? No. No," Aunt Maria said. "She is a tailor."

Gianna's eyebrows shot up. "Like, she makes things? I'm great at that."

"*Sì?*" Aunt Maria asked.

"Yeah. See these jeans?" Gianna stood and showed the rhinestone embellishments on the back pocket. "I added them myself."

"*Bella!* You are good at the designs," Aunt Maria said, admiring the bling. "You will like to work with Signorina, *sì?*"

"I think I will."

"Then you are the one," Aunt Maria said to Gianna.

Phew! I would've skinny-dipped in the Fontana del Cuore before I'd have given up working at Amore.

At that moment, a boy walked in Amore's front door. Not just any kind of a boy. He was extremely cute, with a thick head of dark hair to match his thick arm muscles. He looked like he was Gianna's age. Gianna's eyes popped out of her skull at the sight of him.

"*Buongiorno*," he said.

"Hi," we said.

"I am Lorenzo," he introduced himself in English.

"*Tu!*" Aunt Maria pointed at him. To us she said, "I know who he is. He cannot come in here!"

4

Lorenzo set a Vera Bradley bag on the counter next to the cash register and held his hands up in surrender. "I just wanted to deliver this. It was on the ground at the end of the alley." One of Gianna's bags must not have made it back into the Fiat. "The tag says it belongs to Gianna Rossi. Since your last name is Rossi, I figured I'd bring it over. You are lucky it wasn't stolen!"

"Yup, that's mine," Gianna said. She got up and took the bag from him. The luggage tag clearly stated her name and cell phone number. "*Grazie,*" she said. Her eyes locked with his.

"*Bene.*" Lorenzo stared at Gianna. "You are *bellissima,*" he said to her. "Pretty."

Gianna flipped a few locks of hair over her shoulder. "*Grazie,*" she said again, this time with a blush and a shy smile.

I rolled my eyes at her flirty maneuver.

"Are you American?" Lorenzo asked.

"*Sì.*"

"*Vai!*" Aunt Maria yelled at him. "Go!"

Lorenzo pointed to the cell phone number on the luggage tag, moved to the door, and mouthed, "I'll call."

Through the window we watched him strap on a helmet and vroom away on a bright-red Vespa scooter with an unusually loud motor.

Aunt Maria placed her hand firmly on Gianna's. "He is with the Pizzeria de Roma. He must stay away."

"But he seems so nice," Gianna said.

"And he ain't bad to look at, if you know what I mean," I added under my breath.

"Do not think that his words and beauty are true. He is very bad. They take my customers," she said. She gave us both a look that meant business. "Promise me you will not talk to him again."

"Okay," Gianna said. I watched her cross her legs under the table. "I promise." I was pretty sure she wasn't planning to keep that promise.

"*Buono*," Aunt Maria said. "Now I tell Signorina Attilio to come down." To me she said, "I am going to teach you my sauce this summer. It is true."

"Yay!"

She shuffled to the back of the shop, picked up a broom, and klonked the handle four times on the ceiling, knocking.

Knock—knock—knock—knock.

"Are you going to stay away from him?" I asked while Aunt Maria was away.

The knocks were followed by the sound of four stomps coming from the floor above.

"You saw him. Is that even humanly possible?" Gianna asked. "Besides, it's summer break. We have two weeks in Italy, one of the most romantic places in the world. And I don't have a boyfriend."

I didn't say anything to Gianna, but I'd had a strange feeling in my gut when she spoke to Lorenzo. It was a feeling I'd been having kinda a lot lately. Like bubbles spilling over the edges of a glass of Coke.

Aunt Maria returned. "Signorina is on her way down." She left again with our dirty plates and empty bottles.

I felt something brush against my leg under the table and reached down to swat it. It wasn't something swat-table.

"Meataball!" I exclaimed. "You're alive!" I bent down to lift him for a hug. Lifting Meataball was no small task. I kissed him. "I'm so happy to see you."

Gianna said, "He's gotten *bigger*."

"And heavier." I sat down with him in my arms and scratched his ears. He purred and exposed his belly, inviting me to rub it.

As a kitten, Meataball found himself trapped in a trash can behind Amore Pizzeria. Aunt Maria kept him and called him Romeo, *her* Romeo. And Romeo, a beautiful gray tabby, grew, especially in the belly zone, and was lovingly nicknamed Meataball.

I petted him and he purred. "That is one impressive hunk of cat tummy," I laughed.

Meataball yawned.

"He's so sweet," Gianna said.

While we spoiled the cat, Jane Attilio swooped in from a door in the kitchen that was visible through the opening in the wall between the kitchen and dining room. She was now wrapped in an extraordinarily long plaid pashmina. I'm no fashion expert, but it didn't go with any of the other crazy stuff she was wearing.

She joined our table and patted Meataball's belly like someone looking for good luck from a Buddha statue.

"So, which one of you is going to work with me?" Jane poked a straw into the extra Aranciata bottle and sipped.

"Me!" Gianna raised her hand. "I love that wrap and those glasses."

"Thanks. I painted them with nail polish."

"Nail polish? Great idea. I could probably Gorilla Glue some bling on those," Gianna said.

"Bling? I love bling!"

"The bling-ier, the better, I always say," Gianna declared. She had just found a new BFF.

"Let me guess," I said to Jane. "You like mushrooms on pizza."

"It's my favorite. How did you know?"

"I haff my vays," I said with squinty sort of mysterious eyes.

Gianna glared at me with a raised eyebrow. "Don't start with that."

Jane asked, "What's 'that'?"

Gianna shook her head subtly so that only I could see. She didn't want me to tell Jane about "that."

I ignored her. I said, "'That' is my unusual ability to tell things about people based on their pizza preferences.

People who like mushrooms are creative types, generally; it isn't an exact science."

"That's fascinating," Jane said.

"That's not all," I said.

Gianna said, "Yes, it is."

"No," I added. "There's more."

"Do tell." Jane leaned in and flipped her nail-polished glasses onto the top of her head scarf.

The sound of a plate scraping against the tile floor came from the kitchen, and Meataball struggled to jump off my lap.

"Meataball! *Mangia!*" Aunt Maria called.

He hustled, his belly swinging beneath him, to lap up whatever had just been set on the floor for him to eat.

I explained, "Once I know someone's pizza type, I can create a couple with someone else based on *their* pizza type."

Jane asked, "Like a romantic couple?"

"She's only done it once," Gianna interjected.

I clarified, "I've only *actually* done it once, like for real, but I've made lots more couples in my head. Those should count."

"And the one you did for real, it worked?" Jane asked.

"So far," I said.

"It's only been a few weeks," Gianna said.

"Six," I said.

"This is very cool," Jane said. "You're like a live, one-girl dating service."

"Except that dating services use science or formulas," Gianna said.

"But in Italy, people like tradition. I think they'd be excited about a good old-fashioned matchmaker that they can meet face-to-face right here in a pizzeria in Rome," Jane replied.

"And," I added, "if dating services ever suddenly just disappear, due to something like a zombie apocalypse, we'll have an experienced matchmaker ready to go."

"Zombies?" Jane's face scrunched.

I remembered what Dad had said about cooling it with my stories. "Or something like zombies," I said.

420

5

Gianna went upstairs with Jane, while I went to the kitchen to see Aunt Maria.

"This is AJ." Aunt Maria pointed to a boy about my age who was tearing romaine lettuce into bite-size pieces. "And this is Vito." She indicated a man pounding chicken breast with a wooden mallet. "He no speak English." She said something to him in Italian, and he waved to me.

"*Buongiorno*," he said.

I waved back with a smile.

To AJ she said, "This is Lucy. I told you about her. Please show her the things around here." Aunt Maria took off her apron and hung it carefully on a hook. "I go to the bank and be here in one hour." With her black purse over her shoulder, she left through the back door.

"Hey," AJ said to me, and held out his fist for a bump, which I gave. Nothing about AJ seemed Italian: bushy blond hair, blue eyes, light skin. "Your aunt told me a lot about you."

"You know about me, but I don't know anything about you," I said. "Doesn't seem fair. What's your story, AJ?"

"Let's see, I've been working here for about a year."

"Do a lot of Americans work at pizzerias in Italy?" I asked.

"Hardly any," he said. "My dad was transferred here for his job. I started coming in here every day to pick up dinner. Sometimes I would help Maria talk to tourists or translate things for her."

"You speak Italian?"

"Not like, fluent, but I took a class in school and I had a special tutor for a few months before we moved here." He continued, "Anyway, I asked her if I could have a job. I needed the money and she needed a translator and I had some experience as a busboy. The waiter quit,

so now I'm a one-man show. Let me show you around."
He pointed to glass containers. "These hold oil."

"Got it. Oil."

He walked past the ovens. "This is where we cook the pizza."

"Why are they empty?"

He pointed to the dining room. "No customers." I looked at my watch. It was still set to Pennsylvania time, where it was nine in the morning. "What time is it?"

He pulled his phone out of his back pocket and checked. "Three."

"So you'll probably start getting ready for the dinner crowd soon," I said.

AJ laughed. "We can roll out some dough, but since Pizzeria de Roma reopened, we don't get crowds the way we used to. In fact, if something major doesn't happen soon, your aunt will probably close this place."

"Close it? It's been in the family for years," I said. I pointed to a faded black-and-white picture that hung on a wall in the dining room. The glass covering the picture was smudged with grease. "Do you know what this is a picture of?"

He shrugged.

"These are my great-grandparents and their six children." I pointed. "This is Aunt Maria, and this little boy is my grandfather, Luciano—I'm named after him. He left for America with his brother when he was only eight."

AJ looked unimpressed, so I added, "It took ten stormy nights by sea for them to arrive in America. They'd lost their shoes and had to walk miles through snow to meet people they were going to live with. They lost a few toes but managed to start a family." *Man, I could make up a good story.*

He'd perked up around "stormy night." I showed him another picture. "And this small house was the original Amore Pizzeria. My great-grandparents started making pizza and invited friends over on Sunday nights. The crowd grew, so they added tables into their living room. People started placing orders to bring the pizza to their own homes. Soon they had so many customers that they built a restaurant at the end of a narrow cobblestone street near Fontana del Cuore. It's been a landmark ever since."

At the last sec, I added, "It's rumored that the Pope himself orders his pizza from here under a different name."

AJ raised his eyebrows at me and said, "I think maybe you made that part up."

Sometimes a story needs extra spice. My teachers all say I'm good at those little details that make a story really interesting. Although I might go overboard sometimes.

"You may not be able to relate to this the way I can, but trust me, Amore Pizzeria can't close. I'll do whatever it takes to keep it open," I promised.

"How are you going to do that?" AJ asked.

I paused. "I don't know yet, but I will!"

He lifted his hands in an *I give up* gesture. "I believe you. I'll even help."

"Really? Why?"

"I might not be related to Maria, but I like her and I like this job. I need to save money."

"Well, let's get started with a little old-fashioned detective work," I said.

He scratched his head, signaling that he didn't understand what I meant.

"We need to spy—check out Pizzeria de Roma," I explained. "To understand what we're dealing with."

"I'm in, but don't tell Maria. She wouldn't like us going to that place."

"Roger that." I walked to the door. "*Andiamo.*" I'd figured out that meant "Let's go."

6

We strolled down the alley, which was complete with a trio of stray cats who, all put together, were smaller than Meataball. The stores—a bakery, a handbag store, and a butcher shop—that lined the quiet street were dark, closed, out of business. Sprigs of ivy that had sprung up between the cobblestones crept up the buildings' facades, and terra-cotta pots were overgrown with weeds.

"What happened to the stores?" I asked.

"The same thing that's happening at Amore," AJ said. "At the end of this road is a piazza built around the

Fontana del Cuore. There are bigger, brighter, and more modern stores there," he explained. "They may not be better, but you know what they say . . . location, location, location."

We came to the end of the alley.

I had to shade my eyes from the sun, which drenched the crowd of people in the square. It bustled with tourists snapping pictures of the ancient Roman architecture, throwing coins into the Fontana del Cuore, kissing under marble statues, and painting at easels. I had to admit that both the beauty and excitement attracted me.

There was one wide main street that led people, bikes, and motor scooters to and from the piazza. The little roads and alleyways off the square were like unnecessary tentacles around the big attraction that had everything: shops, cafés, restaurants, and carts selling souvenirs, trinkets, key chains, and Pinocchio puppets. It was strange that the crowds and hubbub were so close to Amore Pizzeria without any of it being seen. Of course, that also meant that all these people couldn't see Amore either. That was a problem.

"Isn't there a story about this fountain? I think Uncle Ferdinando told it to me once, but I can't remember it."

"You throw a coin in and wish for your true love, blah blah blah."

"Blah blah blah? You're such a guy." I looked into

427

the fountain. There were enough coins to make some-one very rich. Apparently, lots of people were looking for their true love.

Shining on the other side of the Fontana, like the big deal of the piazza, were multicolored letters spelling PIZZERIA DE ROMA. We entered. Inside, a small group of people waited near a podium for the hostess to seat them.

"I'm going to the restroom," I said, and followed an arrow down a hall. There were three doors. Two were restrooms. The third was cracked open, so I peeked in. It was a small office. There was a red motorcycle-type helmet on a desk and a pile of clothes—jeans, oxford shirt—on the floor. I wanted to go in and snoop around at the papers and files on the desk, but I was too nervous.

When I returned to AJ, he had moved up a bit in the line. It seemed like the hostess was super slow. The place wasn't even that busy!

"Where are you from?" I asked AJ.

"I was born in California."

"And what are you saving money for?" I asked.

"A new guitar," he said. "Right now I play the ukulele."

I asked, "Can you sing?"

"Sure. Who can't sing?"

"Well, everyone thinks they can sing, but not many actually can. Let me hear," I said.

"Now? Here?" He pointed out that we were in a crowded line.

"No time like the present," I said.

"Unless we were in the past or the future," he suggested.

I thought. "Maybe. But we're not. So, stop stalling, SpongeBob SongPants."

AJ cleared his throat. "All right." He sang, "Pizza! Ohhhh, how I love pizza!! Pizza, ba-a-a-by."

Maybe I should tell you about AJ's singing: It wasn't great, but it didn't matter, because he was cute in a California surfer kinda way. The cute and not-great (okay, "bad") singing combo somehow worked for him.

I started clapping, and everyone else joined in. A few people hooted and whooped. The crowd parted, creating a path for us to move to the front of the line. We got seated right away. I guess they must've been hungry for live music if they thought *that* was good.

Pizzeria de Roma was definitely decorated to stand out. The lights were bright, and the walls were painted lime green. It looked more like an American frozen yogurt place than a pizzeria in Rome. There was a stage and a dance floor, both covered with old-fashioned pinball machines that were unused and seemed out of place.

I studied the menu, which was not only in Italian but also in English, Spanish, French, and German. We ordered two Aranciatas and three kinds of pizza. I chose eggplant and sun-dried tomatoes. AJ went with two orders of anchovy. *Blech!*

Not surprisingly, they didn't have ham and pine-apple (my fave)—that was more of an American thing.

"What do you think of this place?" AJ asked.

"It's nice, I guess. Exciting and colorful, but it lacks . . . something. . . ."

"What?" he asked.

"Tradition," I said. "I don't even feel like I'm in Italy. I don't even feel like I'm in a pizza place. I mean, this could be an arcade in Pennsylvania."

He looked around. "Yup. You're exactly right." He sipped his soda. "So, Lucy, what do you do for fun in Amer—" He snapped the menu open in front of his face.

"What are you doing?"

He stretched his mouth around the menu to talk, but kept the rest of his face hidden. "Lorenzo," he whispered.

I glanced around and caught a glimpse of him. He wore a crisply ironed white shirt with the Pizzeria de Roma logo and his name on the lapel and matching white pants under a black apron that was tied at the waist.

"Don't look!" AJ snapped.

I casually brushed my hair in front of my face and refocused my eyes to my fork. Aunt Maria was right, they were shiny.

We waited a minute.

I scanned the floor to see if Lorenzo's feet were still there. "He's gone."

AJ lowered his menu. "That was close."

Just then, a waitress appeared with our pizzas. I had to admit, they looked really good.

I hung my nose into the steam. "Smells good," I said. I cut a piece of eggplant, closed my eyes, and slid it into my mouth. I let it sit on my tongue for a second. Then I opened my eyes.

"What?" AJ asked.

I didn't answer, just chewed and swallowed.

"Good?" he asked. "Do you like it?"

Again, I didn't answer. I cut a piece with sun-dried tomatoes. Again, I put it in my mouth, closed my eyes, and let my tongue roll around it.

When I opened my eyes this time, I saw that AJ had finished both of his anchovy pies. BOTH!

How do boys do that?

Through a full mouth, he asked, "Good?"

"No. The crust is doughy and undercooked. And

Aunt Maria's sauce blows this away. This could be"—I lowered my voice—"from a jar."

I looked at all the people in the crowded restaurant. "Look, there's no, 'Ooh. Mmmm.' Or 'This is so good.' They're only here because it's convenient. There's nothing special or memorable about this place except maybe the big dance floor, but they don't even use that. The food is like blah with a side of meh." I smiled and pushed the food away. "This is great!" I said.

"You just said it was 'meh.'"

"That's what's great. Amore Pizzeria is way better. We just need something to attract customers. And the place could use a little sprucing up, if you know that I mean. Luckily, I know the Queen of Bling, who can help with a makeover."

"I like your optimism." AJ eyed my plate. "You going to eat that?" I slid the plate to him. "Do you have a good idea for how to attract customers?" he asked.

I grinned. "Actually, I have *two* good ideas."

7

My ideas: samples and couples.

The next day I started with samples. I rolled the dough for a big pizza, very thin like my dad had taught me—of course he learned from Aunt Maria. I planned to top it with cheese, Aunt Maria's sauce, and an amazing classic Italian topping, sausage. Its deliciousness would lure people down the narrow cobblestone alley. Once they arrived, I'd match them. Then word would spread—maybe it would even trend on social media. All those coin throwers looking for love would come here. If my plan worked, I'd spend the rest of my visit teaching Aunt Maria how to match when I was gone.

Hmmm . . . I should probably start keeping good notes to share with her.

In the kitchen with me was Vito, the cook who didn't speak English. He packed a meat mixture into balls and hummed loudly.

Then I heard something else, a sound coming from a vent near one of the ovens.

It was Gianna's voice from Jane Attilio's apartment upstairs.

I listened harder, but AJ came into the kitchen and interrupted my eavesdropping.

He had tied a red bandanna around his head in a rock star kind of way.

"I want one," I said about the bandanna. He pulled one out of a drawer. My hands were floury, so he tied it for me in a Little Red Riding Hood style—under my chin.

He laughed.

Even I chuckled a little before saying, "Come on, like yours."

He switched it to the back of my head over my long, curly hair. I took a quick peek at my reflection in the stainless-steel oven door; it actually looked cool.

Just then Meataball rubbed against my legs. "Is there another bandanna?" I asked AJ.

He handed one to me, and I tied it around Meataball's neck, so he could be included. He purred.

"So, what are we doing here?" AJ asked.

"Making samples, just like the food court at the mall. It works there. Maybe it will here." I brushed on more sauce, making sure to get all the way to the edges. I dipped a spoon into the sauce and put just a smidgen on my lips. "I just love it. I swear I could sit in this pot all day, like a sauce hot tub."

"I'd go in with you," he said. "We'd need a big pot." He rolled out his own crust and swirled sauce on it.

"What's your fave topping?" I asked.

"Duh! Anchovies."

"Really?" This was a drag. In my experience, ham and pineapple wasn't a match with anchovies. At least I didn't think so. After all, I was still a beginner at this matching stuff.

I finished off my pizza with fresh mozzarella and Italian sausage, with a dash of Parmesan cheese and oregano.

AJ put my masterpiece on a wooden board and showed me how to slide the pizza into the oven and take the board out.

"Do you have little plates that we can serve the samples on?" I asked.

"White paper pie plates?" He indicated a stack resembling the Leaning Tower of Pisa, which I'd called the Leaning Tower of Pizza until, like, two years ago.

If Gianna was here, she'd have used fancy scrapbook scissors to give each plate pretty edges and then decorated them with markers and glitter, and maybe hung ribbon from the bottom. "They'll work."

AJ looked into the pizza oven. "It's done." He went to open it, but I put my hand on the silver handle keeping it closed.

"A few more seconds for *extra* crispiness."

"One Mississippi, two Mississippi, three Mississippi, four—get the pizza cutter—Mississippi," he said.

I grabbed the rolling pizza cutter.

"Five—I think this is a good idea—Mississippi," he said. "Six—and it smells good—Mississippi."

I said, "Seven—but you also liked Pizzeria de Roma's yucky pizza—Mississippi."

He said, "Eight—I was really hungry—Mississippi."

"Nine—you're going to love this—Mississippi."

"Ten—can we stop now—Mississippi?"

"Yes—Mississippi."

AJ opened the oven door and in one quick swoop

slid the wooden board under my rectangular pizza, gently removed it, and carried it to a cutting board that was lightly sprinkled with flour. AJ smacked the round cutter into the crust and quickly ran it from one side to the other, making bite-size squares. I put each one on a paper plate.

Soon I'd filled a tray. "Are you going to try one?" I asked.

"Duh."

We each took a square. I crunched into mine and enjoyed the melted cheese and salty Italian sausage.

AJ said, "Mmm. *So* good."

"That's the reaction we're looking for. Let's go before it gets cold."

On our way out, a deliveryman who reminded me of a tanned Santa Claus came in the back door with bread. "*Buongiorno!*" he cried with a huge smile.

"*Buongiorno!*" I returned the same excitement and gave him a sample.

"*Delizioso!*" His stomach shook like a bowl full of jelly.

We left the cook and deliveryman speaking in rapid-fire Italian and strolled down the alley. I looked in each of the closed shops and thought about how sad it was that these businesses had closed because more modern stores had opened on the main piazza. That was sad with a scoop of bummer on top.

We stood at the end of the piazza opposite Pizzeria de Roma, in sight of the crowds of people—both tourists and locals.

I called, "Amore Pizzeria here! Free samples!"

People looked but didn't come over. I tried again, "Come and get your free sample from Amore Pizzeria!"

A couple of tourists—fanny packs are a dead giveaway—came over.

"Help yourself." I held out the tray.

I saw a girl looking at me from a distance. I called to her, "Would you like to try a free sample? Bring your friends, too."

Soon I was surrounded by people. When *other* people saw the crowd, they came over to see what was going on too. I called out, "This pizza is from Amore, which is behind me at the end of that cute street. It's traditional pizza made with a signature secret sauce that's been passed down for generations. My aunt Maria won't even tell me what's in it. That's how secret it is!"

(Like I said, a good story has a select few perfect details. Like telling them the sauce was from a secret family recipe. People love that stuff!)

Everyone smiled and seemed to enjoy their pizza

samples. Several started walking down the quiet little alley.

I said, "Maybe you should get crust ready at the shop."

"Roger that," AJ said, copying my trademark phrase I'd used earlier. He grinned at me, showing off his dimples.

I can't believe someone this cute could like anchovies.

8

❦

I entertained the sample-eating crowd. "Aunt Maria goes to the vegetable auction every three days for the best, naturally ripe tomatoes." I added, "To keep the recipe secret, she does it late at night when no one's around. She learned from her mother, who learned from her mother. It's written down and locked in a safe that can only be opened upon her death. Her last will and testament specifies which family member will inherit the recipe."

I didn't know that any of this was true, but I didn't know for a fact that it was *untrue*.

The crowd oohed and aahed about the samples and listened to every word.

I said, "Amore Pizzeria is just at the end of this street. Come on down for some traditional Italian pizza. I can smell it from here!"

My tray was empty, and a small group of people started moving toward the alley.

With part one of my two-part plan complete, I hustled back to the restaurant, where three tables had seated themselves and more customers waited by the door.

AJ took orders and delivered drinks. When he walked past me, he said, "More samples are finished in the oven."

"Roger that," I said. I quickly swished the board under the rectangular pie and cut it the way AJ had shown me. Then I walked around the shop, making personal deliveries and refilling drinks—mostly Cokes and fizzy water that they called *acqua frizzante*. I pointed to the family pictures on the walls and explained who was who. There were some people I didn't know much about, so I made up stories about them to keep customers amused until their lunches arrived.

"Grab those dishes and follow me." AJ indicated steaming bowls of spaghetti—of course Amore served more than pizza—that Vito had set on the counter between the kitchen and dining room.

Aunt Maria walked in the front door, followed by a man in a business suit.

"My goodness," she said. "Busy lunch today."

"Yes," I said.

She introduced the man, "This is Eduardo Macelli from the bank."

I smiled. "Hi. Welcome to Amore Pizzeria. Will you be having lunch?"

"*Sì*," he said.

"Follow me to this table just beneath a beautiful painting of the very port that my grandfather sailed from on his way to America. His name was Luciano. I was named after him," I said. "My name is Lucy."

Eduardo Macelli sat down. He was a petite man, bald and thin.

"Let me guess," I said, studying him. "*Acqua fizzante*?"

"*Sì.*"

I returned to the kitchen, where Aunt Maria checked her sauce supply. "Be sure he gets the best service," she said to me about Eduardo Macelli.

"I will." I took him the last sample with his fizzy water. He bit into it. I waited for a reaction but didn't get one.

"Do you like it?"

"Sì." It seemed Eduardo Macelli wasn't much of a talker.

I asked, "Do you know what kind of pizza you want?"

"Surprise me," he said with a thick Italian accent and a straight face.

"I'll do that."

I wrote down one ricotta cheese and one salami. Those might be unusual in America but were pretty standard here in Rome. I gave the order slip to AJ, because I wasn't sure where it was supposed to go next.

Then I watched the customers and started making couples in my head. Since the pizza toppings here were so different from the ones at home, I sort of had to start from scratch. I had pepperoni, mushrooms, and meatball all worked out, but ricotta cheese and salami were new territory for me. This required serious concentration.

A pretty woman with a cute pink purse was speaking French with her female companion while savoring *bianca* (that's white pizza) with asparagus and burrata mozzarella—a cheese with a smooth, creamy center that's spreadable. It is majorly *delizioso*.

A table of four men nearby had ordered a table-size margarita pizza. (Margarita is topped with olive oil, garlic, fresh basil, tomatoes, and mozzarella and Parmesan cheeses.)

When I passed them, my stomach fluttered like a

butterfly had just burst out of a cocoon. And an idea hit me.

AJ had added up checks for the tables. "I'll deliver those," I offered.

First I gave Eduardo Macelli his pizza. Then I placed a leather folio containing a check on the table with the French ladies and gave another to the men eating margarita.

Then I watched and waited.

When the ladies realized I'd given them the wrong bill, they scanned the tables for the order matching the food on the check.

Mademoiselle bianca with asparagus and burrata mozzarella approached one of the margarita men. "*Pardonnez-moi*," she said in French. Then in English she said, "I think this is your check."

Mr. Margarita opened the folio. "And this is the one for you," he said with an Italian accent.

They traded, pausing for only a second when they each had a hand on the same folio.

The butterflies in my stomach flapped their wings.

"What is your name?" he asked.

"Murielle."

He said, "Would you and your friend join us for coffee, Murielle?"

"*Bien sûr*. Of course."

The ladies fitted chairs around the men's table, and AJ brought them espresso and cappuccino.

My first match!

I found a pad used for taking orders and jotted notes about matching margarita and bianca pizzas.

AJ leaned on the counter. "What happened there?"

"Remember I told you that I had two ideas? The samples were just to get people here. That"—I pointed to the table—"is my second idea. You see, I'm kind of a . . . a bit of a . . . I guess you'd call it a . . . romance coordinator. I—"

"Lucy." Aunt Maria waved for me to come into the kitchen.

"I'll tell you later," I said to AJ, and headed to Aunt Maria.

AJ called after me, "Uh, yeah. You will. You can't just tell someone that and walk away."

I turned. "Sorry." Once in the kitchen, I asked Aunt Maria, "What's up?"

"What was that with the check?"

"I thought I would introduce *them*"—I indicated the women—"to *them*." I indicated the men.

"Why?"

"Well, because of the pizza they ordered," I confessed. "You see, I kind of guess things about people based on how they like their pizza. Something told me that the margarita and bianca people would make a good romantic match."

"*Mamma mia!*" Aunt Maria exclaimed. "Who taught you to do that?"

"No one. It was just like a feeling I had in my gut one day at home at a pizza shop. And I went with it. First it was just in my head. Then I tried it for real. And it worked!"

"It is the *matchmaking*. It is not good. Do not mess with the love."

"But it could be good for business," I said. "Look around. They'll totally Instagram and tweet this stuff."

"What is this 'tweet'? Like a bird?" She shook her head, not really wanting an explanation. "No. No more, Lucy. Understand? *Capisce?*"

I sighed. "All right. But it seems a shame to let this skill go to waste."

"No more! Don't mess with the love."

"Okay," I said. I walked back out to the dining room, angry and confused. Why did it bother her so much?

I walked right past AJ without explaining anything and approached Mr. Macelli. "Did you like the pizza?" I asked him.

"Yes. *Buono.* Now I'll try"—he pointed to two items on the menu—"this and this."

"You're still hungry? Super!" I said. "I'll get that for you." I took his glass. "And I'll refill this."

I put the order in, brought the drink, and waited on other tables. As the lunch crowd faded, I wiped down tables and reset them for dinner.

Eduardo Macelli sat for another hour, determined to try as many menu items as he could before exploding. He had taken a pen and paper out of his briefcase and wrote things down.

"Can I get you anything else?" I finally asked him.

"Sì. Your *zia* Maria."

"Okay." I thought he was going to file a complaint about my waitressing or the food. "Is everything okay? This is my first day."

"Everything is *buono*. I want to talk."

I pulled Aunt Maria away from the food prep area, where she was peeling garlic, and sent her to Eduardo's table. She wrung her hands nervously as she approached him.

I walked past the table several times, lingering to catch what they were saying, but I couldn't translate their hushed Italian tones.

What was going on with those two?

9

After all the customers had left, I was so tired that I would've been happy with a cereal bar and a bed. But then I saw the spread of Italian food that Aunt Maria had set on a table in the dining room, and I forgot all about a cereal bar.

A mountain of homemade pasta with an Aunt Maria–invented sauce that had a pinkish tint to it, a chopped salad with vegetables of every color, and crusty bread wooed me to sit at the table set for seven.

"What's all this?" I asked.

"We will eat together," Aunt Maria said. She poured olive oil on little plates and sprinkled it with seasoning. "Sit." She broke off a piece of bread and dipped it in the oil. No one butters bread in Italy.

As if on cue, Gianna, Jane, and a young guy my age, looking absurd in a mid-length black skirt with many layers of pink tulle underneath, entered Amore Pizzeria through the back door.

"Ah, Rico. Here is Lucy. You remember her, sì?" She dashed into the kitchen, calling for AJ and Vito.

"Remember what?" I asked him, confused.

He shrugged. "I guess she meant that she told me you were coming. It's all she's talked about for days," he said. He popped a chunk of bread in his mouth.

"You don't have an Italian accent either," I said to Rico.

"Nope. I was born in the US. But my parents are Italian. We moved back when I was, like, six," he explained. "A lot of tourists come into Amore Pizzeria. It helps Maria to have fluent English speakers around."

That all made sense to me.

AJ sat down and asked Rico, "You the model again?"

Rico said, "Seems that I have the best legs." He jutted his bruised and battered typical boy leg out for everyone to see.

As far as banged-up boy legs go, I guessed his were pretty good. But it wasn't his legs that struck me; it was something about his eyes—dark, dark brown—that was strangely familiar. He reminded me of a boy I sometimes put in my stories.

Did I know him from somewhere? Were we online friends?

I didn't think so. A cute Italian boy who didn't mind wearing a skirt seemed like something I would remember. I got a weird feeling in my gut. Was it telling me to match him with someone? I didn't even know what kind of pizza he liked.

Rico said to me, "I know this might look weird to you, but I'm an unusual guy. I like football, snakes, loud music, horror movies, and"—he indicated the skirt—"I happen to have a knack for fashion. And, FYI, I don't usually wear skirts."

"You're right. That *is* unusual. But I like that." I whispered, "I'm a little different myself."

"Yeah? How?" he asked.

"Maybe I'll tell you one of these days."

"I can't wait."

Gianna looked at me talking to Rico and raised an eyebrow. Recently she'd been asking me if I thought there were any cute boys at school, if I liked anyone, etc.

Maybe she thought it was somehow her responsibility as my older sister to show me how to meet boys. She dropped her brow and said, "Dinner looks great. I'm so hungry."

Rico said, "Those are Maria's favorite three words to hear." His name and appearance were blatantly Italian— dark hair, skin, and eyes—but he had no accent. It seemed that Aunt Maria had somehow attracted Americans.

Aunt Maria said to everyone, "*Mangia*." Then she called, "Meataball! Psst! Psst!"

The cat ran in and sat on his haunches next to a plate of fettuccini that Aunt Maria had cut up and put on the floor for him.

"It's his favorite," AJ said to me.

Then she dished out a generous bowl of pasta for each of us. My stomach growled at the squishy sound of the white cream sauce hitting the plate. I hadn't realized how hungry I was.

"Did you work hard today?" Aunt Maria asked Gianna.

Gianna said, "Jane and Rico don't stop. Not even for lunch."

Aunt Maria said, "Then you eat a big dinner, like AJ."

AJ twirled pasta around his fork, making sure no noodle went astray. Then he crammed the forkful into his mouth. "You can always count on me to be hungry," he said through the mouthful of pasta.

We didn't talk for a few minutes while we all took the edge off our hunger. Then I asked, "What happened with Eduardo Macelli today?"

Gianna asked, "Who's that?"

Aunt Maria said, "He is a man from the bank."

"Did he agree to give you an extension?" Jane asked.

"We are a . . . a bit behind in some of our payments since Pizzeria de Roma reopened," Aunt Maria explained. "But Eduardo Macelli is going to give me an extra month. This is good."

"That's great news," Jane said. She held up her Coke. "*Salute!*" she said.

We all repeated, "*Salute!*"

"What changed his mind?" Jane asked.

"He loved the food and thought there was a lot of customers," Aunt Maria said. Then she asked, "What happened? Why so many customers today?"

I explained about the samples and the stories on the square. "It seems they like good food, a good story, and a traditional Italian experience. You can give them that," I said.

You can give them more, but you put the kibosh on matchmaking.

452

"You know," I said, looking around the restaurant. "The place could use a little refresh."

"Refresh?" Aunt Maria asked.

Gianna clapped her hands. "Oh, I'm so good at refreshing. We can go with colors like red wine and espresso brown. And we can get fresh plants and cut flowers and pretty little candles on the tables. Plus, it will give me something to do while I'm here, since I'm not working in the shop."

Aunt Maria looked around. "Maybe the place does need a—what you call it?—refresh."

Gianna said, "It's kind of a big job. We're gonna need some help."

"No worries." Rico leaned back in his chair. "I know a few guys who can come over." He crossed his bruised legs under the pink pouffy skirt.

"I'll help too," I volunteered.

AJ's mouth was full again, so he raised his hand, indicating he would help too.

Gianna walked around, explaining her vision for Amore Pizzeria's face-lift. "A mirror could go here, and I can dress up all these frames and rehang them."

"I have any dress-up supply you could ever need," Jane offered.

"And I never travel without my bling kit," Gianna

said. "Then we can get a few trees, maybe a ficus, and wrap them in little white lights—a very classy and romantic feel."

Romance. That was exactly the direction I wanted to go. But *nooooooooo*.

"I'll make a new curtain," Jane added.

"Oh, and get this: when it gets dark, we can line both sides of the street with LUMINARIES!" Gianna squealed. "Oh, I love, love, *love* luminaries."

Aunt Maria said, "This sounds all very good, but like a lot of money."

Rico said, "I know a guy who owns a florist shop. He owes me a favor. He can bring the stuff you need."

"Okay. Is a good idea. A little refresh," Aunt Maria relented. "Tomorrow is Wednesday and we no open. This is the day I go around Rome for my ingredients and make sauce. Can you do it in one day?"

"Totes," Gianna promised. "Except for the walls. It could take some time to get that paint off the brick. We can do that at night. The rest is easy peasy."

"'Totes'?" Aunt Maria looked confused. "'Peasy'?"

10

The next morning I found Gianna in the pizzeria early. She studied the current decor with a tilted head and occasionally wrote things on a clipboard. She would DIY this place from falling apart to fabulous.

"Aloha!" Rico said, walking through the back door. No skirt today. Ripped jeans and worn black basketball high-tops.

Aloha? Random.

Rico led three people who I guess were his "guys." Their tool belts told me they were ready to work. He said, "These are my friends." I gave them a wave. "They're good at hammering and stuff."

"I'm sure Gi has stuff to hammer," I said. "I'll head upstairs to see if I can help Jane with curtains, but I'm not really the sewing type."

"Okay, but promise me one thing." He looked very serious.

"What?"

"Please help her choose the colors. She is an amazing designer, but her fabric selecting? Ugh!" He covered his face.

"I'll do my best," I said, but the truth was that I was kind of "ugh" myself.

Jane dashed from one side of the apartment to the other, throwing around balls of yarn, yards of fabrics, spools of thread, and measuring tape. I had to duck or a flying sketch pad would've clocked me right in the noggin.

"Redecorating Amore Pizzeria is a great idea, Lucy," Jane said excitedly without looking up from her searching.

If she thought that was good, she hadn't heard my best idea of all. "Thanks."

"Here it is." She pulled a key ring with swatches of fabric from under a stack of fashion magazines and flipped through them. "Oh, I can't decide. I like this one and this one and this one. And this one is pretty." She stared at them. "Hmmm . . . What do you think?"

"Um, I'm really not great at this stuff." I remembered what Rico had said. "Maybe we should call for backup."

She nodded and stomped on the floor four times.

Bam—bam—bam—bam.

"We'll ask Rico," she said. "He has a great eye for color."

"I wouldn't have guessed," I said.

"Why?"

"Maybe because he's a boy."

"True, but he's a boy with an eye for fashion," she said. "A good eye too. I like that he is confident enough to be this tough guy who likes typical boy stuff, but this stuff too."

I nodded. That *was* pretty cool.

I was walking around the apartment/sewing studio waiting for Rico, when I heard a sound coming from downstairs. I walked toward it. It floated up from a vent. The same way I had heard what was happening up here when I was in the kitchen, I could hear people downstairs.

It was Gianna. She said, "What are you doing here? My aunt would flip out if she knew."

The only person I could imagine she would say that to was Lorenzo from Pizzeria de Roma. He was here early.

457

I didn't like that Lorenzo was in Amore's kitchen. I had just made up that stuff about the recipe being locked in a safe. For all I knew, it was written on a Post-it or sitting on a counter somewhere.

I heard Lorenzo say, "I wanted to tell you something."

I waved to Jane. "Come here. Listen," I whispered.

She bent toward the vent.

"Really, you can't be in the shop," Gianna said. "Maybe we can go out for a walk or something?"

Lorenzo asked, "Can I have a Coke?"

Rico walked into the apartment to find Jane and me crouched on the floor. "Looks like fun," he said.

We both shushed him.

"Jeez," he said, and bent down next to us.

Lorenzo was saying, "I am very thirsty."

Gianna said, "Fine. I'll get you some Coke, but then you have to leave."

"*Sì.* That is good."

I could hear Gianna's wooden sandals clopping on the floor as she left the kitchen and walked to the bar area, where the soda was kept in a refrigerator. I wished I could see what Lorenzo was doing.

Gianna and her shoes came back in. "Here you go."

"*Grazie*," he said. Then he exclaimed, "Whoa! That is a *grande* cat."

"Lots of him to love," Gianna said, and I imagined her scratching Meataball's ears.

Then I guess Lorenzo had sipped his soda, because he said, "Oh! It is great. And you know what else is great? You. You look very pretty today. I love your hair."

"Thank you," Gianna said. She was probably twirling a lock of it and blushing.

Rico whispered, "He's smooth."

"Shhh!" we snapped at him.

"What was that?" we heard Lorenzo ask downstairs. Had he heard us?

"Some friends who are helping me redecorate," Gianna said.

"What are you redecorating?" Lorenzo asked.

"The dining room," Gianna said. "Did you have something to tell me?"

"Sì, I came to tell you that I would like to see you again," Lorenzo said. "I want to show you Rome. Can I come get you later?"

"I'd like to see you, too," Gianna said. "Maybe I can sneak out for a while. Text me."

We heard the back door of the restaurant close.

Rico laughed, "She's a rebel, defying your aunt Maria. Not many people do that."

But if she had, maybe I could too. . . .

"Love makes people do crazy things," Jane pointed out.

"They just met," Rico argued. "How could it be love?"

"You don't believe in love at first sight?" I asked.

"I think maybe there is a spark or something at first sight," he said. "But—"

"Shh," I said, because I heard another sound. Noises came from downstairs: boxes sliding on the floor, the walk-in refrigerator opening and closing, and the whistling of a cheerful tune.

"It's just the deliveryman," Rico said. "He's here, like, every day."

Rico took his messenger-style bag, which hung diagonally across his chest, and tossed it into a chair. "You banged on the floor. What did you need?"

Jane held up the four swatches.

"Curtains?" he asked.

Jane nodded.

"This one." He chose the plainest of the three. "It'll be perfect."

"Wow," I said. "That was fast."

He shrugged. "I have an eye. Not sure if it's a blessing or a curse."

"You mean because fashion and sewing are usually for girls?"

"No. That doesn't bother me. I meant because everyone always wants my fashion advice. I get lots of calls and texts from guys who want me to help them pick out clothes for a job interview or a date."

"Do you help them?" I asked.

"Yeah. I have a gift, and it wouldn't be fair if I didn't use it to help people who need me," he said. "But I get something too. Then I can call and ask them for favors. It's not a bad deal."

"I guess that explains all the guys you know."

"Yep."

He picked up the worn leather bag, tossed it over his shoulder, and said, "And for the record, fashion isn't just for girls."

"Oh. Sorry. You're right."

"Don't sweat it." His cell phone rang. He answered it, and after a few one-word responses, he said, "I gotta go for a while, but I'll be back."

"A fashion emergency?"

"My mom. I left without cleaning my room," he said. "She gets mad about stuff like that." He shrugged.

"Mine gets mad about that too," I said.

As he left, I got another weird feeling, like I'd seen him do that shrug before. But I couldn't have seen him do that before—I'd just met him yesterday.

Weird.

11

~~~

It was late in the day and time to show Aunt Maria what we'd done with the dining room.

She'd finished making sauce a few hours earlier and had gone to her apartment for a nap. AJ, Rico, Gianna, and I were sweeping the tile floor when Jane pushed the door open with her butt.

One of Jane's hands covered Aunt Maria's eyes while the other guided her to sit on a stool. Jane held the door open with her foot for an extra second, allowing Meataball to waddle in behind them.

"I found her baking at the apartment," Jane said. A basket of something steamy hung from her wrist.

"Thank goodness," AJ said. "I'm starving."

"I cannot wait to see what you kids have done." Aunt Maria giggled.

Gianna said, "One, two, three, TA-DA!"

Jane moved her hand.

"*Mamma mia!*" Aunt Maria cried. "It look so lovely. How did you do all of this so fast?" She wiped away a tear.

"Rico's friends were very helpful," Gianna explained. She started the tour with the biggest wall. "The pictures are in their same frames, but I added an antique finish, so they all match." They'd been hung in a lovely pattern around a huge mirror whose frame was also antiqued. The mirror made the whole dining room look bigger and brighter.

Gianna continued, "Each table has fresh-cut flowers. The tablecloths, which Rico hemmed, match the curtains." To Rico and Jane she said, "Thank you."

"What can I say?" Rico sipped espresso from a little white mug. He had proven that he was as good with a hammer as he was with a sewing machine—definitely an interesting combination for a teenage boy.

"The seats have been re-covered with black fabric."

463

Gianna held one up to show everyone. "Tonight while we're all sleeping, someone is coming to scrape the paint off the brick. *That* will really look great, but it might take several nights."

"*Perfetto!*" Aunt Maria gasped. "Since Ferdinando passed away, I have not been keeping up on these things."

"The menus need updating too," Gianna said. "I'll work on that tomorrow."

"Can I help?" I asked Gianna. "I have a few ideas for some new pizzas—with a little American inspiration, if you know what I mean."

"Sure," Gianna agreed. "You can help me before I show it to Aunt Maria for her approval."

Aunt Maria gave Gianna the first big hug, then the rest of us. "You must all be very tired. Why don't you get some rest?" She pulled a napkin away from the contents of her basket and a puff of sugary sweetness floated upward, covering the smell of cleaning products. "Not without a little food in your stomachs. Something that will stick to your ribs."

Let me tell you about a warm *sfogliatella* pastry. It's amazing with a side order of WOW.

"Oh yeah!" Rico grabbed a pastry and left the restaurant. I watched him through the front window as he rode away on his bike. Rico was an interesting guy. Probably pepperoni or onion. It was hard to peg. I wished I could figure out who he reminded me of. Someone—but I couldn't put my finger on it.

I was almost too tired to eat. Almost. So I took a pastry and walked out the front door, practically bumping into a woman on my way.

"Oh, *pardon*. So sorry." It was the French woman from yesterday, a.k.a. Bianca with asparagus and burrata mozzarella cheese.

Gianna said, "We're closed on Wednesdays."

"*Oui*. I know. I came to talk"—she gestured toward me—"to you."

"Huh? Me? Why?" I asked, confused.

"You mixed up my lunch check yesterday with Angelo's." She sighed when she said his name.

"Angelo?"

"The man at the other table." That must be the man who'd ordered the margarita pizza. "We walked around Rome all afternoon. We have so much in common," she said. "I just wanted to say thank you. So, *merci*!"

Gianna whispered to me, "You didn't?"

"Just a little," I whispered back. "She was the only one. Aunt Maria saw and told me, 'No mess with the love.'" I imitated Aunt Maria.

The woman heard me. "Mess with love?" she asked.

"You see, I think maybe I can make love matches based on what pizza people order," I explained. "No biggie. But I tried it on you and Angelo."

"Not *maybe*. You can!" she squealed. "You're a *matchmaker*? *C'est fantastique!*" She held out her hand. "I am Murielle duPluie. I used to be quite a popular TV news reporter in Paris. Now I work for the Rome newspaper. All of Rome needs to know about this. I will come back tomorrow with a photographer." She looked out into the open air and moved her hand along words that weren't there. "Pizzeria Matchmaker."

Gianna and I stared at the imaginary letters.

"You may get famous," Murielle duPluie said. "And Amore Pizzeria, too!" She skipped down the alley. I looked at it for a minute and imagined what it would look like lined with luminaries on either side.

"Wait," Gianna called out after her, but Murielle duPluie had already lifted her cell phone to her ear. Gianna said to me, "That's not good."

"It's not *good*; it's great! Maybe I am a"—I looked out into the open air and moved my hand along words that weren't there—"Pizzeria Matchmaker! Just think, people could get awesome food and meet the love of their life. What could be better?" Without waiting for an answer, I said, "If Amore Pizzeria is famous, it'll make lots of money and stay in business. That's the best thing we can do for Aunt Maria."

"I don't know, Lucy. You know what Aunt Maria said. I don't think she'll go for it."

"She wouldn't *if she knew*."

"You're not gonna tell her?" Gianna asked. "I think she'll notice a reporter and photographer in her restaurant."

"Not if we get her out for a few hours."

"How are we gonna do that?" Gianna asked.

"I have an idea."

Gianna grinned. "You always do."

12

The next day, well rested and refreshed, Gianna and I walked from Aunt Maria's apartment to Amore Pizzeria.

"You think it'll work?" she asked.

"Yep," I said. "When I give you the sign, you go for it. Until then, act totally normal." I handed her the slip of paper she would need to get Aunt Maria out of the pizzeria for a few hours.

"Fine, but for the record, I don't like this."

I said, "Okay. I'll make a note in the official record." I pretended to open a big, heavy book. I grunted when I opened its huge cover. I dipped an imaginary quill pen in ink and as I wrote, I said, "Gianna doesn't like it." I put the pen back in the ink cup, closed the giant book, and said, "Done."

Gianna rolled her eyes at me.

We found Aunt Maria kneading dough as AJ filled salt and pepper shakers.

I gave Gianna the signal—a thumb in my ear and wiggling my other four fingers.

Gianna flipped through some papers and said, "Oh, Aunt Maria, there's a phone message here for you."

Aunt Maria was up to her elbows in dough. "What's it say, the message?"

"Um—it's from the bank, I think. Um, I'm not sure."

Snap! Gianna was gonna crack under the pressure; I could feel it. Gianna Rossi could sneak around with Lorenzo from Pizzeria de Roma, but ask her to feed a fake phone message to Aunt Maria, and she crumbled like a block of extra-sharp Asiago cheese.

I took the slip of paper and read it. "It's from Eduardo Macelli. He wants to meet you at the bank at one o'clock. It says you should bring your business plan."

"The business plan?! That is all the way across the city with my friend Anna. She is very smart with the numbers."

469

"Maybe she can e-mail it to—" Gianna started saying, but I stomped on her foot. "Ah!" she cried.

Aunt Maria ignored her. "E-mail? Pfft! I take the bus. That's how we get things done. On the bus. I do not need the e-mail or the wonder web."

"You mean the World Wide Web?" Gianna asked. "The Internet?"

"Neither of these. If I want to tell you something, I call on the telephone. Not this kind"—she pointed to my cell phone with floury hands—"the regular kind. Or I write a letter with the paper and pen. Remember paper?"

"Yes. I remember paper," I said. "So, if you have to take the bus all the way to your friend's apartment before the bank, you should probably leave around noon. And I guess you won't be back until two, right? Because you'll have to bring the plan back to your friend."

She studied the wall clock. "Sì. Two. *Mamma mia!* I'll miss lunch. That is no good."

"Don't you *mamma mia* yourself. We'll be cool," I reassured her. "We can totally handle it. It's like, mega cool."

"What is this 'mega cool'?"

"She means it's all fine," Gianna said. "We can handle it. Jane, Rico, and I will help."

Aunt Maria looked at AJ.

"It's okay," he added. "I'm all over it."

"All over what? I just want you working at the lunch. Do not go all over anything," Aunt Maria said to him. She stirred sauce, checked on a tray of lasagna that was cooking in the oven, and gave a whole bunch of instructions to Vito, the cook who didn't speak English. At exactly noon, she hung her apron up and left through the back door.

"What are you gonna do when she goes to the bank and Eduardo Macelli doesn't know what she's talking about?" Gianna asked.

AJ interrupted, "Do I want to know what's going on?"

"No!" Gianna and I both said to him.

I said to Gianna, "Don't worry about Eduardo Macelli. He won't be at the bank. I took care of that."

The back door opened. It was Rico. "*Aloha*, pizzeria peeps," he said to AJ and Vito. "And Madame Big Idea."

"Big idea?" AJ asked. "Are you talking about the matchmaking?"

"I was talking about the redecorating," Rico said. "But matchmaking sounds . . . well . . . weird."

"I don't believe in matchmakers," AJ said.

Rico said, "I definitely want to hear more about this, but I understand there's a rogue chair cover needing attention pronto." He held up a staple gun as if it was a chain saw. "It had better prepare to be stapled."

"I'll get that." Gianna took the stapler from him. "We don't want anyone getting hurt."

"You can use a staple gun?" Rico asked her.

"You should see what I can do with duct tape." She ran out and pounded the silver stapler into the chair. That flapping piece of fabric didn't stand a chance.

I asked AJ, "How do the samples look?"

He said, "Almost done!"

There was a knock at the back door. Rico opened it and held it for the deliveryman with the big Santa Claus belly. Santa pushed in a wheeled cart stacked with pasta—gnocchi, linguini, ravioli, and cavatelli. "*Buongiorno!*" he cried.

Then the front door opened, and potential matches walked in. Through the opening between the kitchen and dining room, I said, "Welcome to Amore Pizzeria."

I glanced at Gianna. She sighed. "Go ahead. Do your thing."

"Now? You're doing it *now*?" AJ whispered. "The matchmaking?"

"Yep," I said. "Here it goes."

"I gotta see this," Rico said. The three of them stood at the counter between the kitchen and dining room, leaned on their elbows, and watched me work my magic.

13

❧

"What kind of pizza do you like?" I asked the first pair of women.

"Kalamata olives," one of them said. "We get it every time, but we've never had it here."

"You'll love it." I started thinking about a match for kalamata olives. People in America usually don't get that, so I figured it would be the same as black olives, which I would probably match with mushrooms, but it wasn't an exact science. I had a hunch about what else might do the trick. And if my plan worked like I hoped it would, the match I was looking for would come through the door soon.

I put the order in and sat more tables.

"I'm heading out with samples. Vito can read English, so give the orders to him," AJ said. "Gianna will handle drinks, and Rico will clear dirty dishes."

"Gotcha." AJ left, and the next customer walked in. It was the person I was waiting for—Eduardo Macelli from the bank. "Welcome back," I said.

He asked, "Is your *zia* here? I received the message to meet her."

"You did?" Of course he did—I'd left him the message to come here. "I think maybe there's been a mix-up, because she went to meet you at the bank," I said. "I'll call her on her cell phone." I knew Aunt Maria didn't have a cell phone. "Why don't you eat while you wait for her?" I was going to set him up with more than lunch.

"*Sì.*" He looked around the dining room. "Looks different," he said. "*Buono.*"

"Thanks. It's a work in progress." I hooked my arm into his. "You know, some of the glue on the chairs is still drying." I didn't even know if the chairs had any glue. "I hope you don't mind if I seat you with these two ladies just for a little while." Before Eduardo Macelli or the ladies could object, I dashed to get him fizzy water.

474

I remembered that Eduardo had liked the ricotta that I'd brought him yesterday. It wasn't a precise match with kalamata olives, but I had a feeling about this—bubbles in my gut. It felt right.

I told Gianna the drinks I needed. She pointed to Eduardo Macelli. "Why is he here?"

"So that he won't be at the bank when Aunt Maria gets there."

"Oh. Makes sense," she said.

"And who knows. Maybe he'll meet a lady," I added. I'd made a mental note yesterday that he wasn't wearing a wedding ring.

"Oh jeez," she said, and delivered the drinks.

When I returned with Eduardo Macelli's pizza, he and the two ladies were busily chatting about banking and football—that's soccer to you and me.

I continued to seat people in the newly decorated dining room.

A group of four giggly girls came in, holding white paper pie plates from AJ's sample tray. One said, "We're here for—" She hesitated.

"Pizza?" I asked.

"Our love match." They sounded American. Probably here for summer vacation or a school trip. She said, "The guy handing out samples told us to come here to meet the matchmaker." She glanced at the customers and asked me, "Can I get him?" She indicated a certain guy.

"Well, it doesn't really work that way," I explained. "What kind of pizza do you like?"

"That depends. What kind of pizza does *he* like?"

"He hasn't ordered yet, but I need to know your favorite kind in order to match you."

"*You're* the matchmaker?" she asked.

I nodded. "In the flesh."

"Huh. I thought you'd be an old lady with a crystal ball or something. You're not even Italian."

"Nah," I said. "More twenty-first century. And American matchmakers have come a long way since the Victorian era."

One of the girls, whose mouth was full of complicated orthodontic equipment, asked, "Why do you need to know our pizza?"

"It's just the way it works," I said. "What kind do you like?"

The first girl tapped each of her friends' shoulders one at a time, telling me their faves. "And Riley"—that was the girl with the braces—"she likes bacon, piled real high. And I just like mine plain."

"Well, in Rome we have an Italian bacon called pancetta. You'll love it," I said to Riley.

She smiled, revealing the metal.

I wrote down the orders. I already had a few ideas for three of the girls, but I didn't know what I was going to do with a pile of pancetta. I had never even dealt with regular American bacon. "Wait here," I said.

I walked around and looked at the pizza orders. I got a good feeling when I passed a table of four younger guys who all spoke English and looked like American tourists. I thought maybe I could match two of the girls. Fifty percent wasn't too bad for a beginner.

I pulled an empty table next to the boys' and said, "Hey there, I have a bit of an issue. I hope you can help me out. We just redecorated, and the tiles on the floor are loose in some places where we repositioned them. Do you mind if I put this table closer to yours so that no one trips?" I didn't let them answer. "Of course you don't mind. You look like nice guys." I pointed to one of them. "If you could just move down here to this chair—" The boys looked at each other, confused, but one of them started getting up. "Oh, not you." I pointed to a different guy. "You."

"Why me?" he asked.

"You have—um—a better—um—center of gravity. It will help equilibrate the tile sitch we've got, if you know what I mean."

"Gravity?"

"Yup. It's all about gravity. Am I right or am I right?" I rambled. "Very scientific."

One of them said, "Luke, dude, it's scientific. Just move."

Luke moved where I'd said.

"And you." I pointed to another one of them. "You sit here." He moved where I said. I waved to the girls to fill in the empty seats. "These girls have higher gravity and better—um—cerebellum. It's a girl thing, you wouldn't understand." Everyone got comfy. "Thank you all so, so much! You have no idea how helpful you've been." I scooted away before anyone could object.

AJ returned with his empty sample tray and helped Vito cook. This lunch was going well.

At one o'clock Murielle duPluie from the Rome newspaper walked in with a photographer on her heels.

She and I sat at the two-top (that's a table for two) near the door, so I could hear if any more matching requests came in.

She said, "I always record interviews so that I'm sure to get the quotes just right." She turned on a small tape recorder. "So tell me. How does this all work? The matches? And how did you get into this?"

"Well, I guess it all started because I like to be around

people. If I'm ever home alone, I walk down the street to visit my mom at the office where she works. It's next to a pizza place. She gives me money to get a slice. Sometimes I hang out there and watch people. I started to notice things about people and their pizza."

"Like what?"

"Like personality stuff."

"For example?"

"People who like everything on their pizza—I call them 'Everythings'—they're probably the easiest to describe. They're really outgoing, talkative, maybe a little loud."

"And who do these Everythings match with?" Murielle duPluie asked.

"Well, there are a few possibilities. I can't really reveal my secrets, if you know what I mean. Plus, it isn't an exact science."

"I understand. If you gave out all your formulas, anyone could be a Pizzeria Matchmaker."

"Too true. But it's not just the pizza. I get a certain, I don't know, like a feeling from people. When I mix that feeling with the pizza—KABOOM!—I make a match."

I saw her write "kaboom." "And you knew when I ordered that I would match well with Angelo?"

"I looked at the pizza options in the room and went

with my gut," I said. "When I mixed up your checks, it was sort of an experiment to see if there was a spark. I provided the intro, and you did the rest."

Just then I glanced over Murielle duPluie's shoulder to the window that looked out on the cobblestone street. Aunt Maria was coming back, earlier than planned.

Oh. No.

14

My thumb went to my ear, and I wiggled my fingers.

"Are you okay?" Murielle duPluie asked.

"Fine." I called, "Gi!" into the kitchen.

Gianna saw my signal and Aunt Maria. She raced to the door to intercept her. "I'm so glad you're here," she said to Aunt Maria. "Mmmm . . . errr . . ."

Gi, think fast.

"It's the sauce," Gianna blurted out.

Meanwhile, I pointed to the pictures hanging on the wall facing away from the door and said to Murielle duPluie, "Let me tell you a story about this picture right here. You'll love this, really."

I said, "That one is the house where this restaurant started."

I glanced over to Eduardo Macelli. He was in such deep conversation with the two ladies I'd sat him with that he didn't notice Aunt Maria.

I continued, "People came from all around. . . ." I heard Aunt Maria say, "*Mamma mia!* What is this about the sauce?" She hurried toward the kitchen without noticing Eduardo Macelli, the reporter, or someone taking my picture. That's how important sauce was to Aunt Maria.

AJ appeared with a stack of take-out containers. "You must be in a hurry," he said to Murielle duPluie and the photographer. "I wrapped up some tiramisu and rum cake for you guys to take with you." To me, so that Murielle duPluie could hear, he said, "We have a matchmaking request for you. High priority. A complicated case."

"Duty calls," I said.

Murielle duPluie looked at her watch. "Just one more question. What's *your* favorite topping?" she asked me.

I smiled. "Umm. I, umm . . . I like ham and pineapple. But you really can't find that in Rome. It's an American thing."

"Maybe you can introduce it to Italy." She held her

mic near AJ's mouth. "And you? What's yours?"

"I'm an anchovy guy. All the way. And you can quote me on that."

She smiled and asked me, "Is anchovy a good match with ham and pineapple?"

"That's more than one question," I said quickly. "I'll just say, 'Come to Amore Pizzeria, and maybe you'll find your love.'"

Murielle duPluie clicked off the recorder. "Thank you. *Merci*. This will be *formidable*. Maybe I can do a follow-up story in a few days and see how your skills are improving?"

"Sure." I led her to the front door. As she walked away, I listened to her stiletto heels *clickety-clack* down the cobblestones.

When she was a safe distance away, I spun around. "That was close," I said to AJ.

"You said 'duty,'" he said. "You know, like doody. Like poop."

Boys!

15

❧

I flew into the kitchen. Aunt Maria was tasting the sauce. "It is perfect."

"Oh, phew," Gianna said. "I thought maybe it wasn't warm enough."

"Oh, you worry too much," Aunt Maria said. She looked at the dining room and saw Eduardo Macelli. "He here?"

"I know," I said. "If you had a cell phone, I could've called you to tell you."

"No cell phone." She went to talk to him. I held my

breath for a minute and watched them talk. They laughed, hopefully over the confusion of the meeting place.

When the lunch rush slowed down, Gianna and I sat at the corner near the register with one of Amore's menus. She had an assortment of glitter pens, stickers, and stampers. Meataball sat on the extra menus.

I studied menu items. There were so many wonderful traditional Italian dishes. I wondered if maybe Amore could add a few American-inspired pizzas. I wrote descriptions of three combos that I missed in Rome, while Gianna doodled around the edges.

"How about we name these after American cities?" I suggested. "This one will be the New York, this one the Philadelphia, and this one the Los Angeles."

"I love that idea. And I'll draw something from each city next to them—the Empire State Building, the Liberty Bell, and the Hollywood sign."

The new menu was going to look great and offer some items that no other pizzeria in the area had.

"So," Gianna began. "Rico's cute."

"Sure," I said.

"You know, it doesn't make sense to me that you're a matchmaker, yet you've never had a match of your own," Gianna continued. "I mean, shouldn't the matchmaker have some experience in romance?"

"Umm . . . maybe. I guess." Hm. I'd never really thought about it that way.

"Maybe this could be the summer that you have your first love?" Gianna teased.

I rolled my eyes. Saving Aunt Maria's shop and making matches were stressful enough—I didn't need any more drama in the kitchen!

16

Aunt Maria usually unlocked the Amore Pizzeria door at eleven o'clock in the morning. But the next day, when we were sweeping up the dining room from the work done on the walls the night before, we watched customers begin to gather out front at ten thirty.

"Who are all these people?" she asked. "Are they here because of your samples?"

"I guess so," I said. "They were really good. After all, they have your sauce." I tucked Aunt Maria's copy of *Il Messaggero* with Murielle duPluie's article under the

487

counter where I kept my matchmaking notes, which were growing to a nice size.

Aunt Maria called to AJ and Vito, "You have some crust rolled out? I open the doors early."

"Yup," AJ said.

"Okay." She asked me, "You can ask Gianna, Jane, and Rico to come down and help?"

I took the broom to the back corner of the store and knocked on the ceiling four times.

Knock—knock—knock—knock.

It was followed by four stomps. A minute later Gianna, Jane, and Rico walked in the back door.

"What's up?" Gianna asked.

Aunt Maria said, "We need the help today." She pointed to the customers.

Rico said, "Food service is not really my gig." He pushed a button on the copper espresso machine and watched hot brown liquid drip into a tiny ceramic cup. Then he leaned on the counter and sipped it. "I'll be your support system."

"What is 'gig'?" Aunt Maria took an apron off a hook and wrapped it around his waist. It was long, crisp, and white. She handed him a pad and pen. "There. You are the waiter. Gianna, you are the hostess. AJ, you are the assistant cook. Lucy, the waitress. Everybody has a job. Now, *andiamo*. Let's Go!"

Rico huffed and took his last sip of espresso.

"Just smile a lot," Gianna said to him. "You'll be fine."

I said to Gianna, "Let's check out those new votive candles you put in the dining room." And I tugged her arm.

"What?" she asked. "I can see them from here. They're fine. But just look at that wall." She pointed to the one that had been scraped with a wire brush last night. It revealed the original brick but still left speckles of white in the grooves. The result was a beautiful old-world feel that really captured traditional Rome and the personality of Amore Pizzeria. "It's more fab than I'd imagined it could be."

"I know," I said. "I just want us to have a plan for the matching."

"You're gonna keep doing it?"

"Look." I pointed to the crowd outside the door. "That's why they're here. I can't let them down." I added, "It's for the good of Amore Pizzeria."

She sighed. "What do I have to do?"

I thought for a moment.

"Put people looking for matches on this half of the dining room. That'll be my half. Rico can wait on the other half."

"Fine. You know Aunt Maria is going to be mad when she finds out about all of this."

"But she's happy about all the customers. Maybe she'll be happy and mad," I said. "Then I'll tell her how hungry I am, and I'll just eat and eat. That will make her more happy than mad."

"Probably."

My section of the restaurant filled up quickly. I took orders and studied customers. Some of the matches jumped out at me right away, and some were more complicated.

I delivered sausage to a woman and called out, "Who ordered the garlic?" A man yelled in Italian, but I figured he was claiming the garlic. "Come over here." I set the garlic plate next to the sausage. "You two enjoy your lunch." They giggled and shook hands.

"Who has sliced zucchini?"

A girl raised her hand.

"Come on over here and sit with this gentleman."

This was the way I made the matches, by moving people around. I watched the customers and took notes on an extra order pad. When I finished, I stashed it under the register. I didn't know if I'd made true love matches, but lots of people looked happy. Obviously, they all loved their pizza.

Aunt Maria came out from the kitchen and manned the cash register as customers left.

"How was your lunch?" Maria asked the sausage customer.

"It was great," she said.

"And the pizza was delicious too," the man who ordered garlic added.

Gianna glanced at her phone. A huge grin crossed her face, and she hunched over in the corner as she thumbed a message. I had a pretty good idea who she was texting.

When she returned to her job, she sat a table in Rico's section, where a waiter who I'd never seen took their order and gave it to AJ. I found Rico sitting at a table, sipping an espresso.

"What are you doing?" I asked him.

"What? You mean that guy? He's a friend of mine." He shrugged. "And he has some serving experience."

Aunt Maria rang up one of the last customers and caught my eye with a menacing glare. Then she stuck out her finger and bent it in, like, *Come here*.

Gulp.

She looked way mad, like, angry with a side of enraged.

I smiled. "I'm starving."

"We talk."

"Can I eat first? I think I'm gonna pass out."

"Fine. Get some food and come right back."

In the kitchen AJ said to me, "She looks pretty angry."

"No duh," I said. "Can you make me a meatball sandwich?"

"One sec. I'm outta sauce." He put the empty pot in a pile of dirty dishes and lifted another simmering pot from the back to the front burner. Then he scooped three lovely meatballs onto crusty Italian bread and covered it with the sauce from the new pot. "Cheese?"

"Why in the world would anyone eat a meatball sandwich without cheese?" I asked. "Do you know the only thing that goes better than cheese?"

"What's that?"

"More cheese!"

He smiled. "Toasted?"

"Put 'er in."

He slid the pan with my sandwich into the oven. It took only a few Mississippis for the cheese to melt.

I took my plate back to the cash register with Aunt Maria and braced myself to be yelled at in Italian.

"Want a bite?" I asked her.

"No." She held up the newspaper. There was a picture of me. The headline read, MATCHMAKER AT AMORE PIZZERIA.

"Look. I'm sorry. I know you said not to. You said,

'*Capisce?*' But then that reporter came in. I matched her the other day as an experiment. And that went really well. She wanted to do an article. She said it would be good for business. And I love you so much and love Amore Pizzeria so much that I couldn't let—"

She held up her hand for me to stop talking.

A few beats later, she broke into a huge smile. Then she pushed a button on the cash register and the drawer flew open. It was full of money. "It worked!"

"So you're not mad?"

"I'm furious. But I'm so happy." She hugged me. "You eat!"

I was just about to sink my teeth into the sandwich when a customer yelled, "Water! *Acqua!*" He grabbed a glass and chugged it, half of it spilling down the front of his shirt. "That sauce! It's too spicy! Are you trying to kill me?"

The sauce?

I touched the sauce on my sandwich with my tongue. "Yowww! He's right," I said to Aunt Maria, and grabbed my own glass of water.

Aunt Maria yelled to AJ, "Where did that pot come from?"

AJ said, "The walk-in fridge. It's the batch you made Wednesday."

She looked at the bubbling pot, grabbed a spoon, and tasted the sauce. She immediately spit it out.

"Someone has ruined my sauce," Aunt Maria yelled. "Who would do that?"

17

❧

"*Mamma mia!*" Aunt Maria shouted. "What happened to the sauce?"

AJ said, "I'll take the extra pot out of the fridge and pop it on the stove."

"Do not 'pop' anything," said Aunt Maria. "Just heat it."

"That's what I meant," AJ said.

"Then do not say 'pop.' I no understand you kids anymore."

AJ retreated to the kitchen, while Gianna told the customer that we were making a new lunch for him.

"The sitch isn't that bad," I said to Aunt Maria, who was now fanning herself with an empty drink tray. "We didn't make any pizza with that sauce yet."

"'Sitch'?" Aunt Maria shook her head. "Is good we have the extra pot, but that will change the sauce-making schedule. We will run out before Wednesday."

"We'll make more! You can teach me."

"*Sì!* But I need very special ingredients. I go all over Rome to get only the best. It takes time. A lot of places. A lot of time," she said. "Without the ingredients, I cannot teach you."

I looked at my watch. "I'll go after lunch. Give me a list of what you need and addresses."

"You do not know Rome. You will not find these places."

I held up my phone. "I have GPS. It works in Rome."

She looked at my phone and shook her head. "'Gee peas'? No. You go with Rico. He can follow the map. You know a map?"

"Yes, I know what a map is."

We looked at Rico sipping another espresso, and Aunt Maria added, "You two cannot carry everything. I make many trips. AJ and Gianna will go too." Then she waved to Jane, who came over with her arms filled with dirty dishes. "Can you stay with me? I need the help for dinner."

"Absolutely," Jane said. "Anything you need."

Rico's waiter guy lingered nearby and called over to us, "I'll help too."

"Who that?" Aunt Maria asked, confused.

"Does it matter?" I asked. "He knows what he's doing, and he wants to stay and help."

"Okay." Aunt Maria pointed at him. "You stay."

He asked, "And I can call *mio amico*?"

"*Sì*," Aunt Maria said to his offer to call a friend.

"What if people come in for matches?" I asked her. "I'll show you the notes I've been taking."

"You no worry," she said. "It is under control."

18

When the lunch crowd thinned, the four of us headed out with the list and instructions that directed us to three very different areas of Rome for garlic, herbs, and tomatoes.

Rico's waiter friend let us use his scooter, so Gianna and I hopped on it while AJ and Rico got on AJ's.

"Do you know how to drive that?" AJ asked me.

"No," I said. "But how hard could it be?"

Rico got off the scooter with AJ and said to me, "Let's switch. You go with AJ and I'll drive this one."

I sat behind AJ. Gianna raised her brows at me

because I was sitting so close to a boy. She motioned for me to wrap my arms around his waist, but I was unsure. . . .

AJ put a helmet on my head and secured it under my chin. Then he hit the gas hard—I almost fell off the back—so I grabbed his waist and held on for my life. It wasn't as weird as I'd thought. Actually, I kind of liked it.

We followed Rico and Gianna.

Gianna filled Rico's ear with chatter and pointed to everything. I was content to look around and take it all in. The sun was warm on my back, and the breeze felt cool on my cheeks. I was surprised at the women on scooters—dressed up, even in spiky heels—with bread and flowers in their baskets. Men also scootered around in suits and ties. My mind spun stories about many of these people, and I wondered if they were looking for matches.

I could've ridden around all day, imagining, but we soon arrived at our first stop.

Garlic.

"Where are we?" Gianna hooked her helmet to the back of the scooter.

I pointed. "That's the Pantheon, Gi. It's kinda famous."

"Oh sure," she said. "I knew that."

I rolled my eyes.

Rico unfolded the paper Aunt Maria had given us. "Well, we're at the Piazza della Rotonda. According to Maria, there's a street vendor who sits next to the water-ice stand that sells *fragola*. That's strawberry. He should have her garlic."

"Why not just get it from a store?" Gianna asked.

AJ said, "Oh, no. She is very specific with her sauce. Everything comes from a vendor she knows and trusts. She's been going to the same places for years. It's one of the things that makes her sauce perfect. The garlic comes from a family that grows it in their yard. It's the only thing they sell. She says there's something about their soil that makes it more pungent than anyone else's."

I was totally gonna use that little deet in a story. "That's awesome," I said. In my mind I pictured a cottage in the country and an old gray-haired Italian man picking carefully selected cloves.

I scanned the piazza and easily counted four water-ice vendors, all next to people selling some kind of herbs or vegetables. "This could take a while. We better split up."

AJ said, "And look for clues?"

"What clues?" I asked.

"Like Scooby-Doo. They always split up and look for clues."

500

We ignored him—although I thought it was funny—and each of us ran to a different vendor. On the way to mine I stopped to eavesdrop on a tour group. Their leader said, "The columns are made of granite. They were floated down the Nile, then the Tiber River, before being dragged here. When you see columns in the US, they were inspired by these."

I wanted to hear more, but . . . the garlic.

I waited in line at the water-ice vendor's cart. When it was my turn, I looked at the ground and mumbled, *"Fragola?"*

He shook his head. *"Limone. Caffè."* He didn't have strawberry.

"Grazie," I thanked him.

On my way back to our agreed meeting place, I lingered again by the tour. The guide said, "It was originally a temple to worship Roman gods, and then it became a church. It's also a tomb."

Oh, how I love a good tomb story.

The guide continued, "That huge dome has an ocular—an opening that looks into the sky. It's quite magnificent. Let's get our tickets and go see."

I wanted to see. I thought maybe I could blend in and tag along, but . . . the garlic.

Rico and Gianna were waiting. I showed them my

empty hands. All our hope was pinned on AJ, who came back with four red granitas. He handed them out.

"*Fragola*," he said. "Strawberry for everyone."

I took my cup and tasted it with a little plastic spoon. It was finely grated ice shavings covered with strawberry flavoring. "What about the garlic?"

AJ took a paper bag out of his back pocket. "I got your garlic, girl," he said with strawberry-red lips.

He concentrated on his ice, then asked, "It's good, huh? Sometimes I eat it really fast to get a brain freeze."

"You do that to yourself on purpose?" Rico asked.

AJ looked shocked. "You don't?"

The ice was good, but we were in a hurry. Aunt Maria wanted us back at Amore Pizzeria before dark. She said the sauce would take about six hours. I can't imagine something taking SIX hours to cook. I looked at my watch. "We better get going. What's next? Tomatoes?"

Rico had a big blob of ice on his tongue, which he tried to talk through. "It's near the Colosseum. Not far."

We finished most of our ices, hopped back on the scooters, and headed toward Aunt Maria's tomato supplier. On the way, we crossed another piazza with a grand fountain. This one was chock-full of kids splashing around. A few adults, too—they'd rolled up their pants legs and waded in to cool off.

Large tents lined the square, filled with anything and everything you could think of: shoes, sundresses, jewelry, paintings, oil, flowers, cheese, fruit, and vegetables. If we weren't racing to get tomatoes, I totally would've shopped.

As I glanced around, I saw the Colosseum from a distance. The first thing that struck me was its size. It was massive, like a huge, ancient, crumbling stone football stadium. The second thing I thought was how strange it was that this ruin was right there in the middle of a city. The crumbling building was surrounded by a busy street, people taking pictures and buying souvenirs from men in red gladiator robes and helmets topped with Mohawk brushes.

I turned my head to make sure I didn't miss seeing another timeworn treasure.

That's when I saw something—well, someone—that surprised me.

Lorenzo.

19

I whipped my head around and said to AJ, "Lorenzo's following us."

He tilted his head, confused. I repeated myself louder, but got the same reaction. That probably meant that Rico hadn't heard anything that Gianna had been saying. *Ha!*

When we parked, I took off my helmet, fluffed my hair, and casually scanned the area, which was crowded with Colosseum viewers.

"Don't look now," I said to AJ, Rico, and Gianna, "but Lorenzo is behind us."

Rico moved the scooter's side mirror so he could check. "Yup," he said. "It's hard to hide that huge head of hair."

AJ said, "If I didn't think he was such a jerk, I might be jealous of it."

Gianna added, "It is kind of fab." And she sighed. I think she really had a thing for him, which wasn't good, since in my book, he was suspect numero uno in the sauce sitch, if you know what I mean.

I guess I was the only one not in love with Lorenzo's hair. "Can we forget about the hair for a minute? Is anyone wondering why he's following us?" I asked. Without letting anyone answer, I said, "I think I smell something."

"It wasn't me," AJ protested.

"That's not what I meant," I snapped. "I think that batch of sauce was sabotaged."

"And you think it was Lorenzo?" Rico asked.

"He was alone in the kitchen," I pointed out.

"How do you know that?" Gianna asked.

Rico said, "It's amazing what you can learn when you're crouched on the floor in Jane Attilio's apartment."

Gianna asked, "What? Crouched?"

AJ said, "Don't worry, I don't get it either."

Gianna finally realized what we meant. "You listened to my private conversation?" she shrieked.

"You let Lorenzo in the kitchen," I said defensively. "Pizzeria de Roma is Amore's biggest competition. Don't you think that was, like, a bad idea?"

AJ said, "Whoa. Stop right there. He was in Maria's kitchen? Lorenzo?" He threw his hands up in frustration. "He would totally ruin the sauce."

"No way," Gianna said. She tilted the scooter's mirror to catch a glimpse of him. She studied him for a second. "You think?"

"Totes," I assured her. "And I think he's following us to find out where Maria gets her stuff."

"Or maybe he's following me," Gianna said.

I loved her optimism, but she just wasn't being realistic. "Don't worry," I said. "We'll get back at him."

AJ asked, "Like, how? Are we talking about food contamination? Or maybe give them a little cockroach infestation? A health code violation? A huge 'closed for renovation' sign?"

"Your mind is way more creative, and scarily sinister, than I'd ever imagined," I said to AJ.

"Really, dude," Rico said. "Remind me not to make you mad."

"So, what's the plan?" Gianna asked.

"It's brewing," I assured them. "You leave that to me. We'll get him when he least expects it."

"Cool." AJ looked at his watch. "But right now we need to track down some tomatoes. Or is it tom-ah-toes?"

No one answered his question.

Rico unfolded the paper with instructions and looked around. "They're there." He pointed to a nearby open-air market.

"But Lorenzo will see where we get them," I said. "He'll try to copy Aunt Maria's sauce."

"Fret not, Pizzeria Matchmaker, I'll take care of that," Rico said. "You get"—he checked the paper—"a hundred tomatoes."

"I'm on it," I said. I ran about two steps, then turned back to Rico. "Don't actually injure him."

"I wouldn't dream of it," Rico said. Then to Gianna, he said, "You're helping me."

"I am? I don't know; that's not really my style."

"Make it your style," I said. "This is kinda your fault. Aunt Maria told you to stay away from him."

"She also told you to 'no mess with the love,'" Gianna said.

"True, but that hasn't been a disaster," I said.

"Yet," she added, and left with Rico.

I hoped that wasn't true.

AJ asked me, "What do you want me to do?"

"Stay here and guard the garlic," I said. "If you see

me do this"—I flapped my arms like a bird—"that means I need help with the tom-ah-toes."

"So, I'm your wingman?" he asked.

"If that's what you wanna call it. Sure."

"I'm calling it that," AJ confirmed.

Maybe I should tell you what my opinion was of AJ at this point. I liked him. Not *liked* liked (well, maybe a little). I thought he was a fun wingman to have around. But if those tomatoes grew feet, organized into an army, and started taking over the planet, I don't know that I would want him in my rebel troop. I didn't think he could handle a serious zombie tomato event.

Zombie tom-ah-toes? Now, that was an idea for a story.

20

I found the vegetable stand in the outdoor market where Rico had directed me. The tomatoes looked red and ripe and without the slightest hint of coming to life with a desire to take over the planet.

"*Buongiorno*," a woman wearing a short black apron with pockets said. "I help you with something?"

"*Sì*. I am Lucia Rossi, Maria's niece. She sent me to get tomatoes for her."

"Ah, *sì*. You are early this week. She was just here."

"Right. I know. We had a little sitch—situation."

She looked at me like she didn't understand.

"You see, my sister Gianna, she likes this boy. The kind that she shouldn't like, if you know what I mean. And, well, she let him into the kitchen of all places, and—"

The woman stared at me blankly. She didn't follow what I was saying. "You know what?" I asked. "Never mind. I'll just take a hundred tomatoes."

She hoisted a jug onto the table and then another, and another and two more. Four.

"What's that?" I asked.

"For Maria, I peel and crush. Always I peel and"— she smashed her fist into her palm, like, really hard— "crush."

Now, *that's* a woman I'd want in my rebel army troop.

"Gotcha. A lot of crushing." I looked at the jugs. Now I knew why Aunt Maria had sent all four of us. I couldn't carry all this. I stepped out into the open space and flapped my arms, but my wingman was nowhere to be found.

Grrr.

The tomato woman looked at me. "You okay?"

"*Sì.*" I took two of the jugs. "I'll come back for those."

"No problem," she said.

I carried one in each arm. Man, they were heavy.

How did Aunt Maria do this? She must've had some kind of system. "Oh." I turned back to the woman. "What do I owe you?"

"You no worry. Maria never need to pay with me."

I nodded.

Then she asked, "You don't have the case?"

"Case of what?"

"Maria, she put the tomatoes in a—" She made a motion with her hands like a big square. "It has a hand-hold, and she pull it on the wheels." She pointed to the jugs. "Too heavy to carry like that."

No duh.

"Box with a handhold, huh?" I set the jugs down and looked around the market. "Gimme a minute, please."

"Sure. You have one minute, two minute, as many minute as you want."

I walked around to the various vendors. I smelled leather and oil, even though I saw neither.

"*Acqua?*" a man selling bottles of water asked me. He kept the bottles in a cooler with a handle that slid out to roll it along.

I looked into it. He only had three bottles left, I guess because it was late in the day. "Can I have all three bottles?" I asked.

"*Sì!*" He seemed excited to sell out.

"And your cooler, too?"

"This?" He pointed to the cooler. "No. No. Not for sale."

I reached into the back of my pocket. "How about five euros?"

"No. No." He shook his head.

"How about ten euros?"

"No." He considered. "Fifteen euros?"

"Deal," I said, and *BAM!* I had a way to get the jugs to Aunt Maria's without my arms falling off.

I rolled it behind me, loaded the jugs, and returned to the scooters, where AJ stood eating a *panino*.

"Seriously? You left your wingman for a sandwich?"

He looked at the sandwich. "Sorry." Then he said, "I thought I was the wingman."

"You're mine and I'm yours. We're each other's wingman. That's the way it works."

"Really?" AJ asked. "You think?"

"Yeah, I do."

He looked at the cooler. "What's that?"

"One hundred tomatoes. Peeled and"—I smashed my fist into my palm—"crushed."

"Sweet." He bit the *panino*. "You want a bite?"

"I guess."

. . .

By the time Rico and Gianna returned, laughing, AJ and I had lifted the cooler onto the back of one of the scooters and secured it.

"What's so funny?" I asked.

"You should've seen how Rico distracted Lorenzo," Gianna said.

"That dude is such an idiot," Rico said. "I blew cherry pits through a straw and pegged him right in the face." He laughed so hard he could hardly get the words out. "I was hiding, and he was looking all around, like 'What was that?' And he ran in our direction, but we had moved."

Gianna said, "When he got to the place where we had been, Rico blew another from a totally different spot."

"Then we split up and pegged him from two sides. He didn't know what to do with that," Rico added. To Gianna he said, "I swear you've done that before. Your aim was on the money."

"First time, I swear."

"Where is he now?" I asked.

"He took off," Rico said. "I don't think we have to worry about him anymore today."

"Today," I repeated. "What about the rest of the week?"

"What's your plan to get even with him?" AJ asked.

"The details are still coming together in my head," I said. "This type of genius takes careful consideration, but it's gonna be good."

21

❧

"To the Piazza di Spagna and the Spanish Steps," Rico said, starting up his scooter, the back end of which sagged due to a cooler with four heavy jugs of crushed tomatoes.

He gave us a forward wave and rode off. Slowly.

The other motorists honked at us, and a few yelled. Luckily, I couldn't understand their Italian. Slow was not the Italian way of driving. A group of teen boys on bicycles chuckled as they pedaled past us.

I had come here to the Spanish Steps the last time I was in Rome, but that was such a long time ago that

I hardly remembered. The Piazza di Spagna was huge and very crowded. The Fontana della Barcaccia sat in the middle of the piazza. People of all ages sat on the edge of the fountain, sipping coffee or eating granitas or gelato with little plastic spoons. Shopping bags from Fendi, Prada, and Gucci sat on the ground next to them.

Behind the fountain was a grand staircase—I mean it was *HUGE*, and beautiful. I didn't count, but it looked like more than a hundred massive stone steps. At the top was an ancient church. Flowers—pots of colorful violets and daisies—lined the steps on either side.

Ladies in flowing skirts, carrying baskets filled with long-stemmed red roses, strolled up and down the steps. When they saw a couple posing for a photograph, one of the ladies would encourage the man to buy a rose for his date.

"We have to go up there." Rico pointed to the top of the steps. "There are shops. One of them sells herbs."

As I followed Rico up the steps, I was totally overcome with déjà vu. You know the feeling like you've been somewhere or done something before? Well, I had actually been here before, but it was more than that—I felt like I had been here before *with Rico*. And as fast as the feeling came, it left.

AJ and Gianna walked up too. Our climbing was

interrupted by a woman selling roses from a basket. "For your girlfriend?" she asked AJ.

"Oh, she's not my girlfriend. She's a friend."

The woman said, "And she's a girl. So, she is your girlfriend. Buy her a flower."

"Um . . . er . . . um." AJ couldn't form a single non-mumbled word.

"No, thanks," I said.

We caught up to Rico and Gianna, who were taking a rose from a different woman. I imagined Rico couldn't say "No, thanks" either, and Gianna probably really wanted the rose.

The woman handed one to me.

"No, thanks," I said again.

"Oh, you take this. You are Maria Rossi's niece, sì? You must have a rose."

"How did you know that?" I asked.

"It's all she's talked about for days, and you look just like her."

I took the rose. "What do we owe you?"

"Nothing. I'd do anything for Maria."

"Wow. Thanks." I wondered what Aunt Maria had done for her.

"I am Carina." She shook my hand.

"Hi. I'm—"

"Lucy. I know. I hope you have a wonderful visit." She turned to another customer after saying "*Ciao*" to us.

We made it to the top of the steps and found the shop that had the herbs for the sauce. Thankfully, herbs were much lighter than jugs of crushed tomatoes. Then we headed back to Amore Pizzeria, with the tomato jugs weighing us down. After safely tucking the coveted ingredients way in the back of the walk-in fridge, we all helped with the few remaining dinner customers.

"Do you need me to, you know . . . make any matches?" I asked Aunt Maria.

I followed her eyes to the dining room. "Is all taken care of," she said.

There were couples holding hands, giggling, smiling, and exchanging phone numbers.

"How did you do that?" I asked her. "How did you know who to match with who? I didn't ever show you my notes."

She rang up two customers at the cash register. "*Grazie*," she said to them. They walked down the cobblestone alley arm in arm.

"The notes do not matter. Is not like sauce. There is no recipe you can follow," she said. "It is a feeling. A gift."

"Matchmaking is a gift?" I asked.

Aunt Maria smiled. "*Sì*, one that runs in the family. You aren't the only one who knows the matchmaking."

518

22

I couldn't believe it. "Whoa! You can do it too?"

She laughed. "Yes, I can."

"That is, like, cool with a side of oh yeah!"

"Right. 'Cool,'" she said. "Yeah."

"I can't believe this! Why didn't you tell me sooner?" I asked.

"Meddling in matters of love is big responsibility. Some matches go wrong. I know this."

"But lots go right." I pointed to the backs of the couple who had walked out a minute ago.

"Oh, I know. I make many, many good matches, but then I stop."

"Why?"

She looked at the clock. "For another day," she said, and reached under the counter. "But look at this." It was a basket with three envelopes.

"What are those?"

"Letters from people asking the Pizzeria Matchmaker for help," she said. "They think you are the new Beatrice."

"Who's Beatrice?"

"I tell you the story later. You are not the only one who can tell the story. That run in the family too."

"We have a lot to talk about," I said.

"*Sì*. We will talk while we make the sauce."

Then she pulled a large piece of laminated paper from under the cash register. "Salvatore the deliveryman leave this here on the counter today." She handed it to me.

"The happy guy who brings meat and bread? He brings menus, too?"

"*Sì*. Salvatore. He bring everything. That is the job of the deliveryman."

"I guess," I said. I thought it was a little strange that he would deliver pasta *and* menus—very different things.

She pointed to an item on the menu—the New York—that I had added. "What is this?"

"It's great," I said. "I'll show you how to make it."

"I hope you will. Now, we better start on the sauce. It take six hours." Aunt Maria announced, "No big dinner tonight. Me and Lucy, we make the sauce. We will eat while we clean up."

I followed her into the kitchen.

Vito had a big pot of leftover spaghetti. He put some on a plate and cut it up for Meataball, then made a plate for himself.

I took a round roll and hollowed out the soft middle. Then I filled it with spaghetti, sauce, and mozzarella cheese. I set the other half of the roll on top and pushed down.

"What you doing?" Aunt Maria asked.

"It's a spaghetti Parmesan sandwich. I made it up." I took a bite.

"Mamma mia."

"It's good." I handed it to her, and she took a bite.

"Sì. It is good," she agreed. I think she was surprised she liked it!

I made one for everyone.

AJ bit into his. "It's the perfect way to take spaghetti on the go. The only thing that would be better would be if we could put it on a stick."

I thought about this while I cleaned. Spaghetti on a stick? Good idea! Could it be done?

521

With everyone helping, it didn't take long to reset the dining room for lunch tomorrow.

Aunt Maria waved her arms. "You are all done with the cleanup. *Grazie*. Now, you go. Lucy and I have to work." She shoved everyone out the door.

The gang left. Aunt Maria locked the door behind them and turned off the lights except for the kitchen. "Get the ingredients."

I did as directed while Aunt Maria lifted a huge metal pot akin to a cauldron onto the stove. She slid a little step stool over so that she could get high enough to see inside the pot.

She poured in olive oil without measuring and put the burner on low-medium while she showed me how to use a garlic press.

She said, "You put the garlic in the oil." She waited for me to press seven cloves and add them to the oil. I added it carefully and snapped my arm back when the garlic popped and sizzled.

"Now you stir." She took a very long silver spoon off a hook on the wall. "Only this spoon."

"How come? Does it have some special Italian magical power?"

"Always with the story, you are," Aunt Maria said. "It is the spoon I always use to make the sauce, and the sauce is always good, so that is the way to make it."

"My explanation is much more interesting."

"Sì," she said. "But just a story."

We carefully worked through the rest of the secret recipe, adding tomatoes and herbs. She measured nothing, and I wasn't allowed to write anything down. "That is how it stay a secret. It is here." She pointed to her head.

"How do you know you're getting it right if you don't measure?"

"You taste every time. Your taste know if it is right." She took a plastic spoon and touched the garlic and oil with it. She let it cool for a sec, then let me lick it. "Close your eyes. This is how it should taste right now." She paused. "Remember it."

I wasn't confident I was going to remember, so I concentrated.

Aunt Maria threw the spoon away and continued her sauce routine.

"You have a lot to tell me," I said. "What's with this family 'gift' that I seem to have inherited from you? You know, I always thought there was something special connecting us."

"I did too." She pinched my cheek.

"How did it start?" I asked her.

"I was making the pizza." She pointed into the dining room to the picture on the wall. "Right there."

I nodded and continued to slowly stir with the silver spoon and commit the details of the recipe to memory while listening.

"I was young and married to Ferdinando. My lady friends were not married. They would come over for the pizza. Ferdinando's friends would come over for the pizza too. I started getting ideas in my head about the pizzas they liked and a feeling in my heart about which lady would match well with which man."

"That's exactly what happens to me."

"The matches, they worked." She used the tips of her fingers to sprinkle sugar in the bubbling red liquid, stirred, and dabbed a bit on the end of a plastic spoon for me to taste. "Remember that," she said about the taste. "Sometimes you need a little more sugar, sometimes less."

I tried to memorize the taste—not as easy as it sounds.

"The matches is how we got the name Amore Pizzeria. *Amore* is love in Italian," she said. "Everyone loved the matches."

"Then what happened? How come you 'no mess with love' anymore?"

"Because of a bad match I made. I paired a woman with a man, and they go off to America. Then I met another man who I just know is the perfect match for her, but she is gone." A sad look came over her face. "He never marry. I always see him and he so sad. I think this is my fault. I feel so guilty, I stop the matching."

Everything had been added to the pot. Aunt Maria turned the heat down and stirred the deep-red liquid with a long wooden spoon. "Now, we let it simmer."

23

~~~

Dear Pizzeria Matchmaker: I like
pepperoni pizza. I'm coming into Amore
tomorrow. Please make a match for me.

Dear "Beatrice": Please help me find my
true love. From Kelsey

Dear Beatrice II: Please make me a match.
Love, Basil and Tomato

Cara Beatrice: Voglio incontrare il mio vero
amore. Da Bianca

I piled the four new letters on top of the old ones. AJ rolled out dough. "What are you going to do with those?"

"I'm not sure yet," I said. "I don't even know anything about Beatrice. Aunt Maria was supposed to tell me about it last night, but we got so preoccupied with matchmaking that we didn't have time. Do you know she does it too?"

"Matchmaking?"

I nodded and helped spread sauce on the dough. "Well, she used to, but not anymore."

"How come?"

"She made a bad match and felt so guilty about it that she swore she wouldn't do it after that."

"Oh man, that's heavy stuff," AJ said.

"Yeah. I don't know how I would feel if a match I made went bad. I mean, should a matchmaker really be responsible for what happens after the intro?"

"*That*, Lucy, is a question for a matchmaker, which is your department," AJ said. "I roll dough. You make matches. It works for us."

I sighed. "I don't know." I wiped my hands on a towel and picked up the small pile of letters. "I guess I'll just hang on to these for now. What did Beatrice do with them?"

"Well, she was dead when she started getting letters, so I don't think there really was much she *could* do with them." He slid the crusts into the oven. "How can you be Italian and not know about Beatrice and Dante?"

"Well, I don't. So tell me."

"It's a love story," he said, and made a face, like love was gross. "Beatrice Portinari lived in Florence about a bajillion years ago. As a child she met Dante at a party. For Dante it was love at first sight. Supposedly, they wrote letters to each other for many years."

"How romantic. No one does that anymore. Maybe a text sometimes."

"Whatever," he said. "Eventually they each married other people, but it is said that Dante always loved her."

"And they reunited?"

"No," he said. "She died, remember?"

"Oh, that's a terrible ending," I said.

"Blahbity blah," he said. "But there's more."

"Well, don't keep me waiting. Bring it on," I said.

"In Florence there is a tomb for Beatrice. Letters started mysteriously appearing. They asked Beatrice, or her ghost or spirit or whatever, for help finding love."

"People think I'm Beatrice?" I said. "Like, reincarnated? Or back from the dead?"

"It's more likely that they think you're *like* Beatrice," AJ said. "Maybe that you can help with their romantic needs."

"But a modern version," I added. "What does the dead Beatrice do for them?"

"I don't know. Maybe makes their wishes come true, I guess. Like a wish in a fountain."

I looked at the letters. "I can't make wishes come true. I'm not a magician. If they think I am, I'm going to disappoint a lot of people," I said. "It's just pizza and a feeling in my gut."

"I guess they'll take whatever they can get."

"What do you think I should do with these?" I indicated the letters in my hand. "They don't have addresses, so replying isn't an option."

He tied a bandanna around his head and headed toward the walk-in refrigerator. "I bet you'll think of something."

I was left wondering about a lot of matchmaker-y things and something else. The Beatrice and Dante story was bothering me, and I wasn't sure why.

AJ had propped the refrigerator door open and

called out to me, "We'll go to the Festa de Santa Elizabeth tomorrow night and take your mind off it for a while."

"What's that?"

He brought out a crate of cheese and sifted through it. "It's only one of the biggest, funnest summer events in Rome. It's a street festival that lasts all night. There's food and dancing and music. It's a total blast," he said. "If there was a place like that where we could go every night, that would be awesome."

"Sounds great. But won't we have to work?" I asked.

"Nah. All the businesses close. Everyone will be at the Festa."

"If there really was a place like that all the time, no one would ever work," I said.

"I guess, or maybe then it would be more usual," AJ said. "You know, like, normal and not such a big deal."

"Maybe," I said. "Well, it sounds like fun."

"Oh, it is."

"What should I wear?"

"That's really more Rico's department. Besides, we've got customers."

I could tell by the smirks on the women's faces that they were looking for more than pizza.

"Table for two?" I asked them.

530

"Yes. And two matches, please."

No one else was here for lunch yet, but they would be soon. I sat them smack-dab in the middle of the dining room, thinking that would give me lots of options.

"Tell me about your pizza. What do you like?"

One of the women said, "Roasted vegetables."

The other said, "Mushroom."

Mushroom was easy peasy, but roasted vegetables? I didn't have an immediate idea in mind. I went to grab my notepad.

I kept it under the register, but when I went over, it wasn't there. I looked on the counter, near the bar, on the ledge between the dining room and kitchen.

It was gone.

24

I hustled into the kitchen and found Meataball keeping AJ company while he moved stuff around in the walk-in refrigerator. "Have you seen my matchmaking notepad?"

"It was under the register."

"It's not there now."

"Dunno," he said. "Can you do it without your notes?"

"I guess I don't have much of a choice."

I sat more customers, and soon I had a selection of men to choose from: pepperoni, plain, basil, and jalapeño peppers.

I'd never worked with jalapeños before, so I left him out.

"I've matched basil and mushroom before. It's a tried-and-true combo, but what about the lady with roasted vegetables?"

"What is your gut telling you?" AJ asked.

"Strangely, it's telling me jalapeño."

"Then go with it."

"What if it's a disaster?" I asked.

"You won't know until you try," he said. "It might not be."

"I guess," I said. "Let me know if you see my notes."

"Will do."

I switched the customers' seats around. Then I watched and waited. Right away I could tell something was up with mushroom and basil. The woman's face grew redder with each passing minute, and as I delivered her pizza, she tossed her Coke in Mr. Basil's face. He jumped up and yelled, "What? Are you crazy?"

She looked at me. "You are a terrible Pizzeria Matchmaker, and I'm going to tell everyone." She slid her phone out of her purse and tapped the screen. "There. It's posted. Now everyone knows you're a fraud." She stormed to the door.

"Wait," I said. "I'm sorry. Let me try again."

"No way. I'm never coming back here." She left Amore and I could hear her yelling down the cobblestone alley that I was not a real matchmaker. The would-be customers turned and walked away.

My heart raced.

A bad match.

I went into the kitchen to the walk-in refrigerator and stepped inside. I sat on the floor and held my head in my hands. A second later there was a knock on the door.

"What?" I called out to AJ.

A voice that wasn't AJ's asked, "Can I come in?"

Rico closed the door behind himself. "Bad day?" he asked, and sat down next to me.

"Pretty much."

"AJ filled me in. Was it the jalapeño?"

"No. It was mushroom and basil," I said. "You know, when I moved them together, I had a feeling it wasn't a good match."

"Then why did you do it?"

"Because to me, mushroom and basil just go together. Like peanut butter and jelly."

"Maybe you underestimate your gut."

I thought for a second. My gut was bubbling like a pot of simmering sauce at the moment. "Maybe I do."

We sat in silence for minute. "It's cold in here."

I didn't respond to the comment. "Maria, she used to be a matchmaker—"

"We went from zero matchmakers to two. Big week in Rome."

"And she made a bad match that made her feel so guilty that she stopped doing it." I explained Aunt Maria's story.

Rico asked, "Are you wondering if you should feel guilty?"

"The thought crossed my mind."

"I don't know what the Webster's Dictionary definition of matchmaker is, but I think you're just the thing that puts two people together. You create an opportunity to see if there is an initial spark," he said. "I don't think the matchmaker is in charge of everybody's happily ever after."

"Maybe," I said.

"That's the job of the fairy godmother."

That got a smile out of me. "It is?"

"Sure. They handle the whole bippity boppity boo." He asked, "Don't you guys get together for annual meetings or something?"

I chuckled.

"Well, you should."

"I guess we should," I said. "My notes, the ones about the matches, are missing. What am I gonna do about that?"

"I don't know, but we better find them before someone else does, or people all over Rome could be matching themselves based on pizza," he said. "That would be terrible. The city could crumble." He stood and held his hand out to help me up. When I stood, we were face-to-face.

His eyes.

I knew them.

I had definitely written about eyes exactly like his, or dreamed about them, or something. I had that déjà vu feeling again.

"Are you making fun of me?" I asked about Rome crumbling.

"Never," he said.

He opened the refrigerator door and let me leave first.

A loud burst of laughter came from the dining room. It was Jalapeño.

AJ fiddled with his phone while watching the dining room. "See." He pointed to my stomach. "Your gut did that."

Rico said, "Who needs notes?!"

Then AJ held up his phone. "You won't believe this."

"The post from that lady?" I asked, figuring the unsatisfied customer's words had jettisoned through the "interwebs" as Aunt Maria called it.

"No. I was flipping through FaceSpace to see what was going on, and guess what someone posted?" He didn't wait for us to answer. It says, 'Pizzeria Matchmaker's recipe for romance for sale.' And there's a photo." He showed me.

"Those are my notes!" I yelled.

"I guess we know what happened to them," Rico said.

I pointed to the background of the picture. It was a tiny silver corner of an old pinball machine. One I'd seen before.

"Oh no, he didn't," I said.

I picked up the broom and bopped the handle on the ceiling four times. Then I yelled up the vent, "Gianna Rossi, we need to talk!"

Four stomps followed, and a second later Gianna came in the back door. "What's up?" she asked.

AJ showed her the post.

"Oh my God. Are those your notes? You lost them?" she asked.

"No. I left them by the register, and now they're gone."

"Isn't that sort of the definition of lost?"

"Lost? They were *stolen*." I stared at her, waiting for her to catch on to my line of thought. "And I know by who."

"Who?" she asked. "You think *I* took them?"

"No. I think Lorenzo did." I pointed to the pinball machine. "Do you know where this picture was taken?"

She shook her head.

"At Pizzeria de Roma," I said.

She asked, "How do you know what Pizzeria de Roma looks like?"

Busted.

"That's not important. What we're talking about is that we heard Lorenzo and you talking through the vent the other night. Has he been back?"

"I haven't seen him since the spitball thing."

"I had my notes after that. How did he get them?"

"I don't know," Gianna said. "Maybe it wasn't him."

I looked at AJ's phone again. "People are bidding. It's up to eighty euros!"

Rico tapped numbers into his own cell phone. "Don't worry. I'm on it."

"What are you gonna do?"

He whispered, "I know a gu— Hey!" he said into the phone. "*Come stai, mio amico?*" He walked away so we couldn't hear him.

Just then our friendly neighborhood deliveryman came in, pushing a dolly stacked high with cardboard boxes. "*Buongiorno!*" he cried, the same way he had every other time he'd come into Amore Pizza. "Today I have butter and sugar and flour. Lots of flour." Vito spoke to him in Italian. I guess my Italian had improved, because I understood that Vito referred to our delivery guy as Salvatore and asked him about a man named Mossimo.

Salvatore asked Gianna, "Did you get the sample of the menu I left for you?"

"Yes. Thanks. I have just a few changes." Gianna went to the front of the store by the register to get the sample menu. She handed it to Salvatore.

He said, "I take it to the printer."

"Okay. Thanks," Gianna said.

I asked, "So you deliver everything?"

"I have a truck. I deliver anything anywhere. I used to run a restaurant myself, but I like to be out in the city. Not all day in the kitchen. So now I am silent partner. My brother and grandnephew, they run the restaurant. I do the accounting books at night, and all day I ride around and deliver stuff. Lots of sunshine."

"Which restaurant?" Gianna asked.

"Pizzeria de Roma. You know it. It is in the piazza by the Fontana del Cuore."

539

"Yeah," I said very casually. "I've seen it."

"I go now," Salvatore said. "*Ciao!*" he cried with his standard level of pep.

"*Ciao,*" we echoed with much less excitement.

Once he was gone, I said, "He's Lorenzo's *great-uncle*."

"Seems that way," Rico said.

AJ asked, "Do you think he knows what Lorenzo did to the sauce and that he stole the matchmaker notes?"

"I don't know, but maybe Lorenzo will need to explain it to him when we give him a dose of his own medicine."

"Now?" Gianna asked.

"Tomorrow."

"What exactly is this master plan?" AJ asked.

I supplied the deets.

"I like the way your mind works," Rico said.

25

〜✦〜

The next morning it was time to put my plan into motion. We walked through the piazza, past the Fontana del Cuore, and hid behind a statue near Pizzeria de Roma. Lorenzo's scooter wasn't out front. We waited for him to arrive and unlock the doors.

For this plan to work, Gianna was going to distract Lorenzo.

"Are you ready?" I asked her.

She chewed on her nails.

"Just like we practiced," Rico said. "You can do it."

Vroom!

"There he is," I said.

He parked his scooter, tucked his helmet under his arm, and headed for the door with keys in his hand.

"Now?" Gianna asked.

"Wait—wait—"

Lorenzo unlocked the doors and was just about to step inside when I said, "Now!"

Gianna walked toward Pizzeria de Roma with a hair flip, like we'd discussed, but—

Oh no!

The heel of her sandal caught between two cobblestones, and she fell.

Epic fail.

"Ah!" she called out, getting Lorenzo's attention.

"Ouch." AJ winced. "That's gonna leave a mark."

"Not exactly like we rehearsed, huh?" Rico asked us.

"But it'll work," I said.

"Mamma mia!" Lorenzo left the door and hurried over to her. He bent down with his back to the door.

Gianna said, "I'm okay."

"Let me get you some ice," Lorenzo offered.

"Wait," she said to him. "Look at it. Do you think it needs a bandage, too?" She was improvising. I was proud of the improvement in her skills.

542

Perfect.

I tiptoed to the door and slid in, totally unnoticed.

I went down the hallway and entered the small office. I reached into my pocket and took out a paper bag filled with itching powder—something that Rico got from a guy who owned a joke shop.

I found the crisply ironed white uniform hanging on the back of the door and sprinkled the shirt and pants generously, especially in the butt region, if you know what I mean.

I went back to the front door and cracked it open to see if the coast was clear. Gianna still had Lorenzo perfectly distracted.

I dashed back behind the statue.

"Mission complete," I said to the guys.

"Roger that," AJ said.

Rico looked at us. "FBI? Secret agents?"

"I always wanted to write a story about a secret agent. Now I know how it feels."

Rico said, "Somehow I think secret agents are in a little more danger."

"Well," I said, "I just meant in general."

We watched as Gianna began to hobble to us with a napkin on her knee.

"Do you want me to bring you back to Amore?" Lorenzo asked her.

"No, thanks. I'll be okay."

"I'll see you tonight." He sounded genuinely sweet. "At the Festa."

She waved and he went inside.

When she was safely behind the statue, I asked, "Are you okay?"

She tossed the napkin in a nearby trash can and flipped her hair. "*Perfetto.*"

She'd faked that fall?

Her skills had improved more than I'd thought.

26

"What do we do now?" AJ asked.

"Look through the windows and wait for the show," I said. "Then we complete phase two."

"There's a phase two?" Gianna asked.

"There's always a phase two," I assured her.

Lights inside Pizzeria de Roma came on, the hostess arrived, and just a short while later, customers walked in.

Through the windows we saw Lorenzo walk down the hall in his jeans and oxford shirt. A minute later he walked by wearing his white uniform.

"It won't be long now," I said.

Lorenzo walked to a table and talked to the customers. He rubbed at his collar.

More customers sat, and Lorenzo moved throughout the pizzeria. He began rubbing his shoulders, then his stomach, and finally his butt. And his butt some more.

We all laughed.

"It's perfect!" Rico said.

"Oh, I just don't want it to end," AJ said.

I looked at them. "Okay. It's time. I'm going back in."

"Good luck," they called to me as I scurried in, flew past the hostess, saying, "Sorry, I have to use the restroom," zipped down the hall and into the office, snatched Lorenzo's clothes off the floor, and ran back out.

I paused to see if the hostess was standing guard at the door, but she wasn't even there. She was in the dining room with her mouth hanging open, watching Lorenzo's spectacle. He wiggled and wriggled and danced from table to table, scratching every part of his body.

I laughed the entire way back to the statue.

AJ and Rico were rolling on the ground. "Itching powder is just so classic," Rico cried.

"You took his clothes?!" Gianna asked, surprised and maybe even angry.

I nodded while I laughed.

A second later Lorenzo hopped down the hallway toward the office.

"Oh, how I wish we could see what was happening now," I said.

Another minute later Lorenzo came out wrapped in a tablecloth toga. He got on his Vespa and took off with white flaps of cloth waving behind him like a cape.

27

Gianna braided my hair for the Festa. It was like a craft for her; she had a knack for it. I wore a supercute dress that I'd been saving for something special.

Gianna studied me in the mirror. "This is weird, but I think you look more grown-up than you did a week ago."

"Thanks." I looked at myself. She was right.

"What I want to know," Gianna said, "is which one do you like?"

"Which what?"

"Which guy? Rico or AJ?"

I hadn't thought about it that way. But I guess I wasn't thinking about *like* liking either of them. They were very different. And both of them were cute and fun to hang around with. "I don't know," I said.

"I think you like them both." She twirled a tendril of my hair that fell outside the braid.

"Which one should I like?"

"Isn't that *your* area of expertise? I do braids; you handle the romantic pairing." She turned to her own hair and began twisting it this way and that, sticking pins here and there.

"Are you totally bummed about Lorenzo?" I asked.

"Yeah, I am. He was really sweet to me," she said. "I guess some people are good at acting."

The piazza was decorated with streamers and lights. Each corner had live music of a different kind—violins, a mariachi band, steel drums, and a traditional rock band. Everywhere people danced in the street. It was like they'd never heard live music or danced before, and never would again.

Rico got us four Aranciatas and wedged through the crowd, looking for a place where we could stand. He took my hand and pulled me behind him through the crowd.

Did you hear the part where I said he was holding my hand?

Let me tell you what it was like. His skin was rougher and cool. I liked it—*like* liked it.

Rico and AJ turned out to be good dancers. The three of us clapped and sang in the night air.

I thought about how cool it was that in just a few days I'd made two great new friends. They were new friends, right? I was continually nagged by the thought that I'd met Rico before.

The night was fun, exciting, loud, and totally awesome sauce, except for Gianna. She wasn't joining in with us. When we took a short break to replenish our Aranciatas, I asked her, "What's up with you?"

"I'm feeling like that was pretty mean to do to Lorenzo. He's not even here. He probably can't get out of the shower."

"If I didn't think that he sabotaged the sauce and stole the notes, I might feel a little bad for him," I said. "But remember, he's messing with Aunt Maria. With Amore Pizzeria!"

Rico said, "No one messes with Maria."

AJ, Rico, and I tapped our soda bottles together.

"Yup," AJ said. "No one."

Gianna tapped her bottle to ours.

28

⸙

The next morning Aunt Maria took Meataball to get his claws trimmed, and I went to Amore. I was greeted by a handful of notes for the Pizzeria Matchmaker. The sound of Vito pounding chicken with a wooden mallet echoed off the exposed brick walls. The scraping work had been completed, and honestly, the place looked incredible. It was old-world and traditional, yet felt romantic and homey at the same time.

I lifted the humongous pot to a burner and started the ritual of making sauce, on my own, for the first time.

Even though we'd just made a batch, I wanted to try to do it myself.

I followed the directions the way I had memorized. Nothing was written down. And now I understood why. The oil bubbled, the garlic popped. Slowly I added the tomatoes a little at a time, stirring carefully with the very long silver spoon.

Going through the motions of mixing the steaming ingredients, with the rhythmic pounding in the background, allowed my thoughts to drift away in the steam floating from the pot. I wondered about:

1. AJ and Rico: Did I *like* like Rico or AJ? I thought the answer to this question was still "both." And what was it about Rico that made me want to stare at him and try to figure out where I thought I'd seen him before?

2. Letters: What was I going to do with these letters? Throwing away others' wishes seemed wrong. But the pile was getting big.

3. My notes: *Where were they now?*

The back door opened, followed by the familiar sound of *"Buongiorno!"* from the deliveryman named Salvatore. This guy seemed like he never had a bad day.

"Ah, you are making sauce," he said. "Maria taught you her recipe?"

"Yeah, she did," I said. "This is my first time flying solo."

"Really?" He moved closer to the pot and studied the empty jugs. "Where do you get your crushed tomatoes?"

"Can't tell you," I said. "It's a secret. You know that."

"Ha-ha!" His belly jiggled. "Everyone knows that. Between the sauce and the matchmaking thing, you guys are getting all the pizza customers."

"Yeah. I guess the matchmaking gets them in, and the sauce keeps them eating. A good combo," I said. "We wouldn't want to let those secrets out."

For the first time the perma-grin glued to Salvatore's face faded. The sudden change in his expression made the hairs on my neck stick up. Then, just as fast as it had disappeared, it returned, but this time it looked like he was forcing his face muscles to smile. It looked . . . *fake*.

Suddenly I didn't trust Salvatore.

The sauce—he was in the kitchen alone all the time.

The matchmaker notes—he'd delivered the menu sample near the register.

Did I make a terrible mistake?

I think I had.

Was I wrong about Lorenzo?

I think I had been.

29

"It was him," I said to Rico and AJ as soon as they had both feet in the kitchen. "He took my notes and put them up for an online auction."

"Not Lorenzo?" AJ asked.

"No," I said.

"So we—" Rico started saying.

"Yup," I said.

"And Lorenzo didn't—" AJ began.

"Nope," I said.

"Not cool," Rico said.

"Not at all," I confirmed.

"And why was he following us around Rome?" AJ asked.

"Maybe he was really following Gianna to talk to her," I suggested. "Like she thought."

"And we spit cherry seeds at him," Rico said. "Now I feel bad."

"Me too," I said.

"Why did Salvatore do it?" AJ asked.

"That is the one-million-pepperoni question," I said. "And we're gonna get an answer."

"How?" Rico asked.

"We're gonna go over there and ask. No more recon, no more acts of deception, no more stakeouts," I said. "AJ, can you stir this sauce for me?"

"Really? The sauce?" AJ asked.

"Yeah. Look, you have to do it like this." I showed him how to make big sweeping circles with the long silver spoon. "You can't stop." I handed it to him. "Ever."

"You're letting me use the spoon?"

"Yeah," I said. "I trust you."

He took the spoon and stirred it exactly like I had said.

I gave him a thumbs-up.

"You," I said to Rico. "You come with me."

I took Rico's hand and dragged him out the back door.

Did you get the part where I grabbed his hand?

I jumped on the back of his friend's Vespa, which Rico continued to borrow, and secured the helmet like a pro.

Rico took off with such speed that I had to grab him around the waist to keep myself from falling off. He zipped through the streets more aggressively than AJ had. I held on tight. He smelled good, like a familiar soap.

Again, I debated the question about which boy I *like* liked. Right now, it was Rico.

"We're going right in there and ask them why they're doing this to Amore Pizzeria." I set my helmet on the back of the scooter and marched toward the door. "You coming?"

"Um—"

"Wimp," I said.

He swung his leg off the scooter. "Wimp" did it.

I knocked on the back door of Pizzeria de Roma, hard.

Lorenzo opened it.

"I need to talk to you," I said. I saw Salvatore and said to him, "And you."

"Come in," Lorenzo said.

The kitchen of Pizzeria de Roma was very different from Amore's. It was very big, bright, and filled with chefs with tall hats and shiny dishwashers. Every appliance shone and sparkled with newness.

"What's going on?" Lorenzo asked.

"That's my question." I looked at Salvatore. "And I think *he* can answer it."

"Uncle Sal?" Lorenzo asked.

Uncle Sal said nothing.

"He's been in Amore Pizzeria doing a little more than making deliveries, if you know what I mean. And I want to know why."

"No," Lorenzo said. "I don't know what you mean."

"I think he sabotaged our signature sauce with an insane, and potentially lethal, dose of red pepper. I tried it. I almost lost my tongue, literally. It almost fell right out of my mouth and onto the tile floor."

Lorenzo stared at Salvatore and then at his grandfather, who was also in the kitchen. "Did you ask him to do that?"

"I know nothing about this," Grandfather said. "What did you do, Salvatore?"

"I did what had to be done," Salvatore said. "You are blinded by *amore*. And that is going to kill our business. We will be broke."

"So, it is the truth?" Grandfather asked. "The sauce?"

Salvatore nodded. "First I look for the recipe for the sauce. But they no write it down. I look everywhere. It was the only thing keeping them open."

"But why?" Grandfather asked.

"We no make enough money to cover all of this." He pointed to the shining appliances. "With that sauce, people will eat more of our pizza."

"I hate to break it to you, but your pizza has more problems than the sauce, if you know what I mean," I said under my breath.

"The customers, they come once and no come back," Salvatore said. "Then they start with the matchmaking and we have no customers. When I see the matching instructions at the register—"

"What did you do with the instructions?" Lorenzo asked.

"He's selling them online. To the highest bidder," Rico said.

Lorenzo asked Uncle Sal, "So you were trying to put them out of business?"

"I have a lot of money invested in this place," Salvatore said. "It's my retirement. And you, Mossimo, you don't know how to run a restaurant."

Grandfather said, "Salvatore, I cannot believe what

you have done." To us, he said, "I am sorry. I would never want to hurt my dear Maria."

"Your . . . 'dear Maria'?" I asked slowly.

Everyone nodded.

"Yes," Grandfather said. "It is a very old story."

"Those are my favorite kind," I said. "Lay it on me." I hopped on the counter and made myself comfortable.

"It started when Maria and I were about your age."

"What happened?" Rico moved toward the cappuccino machine, pushed a few buttons, and rested a small white cup under a spout. "Does anyone else want one?"

Everyone nodded.

"She was so beautiful. We fell in love. But then I went into the military. We kept in touch for a long time with the letters. One day she write me that she was marrying Ferdinando. I was heartbroken and didn't write to her again."

Lorenzo helped Rico put tiny mugs into tiny saucers with tiny spoons and pass them around.

Grandfather continued his story as he stared at the wall. It was as if he was watching it play out on a movie screen and he was telling us what he saw.

"We lost the contact with each other. I thought I would never see her again. I married my dearest Nicolette. Loved her deeply. She died very young. After two broken hearts, I never looked for the love again. A few months ago I decide to take money that I won from a national bocce tournament and move to Rome."

"He is very good at bocce," Lorenzo added. "And dancing."

Grandfather took a sip of espresso and continued, "I move here to Rome to be with my brother and his little restaurant. We make all the changes. Sal wanted a break from the cooking, so I take over and he start the deliveries. One day I visited the Fontana del Cuore. Like everyone, I toss in a coin. And that is when I saw her. At least I thought it was her. I could no be sure. It had been so many years. I followed her down a cobblestone alley to Amore Pizzeria, where she disappeared. I go in and order. When I try the pizza, I know the sauce. It was my Maria."

"What did you do?" I asked. At the same time I thought about how I was going to write a story about this when I got home.

"I left. I no talk to her."

He continued, "She is happily married and has a lovely life. I no want to interfere," he said.

"You know," I said, "Great-Uncle Ferdinando died three years ago."

"What?!" Grandfather said. He set his small espresso

cup down and glared at Salvatore. "You knew this?"

"I—er—um . . ."

"You are every day making the deliveries. You knew?"

"*Sì!* I knew! If I told you, you would never try to make this business work!" he yelled. "When you came back that day and told me you'd found your true love at Amore Pizzeria, I would not believe it. In all the piazzas in all of Italy, and she owns a pizzeria *here*! What are the chances?"

"*Mamma mia!*" Grandfather smacked his forehead with his hand. "I cannot believe you no tell me, Salvatore." Suddenly he lunged at his brother.

I jumped in between them. "Wait!"

Lorenzo tried to calm his grandfather, while Rico subdued Salvatore.

"I have an idea," I said.

"Thank goodness," Rico sighed.

"I can't wait to hear this," Lorenzo said.

"By the way," I said to Lorenzo, "I am so sorry about the itching thing."

"That's okay," he said. "It's not like you had anything to do with—"

I stared at the floor.

"You? You did that? Why? I was nice to you and Gianna. I liked her. I still like her."

"I thought you had done it—the sauce, the notes."

I expected him to yell and get angry. Instead he combed his fingers through his hair. "No. It wasn't me."

His calmness made me feel worse, if that was even possible.

This story needed a much happier ending.

30

I banged the broom on the ceiling. Jane came in with a big board covered with fabric.

"What's that?" I asked.

"It's a pin board. I'm going to make crisscrosses with ribbon. Then I'll slide pictures or memorabilia under the ribbons and make like a collage type of thing," she said. "Do you like it?"

"I do." This gave me *another* idea. They were coming faster than I could handle now.

"Guys, we need to have a little meeting."

I set myself at the head of a table for six. My sister and friends sat around me. Rico and I related the story about Aunt Maria and Grandfather Mossimo.

"What are we gonna do?" AJ asked.

"What we're good at," Gianna said. "Everyone is going to do what they're good at."

"I resisted my special skill because *someone*"—I eyed Gianna—"told me it was weird. But I'm matchmaking regardless of what people think."

"Obviously Maria is awesome at pizza," AJ said.

"Totes," I agreed. "Grandfather Mossimo—not so much. But he's got other skills he's not even using." To AJ I said, "And so do you." I looked at Rico. His expression said he wanted to hear what he was good at. "You have friends who owe you favors. We're gonna need them." To Jane I said, "I need a special dress made. Oh, and I'm gonna need that pin board thingy too."

"What about me?" Gianna asked.

"We're gonna need signs and flyers made," I said.

"I'm on it."

I laid out the details of my plan.

31

The next day we mobilized the plan we'd created last night. I was on Aunt Maria duty.

"You know, Rico told me the story of Beatrice and Dante," I said as she and I made cannoli filling.

"Yes. You like?"

"I think the ending is sad. And I've been wondering, what do you think would've happened if they'd met again? You know, later, when they were older?"

"I think maybe a love like theirs would not have died. Some love is like that."

I asked, "Do you know a love like that?"

She pinched the dough together and didn't answer right away. "*Sì*. I have, but that was a very long time ago."

"What if you had a second chance at it?" I asked.

Aunt Maria gave me a curious look. Before she could respond, AJ stuck his bandannaed head through the opening between the dining room and kitchen. "Match needed at twelve o'clock."

I looked straight ahead—at the twelve o'clock position. No one was there. AJ didn't know what these positions meant. But it was cute that he tried. "Who?" I asked.

"The girls at table six."

Table six was not at the twelve o'clock position.

He'd sat the four girls who were in the other day. I remembered the girl with the mouth full of elaborate orthodontics. I thought her name was Riley, and I thought she was the one who was all about bacon. Her hair was pulled back in braids that were as pretty as the ones Gianna could make.

"Sorry," I said to Aunt Maria. "I'll be right back."

"*Sì*. You do the matching."

I approached the girls. "Hi there. Welcome back. So, how did the matches work out last time?"

The leader girl said, "I've been out with Evan three times. Your little pizza voodoo worked for me."

Another girl said, "I'm going out on a date with Ashton tonight."

"That's great," I said.

"But we're here to find a match for Riley," the leader said.

"Double bacon, right?"

She smiled. She was a very pretty girl.

"You're a tough one, because bacon is so unusual. I'll be back. Let me think for a minute." I strolled from table to table with a pitcher of water, refilling glasses and hoping I'd get a feeling from someone, but nothing stirred my gut.

That is, until I returned the pitcher back behind the counter to discuss the situation with AJ, who had made himself a big ol' slice of anchovy pizza.

Double bacon and anchovies?

I guess it made sense.

Maybe I hadn't seen it initially because I thought I *like* liked AJ myself.

What does a matchmaker do in a situation like this?

Anchovies didn't go with ham and pineapple.

I knew this.

My gut knew this.

Maybe I just liked him, not *like* liked him.

I said to him, "They asked for bread. And the girl

with the braids wanted an Aranciata. Can you bring those over to them?"

He folded the last quarter of his pizza into his mouth and, without swallowing, said, "Roger that."

I watched. They talked. Riley laughed at something AJ said. I took a cherry from a bowl in the kitchen and ate it, except for the pit, which I blew through a straw and shot at the leader girl.

Bing!

Hit her right in the forehead. She looked at me, and I waved for her to come over.

"What the heck?" she asked, annoyed.

"I need help right away with—with—with—the chocolate mousse pie. I can give you a free slice."

Her expression brightened. "I love chocolate."

Who doesn't?

"It's going to melt if it doesn't get eaten, like, right this second." I ran to the kitchen and got a half-eaten pie out of the refrigerator and put it on the counter with three forks. "Look at that," I said. "I only have three forks. Which of your friends do you think would want to help?"

Vito pushed a little bell, signaling an order was ready for pickup.

"That's probably Riley's double bacon. I'll bring it

to her. Bacon probably doesn't mix well with chocolate mousse pie. Am I right, or am I right?"

"I think you're right. I'll get the other girls," she said.

"Wait a sec," I said. I snatched the bacon pizza. "Would you give this to Riley? And this to AJ." I handed her an orange soda. "I have to get a lasagna out of the oven before it burns, if you know what I mean."

"Sure thing."

As I'd hoped, the three girls left Riley alone at the table and sat at the counter around the chocolate pie.

With three empty chairs now at the table, AJ sat. He started showing Riley pictures on his phone. The two of them didn't stop talking, and Riley laughed at pretty much everything AJ said.

It looked like another successful match! I was happy for AJ.

To the three girls devouring the chocolate mousse pie, I said, "I found another fork after all." I dug into the pie with them.

One of the girls pointed to the basket of letters for "Beatrice." "Can we look at those?"

"I guess so." I brought the basket over and took the empty cake plate away.

They unfolded them and read them to each other. "Can I tweet some of these?"

I said, "I guess that would be okay."

She took pictures of the notes and, with a click, sent them out into social cyberspace. A minute later her phone dinged—dinged—dinged.

"I'm getting tons of comments about these," she said. "You should start your own Instagram page with these. People love it."

It was a great idea.

"I'll tell you what," I said. "If you can do that for me, I'll hook you up with endless chocolate mousse pie for the next few days—for as long as I'm in Rome."

"Deal!" the girls squealed.

The three of them snapped pictures of the letters.

Then Lorenzo and Gianna came in through the front door. I looked back into the kitchen to see if Aunt Maria was watching. She still didn't like Lorenzo. Her back was turned as she shaped cannoli shells. "What's up, guys?" I asked.

Gianna said, "I came in to tell you that I'm taking the night off."

"Um—" I started, but she didn't wait for a response. They left holding hands as they walked down the cobble-stone alley.

32

A few nights later, all the prep work for my plan had been completed. There was only one piece missing. I had my biggest—and most important—matchmaking challenge ahead of me.

"Aunt Maria," I said, "we're going out."

"Okay, Lucy. Have fun."

"No. You're coming too."

"Oh, no. I can't go out with you kids. You'll do all the games." She wiggled her fingers like she was holding a video-game controller. "And the computers." She panto-mimed a typing motion.

"Uh, kids usually don't work on computers when they go out," I said. "We're going to sing, dance, and play bocce!"

Aunt Maria clapped. "I love the bocce. I used to play a lot."

"I'll do your hair," Gianna said.

"Why? Is the place fancy?" Aunt Maria asked.

"No, we just thought it would be fun to dress up. And celebrate!" I said.

"What should I wear?" Aunt Maria asked.

Jane replied, "I have an idea."

On cue, Rico held up a flowery red dress.

"It's perfect," Gianna said.

"It will look great on you," AJ added.

"It is very *bellissima*," Aunt Maria said. "How can I say no?"

"You can't," I said. "Get ready."

We all walked together into the piazza, which looked different now. The colorful sign for Pizzeria de Roma had been replaced with a DANZA ITALIANO sign.

"What is this?"

"Surprise! It's not a pizzeria anymore," I said.

AJ explained, "They have dancing and singing and indoor bocce."

We went inside and saw Lorenzo standing at the podium. "Your table is waiting for you," he said.

We followed Lorenzo to a large round table close to the stage. The lights had been dimmed, the music turned up. AJ didn't even sit down. He walked to the stage and pressed a few buttons on a big piece of stereo equipment—which I guess was kind of video gamey and computerish—and a second later the beat of a popular dance song came on.

Then AJ started singing. *That's* what he was good at.

Okay, so I'll tell you about his karaoke. It wasn't terrible, but he was far from good. It didn't seem to matter, because people of all ages jumped to the dance floor. Even Aunt Maria left her Aranciata on the table and danced. That is, before she froze.

She looked like she'd seen a ghost.

"*Mamma mia!*" she said. "Is that you?"

"Yes," Mossimo said.

She walked up to him, and they hugged. A tear rolled down Aunt Maria's cheek.

Mossimo wiped it off. "I've thought about seeing you again for a very long time," he said. "You look exactly the same."

"Um," I said to Rico. "How about a game of bocce?" I had never actually played the game, but I wanted to give

Aunt Maria some privacy. Rico and I challenged AJ and his new "friend" Riley.

Mossimo led Aunt Maria to a small table in the back corner. I spied as they looked into each other's eyes and talked.

I hadn't been a matchmaker for very long, but if this was what it felt like, I wanted to do it forever. I was so happy to have helped them find each other again—and write the perfect ending to their story.

33

Pizzeria de Roma's transformation to a singing, dancing bocce club was a huge success. All the pizza lovers in the piazza now came to Amore to eat, then went to Danza Italiano to have fun. AJ's new friend Riley and her three social-media-maven girlfriends maintained our website and also got jobs at the pizzeria for the rest of the summer. Rico and his friends had set up tables and chairs outside so we could offer dining alfresco.

The first order I took a few nights later was from Murielle duPluie and Angelo.

"*Bonjour*," she said.

"Hi!" I was excited to see her.

"I am going to do the follow-up article we talked about," she said. "And have dinner with *mon amour* at the same time."

"Great." To Angelo I said, "Nice to see you again."

"The place looks different," said Angelo in perfect English. "I love the outside seating and new menu."

"Thanks."

"I just *adore* the walls," Murielle duPluie said. "The exposed brick is *très jolie*." The paint had been scraped from the rest of the bricks and the walls really did look great.

I took their order and was about to leave when Carina, the lady selling flowers who I'd met on the Spanish Steps, walked by with her basket. "Flower for the lady?" she asked Angelo.

"Of course," Angelo said. "I'll take two." He gave one of them to me and the other to Murielle duPluie.

"*Grazie*," I said, and walked away with Carina. I asked her, "I'm just wondering, what did Aunt Maria do for you that you would do anything for her?"

"She introduced me to my husband." She smiled and offered roses to two more customers.

Ha. Even when Aunt Maria had stopped officially matchmaking and was "no messing with the love," she'd still managed to create some very happy couples on the sly.

AJ called to me from the kitchen, "You have a phone call at twelve o'clock."

I looked straight ahead.

The only thing there was the men's room.

"No. Sorry. I meant right here." He held up the phone.

Who would be calling me at Amore Pizzeria?

"Hello," I said.

"Hi, honey."

"Hi, Dad. I'm kinda busy right now."

"I know. I just wanted to tell you that Mom and I are reading all these letters on the website and looking at the pictures of Amore Pizzeria. It's just incredible."

"Thanks. There's actually a lot more I can tell you. Like Aunt Maria reconnecting with her Dante, whose name is Mossimo, and the menu and the dance club, but I've got a lot of hungry people here who need me to match them."

There was a long pause. Finally Dad said, "Okay, honey. I didn't understand all that, but I wanted to tell you how proud we are of you."

"Thanks, Dad. Bye—"

"Lucy! Wait."

"What?"

"I was wondering if you ever met Enrique. He used to hang around the shop."

"Who's that?"

577

"A boy you were friends with last time we went to Italy. You were in, like, first grade then."

"I don't remember any boy."

"Sure you do," my dad said. "He's in your stories. You call him something different every time, but I recognize him."

I knew the character Dad was talking about, but I didn't know anyone named Enrique.

"No, Dad, I haven't seen him."

"Too bad. You were pals back then," he said. "I'll see you at the airport tomorrow night, honey."

I hung up.

I finished the dinner crowd, wondering if I had a Dante of my own and didn't even realize it.

How would I find him in a huge foreign city like Rome?

Vito tapped my shoulder and pointed to several take-out tins of food filled with pizzas and spaghetti Parmesan sandwiches. He chattered something in Italian. I understood that he wanted me to deliver that stuff to Rico, who was in charge of the Amore Pizzeria mobile cart, which sold food in the piazza. It had a huge Amore Pizzeria sign and an arrow pointing down the alley.

I took the warm tins toward Rico. On my way I passed the Fontana del Cuore. I set the tins on the ground, reached into my pocket, found a coin, and tossed it in. I closed my eyes and thought—*Enrique*.

When I opened my eyes, Enrique hadn't miraculously appeared, so I took the tins to the cart, which was manned by Rico and one of his buddies.

"Who's hungry?" I asked.

"Actually," he said, "I'm starving. Do you want to take a break and chow with me?"

I untied my apron. "Yup. I absolutely would."

He asked, "What can I get for you?"

"Spaghetti Parmesan sandwich," I said. "I hear they're fabulous."

"If there was a zombie apocalypse and all we had were spaghetti Parm sandwiches, we would never have to worry about zombies wanting to eat brains. They would be totally satisfied with these." He handed me a warm sandwich wrapped in foil.

Had he seriously just referenced a zombie apocalypse?

"What are you going to have?" I asked him.

"Duh. My favorite. I haven't been able to get it anywhere. Until now, that is. You added it to the new menu." He held out a plate of ham-and-pineapple pizza. "The Los Angeles."

Did you get the part where I said Rico's favorite pizza was ham and pineapple?

That's my favorite too, and best matched with *another* ham and pineapple, generally speaking. Of course, it isn't an exact science. I use my gut, too. And right now my gut was tangled like linguine al dente being dumped into a colander.

"When my parents decided to move back here from the US, I was homesick for my American friends. Then I met an American girl here on vacation. She introduced me to it, and ever since then it's been my numero uno favorite."

"As a kid? An American?"

"Yeah. She was on vacation here in Rome and I met her. We hung out for a week and then she was gone. I never saw her again." He bit into the pie. "But she left me with ham and pineapple."

"Enrique?"

Rico made a face. "Oh man, I hate that name. Don't call me that. Rico is much more fitting to my personality, don't you think?"

"Totes." He didn't put it together that I was the American girl, and I didn't tell him. At least not yet.

This was going to make a great story someday.

Then it happened.

Rico reached into his back pocket and took out my matchmaking notes. "I won the auction," he said, and gave them to me. Then he took me by the hand. We walked down the cobblestone alley—which was now lined on either side by glowing luminaries—with Meataball waddling behind us.

Looking for another great book?
Find it
IN THE MIDDLE.

Fun, fantastic books for kids
in the in-be**TWEEN** age.

IntheMiddleBooks.com

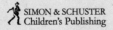

READ & LEARN

with *simon* kids

Keep your child reading, learning,
and having fun with Simon Kids!

A one-stop shop where you can
**find downloadable resources, watch interactive author
videos, browse books by reading level, and more!**

**Visit us at
SimonandSchusterPublishing.com/ReadandLearn/**

And follow us @SimonKids

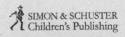

SIMON & SCHUSTER
Children's Publishing